T0299511

A
CROWN
SO
SILVER

By Lyra Selene

Fair Folk

A Feather So Black
A Crown So Silver

LYRA SELENE

A CROWN SO SILVER

orbit-books.co.uk

ORBIT

First published in Great Britain in 2025 by Orbit

1 3 5 7 9 10 8 6 4 2

A CIP catalogue record for this book
is available from the British Library.

HB ISBN 978-0-356-52494-8
C format 978-0-356-52495-5

Printed and bound in Great Britain by
Clays Ltd, Elcograf, S.p.A.

Papers used by Orbit are from well-managed forests
and other responsible sources.

Orbit
An imprint of
Little, Brown Book Group
Carmelite House
50 Victoria Embankment
London, EC4Y 0DZ

The authorised representative
in the EEA is
Hachette Ireland
8 Castlecourt Centre
Dubline 15, D15 XTP3, Ireland
(email: info@hbgi.ie)

An Hachette UK Company
www.hachette.co.uk

orbit-books.co.uk

*For the soft ones who were made to be hard,
and the hard ones who learned to be soft*

Before

Irian

Irian watched Fia die.

He would never forget the moment. There, beneath the colossal Heartwood, with the Ember Moon lofting toward its zenith, when she chose to sacrifice herself, instead of him. Bent the sword meant for his chest toward her own heart. Spared his life and took her own.

Paid a tithe that was his to pay.

For such a palpable decision, it was made so swiftly. There was a fleeting stillness, where before she had trembled. A momentary widening of her lovely mismatched eyes as the terrible idea bloomed inside her. A sudden stubborn angle to her delicate jaw. A flurry of emotion blowing ephemerally across her expressive features— regret, sorrow, tenderness, resolve.

She stepped away. Shifted her grip on the Sky-Sword—*his* sword, *his* emblem, *his* sacrifice—and slid the blade against her chest.

No.

Too late, he realized what she was doing. Horror screamed

through him, hollowing his bones and tattering his muscles. He staggered to his feet. Lunged for her. But she was fast—far faster than he, weighed down as he was with the crushing burden of his own dying magic. She danced out of his reach. Lifted her eyes to the Heartwood. Murmured words he could not hear over the percussion of his panicked blood pounding in his ears.

She plunged the Sky-Sword into her heart.

For thirteen years, Irian had been that sword, and the sword had been him. Its length of metal—shifting color with the skies—was an extension of his own body, his own mind, his own magic. Its keening song was the melody of his own soul. So when it took his new bride's life, he *felt* it. The razor edge slicing into warm skin. The burst of hot blood sliding along its curving bevels. The blade punching through muscle, carving out bone, biting into her throbbing heart. He felt it as surely as if he had slaughtered her with his own hand. As if he—instead of dying as he'd planned—had *become* death and stolen the life of the only person he had ever dared love.

He caught Fia the moment before her body struck the ground. He tore the shard of night from her shattered chest. Pressed his hands over the wound. Tried to stanch the life ebbing from her.

It was no use. Steam pale as a ghost blossomed above her lifeless form as her green-dark blood welled hot around his fingers, making his hands slip. Its scent filled his nostrils—wet loam and turned earth and the metallic tang of creeping rot. Where the rivulets touched earth, tiny blossoms sprouted—white and black as stars in a night sky.

He gathered her up, clutched her to him. Although she was physically petite, Fia had never struck Irian as small. There was so much of her—so much sharp beauty and biting wit and searing emotion—that it had rendered her more expansive in his mind than her mere body could contain. Yet now, forsaken of all the inimitable qualities that had made her *her*, she seemed tiny in his arms. Her limbs fragile as birds' bones. Her eyelids the color of bruised lilies. Her skin going gray as the underbelly of a storm cloud. He buried his bloodied palms in her tangle of dark hair, brought his lips to her forehead. He clenched his eyes shut, whispered meaning-less words against her cooling skin.

"Come back. Let it be me. Live, Fia. *Live*."

The ground shifted beneath him. His eyes flew open. Roots churned up from the dark earth, curling around Fia's limbs. Branches groaned down, bark lengthening to cradle her form. He tried to keep hold of her, but his hands were slick with blood, his arms sapped of strength, his mind slack with shock. He thought he must have roared as the forest carried her away, but the sound in his ears was hoarse and raw. He did not register it as his own voice, only as the sound of his heart breaking.

The Heartwood pulled Fia toward itself, as gently as if she were a sleeping baby. Its roots lifted upward; its branches stretched downward. Opening itself up and swallowing her whole.

Leaving Irian alone.

For an unknowable time, his mind echoed with emptiness. But thoughts crept in, inexorable.

The Sky-Sword.

He crawled to where he had flung it, took its hilt in his green-streaked palm. The blade cried out a lament. He wondered whether it mourned for him. Or for her.

The Ember Moon.

He squinted up. Between the colossal branches of the Heart-wood, he could not tell whether the moon had reached its zenith. It must be soon. Which meant—

The tithe.

He ran his palm along the sword, letting its singing edge slice his skin. A trickle of his own silver blood mingled with the green already staining its length. The bright line of pain focused his mind. So, too, did it sharpen the anguished elegy screaming through him.

All was lost. He did not know what Fia had meant to do by tak-ing her own life instead of his. Had she meant to pay the tithe on his behalf? To trade her life for his? If so, it had not worked. The last of the Sky-Sword's strength sapped from his limbs; its powerful pulse dripped from his veins. Warped wild magic shoved at the fraying edge of his consciousness, seeking its freedom.

The tithe had not been paid—his Treasure had not been renewed. And without Fia, there was no heir. Even if he bent the blade to his own chest—paid the tithe as he had intended—there was nowhere for the magic to go.

So—Irian would still die. The wild magic of the Sky-Sword— the last Treasure of the Septs—would go free. The blight of tainted magic would spread throughout Tír na nÓg, warping as it spread. The Gates would shatter. Violence would escalate through mortal and Folk lands alike. Eala would have her war. Both worlds would burn.

The knowledge should have tormented him. But Irian found he could not muster up the energy to care. About the Gates, about Eala's treachery. About his own worthless life. All he cared about was *her*. Fia.

And Fia was gone.

Gone beyond where he could reach her. He could only wait to die, and pray that in death, he would somehow be reunited with her.

Weak and bloodied, he rested his head on the cool earth and waited for the magic to seep away from him completely. For his heart to stop.

The change was nearly indiscernible. A slow, silent stirring inside him. A kind of *lightening*—a strange counterpoint to the dimming moon sliding down behind netting branches. He rolled out his stiff shoulders. Shifted his weight on legs numb from kneeling on cold ground. Gripped blood-crusted fingers around a blade that had long gone silent as its magic died.

But no. It *hummed*—so softly Irian couldn't hear it at all, could only feel it purr along his wakening bones. The lightness inside him responded, unfurling slow wings around the painful throb of his heart. A weightlessness—like falling, like flight—lifted him to his feet. When he looked up, he saw a brightening sky painted in broad strokes of vermilion and rose, pricked with distant, dimming stars.

Dawn.

Dread clenched his spine and beat back the growing lightness at his core. Dawn was when he changed—when he became *other*. He did not know why he was still alive, when *she* was not. But he had lived with the cost of his arrogance—the price of his selfishness— for too long to assume it could be wished away. For years, this had been the way—shadow and fury until sunset set him free.

He steeled himself for the pain, for the mutation, for the loss of self.

With a distant sigh, the sun rose.

Irian shielded his eyes from piercing golden light with a hand blackened by tattoos, but not real feathers. A brisk wind smelling of frost swept the forest, chasing the last of autumn's leaves and lifting the short hair off his neck. Hair, not feathers. Slowly, he glanced over his shoulder. But the stiff pinions of shadow that had haunted him for years were evanescing in the cool bright morning. He reached for them, but they were nothing more than tatters of night; scraps of bad memory; a curse, lifted.

And when the Sky-Sword began to sing—a full-throated aubade to the glory of day—he knew.

Somehow, Fia had done it. She had paid his tithe with her life. She had broken the curse. She had saved the magic of the Sky-Sword. She had saved *him*.

He was not sure he could bear it.

He preferred the days. It had been so long since he had been himself during the day, and he glutted himself on it. With his anam cló under his control once more, he flung himself into the blue sky, the high wind, the rippling sunlight, soaring high and higher. Until the air grew thin in his lungs and flowers of frost blossomed on his inky wings. He screamed at the sky until he had no voice left to rage with.

He watched the landscape of Tír na nÓg shift far below him. Warriors marched across sighing plains, the colors of the bardaí's fianna blending in ways he did not expect. Trees were felled. Camps were pitched, then dismantled. Skirmishes broke out, and the stench of rotting corpses mingled with the carrion reek of warped magic wafting over the hills.

Irian could not bring himself to care. With his Treasure renewed, his borders were secure. His Gate, strong. His magic, unassailable.

But she—she was gone.

One. Two. Seven. Twelve days.

There became a rhythm to the thing: a song of inevitability, notes composed in a nightmare of grief and performed in a solitude of sadness. There were the shadows, creeping long and longer as the light faded. The unclenching grasp of the sun's rosy fingers on the windowsill—the touch of daylight fading. The calls of nesting rooks. The distant yip of kits returning to their dens. The settling of stones into the earth.

And him, alone.

Sometimes he was calm. He slept and dreamed of never waking up.

Most times he was not calm. A spray of glass breaking on flagstones: shards sparkling bright as the tears of those who had died for love. A cracked and broken voice dying in a hoarse throat.

Chairs broken into matchsticks against vine-climbed walls.

Fire-scorched logs scattered from the hearth; palms charred and blackened like overdone meat; the stink of roasting flesh.

Dark, hungry metal biting tattooed skin. The lure of steel. But no matter how he wished it, he knew the Sky-Sword would not let him die. Not until he had served his second sentence—however long that might be.

It did not mean he did not try.

On the thirteenth night—when the sky was black, black without a moon to light it—Irian noticed the swan.

He had tried to stop looking at the lough. The swans were gone—Eala's treachery had torn them all from his influence. He was glad for it. He had never liked the sight of them—it reminded him of all the things he had done wrong. The poor choices he had made. The power he had misused. The years he had squandered—not for himself, but for *them*. He had loved them, in his own way. They were the only ones who had passed for friends these past thirteen years. But he had hated himself for what he had done to them. As he knew they hated him.

He had spent thirteen years' worth of nights looking out at that lough. Counting. Naming. Worrying. He supposed it was a hard habit to break.

He saw it only in absence, at first. White ripples creasing black water. A soft, soundless splash. A vibration in the air as stiff pinions sifted wind. He looked closer, forcing his eyes to distinguish the shape by its outline.

Dark wings, outspread. An elegant, curving neck. A tilted beak. Depthless eyes.

A black swan.

A hollow, consuming darkness reared up inside him. For a long, ungenerous moment, Irian thought to run the bird off. To frighten it so that it took to the air. Let it make some other lough its home—he had had enough of swans for one lifetime.

But then he remembered. Remembered how *she'd* looked that fateful night two weeks ago. What she'd worn the night of her death.

Feathers. Feathers so black they'd stolen the light. Feathers in her hair, on her gown, sweeping from her shoulders in a magnificent train of night. It had been a statement—a symbol of intent. Fia had meant to swear herself to his Sept the night of the Ember Moon. To declare herself as his heir, his tánaiste. To accept his tithe and inherit the last Treasure, the Treasure of the Sept of Feathers.

But she had only gotten as far as the handfasting. She had wed him, only to tithe herself. She had become his wife, only to die. The darkness inside him gnashed sharp teeth and threatened to swallow him whole. But in that yawning maw of grief, a tiny star kindled. A spark of light that seemed to sing, *What if?*

He dared not voice the rest of the question.

Irian was not accustomed to hope. He had forgotten how much it *hurt*—a punch to the chest, an explosion behind the eyes, a precipitous tilt toward a future he dared not dream. An unbalancing, a mad slide away from despair toward—

He dared not let himself fall. Not now. Not yet.

Instead, he paced.

For fifteen days, he paced the edge of the lough. He followed the black swan as it sailed around the water. Napped on broad stones. Dived for pondweed. Tucked its head behind ruffled black wings when the wind rose. He stared at it, searching for some glint of recognition, some hint of consciousness. Sometimes he swore green glittered deep in its smooth, depthless eyes.

All the while, the Sky-Sword sang to him. It sang of heartbreak. It sang of hope. It sang of healing.

He dared not listen.

The full moon sailed up through a cold sky embossed with silver cirrus clouds, and Irian's hope turned feral.

No longer a quiet whisper he dared not acknowledge, it roared inside him—a gale of conflicting emotions lashing his thoughts into chaos. A storm howling treacherous, wondrous, delirious promises in a voice he did not know if he could trust.

He wildly paced the shore. The night seemed to last forever. And yet as the moon descended and dawn touched the horizon with ghostly fingers, he wished it might last forever. He was falling, and if he did not have wings, he did not want to know.

If he was truly alone, he was not sure he could bear it.

The sky turned restless with color. Irian's hope began to die, burning out like a falling star in an endless night. He turned his back on the lough. On the black swan. On his own desperate foolishness.

A flash of green split the dim. A breeze kissed his neck, smelling of summertime. He spun.

A splash. A cough. A pale, indistinct form rising from dark water, shedding black feathers as she stood.

He was not alone. Gods alive—*he was not alone.*

His hope exploded like a sunburst against the dawn.

Irian strode into the lough. He barely noticed the icy black water biting his thighs—only that it weighed his footsteps and made him slow, clumsy.

He could not reach her fast enough. He gathered her up, clutched her to him. Despite the cold water, her skin was warm. Her heartbeat pulsed strong, her chest against his chest. Color touched her pale cheeks. He buried his palms in her tangle of sable hair, brought his lips to her forehead. He clenched his eyes shut and bent to kiss her, whispering meaningless words against her mouth.

She broke away, stared up at him. A delicate fear crept onto her face—a dread he could not fully fathom. Her eyes jerked toward the horizon, where swords of golden light pierced the canopy of trees. Worry twisted her mouth.

Irian understood.

She did not know. Whatever miracle she had performed— whatever unknowable magic she had wrought—she did not know she had broken the geas. She did not know she had saved the Sky- Sword. She did not know she had saved *him.*

The sunrise was its own explanation. He pulled her close, savoring the heat of her skin, the rush of her breath, the steady throb of her heartbeat.

A morning star pricked the dawn, then flung itself down in a line of fire. Only, Irian no longer felt as if he were falling.

Fia drew back. Her mismatched eyes shone, huge in her lovely face.

"Irian," she whispered. "*Irian.*"

He lifted his head from her hair, slid his hand along the delicate angle of her jaw. Put his hand over her heart, only to touch a blue-green stone hanging above her breast. Wonder rose up in him. He had never seen the Heart of the Forest—he had been a little boy when the Sept of Antlers' Treasure had been lost. But he *knew* it—knew it by its slow, deep pulse, like dark earth and green growth. Knew it by the way it hummed in counterpoint to the Sky-Sword belted at his waist and anchored in his soul. Knew it by the way it shone the same elusive green as the inquisitive eyes of his childhood friend Deirdre.

The same elusive green as Fia's right eye.

He did not know how or why. But somehow, Fia's sacrifice not only had renewed the magic of the Sky-Sword but had resurrected the lost Treasure of the Sept of Antlers too. She had mended the broken Heart of the Forest. She had ended Deirdre's sorrow.

She had changed their story's ending.

Fia looked down at the stone shining at her breast, then lifted her arms, which were newly embossed with tattoos like creeping, coiling vines. And tangled amid those vines—feathers. Gleaming, razored pinions, a mirror to his own magical markings, which were shot through now with delicate vines. Tiny flowers. Needle-sharp thorns. She drew him down, tilting her chin as her mouth parted. She kissed him. He kissed her back, lingering on lips that tasted of moss and miracles and the aching promise of a future yet untold.

"Good morning," she whispered for the first time.

The smile creasing Irian's face came slowly. Not because he was not happy, but because he could not yet forget what had happened. Memories of her death lingered, beating at his head and shoulders like wings of night. Specters of grief clutched sharp fingers around a heart that had not yet healed. That might *never* heal.

Still, he made himself smile. "Good morning, colleen."

He kissed her as dawn bled into morning—kissed her long and slow and deep. And he swore—silently, savagely, solemnly—that so long as he lived, so too would she.

Irian would watch both worlds burn before he would ever watch Fia die again.

Part One

The Isle of the Happy

To be without grief, without sorrow, without death, without any sickness, without weakness; that is the sign of Emain...There is nothing to liken its mists to, the sea washes the wave against the land; brightness falls from its hair. Golden chariots in the Plain of the Sea, rising up to the sun with the tide...It is a day of lasting weather, silver is dropping on the land; a pure white cliff on the edge of the sea, getting its warmth from the sun.

—"The Call to Bran," translated
by Lady Gregory

Chapter One

The beach rattled with the footsteps of advancing warriors. Crouched in shadow at the edge of the trees—a mere stone's throw from the approaching fiann—I felt every footfall as if it were my own skin they trod on, instead of pebbled sand. My awareness darted over the landscape toward the fénnidi like fireflies.

I sensed the stones beneath their boots that clutched fragments of afternoon's warmth.

The stubborn weeds growing upward through sand and shale, crushed beneath their careless boots.

The rich muck at the edge of the lough…its pondweed and algae and stiff reeds guarding minnows.

The trees at the edge of the wood, reaching leafless branches toward the interlopers.

I leaned forward, nerves and anticipation braiding up my spine like knotty vines. The trees whispered around me. The green-blue stone above my breast throbbed, sending a coil of leafing warmth through my veins. My hands twitched toward my skeans.

"Colleen." Irian's whisper was hoarse with unease. "Easy."

I looked up at him. His silver eyes glittered in the dim, intent on my face. He hadn't wanted me to attend this negotiation tonight. It had been a week since I'd splashed to life in the middle of the lough, coughing black water as I shed black feathers. Irian had wanted me to rest, to recuperate, to acquaint myself with the riot of new, powerful magic roaring through me—the magic I'd inherited from the Heart of the Forest, the lost Treasure of the Sept of Antlers.

But I felt *fine*. Better than fine—*wonderful*. Exquisite. Invincible. I felt like I could do anything. Birth forests on a whim, invent flowers that smelled like rain, bid the earth to open up and swallow whole fianna of Gentry warriors.

In retrospect, that was probably why Irian had wanted me to stay home.

"Easy," he said again. "These fénnidi are the She-Wolf's sworn men. I have let them into my domain under the strict geas of parley. Almha never hated me as much as the other bardaí—perhaps she can be reasoned with."

Almha. I remembered that name from last year, when Chandi took me to the Feis of the Nameless Day. Almha was the so-called Silver She-Wolf, barda of the Elder Gate. But we did not know where her loyalties lay. In the five weeks since my adoptive sister, Eala, had sacrificed the hearts of her swan maidens for control over the Gates, many of the bardaí had fallen under her influence. Some because of the potent geasa Eala had wrought with unthinkable magic. Others had joined her of their own free will, eager to wage war on their Folk rivals...or the human realms. From what Irian had learned, Eala now commanded seven out of the thirteen Gates. Not counting Irian himself, that left five bardaí whose loyalties remained either neutral or opposed to Eala.

Almha was one of those. But I couldn't help but shiver as I watched her warriors approach. At first glance, they were merely Folk Gentry. But in the waning moonlight slicked over their tall, muscled forms, they appeared more grotesque. The pelts of wolves ruffled over their backs and shoulders, tufts of fur fusing to skin. Their faces seemed unnaturally elongated, scenting snouts smiling with rows of glittering white fangs. The breeze carried the stench of carrion in their wake; strange shadows snapped and scratched at their backs. Wrongness slithered up my throat and filled my mouth with grave dirt.

Almha and her fianna had tampered with wild magic; that much was obvious. And these warriors did not look like Folk who could be reasoned with.

"Wait here."

Irian's sharp command grated against my fervor, but he was already stepping out of the shadow of the forest, an arrow nocked on his drawn bow and his hood shadowing his features.

Sudden recollection tangled me up in memory as I watched his towering, menacing figure approach the intruders. This—this was how I'd met Irian, that fateful night over a year ago. He'd been terrifying and so beautiful I could hardly comprehend him. He'd thought me a ghillie, and I? I'd thought him a monster without equal. What had he said to me?

This is no place to be lost. Nor found.

My quiet, private laugh puffed pale vapor past my chilly lips. Would I have run from him, panic snapping at my heels, if I had known those words had not been a threat, but an unintended promise? For, in the end, I had lost myself in this place. And in the losing, found everything I had never known I was looking for.

Magic. Destiny. Home. *Him.*

Myself.

The She-Wolf's fiann caught sight of Irian and halted, fanning out in an attack formation. I tucked my memories away, creeping closer to the edge of the trees. I wanted to be in earshot of this sup-posed parley. My skin still vibrated with the pressure of the fiann's boots on the shore, even as my nostrils filled with their tainted scent.

I knew enough of violence to tell when warriors wanted to talk. And when they wanted to fight. But this was still Irian's domain. So I'd let him figure that out on his own.

"Hello, She-Cub." Irian's voice was a knife, keen edged and savage. "You have...changed."

The woman at the head of the fiann shifted her stance. Turned her head. Spat on the beach. Nearly as tall as Irian, she had long silver hair tied in complicated braids around her head. Her eyes—blackened with kohl—shone yellow in the dim. When she grinned, teeth thronged her mouth, long and white and sharp as a predator's.

She-Cub. She must be the She-Wolf's daughter. But in command of her mother's fiann, she clearly wasn't much of a cub anymore. If Irian wanted to keep this conversation civil, he had picked a fine point to start with.

Good. Thorns nettled through my veins, sharpening my pulse and bunching my muscles. Let them have their parley.

Then let us have our fight.

"As have you, Shadow Heir." Her voice was a snarl. "Last time I saw you, you were a dead man walking. But you are quite talkative for a corpse."

"Sorry to disappoint." The hardness of his voice belied his easy stance. "As you see, I am restored. As are the boundaries of my realm. You are here at my pleasure, She-Cub. If you have terms to offer me, speak them now."

"Offer *you*?" She laughed, and her pack laughed with her—a baying, howling cacophony that raised the hairs on the back of my neck. "Things are changing in Tír na nÓg. You have never been heir to much, tánaiste. But now you are heir to nothing. We offer you survival. And the cost will be high."

"Then you have thrown in your lot with the mortal princess." Irian did not so much smile as bare his teeth. An echo of his hostility ripped through me, tinged with a sour flicker of resentment. Another Gate fallen to Eala. Another of the bardaí allied with my adoptive sister. My bright-haired, dark-hearted twin. My nemesis. "I knew you and your mother were willing to forsake much of what made you Gentry in return for power. But I never thought you'd betray your own kind for someone like *her*."

Aggression buzzed through the fiann, raising furred hackles and sharpening fangs.

"Someone like *who*, Irian?" Almha's daughter vibrated with fury. "Someone who would unite us lower-born Folk in a common cause? Rally us toward a common enemy? Help us take back the human realms, which should always have belonged to us?" Again, she spat. "It was more than the Septs ever did."

"You are all always so quick to blame me for the sins of my parents." Irian's low laugh rang harsh. "This is not a feud we started, She-Cub."

"And it is not one we must end tonight." Almha's daughter spread her arms in false placation. "We truly did not come to quarrel, Shadow Heir. Give us what we want, and we will let you live."

"What could you possibly demand from me?"

"The changeling girl." The She-Cub's yellow eyes glittered. "The swan princess wishes to speak with her sister."

Irian's shoulders bulged. A stiff breeze swept suddenly down through the valley, ruffling the inky water of the lough and knitting ice along its shallows. Irian dropped the bow and drew the Sky-Sword in one smooth motion. The blade began to sing—a keening, heartrending complaint. My own Treasure responded, humming in antiphony. Emotion churned through me. Regret for who Eala and I could have been to each other, had we truly been raised as sisters. Resentment for how swiftly she had been able to rally Folk to her cause. Anticipation for the thrill of the fight.

And, perhaps, tonight—the promise of a kill.

"Gods alive," Irian intoned, "I swear I will hang you upside down from your own intestines before I let you touch her."

The She-Cub drew her own wicked blade. "Try."

Parley over.

Oh well.

I stood up and strolled out into the light of the waning moon.

"While I do appreciate your inventive imagery, sweetheart," I said, pitching my voice toward Irian, "I'm sure that's not necessary." The fiann of warriors turned at my voice, their lupine faces hungry. "You're welcome to take me wherever you please. But you'll have to come and get me first."

"Fia." Irian's voice was rough, urgent. "Do not."

But I already had. Tufted helms snapped down over gleaming yellow eyes. Blades rang from scabbards. The fiann started forward. Irian, too, turned. He sprinted back toward me, his dark hood falling away from his face. His opal eyes snagged on mine, jagged with...*fear.*

Surprise jolted me back a step. In all the time I'd known Irian, I'd never known him to be afraid. Not even the night of the Ember Moon—when I'd held the blade of his own Treasure against his neck and prepared to end his life—had he been afraid. Sorrowful, perhaps. Regretful, almost certainly. But never *fearful.*

But I didn't have time to wonder what had frightened him— the She-Cub's fiann was almost upon us. I sidestepped Irian as he reached for me. Whipped my twin skeans from my belt, swirled them around my fingers. Slid into a wide fighting stance. And stomped my foot.

My boot heel met the dirt with a sound like thunder. The ground—half-frozen in early winter's grasp—convulsed. Mounds of loam and shale heaved upward like the death throes of a great dark beast. The warriors lifted with it, howling as they were thrown backward onto the rocky beach. Groaning, some of them managed to climb back to their feet on the shuddering ground. Others were not so lucky—the pondweed at the edge of the lough turned predatory, curling around ankles and wrists. Dragging unsuspecting warriors down into the shallows.

I didn't bother to count how many. It wasn't enough—the She-Cub was back on her feet, staring murder from twenty paces away. With her were enough of her fiann to merrily drag me back to Eala.

But I had no intention of letting that happen. I took a few steps back, until the shadows of the forest caressed my back. I flicked one of my skeans at the She-Cub, beckoning. I smiled.

She growled. Then charged, what remained of her fiann falling into formation behind her. Beside me, Irian cursed, ripped off his mantle, and raised his singing sword.

We met the fiann with a clash. The She-Cub's steel screamed against mine, the impact jarring me to the elbow. I cried out. But the powerful magic of the Heart of the Forest was already cooling the hot stab of pain that laddered my arms. Cushioning my bones. Filling my veins with the calm peace of summer forests.

But I didn't need peace. I parried the woman's strike, shoving her blade to the side. I kicked one of her knees, hard. It wasn't elegant, but it worked—she stumbled off-balance, catching herself with the wicked tip of her claíomh in the dirt. Thorny vines sprang from the earth, swiftly twining around the blade. The She-Cub cursed and tugged at the hilt, but the briars made no distinction between steel and flesh. They whipped around her hands, her wrists, biting and piercing skin where they found it behind her armor. She yelled and jerked her arms away. Blood dripped scarlet down her forearms, staining the white fur lining the backs of her hands.

"I do not need a sword to best you, little changeling." Her yellow gaze was violent. "And I'm afraid your sister never mentioned in what condition she wished you brought before her."

She lifted her hands. Where before there had been fingers, there were now claws—brutally long and wickedly sharp. She slashed out at me. I dodged, whipped my blades up to guard my face. But she was fast and furious and unnaturally strong. She attacked me with the single-mindedness of a predator, her reflexes as swift and canny as a true wolf's. It was all I could do to stay on my feet, let alone defend myself against the barrage of razored blows she rained down on me. I retreated. My heel caught a tree root. I went down, falling gracelessly onto my arse. I fumbled for my fallen blade, but she was too fast. One of her ruthless paws gripped the back of my neck, her claws scoring my skin. The other found the waist of my breeches.

She lifted me bodily above her head and flung me. For a moment,

I hung weightless in the night. Then my back collided with a tree, knocking the breath from my lungs and sending blackness to tug at my vision. I slid, rough bark scraping lines of agony down my spine. I fell on my hands and knees in a cradle of roots. Broken bark and spiny needles and splinters of wood rained down around me.

"Finish him!" The She-Cub's voice filtered through my ringing ears. "Then we take the girl and go."

Shite. I forced myself to look up through the haze of pain. A few paces away, Irian toiled against three huge assailants. His sword was a halo of wailing blackness as he whirled and feinted and ducked and parried. My throat tightened at the sheer beauty of his skill—the finesse of his fighting never failed to impress me. But creeping worry mingled with my awe. Even he was beginning to flag, and for every warrior he cut down, there was another waiting to take their place.

I'd gotten us into this fracas. I would be the one to get us out.

My fingers convulsed in the litter of wooden splinters beneath me.

An idea green as leaf-glass coiled through my veins. I looked back at the tree Almha's daughter had thrown me into—a juvenile larch, its soft lower branches now crooked and damaged from where I'd struck it. It might survive the insult; it might not. Regret slowed my decision, but I heard the She-Cub's footsteps prowling toward me. She did not hurry—she thought me beaten. Which meant I had only a few moments to best her.

I looked down at my wrists, as I had so many times in the past week—at the tangle of unfamiliar brambles and slender feathers coiling toward my shoulders. It wasn't hard to understand what the tattoos symbolized. Although the black ribbon and green vine Irian had used to handfast us were both long gone—lost beneath the Heartwood on that terrible, fateful night—they lived on in the markings we wore. In the last moments before I'd planned to take Irian's life—and his magic with it—he and I had been wed. Our lives had been bound together, in black feathers and green thorns and spilled blood.

Neither of us could have guessed what would happen when I sacrificed myself, instead of him, to the Heartwood. I had died. I had been reborn. And now—now I was bound to the Sept of Feathers, by the promise of my human heart. Bound to the Sept of Antlers, by the promise of the Heart of the Forest. And bound to Irian in ways I was only beginning to understand.

I slid a finger over my wrist, gliding it along the edge of a sharp black feather.

"Irian," I cried out.

His head whipped up. His raven hair—long enough now to kiss the nape of his neck—whirled around his ears as he looked for me. Across the melee his gaze fastened on mine, pale as the moon and sharp as a sword.

"Wind," I screamed, and prayed he understood. "Give me wind!"

The breeze at my back gathered speed. I bent, laid my hands against the roots jutting from the ground.

"Sorry, friend," I whispered to the tree in the moment before I shattered it.

The air exploded with shards of wood, splinters of branches, sharp corners of pinecones. The wind turned vicious, a sudden gale-force tempest lacerating the glen. Trees bent so far forward their branches touched the ground. White-foam horses raced across the lough. And a thousand blade-sharp splinters of larch whistled deadly toward the She-Cub's fiann.

Not all found their mark. Some landed harmless on the beach or knifed into the calming lough. But when I dared look up, nearly all the warriors lay injured or dying on the beach. Many were blinded—they howled at a moon they could no longer see. Ragged punctures wept blood over pelts of white fur; uneven slashes mutilated faces. And Almha's daughter—standing a few paces from me when the splinters flew—was dead, her throat ripped out by my vengeful magic.

"Colleen." Irian fell to his knees beside me in the litter of needles and pinecones and splinters. He gathered me against him. I tilted my face up to his, letting him rain kisses on my cheeks. My forehead. My lips. I shuddered with adrenaline and relief and the comfort of his closeness. "You mad, wild, reckless thing. She could have killed you. And if not her, Eala."

I wasn't sure that was true. Nearly a year ago, Irian had said about his Treasure, *It won't let me die.* In the same way, I didn't think the Treasure now tethered to my heart, my soul—my very being—would let me simply *die.* And although I wasn't sure what my adoptive sister wanted from me, I had to believe murdering me wasn't top of her list.

"You can yell at me later." I drew away from him, turned my attention toward the fiann of warped Gentry warriors writhing and dying on the beach. I didn't regret what I'd done to protect myself, but this was…messy. Shards of wood had shredded skin, pierced bone, mangled muscle. Those who survived would be maimed or crippled for life. Those who didn't would die long, agonizing deaths. Ravens would peck out their eyes; bone-foxes would feast on their flesh. "They don't deserve to die like this."

Irian stared at the destruction I'd wrought, his pale eyes opaque as the moon sliding behind the trees. Then he stood, hefting the midnight length of the Sky-Sword. Its carven metal was already stained with half-dried blood. "A swift death is the best mercy."

"There's no need." I also stood, laying a forestalling hand on Irian's arm. I glanced at the ragged stump of the larch I'd shattered, then back at the mangled fiann. "I started this. Let me be the one to finish it. Let the forest have them. At least then they might still live. In a way."

I had barely thought it before it became so. The blue-green stone above my breast throbbed hard above my heart. Veins of green and brown blurred out from the edge of the forest toward the fallen warriors. The shards of larch wood embedded in their flesh—the needles and pinecones and splinters—burst to life. Rough brown bark crusted over their skin. Their bodies went rigid as wood.

Their limbs split and fractured, fractal fingers becoming a thousand reaching twigs. The blood speckling the beach erupted into undergrowth—ferns and mushrooms and flowering vines.

Within moments, there were no remnants of the Silver She-Wolf's fiann. Only the ravenous forest marching a little closer to the lough.

I turned toward Irian, sudden exhaustion tugging at my limbs. He folded me against him, sweeping the length of his discarded mantle around my shoulders. The edge of his jaw slid over my wind-tangled hair; his lips brushed the seashell of my ear.

"Am I allowed to start yelling at you yet?"

"You could." My arms looped around his tapered waist. I slid one finger, then two, then my whole palm beneath the fabric of his shirt. He jerked at the touch, the ridges of his stomach flexing hot and hard beneath my palm. I smiled up at him. "If that's what you want to do."

He tilted his face down toward mine, closing what little gap remained between us. The waning moon had set, rendering the predawn darker than the night, and Irian's features abstract. A dark, arching eyebrow. A sculpted cheekbone. His plush lips, lifting sideways over a polished canine.

"Not anymore, colleen."

I looped my arms around his neck and drew him down for a searing, simmering kiss. He tasted like ice water and the hour before dawn. "Then hurry up and take me home, Sky-Sword."

Chapter Two

The night sky bent, churned, turned itself inside out around us. A momentary wave of dizziness. A brief, blistering urge to vomit.

Irian's favorite mode of travel was my *least* favorite.

But as Irian had once promised, I was getting used to it. Or perhaps I was more focused on his fingers tangling in my hair and cupping the nape of my neck. His mouth dragging fire up the column of my throat. His hard body fitting against mine in a way that still felt deliciously new and irresistibly alluring.

His tower room was unlit save for the gray line of false dawn ringing his windows. We fumbled in the dark, tripping over discarded blankets and careless pillows. Three months ago, I had nearly Greenmarked his chambers to oblivion. Dried goldenrod and drooping asters brushed us as we stumbled toward the half-rotted mattress.

"Have you ever considered," I asked, my voice a breathless whisper in the dim, "buying candles?"

"Have you ever considered, colleen," he breathed back, "that I possess the enviable talent of being able to see in the dark?"

Proving his point, Irian bypassed the mattress completely, lifting me deftly over a row of cantankerous gorse bushes intent on ripping my trousers. My spine collided with the wall. Remembering how Almha's daughter had thrown me into the larch, I hissed against anticipated pain. But none came.

"My back," I gasped out. Irian froze, concern icing over his desire. I laughed, squeezing his bicep in reassurance. "No, I mean—it feels *fine*. Good as new. Yet another benefit of becoming a Treasure, I assume?"

"Accelerated healing is part of the package, yes." He dropped his head beside mine, whispered his next words onto my throat. "But do not think yourself invincible, colleen. Burns or lacerations may knit up in hours. But deeper wounds can be unpredictable. Internal injuries may take far longer to heal, leaving you vulnerable."

"So you're saying I should avoid getting stabbed?"

His laugh ruffled my hair. "Please."

Irian's hands slid down from my waist to cup my rear. I hooked my legs around his waist. Wordlessly, he slid one hand down the length of my leg. Untied my boots. Nudged them off. Tossed them to clatter in the corner.

His hand on my chin was a question. I answered, tilting my face toward his and sliding my tongue over his bottom lip. He caught my mouth and kissed me deeply. Leisurely. As if now that he had me in his arms, he was in no hurry to do anything but enjoy me.

After a moment, he drew back. In the dim, his expression was a puzzle.

"Colleen," he murmured. "I have something I wish to ask you."

A giddy flush of nerves burned heat onto my cheeks. "Then ask."

"Tonight, down on the beach." He paused, as if searching for the right words. "Did you call me *sweetheart* for all the She-Wolf's fiann to hear?"

Surprise made me still. Then I burst out laughing, laying my forehead against his shoulder and cackling into his chest.

"Did you not like it?" I finally managed.

"I liked it about as much as *Beefswaddle*," he growled. "If you are to call me by a pet name, colleen, then I insist you choose something better."

"Why?" I lifted my head, searching for his silver eyes in the dark. My hands found the sharp curve of his jaw. Traced the hollows of his cheekbones; the elegant angle of his eyebrows. "Do you object to being called my *heart*?"

"Never." His fingers brushed over the Treasure at my chest, glowing faintly in the dim, then trailed lower. "I object to being called *sweet*."

He unlaced my shirt deftly, each motion of his hands keeping time to the throb of my heart. The garment fell open, and he palmed my breast, brushing a sword-calloused thumb over one peaked nipple. I gasped, and he caught the sound with his lips, dragging his mouth over mine. His hand roamed lower, gliding over the plane of my stomach until it found the waistband of my trousers. He unlaced them with the same easy speed as my shirt. His hand glided hot between my legs, against my ready slickness.

His mouth dropped to my neck. He slid a finger inside me. Two. I closed my eyes and rocked against him, his touch burning heat through my veins. I moaned at the slippery ache coiling tight in my belly, and he made a sound deep in his throat. His fingers never stopped. I hooked my heel deeper into his back and let him drive me toward the edge—until I was gasping in his ear and digging my fingernails into his shoulders. Only then did I stop him with a hand on his wrist; a palm in the center of his chest. He stilled but didn't take his hand from my trousers.

"Tell me, colleen." His words rasped with desire. From the window, a marigold flush of dawn kissed his hard jaw. "Tell me where you want me."

"You know."

"Tell me anyway." His plush mouth curved. "I want to hear you say it."

A glittering thrill sped my heartbeat and bathed my spine in warmth. My gaze collided with Irian's—in the rising light, motes of gold touched the silver of his irises.

"I want you inside me, Sky-Sword." I reveled in the way my words transformed him. His pupils blowing dark in his metal eyes...his whole body going rigid...his mouth softening. "But slowly. I want you to fuck me until the morning comes."

He didn't need to be told twice. He tore his shirt over his head, slipped off our trousers, then lifted me back to the wall. My spine pressed against cold stone as my front molded to his marvelous muscular heat. His fingertips burned divots into my hip bones as he hooked my knee over his elbow...then pushed inside me, inch by glorious inch. Slowly—achingly slow. The sensation broke my control. I writhed against him, crying out as pleasure tangled sharp thorns in my core. Burned summertime heat up my back. Burst leafing green behind my eyelids. The wall at my back exploded with growth—an emerald corona of pillowy moss and creeping phlox and flowering vines. The masonry protested, stones groaning.

Irian smiled and slowed his movements further. Red winter sunlight slit through black branches and clawed for the windowsill. My breathing came rough and ragged. I arched my back, dug my fingertips into the spray of soft black hairs at the nape of his neck, wrapped my thighs tighter around his waist. I slid my tongue along his ear, nipping gently at the lobe.

"Irian," I whispered. "The sun is almost up."

He made that low sound in the back of his throat and drove so deep inside me stars shattered behind my eyes. He pushed me faster, although his movements never lost their precision. He fucked like he fought—methodically, gracefully, enthusiastically. His fingers brushed the side of my breast, his thumb drawing circles around my nipple. Renewed pleasure bloomed inside me.

Sunlight burst over the sill, crowning Irian in gold. His hand slid up the column of my throat, applying gentle pressure to my chin, until there was nowhere to look but at him. His eyes bored into me, losing their moonlit glow as they transformed with the morning. Blue as an azure sky ringed with gold, with a shadow of night lingering in their depths. I gasped, the intensity of our physical connection mingling with the overwhelming intimacy of his direct gaze. My breath rushed hot in my lungs. My back went rigid, and the wall behind us complained again.

Never breaking eye contact, Irian slid his hand down my stomach. His fingers again found the peak of my pleasure, slippery and hot. The barest touch pushed me over the edge. He held me as I shattered against him, whimpering and shuddering. Greenery whispered and convulsed on the wall behind me, raining fragments of stone and mortar onto our heads. Only then did Irian finally take his own pleasure, his movements turning relentless until he finished with one last heaving thrust.

The wall at my back shivered, splintered, then caved in. Crumbled stone and mortar and a thousand tiny white flowers showered down around us. Irian cursed as he cupped the back of my head and twisted me around, shielding me from the detritus with his body. I yelped, flailed. We both lost our balance. We collapsed onto the edge of the flowering mattress, which in turn disintegrated in a puff of pollen and dried flowers. We fell with a thump onto the floor.

"Colleen!" Irian's voice was rough with concern. "Are you all right?"

I brushed dried petals out of my eyes and looked up at him. Motes of golden dust danced around his face, contorted with worry. I looked beyond him, at the crumbled wall and the rising dawn and the botanical mayhem. Then I was laughing, choking on pollen. I buried my face in his shoulder, giggling with absurdity and joy and the afterglow of pleasure.

"You *are* mad, colleen." Irian dragged his mantle from our tangle of clothes. He curled it around my shoulders as he tucked me close into his chest.

"*Wonderfully* mad." Exhaustion pulled at my eyelids. "Right?"

"Yes." His smile dazzled like sunlight. He brushed a calloused thumb over my bottom lip, then kissed me. "Magnificently mad."

But in the moment before he closed his eyes, a flicker of darkness crossed his expression. A shadow—a shadow shaped like the same inexplicable fear I'd seen earlier tonight.

A cold, sunlit breeze needled over the windowsill and bit through Irian's heavy woolen mantle. I shivered and nestled deeper in his arms.

I was the forest.

I was huge, ancient, infinite. The shaded path between the trees. The touch of sunlight on half-buried stones.

In the dappled light, the doe was nearly invisible. I could see only her mournful, depthless eyes. They pierced me between the shifting shadows. She lifted her head, flicked her ears.

When she opened her mouth, she had human teeth.

"A long time ago," she said, "you were given away for safekeeping. Now you have been given back to yourself."

I surged awake, the dream already cleaving away from my mind. A riot of sunshine burned over my face—late morning, if not yet noon. I reached for Irian's comforting bulk, but my fingers found only chilly air. I cracked bleary eyes and levered myself up onto an elbow, winding the rumpled mantle around my nakedness as I looked around the tower room.

Irian curled in the window casement, his long legs slung against the sill and his sculpted cheek pressed to the glass. His gaze was fixed somewhere out the window—he hadn't yet noticed I'd awoken. It was rare to observe Irian alone—unguarded. He held himself nearly motionless—a statue in repose. His raven hair—longer now than when I'd first met him—flopped, unruly, over one eye and curled behind his ears. Only his hand moved, sliding restively up and down the windowpane, coalescing lines of condensation in its wake. He seemed to revel in the morning—lifting his angular chin so his face caught the sun. Sliding his blue-and-gold eyes along the curved bellies of clouds. Inhaling the high, bright wind slicing in off the lough.

It occurred to me—blazingly, uncomfortably—that for someone I'd shared so much with, I knew him so little. It also occurred to me that he had been alone for much, much longer than he'd been with me.

My enemy. My lover. My *husband*.

The thought unearthed jagged roots of uneasy emotion. I stamped them down before they had a chance to blossom beneath the light of my attention.

My observation began to border on voyeurism. I coughed. Irian turned. A brief shadow winnowed over his gaze before it settled toward warmth. He smiled halfway, his plush lips crooked.

"Good morning, colleen."

"Good morning, darling."

"Darling?" Irian grimaced. "Still objectively worse than *Beefswaddle*."

"I'm just going to start calling you *Beefswaddle* and be done with it." I narrowed my eyes at him. "Are you planning on coming over here and kissing me anytime soon?"

"And miss the opportunity to watch you saunter across my room clothed in nothing but my mantle?" He said it easily, but the weight of his eyes sparked heat in my belly. "Not likely."

A challenge. I climbed to my feet in the wreckage of the bedroom, curling his dark mantle immodestly around my waist and chest so that most of my back and the outer curve of my breasts were still on display. Running a hand through my messy hair, I crossed slowly toward the window. His eyes followed the sway of my limbs, grazing the arch of my waist, the length of my neck, the curve of my hips. He shifted on the sill, bending toward me as I approached. He kissed me deeply, lingering on my lips, then lifted me against him, curling my back to his front and resting his jaw on the top of my head.

I looked down through the window. Winter gripped Tír na nÓg in shades of gray, but color still found ways to flourish. Brilliant feathers ruffled from the tails of glass-bright songbirds; winter berries clustered like rubies and sapphires on trees pebbled with frost. The sky was a shade of blue I'd never seen in the mortal lands—luminous as a wish and cold as a secret. Far below, the lough was a dark circle of slate. A family of extravagantly crested ducks left tiny white wakes behind them.

"You said I was a swan when you found me." The question left me abruptly. Irian tensed at my back, and I almost regretted bringing it up. But I still had questions about what had happened after the night of the Ember Moon. Over a month had passed, and while I had my own recollections, they were like a fading dream. A warm, calm expanse of roots and branches; an endless sky; the sensation of being infinitely known, infinitely accepted.

"Perhaps it is your anam cló—your soul form."

"Yet the night of the Ember Moon, I gave myself to the Heart of the Forest—to Deirdre's Treasure. I sacrificed myself for the Treasure of the Sept of Antlers. Why would I be transformed into a swan?"

Irian twined his fingers in mine, twisting my wrist so our tattoos lay against each other. My new markings were a tangle of thorny vines, interspersed with sharp black feathers arranged in loose, harmonic circles—almost like the petals of a flower. His were the same stiff black pinions layered in sharp, harsh angles climbing his arm. Yet where I'd once thought his markings unchanged by our handfasting, I now knew that was not the case. Slender vines snaked between the feathers, studded with tiny flowers and tinier thorns.

"You and I were wed, colleen." Irian's voice bruised with emotion. "Among the Folk, the magic of handfasting is not unlike the magic of a geas. It is a binding, an obligation—a knitting together of two into one. Two bodies. Two hearts. Two souls."

The words of the oath we'd made to each other echoed in my

ears, little more than a month old and yet so strangely distant. As if it had been someone other than me who'd said them. *Blood of my blood, and bone of my bone, I shall not permit thee to wander alone.* Heat and shadow choked me when I remembered that night. The piercing ache of feathers tearing from my hair as we fled into the forest, away from Eala's terrible coup. Irian's huge hand gripping mine as he looped makeshift ribbons around my wrist. Thorns biting the skin of my arm as I whispered hurried, frantic words to a man I barely knew. A man I had nevertheless begun to love. A man I had never intended to marry—at least, not so soon. *Give me your heart and let it be known: that then, now, and after, you are my home.*

I had promised myself twice over that night. Once to Irian. Again to the Heartwood. In both cases, I wasn't exactly sure what I'd bargained in return.

"Colleen." Irian's hand found my chin, pulled my gaze to his. His gilded eyes burned blue, so unfamiliar to me after a year of seeing nothing but his nocturnal silver. "Do you regret it?"

"No." The refusal came easily—I meant it. I shifted in his lap, swiveling until I sat facing him, my legs looped around his waist. Under other circumstances, the position would have been carnal. But here—now—it wasn't. It was just intimate. "But I'm trying to understand. Nothing happened the way I thought it would."

"Indeed. I did not die." Irian grinned, a brilliant flash of his lovely white teeth. But the smile didn't quite reach his eyes. "You did."

"About that." I brushed my hand along the plane of his cheek, curling an errant strand of midnight hair behind his ear. A thrill sang through me when he leaned into the touch. "Why did we both live? Two Treasures were renewed that night. Yet only one life was tithed. And then, only temporarily."

"I do not know." Irian caught my hand, kissed my palm. His eyes flicked toward the sky outside, where scalloped white clouds swept over the sun. "You are a changeling, Fia. Fair Folk blood runs in your veins. Our lifespans are long—hundreds, sometimes thousands of years. When you resurrected the Heart of the Forest—bargained with the Heartwood to renew its magic—you traded that unknowable time for a mere thirteen years. Perhaps my own reprieve was stolen from the same lifespan." He paused for a long, tense moment. "We both survived the Ember Moon, colleen. But we are not delivered from our fate. We have simply put it off. Both our lives are still forfeit to the magic holding this land together. Our power is great, but the cost is high. You and I—we are both waiting to die."

"How can you be so sure?" The certainty in his words chilled the warmth passing between our bodies, leaving me hollow. I gathered the folds of his mantle closer around my nakedness. "The resurrection of the Heart of the Forest was a miracle. You said it yourself—I changed our story's ending."

"For now." He sighed, his gaze winging away over my shoulder. His expression turned rueful. "That wall is somewhat worse for wear for your ministrations, colleen." For a moment, I didn't know what he was talking about. "I confess, I am surprised the whole tower did not come down around us."

Oh, *that.* I lifted my chin and quirked a brow at him. "Take it as a compliment, Sky-Sword."

A flash of dark heat seared his eyes. "I cannot pay the mason in compliments."

"*I* could try."

"You would not dare." His hands found my waist. His fingers—less scalding now than they'd once seemed—were deft beneath my ribs as he tickled me in earnest. I squealed, writhing in his lap. He jerked me closer, his hands dropping from my waist to my hips. He curled his palms around the fullness of my rear, gathering me closer. My dark, tangled hair made a curtain around us. But even as desire kindled in his eyes, the shadows I was beginning to despise cooled it. "Did you think on what I asked you, colleen?"

I rocked my hips against him. He was too close; I, too naked. His words barely made an impact. "Hmm?"

"How do you plan to harness the new power of your Treasure?"

I stilled. Now I remembered—he had asked me that two nights ago. And possibly the day before that. In fact, he'd *maybe* mentioned it every single day since I'd arisen, drenched and dazed, from the darkness of the lough. Almost against my will, my eyes drifted toward the wall I'd ruined last night. Vines thick as my wrist choked huge slabs of granite; a kaleidoscope of unseasonable flowers blazed glory across the rubble.

My eyes jerked back to Irian's, and I was unsurprised to find them churning with shadows. Fear—so palpable it took my breath away.

"Is that what you're afraid of?" I whispered. "Me?"

"I do not fear you, Fia. I fear *for* you." Worry made his gaze stark. "The innate magic you once called your Greenmark is gone, replaced by something infinitely more powerful. Ten—a hundred—times stronger. The experience of inheriting a Treasure is complicated—"

"I have it under control, Irian."

But that wasn't true, and we both knew it. Since the Ember Moon, I barely had to look at something before it burst with flowering vines and leafing greenery. I'd easily torn that larch to deadly shreds, returned the She-Wolf's fiann to nature within mere moments. My passion—my pleasure—had nearly destroyed the tower. And I hadn't even told Irian about the dreams—about the surreal images that flooded my mind when I slept. Images that felt somewhere between memory and prophecy. Images that frightened me. Fascinated me.

"If you are not careful, you could become a danger to yourself. Or others. The power could consume you—transform you. Please— there are methods I can teach you. Mantras and meditations—"

I clutched at the blue-green stone throbbing above my breast. "I don't need *mantras*—"

"Hey! Hellooooo?" A strident, feminine voice echoed up the coiled stairwell, startling us both and breaking the tension. "Are you two lovebirds wearing clothes? Or do I need to blindfold myself before entering the sanctum of the beloved?"

Irian looked at me for a moment longer, shadows still clouding the unfamiliar blue of his gaze. Then a small smile touched his face. He rose from the windowsill, setting me gently on my feet in his demolished bedroom.

"I nearly forgot," he said. "Chandika returns today."

Chapter Three

Irian and I dressed hurriedly, fumbling for mismatched clothing scattered around his tower room. Over the past week, I'd discovered that Irian's wardrobe consisted of a whole lot of once-fine but now-threadbare tunics in indiscriminate dark colors and breeches that invariably had holes in awkward places. And since I'd sloshed out of the lough wearing nothing but the Heart of the Forest and a scattering of black swan feathers, I'd lamentably had to rely on said disagreeable wardrobe for my own outfits.

Considering Irian towered over me by more than a head and boasted muscles to match his height, to say his clothes didn't fit me was a significant understatement.

Irian swiftly dragged a dark blue shirt over his head—not bothering to tuck it into the pair of gray trousers hanging low around his hips—then observed me getting dressed with a smile I wasn't sure I appreciated. The sleeves on his borrowed tunic were so long I had to cuff them nearly to the shoulder; the shortest pair of his trousers puddled around my feet and dragged on the floor. I hopped on one foot as I tried to roll them up to my ankles, then strapped them high above my hips with a belt that went around my waist nearly twice.

When I looked up, Irian was still watching me. His smile widened, and—had he not been teasing me—the sharp beauty of it would have carved the breath from my lungs.

"What?" I demanded, narrowing my eyes and cinching the belt even tighter. "Something funny?"

"Not funny, no." He closed the distance between us and slid his hands around my waist, where his trousers gaped despite the belt. "Adorable."

"I look like a sheerie dressed in leipreachán's clothing," I griped. "It's embarrassing."

"It is adorable." His eyes were azure and gilt. He pulled me closer, the hands roaming up my ribs sending heat to spike my spine. His touch, once so hot against mine that it nearly burned, was now only pleasantly warm. The heat of a man, not a demigod. I wondered—not for the first time—whether his skin had cooled with the renewal of his Treasure...or whether mine had risen in tenor to meet his. "Impossibly, unbearably adorable."

"Chandi's waiting for us." I swatted his hands away. "And she's not a very patient person."

"No." He relented with a sigh. "Last time I made Chandika wait in the fort, she dismantled all the wall sconces and set a fire in the cellar. And after last night, I am not sure the fort can stand any more damage."

"I did already apologize for that." I dragged him toward the stairs. "And I'm sure Chandi isn't going to start any fires."

I immediately had to eat my words. At the bottom of the stairs, Chandi crouched before the hearth, swathed in lengths of furs, blowing forcefully over scattered kindling and sparking coals. Her long black hair dangled over her shoulders, drifting dangerously close to the uneven blaze she'd lit.

"Chandika," Irian said levelly. "What do you think you are doing?"

She rounded on us, the fire's warmth pinking her brown cheeks and putting flames in her amber eyes. "Do you two have *any* idea how cold it is in here?"

I laughed, giddy, and flung myself at her. Although Irian had repeatedly assured me she'd survived Eala's Gate coup with little harm, I hadn't seen Chandi since the night of the Ember Moon. It felt like longer than five weeks—it felt like a lifetime. So much had passed between us, in those final moments before I'd fled to the Heartwood with Irian. I remembered how I'd begged Chandi not to let Eala take her heart—how every imperfect interaction between us had fallen away because all I'd wanted was for her to *survive*. And I remembered how she'd helped us flee—how she'd sacrificed her own safety to stand up to Eala, to stand up to—

I pushed away the pernicious thought lapping at my attention before it had the chance to swamp me. I hugged Chandi harder, until she whimpered theatrically and pinched my arm in self-defense.

"You're strangling me."

"Only a little." I swiped a surreptitious hand over my eyes before I drew away. "I'm glad to see you."

"Hmm." She looked me up and down, her eyebrows rising as she took in my attire. "What happened to you? You look like a little lad dressed up in his father's castoffs."

I shot Irian a look that said, *I told you so.*

"And you look like a skinned bear." I glanced askance at her layers of furs. "What happened to swanning around the woods wearing nothing but your birthday suit?"

"Eala happened." Chandi's expression barely changed, but when she turned her head to look at Irian, I noticed a slender pink scar snaking along her collarbone and down her chest. "When she broke Irian's geas over us swan maidens, we all reverted back to our mortal forms. Whatever magic kept me warm in the depths of winter is sadly gone. As is my ability to drink liquor from dusk to dawn without consequence. Did you know that humans get *hangovers* when they drink too much? Oh, and I have to eat food three to four times a day, or else I feel like I'm dying. Do you *know* how much food that is? It's piles of it. Literal pounds and pounds of food. Every single day."

"Chandi—" I tried to interject.

"On that note." She indicated the basket beside the hearth. "The Summer Twins send their regards."

"What—" I flipped up the basket's lid. Nestled inside were piles of lush pastries and crusty breads studded with fruit and glazed with honey. My stomach grumbled, although I wasn't entirely sure whether it was from actual hunger...or old habit. I inhaled a pastry that looked like a bird's nest and spoke around a full mouth. "You absolute paragon of personhood. This is exactly what I needed."

"You do not actually need physical nourishment, you know." Irian's voice remained meticulously even as he approached the flagging fire. He kicked dying embers into the grate and rearranged the kindling until flames licked upward. "The power of your Treasure will sustain you in a way that food and drink will not."

Yet another consequence of my mystical transformation. An unexpected tendril of longing turned the food to ash in my mouth. Longing for a self I'd sacrificed, in return for unknowable and unexplored new characteristics. Longing for what had been, if only because I could never have it back again.

"Where's the fun in that?" I rolled my eyes at Chandi, who cracked a smile. "Now, if only you'd brought me a strong mug of life-bestowing coffee, I could die happy."

"In Mag Mell, they make a brew from mushrooms that heats the blood and sustains energy." Irian's voice remained so expressionless that it had the opposite effect as he intended. Once upon a time, this was the only Irian I knew—cold, controlled. But his true disposition was as shifting as the winds he commanded—his mouth sliding from a grimace to a grin with his emotions, his eyes intense with mercurial thoughts. This flat, forced affect made me nervous. "Perhaps that might satiate the craving."

"I've tried that." Chandi selected a round bread jeweled with winter pears and glazed with syrup and picked it apart with deft fingers. "I'm convinced it's just mud."

For a few moments, we munched in peace. Then Irian lifted

his gilded eyes from the fire, sliding them first to Chandi, then to me. His gaze lingered on mine, jagged tenderness lurking behind a bank of dark resolve. My anxiety grew unwieldy, scratching the inside of my skin with sharp thorns.

"What news from the twins, Chandika?" Irian asked.

Chandi set down the uneaten portion of her bread and brushed a finger over her scar—a new, unconscious gesture. For the past five weeks—since Eala's coup of the Gates on Samhain—Chandi and the remaining swan maidens who had defied their princess had escaped to the Holly Gate—Geata Tinne. Siobhán and Seaghán, the Summer Twins—bardaí of the Holly Gate—were the first to set themselves against Eala and had become de facto leaders of the Folk opposition to her ambitions. But if Almha's daughter's loyalties last night were any indication, that opposition was shrinking by the day.

I swallowed another bite of my pastry, but it stuck in my throat like dirt.

"The Summer Twins have made their position clear—they do not wish to see Eala consolidate more power. Nor do they wish to wage war upon the human realms, should she succeed in somehow dismantling the Gates and attacking the high queen of Fódla." Chandi's expression bordered on grave, and it sent another tendril of yearning to scrabble up my ribs. I missed the Chandi I'd come to love last year. That girl's face had not been suited to war—it had been meant for laughter and strong drinks, daring fashion choices and devilish commentary. I did not know this Chandi—scarred, weather whipped, grim. "They are taking dissenters and refugees under their protection. But they have not outright stated any intention to mount an offensive against Eala. They are but one realm among thirteen. Their position is precarious."

Irian nodded as if he'd already known what Chandi was going to say. "What of the other three Gate bardaí who have also declined to join Eala?"

"They remain neutral—for now." Chandi made a helpless

gesture. "But if I know anything about Eala, it is that she is persuasive. She has a knack for finding the chink in a person's armor—the soft spot they would do anything to protect. She will not bide her time in this conflict—I daresay she has been planning it for longer than any of us knew. By the next full moon, everything could be different."

A green log popped in the hearth. Irian jerked at the sound. Light flared across the room, and in its wake a shadow seemed to beat around his shoulders and darken his gaze. Some decision—or hesitation—made a wasteland of his face.

"Then our path is clear." His voice lost its level. "It is time for us to leave this place."

The statement thudded through me. Irian kept speaking, but the rest of his words fell away like autumn leaves from a barren tree, meaningless in the wake of the ones that had come before it.

It is time for us to leave.

My palm crushed the greasy remnants of a pastry I didn't realize I was still holding. When I forced my fingers to unhinge, I saw the raisins studding the tart had turned back into grapes, their wrinkled skins expanding until they glowed with plumpness and moisture.

"Leave?" The word burst out of me, more forceful than I'd intended. Irian and Chandi broke off the conversation they'd continued without me. "We can't leave."

Irian frowned. "Colleen—"

"We can't leave." I stood. The pastry fell from my lap, and the fat, lush grapes burst where they met the stone floor. Where their moisture spattered, small ugly plants sprang up—birthwort, snake lily, sedge. Chandi's eyes widened. "My sister has stolen what does not belong to her. The hearts of her maidens. The Gates of the bardaí. The loyalty of misguided Folk. And she won't stop there. Once she has enough support, she will break down the Gates and assault the human realms." My words came out rushed, imperfect. "We have a duty to defy her. Like Siobhán and Seaghán. We have to stay—to wrest back the Gates from her control, to rescue the Folk from her dark ambitions, to protect the human realms, to—"

Abruptly, my tirade ended, foundering on the thought I had refused to confront.

Irian's mouth was a sharp cut across his face. "To save Rogan?"

His words knocked me over. I sat down, hard. Around me, the plants I'd conjured withered, desiccating in an instant until nothing was left but brown petals and moldering leaves. Irian uncrossed his arms. A faint breeze rose up, swirling the dust and decay away from my bare feet.

"What do you know?" Chandi stood, forcing nonchalance as she gathered her furs around her. "That fire is burning mighty low. I suppose someone had better go hunt for more firewood."

She fled. I barely registered her leaving. The mention of Rogan— the thought of whom I had been meticulously keeping at bay since I'd risen from the lough—pummeled me with a tide of bittersweet emotion. Almost from the first moment I'd arrived in the high queen's keep in Rath na Mara as a child—an unexpected and unwanted changeling—Rogan had been my only friend. My confidant. My partner in crime. As we grew from children, our relationship shifted toward something both sweeter and harder to bear. But our love story was not one that was ever meant to be told. He had been betrothed to the high queen's true daughter, Eala, from birth. Last year, he'd accompanied me to Tír na nÓg in order to rescue her from Irian's geas even as I sought to take Irian's Treasure for the good of Fódla.

But Eala had been the cunning architect of her own freedom. She had wrested powerful, bloody magic from the hearts of her maidens in order to seize the Gates. And she had stolen Rogan's free will by forcing him to devour the small black blossoms born from wild magic. The last time I'd seen the prince, on the night of the Ember Moon, he was Eala's thrall, his self subsumed to her control.

And I wasn't sure I could bear it. Rogan was still important to me. Despite everything that had happened between him and me—misunderstandings and misery, heartbreak and healing—he still held a piece of my heart. The heart of my childhood, of my innocence, of my *humanness*. And here—now—in the wake of a supernatural transformation that had stripped away so much of who I'd been and left something inescapably *other* behind, I wasn't sure I could let that part of me go. I wasn't sure I could let *him* go.

Not if there was any way to save him from Eala.

"We can't leave." The repeated words left my lips like a prayer, whisper soft. "Not yet. We can't."

"Fia." Irian knelt before me. His huge, warm hands braceleted my wrists, and our complementary markings seemed to tangle together, thorny flowers and black feathers punctuating our skin. "You cannot save him."

"You don't understand." I looked down at our joined hands. "I ate that black flower last summer. I felt the way it crawled through my veins and warped my perceptions. The way it ground down my will until I could no more have disobeyed its influence than commanded my own heart to stop beating. Rogan has no Folk blood to protect him from its full power. I don't blame you for wanting to keep me from him—"

"Do not think me jealous, colleen." Irian lifted a calloused palm to my face, gently tilting my chin up. "How could I be jealous of him when it is me you have chosen?"

His thumb brushed my bottom lip before he bent to cover my mouth with his. I kissed him back—sweet heat and kept promises— but in the back of my throat I tasted unshed tears and the earthy tang of creeping rot.

Regret shone in his eyes as he drew back. "You cannot save him, because I am not sure there is anything to save. No one knows what extended exposure to the black flower does to a human. They only began to grow after wild magic was freed. It has been over a month since Eala made Rogan her thrall. He may not still be alive."

"He's still alive. Eala wouldn't kill him—he's too useful to her."

"*Assuming* he is still alive," Irian allowed, "the things that made him who he once was may be gone. Wiped away by the inexorable magic of the black flowers." He rubbed a gentling palm up my arm, and I realized I was shivering. "Besides, colleen—how would you propose to rescue him? If he is truly useful to Eala, she will not let you saunter into her stronghold and spirit him away. Or she will, only to force *you* to stay—for whatever nefarious reason she sent Almha's daughter to capture you."

"We are tánaistí, Irian—we are Treasures." The words came out harsh and forceful. Thorns prickled along my wrists at the places where Irian's palms gripped me. His eyes flickered, but he did not let me go. "We wield the most powerful magic in Tír na nÓg. We are practically invincible. What is any of it good for, if not *this*?"

"We are not invincible." The blade of his jaw tightened. "There are only two of us, colleen. We may wield strong magic, but it is not the only magic in Tír na nÓg. And you have barely begun learning your limits."

"That again." I surged up, breaking his grip on my wrists. I paced to the fire and back. "This isn't just about Rogan. Eala is wily—it's been just over a month since Samhain, and she's managed to turn the majority of the Gate bardaí to her cause, through treachery or temptation. How long before the neutral bardaí—or even Siobhán and Seaghán—eventually bow to her? If we have any hope of breaking her control of the Gates and preventing her from waging war on Folk and human realms alike, it has to be now. We owe it to the Folk."

"No." Irian's gaze went flat as fallow fields. "We owe them nothing."

His vehemence pushed me back a step. "We are the only living heirs to the Septs—"

"Have you forgotten why that is?" His voice turned deadly. "The bardaí and their fianna butchered the Septs. Murdered all the potential heirs. Destroyed the Treasures. Eala may be wicked, but so too are the Gate bardaí and any Folk who ally with them. This story has no hero, colleen. It is villain against villain. The bardaí started this when they stole the princess and her maidens from Fódla. Let them be the ones to finish it."

"There will be innocents caught in the fray. Surely if we stay, we could find some Folk worthy of our help."

"If I stay, it will not be to help. It will be to watch them all bleed." His gaze was savage, and for a moment I fancied the shadows lurking beyond the fire's light coalesced at his shoulders. Then his eyes softened on my face. "We are beholden only to each other, colleen. When you tithed your life instead of mine, you changed our story. Let us be the ones to decide how to tell the rest of it. Not Eala. Not the bardaí. *Us*—Fia and Irian."

His words pushed through the thicket I'd built from my fear and anger and worry, startling me with their clarity. Irian might not be jealous of the concern I harbored for Rogan, but he was asking me to choose nevertheless. Him over Rogan. Him over the Folk realms . . . over the human realms.

Him over everything.

They were all choices I had made before. They should have been easy to make again.

"Where would we go?" My words stuck in my throat like wet leaves. "If we . . . left?"

"There are two options. The first is Emain Ablach." Complicated emotions—disquiet and distant yearning—made a martyr of his face. "The Silver Isle."

I'd heard him mention it—he'd been fostered there before he'd inherited the Sky-Sword. "What is there for us in Emain Ablach?"

"Gavida, the smith-king, rules there. He swears no allegiance to the Gate bardaí, nor would he be swayed by Eala's promises. He has his own realm, his own great power. And . . ."

"And what?"

Irian exhaled roughly. "And his son and heir is a potential tánaiste."

A potential tánaiste. The words slid through me in the abstract. Only a moment later did they start to grow thick, dark roots, wrapping around my heart until I could barely breathe from the pressure of frenzied hope and creeping dismay.

"That can't be. You said I was the last—the only."

"I fear it is more complicated than that. You were not the only one—simply the only one available."

Confusion unfurled within me. "I don't understand."

Irian's face warped with indecision in the moment before he set his jaw.

"Once, in a time of worrisome wars and swelling dissent, a smith-king with the ability to forge objects of vast power divined what his son might become if he did not intervene. Gavida had no desire to see his lone heir become a pawn in a conflict he had long ago disavowed, so he curtailed his son's innate magic. He cut him off from his destiny. He prevented him from inheriting anything but what Gavida chose. And when he saw what happened to his foster son—to *me*—a few years later…he felt himself vindicated."

I took this in. "So his son is…what? Imprisoned on the Silver Isle?"

Irian tilted his head. "Something like that."

"This does change things." Thoughts scudded through me, dried leaves blown upon a gale. "This smith-king—Gavida. He was the one who originally forged the Treasures, was he not?"

"He was."

I paced to the window. Five weeks ago, there had been only one Treasure left—the Sky-Sword. Then, at the Ember Moon, through some combination of impossible magic and the force of my will, I'd resurrected the second—the Heart of the Forest. But there were still two Treasures that had been destroyed by the bardaí, releasing wild magic over the abandoned cities of the Septs.

"If he did it once, he could do it again," I said slowly. "If we can somehow convince Gavida and his son to help us reforge the other

Treasures—to resurrect the Un-Dry Cauldron and the Flaming Shield in the same way I resurrected the Heart of the Forest—then you and I truly would be invincible. We could defeat Eala—the Gate bardaí. We could renew the rule of law once wielded by the Septs. We could decisively prevent war between the realms."

"Is that truly what you wish to do, colleen?" A strain of sorrow rasped along Irian's voice. "Resurrect more Treasures? Collar more heirs with a terrible burden of power they may not have asked for? Consign them to unnaturally short lifespans?"

"I don't remember you having any of those concerns," I bit out, my gaze colliding with his, "when you convinced me to inherit your Treasure."

"That was before." Irian drew me toward him—roughly, tenderly. "Before I knew the Ember Moon was not where my story ended, but where *our* next chapter began."

"Is that option two?" I already knew the answer. "To simply run away?"

Tortured longing mingled with the fear still lurking in his eyes. "What if we had the chance to truly change things, instead of simply reinstating what came before? To set ourselves free of our fates, once and for all?"

"When I have only discovered mine?" My rising dismay felt like it might throttle me. "When there are grave wrongs that must be righted? A princess wielding stolen power? Wild magic still warping the land? We did all this so that magic might survive—so Tír na nÓg might once again flourish. We can't abandon that now."

Irian gave his head a swift, decisive jerk—between an acquiescence and a repudiation. "Then it is to be Emain Ablach."

"It's a good plan, Irian." I leaned into him. "A strategic retreat. The potential to forge new alliances—to forge new Treasures."

"All so we may then wage war." He mouthed the words like they were poison.

"Eala manipulated and lied to me, dangling her sisterly love like a scrap of meat for a dog," I reminded him. "She stole the lives of her maidens, stole the will of her betrothed. She has taken too much and has only begun to take. We cannot let her win."

A muscle high on Irian's jaw ticced as he clenched his teeth. A moment later he nodded, clearly reluctant to argue further. But I had a feeling this wouldn't be the last time we'd speak of this. "Very well."

The fort's door banged open, gusting autumn wind across the flagstones. Chandi stomped in, looking aggrieved.

"That certainly took long enough." She sniffed. "Does this mean you're leaving me to fend for myself out in the cold?"

"Never, Chandika." Irian rose to his full height, then bowed. Despite his tattered trousers, rumpled shirt, and bed hair, he looked every inch the Gentry heir. His unearthly grace never failed to take my breath away. "Eala's magic may have torn you from the geas binding us together. But I still consider you a member of my household, so long as you wish to be a part of it. Where I go, you too are welcome—and welcome to what protections I can offer. You and any of the surviving swan maidens who wish to join us. We depart three days hence."

Chandi seemed to hesitate a moment before sliding her amber eyes to me. I understood—I, too, might be loath to put myself under the protection of a Gentry heir who'd cursed me to the form of a swan for thirteen years, however noble his intentions were. But then her mouth lifted into a smile.

"Sometimes I can understand why you like him." Her smirk turned wicked. "On second thought, no, I can't. He is objectively *horrible*."

I grinned back. "And terrible in bed to boot."

Chandi screeched, clapping her hands over her ears. Irian growled and pounced on me, huge hands circling my waist as he lifted me over his shoulder and mimed tossing me out the window. I shrieked, slapping at his hands.

But even as I laughed until my sides hurt, the thick dark roots circling my heart gave a little squeeze. And I had to wonder if Irian had a point. Was it possible to choose all things?

Tír na nÓg *and* the human realms? Keeping the peace *and* waging war? Loving Irian *and* saving Rogan?

Or by failing to choose, would I end up with nothing?

Chapter Four

I sat with my back to the wall in Irian's ruined tower bedroom and tried—in vain—to meditate.

The day was clear and cold—an enamel sky etched with pale, distant clouds. Irian had left mere hours before, flinging himself from the window in an act of hubris I found disconcerting. I knew he'd regained mastery of his anam cló—his shape-shifting ability—when the Sky-Sword was renewed. But it was one thing to *know* and another thing to *witness* my new husband plunge seemingly to his death far below, only to rise transformed into a shining black bird riding thermals toward the horizon.

"We leave for Emain Ablach the day after tomorrow," he'd told me moments before that. "I will be gone tonight—perhaps tomorrow as well. I must see to some preparations."

"What kind of preparations?"

He kissed the question from my mouth, cupping my neck with sword-calloused fingers. "The wards are strong, but as you know, they are meant to keep others out. Not you in."

"You mean I'm *not* your prisoner?"

"I *do* have some manacles lying somewhere around here." His smile was lightning, a glint of a canine over a plush lip. But his eyes held a shadow of worry. "Nevertheless, I would prefer if you did not leave the fort. Not unless you have to."

Already the time seemed to yawn out. Chandi had left after breakfast, intending to return to Siobhán and Seaghán's domain in order to gather supplies and extend Irian's invitation to the remaining swan maidens. I'd gone for a long run around the lough, but though I'd pushed myself to the limits of my speed and endurance, my muscles never seemed to flag nor the breath rush in my lungs. My training sequences were much the same—although I moved through my footwork like lightning and slashed my knives with abandon, I didn't so much as stumble. It was as if my delicate human bones had been transformed into strong boughs; my muscles into supple, flexible vines; my lungs into radiant, light-devouring flowers. A cool, insidious panic had gripped me—something not even the flush of exercise and exertion could quiet.

If you are not careful, you could become a danger to yourself. Or others. The intrepid roots of Irian's words niggled at me. Surely he was exaggerating. Yet I could no longer pretend I was exactly who I'd been before I tithed myself to the Heartwood. The thought clenched my limbs and sent thorns to prick the back of my neck, even as I thrilled with the tantalizing promise of magic untapped and powers unexplored.

Which led me to now, sitting with a stone wall digging into my back and my legs crossed on chilly flagstones, swatting dried fronds of goldenrod out of my face and trying not to listen to the inaudible whispers of the wind. Meditation wasn't a novel concept to me— Cathair had attempted to teach me years ago, when adolescence had sent my temper singing toward new heights and the other fosterlings had started complaining about my violent outbursts. But I'd never taken to it. I found no peace in sitting still—no calm in silence. My thoughts darted to and fro like startled gnats, multiplying even as I strove to shoo them away. My arse was sore and my feet were going numb.

Mantras. Cathair liked mantras. I bit my lip and tried to think of a word or phrase that might focus and soothe the nervous rattle of my mind.

As within, so without. Well, it was a nice thought. But I wasn't sure it was true.

This moment is perfect, whole, and complete. Was it, though? I could think of several things making it less than perfect, and entirely incomplete.

The joy is in the thrill of the fight, not the promise of a kill.

The words sprang to mind unbidden and shattered my already dwindling serenity. I jerked to my feet and paced to the open window. My fingers knotted on the sill as I stared out, unfocused.

Rogan—Rogan had always known how to calm me. How to take the edge off my nerves with his steady presence, how to crack the surface of my fury with his easy smile. But Rogan was gone— gone where I couldn't reach him. My hands curled into fists as my memory slid with unforgiving speed toward our last interaction. Before he'd rejected Eala and she'd subsequently stolen his will, Rogan had waylaid me at the Feis of the Ember Moon. He'd confessed his enduring love for me, but I'd rebuffed him, telling him all the ways we were wrong for each other. I searched my chaotic, shock-stained memories of that night for the last words I'd spoken to him. But I couldn't remember.

A murky possibility made rot burgeon up my spine. Had the last thing I'd ever said to Rogan been how little I loved him?

A thunderous pop interrupted the spiral of my thoughts as the slab of granite beneath my fist split in two. Cruel, thorny vines curled relentlessly through the crack, studded with flowers of hellebore and henbane.

Poisonous flowers.

I jerked away, even as the brambles spilled over the sill and braided themselves along the wall. Sudden resolve put hardwood in my bones. I turned for the stairs.

I might never get the chance to say goodbye to Rogan. But he

wasn't the only person—well, *thing*, really—that was still important to me.

Returning to Dún Darragh felt like trying to remake that which
had been unmade. Winding a ball of string that had come unrav-
eled; restitching a seam that had torn apart. Every step familiar yet
wholly novel. I felt ill at ease in my own skin. I wondered, again,
whether I was truly the same girl I'd been before.

Was a butterfly, emerging from its chrysalis, the same as the cat-
erpillar who had provided the base parts for its metamorphosis?
Or, in transformation, had it become *other* in a way that could
never be reversed?

I made no effort to hide my progress as I passed through Irian's
demesne—even if his wards did not protect me, the forest surrounded me like a solicitous friend, bending bare branches in my
passing and ruffling affectionate billows of leaves against my legs. I
reached my awareness as far as it could go, sliding through the cold
loam to follow the vast network of roots before thrilling up toward
the sky. I smiled as strange flowers burst along bare branches; saplings grew broader, taller, stronger. Here, in the forest, my newfound power did not feel like a threat—it felt like a promise. A
pact.

Not something to be controlled or subdued. Something to
revel in.

Far better than sitting on my arse and trying to meditate.

I experienced a flicker of doubt when I approached the Willow
Gate—I didn't know whether I'd be able to cross over. With Rogan,
the toll had been a few drops of my blood and an incantation spoken in an ancient tongue. But that had been before—before my sacrifice had renewed both the Sky-Sword and the Heart of the Forest
and brought the boundary between the Folk and human realms
closer to its full strength.

The Gate was a bare shimmer of silver amid the sun-streaked forest. I laid a palm against it. Pushed.

The barrier bent, parted. I stepped through, a flare of energy raising the hair on the back of my neck and prickling thorns at my fingertips.

I should not have doubted my ability to pass through. I was a Treasure now. The very magic that had created these Gates surged in my veins.

Although early winter gripped both realms, Fódla seemed almost unbearably dim and drab in comparison to Tír na nÓg. The sky was a flat, leaden gray; the woods were still and bleak, excruciatingly lifeless without magic. No branches waved; no leaves whispered secrets. I almost lost my nerve then. But I forced myself forward, to tread the long hike Rogan and I had followed once a month for a year.

I must have cut a strange figure, in my huge, borrowed clothing and unbound hair. But there was no one to see me pass by.

It was afternoon by the time I reached Dún Darragh. The Longest Night was just two weeks away—the sun would soon be setting. I would have to spend the night in the fort. The fading light spurred my footsteps toward the greenhouse, where I had an errand to complete before I ventured inside the fort.

I'd been gone little more than a month—the greenhouse looked much as I'd left it. During our time at the fort, Rogan and I had repaired nearly all the damage done to the structure—reshaping twisted metal, refitting broken panes of glass, rebuilding rotten trellises. Pots of earth and trays of seeds were scattered between tools and supplies on the long, narrow tables, as if some forgotten gardener had left in a hurry, never to return.

Me. I was the gardener. But I couldn't remember what I had been working on that last day. What chores I had left unfinished, what tasks I had neglected to accomplish.

I strode deeper into the greenhouse. The last of my hothouse flowers had died. I experienced a burst of disappointment before realizing how foolish that was. I sent my eager magic thrumming along vines and stems and roots and leaves. Greenery burst back to life from every pot and tray—colors reviving in explosions of yellow and red and white. Tough-stemmed chrysanthemums, blood-red canna lilies, froth-white flossflowers blooming in an instant, as if spring had returned four months early.

But my power kept rippling outward—greening the shrubs lining the path, growing yellow hazel catkins, ripening fruit upon the blackberry hedge. Plumping vegetables in the dead garden, unfurling paths of wildflowers in the meadow, rattling the very stones of the fort.

And I suddenly knew—all this could be *mine*. My magic was magnificent, monumental, majestic. Why stop at flowers? I could raise forests or bring down mountains. What was a bad harvest in the face of my Treasure? What was winter? What—

I stumbled against the edge of the potting table, gasping. The shock of movement broke my concentration; mercifully, my power furled back inside me like wings. A moment later, the tangle of intrusive thoughts followed. I stared around me at the now lush and verdant garden, ludicrously colorful amid the gray frost-spangled afternoon. Then I slowly did what I'd come to do. I plucked a neat little bouquet of flowers before fleeing the botanical chaos I'd wrought.

Outside, evening descended with a chill I felt only distantly. I climbed the path to the fort, pausing again to pluck another posy— this one made of things a horse might enjoy. Clover, sage, meadow fescue. But the falling darkness was a pulse in my veins, hurrying me forward. I pushed open the great looming doors of Dún Darragh.

The fort that had been my home for a year echoed with darkness and silence. Waves of memory crashed over me, threatening to overwhelm me. I willed them away, stepping softly on the broad flagstones. Last time, this space had been untouched for so long my boots had raised clouds of choking dust. Now the floors were clean. But though I spun on my heel, all the torches remained unlit; all the carvings remained inert. The huge pillars that had always reminded me of massive tree trunks hunched beneath the weight of quarried stone and long millennia.

"Corra?" I called. "It's me!"

Fragments of my own voice jolted back at me, distorted and echoing.

"Did you not once say you longed for a sweet, dark-haired maiden to sing you lullabies and pick you posies of flowers? Well, here's your posy." I held up my unseasonably lush bouquet, but the cavernous hall remained empty and still. "I can try for the lullabies, if you want. But I've been told my singing voice resembles the death rattle of a tone-deaf crow."

I waited. Finally, a torch flared to life, followed by another. Movement oscillated on the far wall: carvings in motion. I tapped my foot impatiently until a twin pair of brazen heads with door pulls clasped in their mouths shuddered awake on the door.

"Who's that?" muttered the left head, around a mouthful of bronze.

"How should I know?" The right head mouthed its own circle of metal, then spat it out with some glee. "I was going to ask you."

"It's me." I pointed out the obvious, although a sudden fist of dread clenched my rib cage. "Fia. Chiardhubh. And I've brought you flowers, you fiend."

" 'Tisn't chiardhubh." Corra leapt out of the pair of heads, moving on to animate a jowly hare with drooping whiskers and ears to match. " 'Tis someone else entirely, we fear."

I jerked back a step. "What are you talking about, beastie?"

The hare considered me with a morose expression. "Diggy and Daggy, two names that rhyme. Neither are real, yet both sound just fine."

"Would you like to call me something else?" I blew out my breath in frustration. "*Chiardhubh* was never my first choice anyway. My name is Fia."

The hare gave me another scowl. " 'Tisn't."

"Call me whatever you like, fiend! But would you mind heating some water and lighting the fires? Whoever I am, I'd be *much* obliged."

Corra rocketed out of the hare, leaving it motionless on the wall. I chose to take that as an acquiescence. I pushed back out into the night, crossing the courtyard to the stall block where Rogan stabled his stallion, Finan.

The black horse was far happier to see me than the hobgoblin was. Finan whickered softly, bobbing his head and turning circles in his box. I looped my arms over the door to his stall and offered him my bouquet of equine delicacies, which he happily munched. I stroked his dark velvet muzzle, assessing his condition. He looked well fed, well groomed, and bright-eyed. I supposed I had Corra to thank for his care—not that I was particularly inclined to thank the sprite for anything whatsoever.

"Hey, old boy," I murmured as I scratched behind his ears. "I'm not sure what to do with you. Much as I hope your master will be back soon to take care of you, I fear it isn't something I can promise. As for me...I'm not sure I'll ever be back. I could take you into the Folk realms with me, but to be honest, I'm not sure they *have* horses in Tír na nÓg." I hesitated, feeling obliquely stupid for talking to a horse. "I could set you free and hope you find your way back to Bridei's royal seat at Glenathney. But you are too fine a beast to be captured by local farmers and forced to plough fields. My only other option is leaving you here...with Corra...who historically has no earthly clue how to provide for mortal beings—"

"Aughhhh!" A trio of knots faintly resembling a mouth and two eyes howled to life on the stall door. Finan seemed unperturbed, stomping a foot and continuing to mouth at my now-empty hands. "Wicked wench! How dare you malign us so? Did we not feed you and bathe you and clothe you and—"

I narrowed my eyes at Corra in triumph. "You do know me!"

"Foul trickery," Corra said, seething. "Unconscionable cunning!"

"I had a delightful teacher." I grinned at the wight. "Now, are you going to stop sulking at me? I'd rather thought by the time I left, you and I had become friends."

"Fia and Corra, friends for life. Together they dance through fields of strife." The knots convulsed. "No, the name still 'tisn't right."

And with that, they were gone, leaving me alone with Finan in the dim, hay-scented stable.

I lingered too long with Finan, breathing in his musky warmth, his comforting animal presence. I was gratified that he did not shun me—my metamorphosis did not seem to startle him. Yet I couldn't forget what I'd done to my own horse, Eimar, when Rogan and I first arrived at Dún Darragh. Nor what I'd done to Irian's fortress... or the greenhouse earlier today. My magic was powerful, wonderful. And unpredictable. So I dragged myself away from Finan, sliding back into the fort like a phantom.

The hall flared with fire- and torchlight. Food was piled on a low table near the hearth. When I drew close, I saw Corra had prepared all my *least* favorites—mutton and mung beans; brown bread and bog butter; beet tart. Remembering what Irian had told me about my need for food, I almost walked away from the spread. But then I treated it as what it was—a test.

"Mmm." I plunged a hand into the tart and brought limp, bleeding beets to my mouth. "Delicious."

A self-satisfied muskrat flopped to life on the wall. "Corra provides for even the most ungrateful of nameless wenches."

I sighed, pulled the platter of overcooked mutton closer, and set to work.

Chapter Five

After my dubious meal of unsavory dishes, I found and uncorked a rather spectacular bottle of wine, drinking straight from the neck as I traipsed around the fort. Although Rogan and I had always known Dún Darragh was a temporary abode, it had become home. For me, at least. So I wandered the echoing halls, the staircases that went nowhere, the halls lined with tapestries. I thumbed through my memories like the pages of a book, but every page seemed smudged by the handling—every memory colored by the act of remembering.

Here was where Rogan and I had celebrated my made-up birthday with cake and too many bottles of honey mead. I got so drunk I told Rogan about Corra. Rogan laughed uproariously and commenced talking casually to the walls. Corra was so vexed, they put all the leftover cake in my bed. I woke up the next morning with a raging headache and icing in my hair.

Here was where Rogan had kissed me beneath the guttering light of a torch that always flamed blue—but we had parted soon after, so the crush of lips and bodies now seemed rushed, uncouth, empty.

Here was where I had touched a pile of ancient parchments that had crumbled away into dust, reducing me to furious tears—but I didn't remember what had driven me to touch them, nor why I had been so upset by their destruction.

And finally, saturated with wine and glutted with memory, there was nowhere to wander but to bed. Still, I hesitated. My lantern cast wavering shadows on the carven walls, and I turned—almost against my will—toward the staircase spiraling away into darkness.

The tower. Rogan's chambers.

I took the first three steps slowly, then began to run. The wine made my steps clumsy and the turns dizzying. I arrived at the apex breathless and vaguely nauseated. The door hung open, which I took as an invitation.

My single flame illuminated little but sighing shadows. The room was freezing. One of the windows gaped at the night, letting icy, smoke-scented starlight gust through. I latched it, then circled the room, lighting blunt nubs of tapers on Rogan's desk and bedside table. Flimsy golden light brushed me as I sat gingerly on the bed, which was rumpled and unmade. I fought a sudden, bewildering urge to bring the sheets to my face, to see whether Rogan's brusque male scent of vetiver and steel still clung to the linens. Guilt hammered through me, and I stood up, turning in an untethered circle in the middle of the room.

I had chosen Irian. I had given my heart to Irian. I had *wed* Irian. What was I even doing here?

I blew out the candles and made for the door. But fragments of shapes inked on the wall caught my gaze. A memory gripped me—Rogan and I tangled on the windowsill, breathless and writhing. My eyes had fallen on this same wall. Then I'd seen his drawings—Eala, always Eala, cool eyed and delicate chinned. And my passion had burned away to shame. Shame for my love—my longing, my yearning—for someone I had always known was not meant for me. I paused, lofting the torch.

All the drawings had been smeared away. Charcoal marred the whitewash in gritty sweeps of gray and black, but Eala was gone. No pale gaze staring me down, no superior mouth lifting in a mocking grin. I frowned. Rogan had been intent on wedding Eala, almost until the end. Intent on fulfilling his duty. Why had he erased his drawings of her?

Perhaps he hadn't been so certain. Another memory crept close on uneasy feet. The last time I saw Rogan before the Feis of the Ember Moon had been here, when I'd asked to borrow Finan. He'd been pensively working with charcoal on a piece of parchment, but he'd hidden it before I could see.

I stalked back across the room. I relit a candle and swiftly riffled through the inked and marked parchment scattered across the table.

There. A sullen sweep of black charcoal spilling over a page crosshatched with smaller sketches. I pushed the other parchments away until I could see the drawing in full. Yet another portrait of Eala—a miniature of the murals that had been smeared away.

But that wasn't right. The hair was shaded in. The eyes were mismatched—one dark, one light. And the expression was one I'd never seen on Eala's face—a peculiar sardonic smile rendered humorless by a line of worry etched between the brows.

My fingers flexed on the table, the long-dead wood purring and shivering at my touch.

The drawing wasn't of Eala. It was of me.

Rogan's words to me a few moments before his will had been stolen echoed relentlessly in my ears: *It's always been you.*

What would have happened if I hadn't been in such a hurry to get to Rath na Mara that night months ago? What would have happened if I'd stayed and actually *listened* to Rogan? Would I have been able to intuit Eala's plan before she had a chance to enact it? Would I have been able to save the swan maidens whose lives had been sacrificed? To save Rogan from the black flowers—from a fate worse than death?

My hand clenched into a fist. The wooden table split, canes of green wood bursting upward, spearing the scattered pages and shredding them to nothing. I staggered back from the oak tree taking root in the tower room, then fumbled for the door, slamming it behind me. I stumbled unsteadily down the stairs toward my bedroom.

Rogan and I were children, playing with wooden swords in the training yard. The wind was cold, sweeping salty from the sea. I shivered in my shirtsleeves.

"I'm cold," I told him. "Lend me your hat."

He dragged off a lumpy gray woolen hat, leaving his golden hair tousled. "What'll you give me for it?"

I grinned, then thumped him with my wooden sword. "That."

He hit me back, a sharp thwack of pain at my wrist. "Give me a kiss."

But I didn't want to kiss him. So I hit him again with my play sword. He returned the strike, until we were fighting in earnest, driving each other around the training yard. Bruises bloomed on my arms and legs. I danced backward, but Rogan was relentless. When I looked fearfully into his eyes, they weren't the familiar blue-green of river stones. They were dull gray. Void of familiarity.

"Stop," I told him.

But he didn't stop. He knocked away my sword. He struck at my chest, pummeling my rib cage as if felling a tree. A great rending sound split the air, and when I looked down, I saw my trunk had split in half, and thorny vines spilled out of me like the tentacles of some sharp and vicious monster—

I jerked awake. My mouth was sour with too much wine; my throat parched and tight. Sheets tangled around my legs. Not even sheets—my mattress and linens had dispersed into stiff straw and brittle flax. I kicked myself free. A jug on the table held icy water, which I gratefully slurped. Cold air sighed through the cracked window and dried the sweat pooling along my collarbones. Dawn's bloody fingers stroked the horizon—I'd find no more sleep tonight.

Fine. I didn't want to sleep. I didn't want to meditate. I wanted to stand against Eala. I wanted to take away the things she thought she'd earned—like confiscating all the broken toys of a spoiled princess. I wanted to punch her in the throat so hard she choked on her own blood.

I wanted to save Rogan before it was too late.

The wooden casement groaned beneath my fist, tiny green buds interrupting the grain. I jerked my hand away, willed calm into my restless bones.

Irian was partly right. Together we might be formidable, but I had not yet learned to control the surges of my new magical capacity. Meanwhile, Eala had spent the past five weeks amassing allegiances and armies. We needed to grow our own power and fortify our position. With more Treasures—more magic, more legitimacy—we would be able to step into the vacuum left by the Septs. To return the rule of law they once wielded over Tír na nÓg's broken domains.

But beneath the violent anticipation spiking my veins, a tendril of guilt tangled. I leaned my head on the cold stones as a rose-petal sky unfurled beyond the dark line of the trees.

So Irian did not relish the prospect of war. I could not blame him—the trauma of his upbringing would make anyone hesitant to choose sides among Folk who had condemned, ostracized, and hunted him. In fact, part of me wanted nothing more than to run away from the world with him—to spend every night tangled in his arms, smoothing each other's broken edges until we were molded to one another.

Yes, I had chosen Irian. But I had also chosen a destiny I had never dared to expect. I had given myself to the Heart of the Forest. I was now married to a story so much bigger than the one I'd ever dreamed of telling.

If Irian and I ran away from all this, what was there for us? Happiness, for a spell. But with a thirteen-year death sentence hanging over us, how long until our love story turned toward tragedy? At least this way, our lives would mean something. Our actions would live on beyond us even if our lives were cut short.

Once, I had been nothing more than a dark ending to a story about war and magic and vengeance. Now I was living another story.

Once—in a time of border conflicts and broken magic—a changeling fell in love with a shadowy heir. She renewed the lost Treasures of the Folk. She defeated her bitch of a sister and saved the golden princeling from a fate worse than death.

Then she got her happily ever after.

I was made of mountains and forests and burned-out stars. I was not made for an ending I hadn't earned.

Chapter Six

There was no point in lingering. This place held little for me now.

It was a relief to dress in clothes that actually fit, although some corner of my mind was almost surprised to find they still did. As though I expected myself to have grown in the past month—tall as a tree, with trunks for legs and boughs for arms. I shoved my feet into my favorite worn-in boots, then hurriedly packed a few of the other belongings I'd left at Dún Darragh. My spare chamois trousers, my fighting leathers, my dark woolen cloak. I hesitated over Corra's moth-wing gowns. Although I didn't anticipate any Folk feiseanna in my near future, I hated to leave them. So I chose two at random and bundled them into my pack.

I trotted down the central staircase. The great hall was shadowed despite the brightening morning. I squinted as I scanned the carven walls, the four massive pillars.

"Corra?" My voice echoed, querulous in the dim. "Aren't you going to come say goodbye?"

A long moment later, a rope-thin stoat wriggled to life on the wall and turned its tapered face to me.

"We already bid farewell to chiardhubh," they said waspishly. "And we are not in the habit of tender goodbyes with strangers."

"Well, go on, then, beastie." I planted my hands on my hips and glared at the wight. "Give me a new name so we can once more be friends."

The stoat stood on its hind legs, fixing me with beady black eyes. "Chroí glas."

"What does it mean?"

Corra flicked their tail. "Greenheart."

Cold vines tangled in my veins. I forced my expression to stay neutral. "Why would you call me that?"

"*A feather so black will rise from pain. A crown so silver will rise to reign.*" Corra's tone was playful, but the frost in my bones crystallized, freezing my feet to the ground. "*Mend the broken heart; end the long sorrow. Give what life is left, so we may see the morrow.*"

"Corra—"

"Now, what comes next?" The stoat romped in a tight circle, heedless of my ratcheting pulse. "*A heart so green, with unwavering might*...No, no, 'tisn't right at all. Perhaps it went something like *with a wing so white, and a star so bright*—"

"Corra!" I nearly screamed the name. The stoat finally stopped frolicking and gave me an aggrieved look. "Are you speaking in prophecy? Or is this your run-of-the-mill fiendish doggerel?"

"*Doggerel?*" The weasel smoothed offended black paws over its snout. "Perhaps 'tis best this way, chroí glas. No one ought to know the ending to their own story. Nothing has yet been written."

"What does *that* mean?"

But the wight was already gone, scudding up along the carvings until the hall was motionless once more.

I shouldered my pack and left the fort slowly, trying to muddle through Corra's nonsense rhymes. For a moment, I had hoped there might be some wisdom—some guidance—the sprite could offer me. But in the end, maybe they were right.

No good had ever come of hearing prophecy.

Movement woke me—a gentle lurch and sway, hands behind my knees, a heavy arm at my back. Panic was a serrated blade in my chest. My eyes flew open to darkness. I tensed, ready to fight.

"Only me, colleen." Irian's voice was rough with affection. Or apology. I couldn't tell.

I relaxed, gathering my bearings in the gloom. Footsteps swayed me up steps. My cheek slid against fabric. Irian's dark, sharp scent of wind-chased water and infinite skies filled my senses. He was... carrying me? Yes—I was clasped against his chest, my body draped between his arms. Inexplicable dread ruffled over me, making me cold despite the warmth of his bulk.

"You fell asleep on the windowsill in a rather dire position," he murmured into my hair. "I did not wish to wake you. But neither did I wish you to suffer a permanent crick in your neck."

I remembered now. I'd returned to Tír na nÓg by early afternoon, only to find the dún still deserted. I'd been restless with energy, jagged with aggression, thorny with resentment. Remembering how I'd lost control over my power at Dún Darragh, I'd spent hours dancing along the limits of my magic. Plunging deep and deeper along networks of roots. Crafting impossible flowers bursting with riotous colors. Growing saplings with glass leaves that chimed like bells.

After, I'd been exhausted. Hollowed out. Hungry not for food, thirsty for something no water could quench.

I didn't remember falling asleep.

"What time is it?" My voice rasped. I fisted one hand in Irian's shirt, reaching for the contours of his face with the other. I fought the grim sensation of being gripped by a phantom—a shadow. By death itself. "Where were you?"

"It is late." He shifted his hold, looked down at me. His eyes shone like pearls, so bright I nearly flinched away. "I am back now."

By the time I realized he hadn't really answered my question, we'd crested the stairs to his tower chamber. I pushed away the inexplicable dread making me cold and forced a smile up at my husband.

"Careful, Sky-Sword. A girl could get used to this mode of transport."

"Could she?" Irian nudged the door open and carried me over the threshold. "Then I shall have to be more diligent in the exercise of my arms."

I pinched his flawlessly sculpted bicep. "Are you admitting I'm too heavy for your weak muscles to endure?"

"Merely commenting that I am unused to such terribly arduous manual labor." His chuckle rumbled through my chest. "And if I am to continue hauling you around like a sack of potatoes, I really ought to receive something in return."

"Oh, I'll give you something in return," I squawked in indignation. "How about a swift kick to the—"

He abruptly dropped me onto what remained of his ruined mattress, burying my threats in a cloud of flax dust and flower pollen. I coughed and struggled to rise to my feet, but Irian was already folding himself over me. Moonlight blurred over his crisp features, soft now with humor and affection.

"Do you know what they have in Emain Ablach, colleen?"

Other than my hope for defeating Eala and rescuing Rogan? "I couldn't begin to guess."

"Mattresses." He reached for me, hooking his fingers in my waistband and tugging me closer. If he noticed I was no longer wearing his oversized trousers, he made no mention of it. "Glorious mattresses. Made of feathers. Covered with silken sheets. Topped with luxurious eiderdown quilts."

"What about pillows?" I let myself be drawn toward him. "A bed is nothing without its pillows."

"Oh, the pillows." He smiled wider, dazzling me. His hand lifted to my collarbone, then dragged up my throat. "Pillows like you have never slept on. Soft enough to dissolve into yet firm enough to

support. I daresay they will be soothing for this terrible...crick...
in your...*neck*."

"My neck is fine." I laughed, batting away his tickling fingers.
"Tell me what else they have in Emain Ablach."

"Many things, colleen." Irian's opal eyes flickered between
mine, his expression losing some of its mirth. "There are sacred
apple trees that bear fruit golden as summer mornings. There are
giant sunken grottoes, artifacts of a time before the Folk ruled
these lands. There are waves blue as day crashing on cliffs white as
starlight." He bent, his breath brushing the shell of my ear. "But I
confess I am mostly looking forward to the mattresses."

I laughed again as I looped my arms around his neck. "We've
been having plenty of fun without mattresses."

"I have had all I can stand of stairs and walls and windowsills
and floors." His lips slid down to my throat, even as his hands
glided down to curve around my waist. I rose against him, wrapping my thighs around the narrow taper of his hips. "I have to
insist on mattresses from here on out."

"Well, if you *insist*." I cupped my palms along the sharp angle
of his jaw, tilting his face to mine. His lush lips parted. "*Lover*."

"Awful." Irian tsked. "And woefully inaccurate."

"Is it?"

"It is, *Wife*."

The ruined mattress disintegrated around us, a riot of straw and
flax and ill-begotten flowers. If the rough ticking bothered Irian
after all his talk of eiderdown, he didn't show it as he moved slowly
against me. And I? After a night and day assailing my senses with
my volatile magic and troubled memories, I was all too happy to
lose myself in something real. Some*one* real.

Irian might prefer to run away from our troubles, but he'd promised to stay by my side. He was warm and strong and stalwart. He
was my husband.

And of all the pieces of myself I'd lost and all the pieces of myself
I'd found? I was, indeed, his wife.

Irian held me.

He gathered me up, clutched me to him. My limbs creaked, fragile as twigs. My skin felt cold. I couldn't *move*. He buried his palms
in my tangled hair, brought his lips to my forehead. He clenched
his eyes shut, whispered words against my skin: *"A feather so black
will rise from pain. A crown so silver will rise to reign."*

I jerked awake. Burrowed between the demolished mattress and
our lumped mantles, Irian's lean, muscled arms were looped heavy
over my chest. When I pushed them away, they left tacky lines of
wetness on my skin. I rolled away from him in the dark and prayed
for no more nightmares.

Chapter Seven

Irian and I waited for Chandi. Mist wreathed the lough, steaming upward in the chilly morning.

"Do you think she's coming?" The vapor of my breath joined the fog.

Irian didn't answer, but his blue-gold eyes scanned the water, the beach, the edge of the trees. His thumb skated over the hilt of the Sky-Sword, the only nervous gesture I'd ever seen him make. Was he expecting someone besides Chandi? And if so, whom? A tendril of apprehension sprouted between my ribs.

We heard footsteps in the undergrowth. A moment later, two girls spilled out onto the pebbled strand, swathed in furs and carrying a few heavy packs between them. I exhaled when I spotted Chandi's glossy black head and flashing amber eyes. The other maiden I vaguely recognized from Eala's entourage, although I didn't know her name.

"Chandika." Irian nodded first at my friend, then turned to the other girl. She was a willowy honey blonde, with startling blue eyes and a smattering of freckles dotted across her upturned nose. "Sinéad. You are welcome this morning." Both girls' gazes on his figure were neutral but wary. Irian had been many things to the swan maidens. Warden, guardian. The reason they were alive, the reason they were cursed. But if he noticed their reserve, he didn't show it. Instead, he slid a hand down the back of my arm and squeezed my elbow. "You have met my wife before, I think."

Wife. The term was still so unfamiliar as to be disconcerting. I managed to contain my involuntary shudder until Irian's hand dropped from my arm.

"Hello," I said weakly. "We're glad you're joining us. Although I thought perhaps there would be more of you, in the end."

The two girls exchanged a heavy glance, and I cursed my careless words. Irian had told me less than half their number had survived Eala's sacrifice. They were surely still grieving their sisters. Perhaps even grieving their own lives both before and after they were stolen away by treacherous Folk thirteen years ago.

"Caoimhe, Aoife, and Áine decided to stay with Siobhán and Seaghán." It was the blonde—Sinéad—who answered at last. "They hope to find a way back to Fódla in time, and be reunited with their families."

"And you?" I asked curiously. "You don't want to go home?"

The girls exchanged another meaningful glance.

"For better or worse, this is my home now," said Sinéad. "Nothing and no one waits for me in the human realms. I would rather forge a new destiny here than return to a past that has forgotten me."

"Then it is decided." Irian's voice was firm. "We will journey to Emain Ablach together. We should only have to wait a few more moments."

Wait? "What for?"

"Not for *what*." Irian gave me a small sideways smile, one eyebrow ticcing up in amusement. "For whom."

I opened my mouth to ask him what in Amergin's blessed name he meant, but he'd already turned to face the lough, where tiny waves lapped insistently against the rocks. The black water began to bubble, and indistinct forms surged upward toward the surface. My boots crunched backward on the pebbled beach as huge heads burst the surface of the water, followed by long necks and powerful bodies. Creatures heaved themselves through the shallows of the lake, shedding water and foam and clinging pondweed. Hooves clattered up onto the strand.

They were...*horses.* A brief image of Finan gusted through my mind, along with the absurd thought that I ought to have tried to bring him with me into Tír na nÓg after all. But the thought of the stallion swiftly cured me of my previous supposition.

They were *not* horses. They were vaguely horse *shaped*—with questing heads and curving necks and waving manes and flicking tails. But their muzzles were too delicate; their gemstone eyes too widely spaced. Their coats gleamed slick as oil, a patina of tiny overlapping scales. The elegant fetlocks draping their fine hooves were not hair, as I'd assumed, but gossamer fins. Not horses, no— but they were an exquisite facsimile. A likeness meant to fool careless eyes, to tempt greedy hearts.

"Aughiskies." My voice was black oil and bad tidings. They were shape-shifting Folk who enjoyed luring unsuspecting humans to their deaths by coaxing them onto their backs before drowning them heartlessly in water, then feasting on their flesh. They were predators. Killers. I had never met one, but Cathair's stories about them were enough to make me fear them. My hands lowered to my skeans, belted at my waist. Roots seemed to grow down from my boots, questing for dark soil. "What are they doing here?"

"Calmly, colleen." Irian's easy smile dazzled through the gray. "I would ask you not to offend our transportation."

Transportation?

He strode out to meet the half dozen menacingly beautiful creatures shaking out their sleek coats and reedy manes. He walked toward the biggest one—pure black and far taller even than Finan, with fetlocks of iridescent purple—and met its eyes before bowing low. The aughisky responded in kind, extending one too-slender leg and bending its fine-boned head to its knee. I only realized my mouth was hanging wide open when Chandi elbowed me in the ribs.

"Behave, won't you?" she hissed. "They're not that bad, really."

I gaped at her. "They're vicious monsters with a taste for human flesh."

"Only when they're hungry." She gave her head an expressive tilt. "They're kind of like me in that regard. Turns out I'm a real bitch when I haven't eaten."

Without another word or an ounce of fear, Chandi followed Irian's example and strode out to meet one of the other aughiskies. She bowed in front of one white as bleached bones. The creature readily returned the graceful gesture. Sinéad followed suit, until I was the only one left—standing rigid and righteously indignant—on the beach. Irian turned back to see what was taking me so long, his eyebrows climbing when he saw me frozen a dozen paces from the water.

"Colleen?" A shard of worry cut through his creeping amusement. "What troubles you?"

I forced myself to march up to him, keeping as wide a berth as possible around the black aughisky. I grabbed Irian's arm and jerked him down so his ear was level with my mouth.

"My past studies suggest aughiskies are, ah, savage, bloodthirsty predators." I kept my tone formal, hoping that made my harsh words sound diplomatic. "Am I to presume that to be inaccurate?"

"On the contrary. They are markedly vicious and violent. However, they are also fiercely intelligent and usually capable of reason." His smile took on an edge. "All in all, quite a bit like someone else I know."

I glared at him and the monster he so casually stroked.

"They will not hurt you, colleen," he assured me.

"That seems like a wild assumption."

"I kept counsel with their matriarch two days ago." He mirrored the gravity of my speech. "And offered them something they have long desired."

"Which is?"

"An expansion of their hunting grounds." Irian's eyes flicked toward the stark-black aughisky, who stamped one impatient foot, then back to me. "Historically, Gavida has banned them from his waters. I have offered an introduction, in return for safe carriage. They will not hurt us."

"Fantastic," I hissed. "So we've muzzled a rabid wolf, in the hopes it won't bite us?"

"I think bridling a wild horse might be the more apt metaphor, colleen."

I gritted my teeth, turned, and marched up to the nearest free aughisky. The slender creature was the color of sea-foam, with emerald eyes and a mane and tail that looked like ink spilled over clear water. It was unconscionably lovely—like wolfsbane or oleander, beauty masking death.

"All right, demon horse," I grumbled. "Let's get this over with."

I bowed, stiffly and shallowly. The water horse followed suit, bending a knee and flourishing its forelock with a mocking air. A sharp sensation rent my skull, followed by a brilliantly vivid image blasting itself across my mind's eye—a still green pond between arching trees, with a vibrant scurf of blue-green algae coloring its surface. I jerked back, tripping over a rock and falling on my arse.

"Oy," I yelped, clapping a hand to my forehead. But the pain was gone, as was the burst of imagery. "What in Donn's black gates was *that*?"

"They communicate telepathically, colleen." Irian crouched beside me, helping me up with his hand. "Did you think them mute?"

"I *hoped* them mute," I muttered. "What was it trying to say?"

"She. And I daresay she was trying to tell you her name."

I looked at the aughisky sidelong as everyone else mounted. She pivoted in a tight, taunting circle, arching her back as if to say, *Mount me at your peril.* But I had already lost this particular battle. So I approached her with a purposeful gait, grabbed a handful of her slick obsidian mane, and vaulted onto her narrow back. She gave a small, peevish buck before trotting after the others.

"Pond Scum, eh?" I gave her neck a light pat. "It really does suit you."

Another image invaded my mind—this time, a lovingly choreographed vision of the aughisky dragging me into the lough, then gleefully and vigorously drowning me.

"Points for imagery." I dug my heels rather viciously into her side and laughed when she shot forward in the wake of the others disappearing into the fog. "But you're going to have to try harder than that if you want to scare me."

We rode all day. We kept to the waterways—striking out first across the lough, then following a broad river between ancient pines, until it split apart into meandering tributaries laughing between rocky gorges. The aughiskies navigated the water in a way I could not fully fathom, rippling over the surface using the broad spiny fins fanning out from their fetlocks. A fine misting spray and narrow white wakes were all that marked their passing.

Except Pond Scum, who kept *accidentally* tripping on submerged rocks so that water sloshed my thighs and soaked my boots, until I was soggy enough to classify as drowned.

Finally, when the aughiskies eventually began to flag and the light blanched flat and gray, we climbed onto the shore to make camp. Irian dismounted, on high alert—all his good humor from that morning evaporating in an instant. A brisk, seeking breeze ruffled around him, raising the ends of his hair before racing off between bare-branched trees. For long moments, he stood still and silent, his thumb moving over the hilt of the Sky-Sword as the wind keened in the trees and his black cloak blossomed around him. We waited with him.

The wind died out. He visibly relaxed.

"There are no Folk patrols for at least three leagues in every direction," he said. "We will camp here, by the water."

"Can we make a fire?" Sinéad asked, exhaustion making her voice thready. Chandi shivered beside her for emphasis.

"I do not think—"

"Of course we can." My voice came out harsher than I meant it to—perhaps my sore arse and sopping boots were to blame. Or perhaps I was still peevish that Irian hadn't warned me about the aughiskies. "We've been riding all day—we're cold, tired, and hungry. A fire won't attract undue attention."

His plush mouth hardened. "Someone will have to keep watch."

"The forest can keep watch," I countered. "All I have to do is ask the trees, Irian. If you can scout our surroundings using the power of your Treasure, can I not safeguard our camp using the power of mine?"

Shadows clustered in his eyes, darker than the twilight wreathing the horizon. But he gave me a brusque nod.

"Chandi, you'll help me gather firewood," I said. "Sinéad, there are mats and bedrolls in the packs—lay them out, won't you?" I cast a dubious glance at the water horses languishing in the shallows. What did you call a herd of aughiskies, anyway? A *drowning*? "I don't suppose you lot want to go hunt before night falls? Something the rest of us can eat."

Pond Scum bobbed her head and showed her teeth, which were razored points layered in rows like a shark's. But she followed the rest of the herd when they dived headfirst into the river and disappeared in a flurry of bubbles.

"And me?" Irian crossed his arms over his chest. He lifted dark sculpted eyebrows over eyes blurring twilight gray. "What am I to do, rígfénnid?"

"Oh, you." I stuck my tongue out at him. "I'm not sure what you're good for."

I turned on my heel and followed Chandi into the darkening forest.

The trees were old, untouched, *alive*, their trunks widely spaced and their grasping branches vaulting toward the dense canopy. I moved between them, inhaling the reverent hush of a forest on the edge of night. These were not mortal trees—no pale speckled alders or diamond-barked ash. These were Tír na nÓg's trees—with silvered trunks and kaleidoscope fronds, whispering secrets and singing like stars. Gemstone leaves lay tarnished in early winter's clutch. Ruffled moonflowers relinquished the last of their parchment petals to the earth.

I paused beside a huge, gnarled tree that reminded me of the Heartwood. Laying my hand on its smooth, scalloped bark, I closed my eyes. My awareness leapt outward, eager as the blood twining green-dark between my bones. I focused on the tree's pulse, slow and dormant in winter's chill, then followed it downward—down to the taproots tangling in warm dark earth. Roots—the bones and veins of the earth, reaching like a vast unseen forest below our feet. My perception splintered into thousands of shards as I followed the immeasurable network of life in every direction. I greeted each tree as I passed, and echoed a formless kind of warning as I went.

Folk bring fire. Folk bring axes. Shield us from invaders.

The forest rustled its willing assent—if any Folk trod this forest for a mile or more, I would know. I reeled back my awareness, but with difficulty—part of me wanted to swarm formless through that living network forever, etching the trees' nameless voices onto my heart. I clenched my fist, grasping each strand of my consciousness and weaving it back into the weft of my bones, the warp of my veins. I returned to my body with a gasp, breath rushing through my lungs and sweat sheening on my skin. When I lifted my palm from the oak, bark peeled away from my skin.

"All right?" Chandi's palm on my back steadied me.

"Fine." My reedy voice betrayed me. "Still…getting used to things."

"Hmm." Her amber eyes lingered on my face. She bent to add a twig to her armful of kindling. "I heard the rumors when I was in the Summerlands. That you renewed a lost Treasure of the Folk. That you died...then came back to life. How?"

A tendril of discomfort climbed my ribs, and the Heart of the Forest throbbed unevenly on my breastbone. "I'm not entirely sure. All I know is I bargained with a power greater than myself. Paid a price I think I was always meant to pay."

"Resurrection seems less a price than a reward," Chandi murmured. For a few minutes, we gathered wood in silence. Then: "It must have been hard on him."

"On Irian?" I huffed, hefting a small log into my arms. "I'm the one who died."

But her words punched a hole in the careful wall of indifference I'd bricked up since the Ember Moon. Because dying *had* been easy—the tithe I'd paid to the Heartwood had been the easiest thing I'd ever done. The memory of that night was like a fading dream now—a watercolor haze of beckoning branches and infinite love and the ecstasy of home. Dying had been easy. The resurrection was the hard part. That, and the weeks since, as I'd stumbled like a newborn fawn through a world that had stayed the same. While I had indelibly changed within it.

"He's been careful with me. Almost coddling. As if he's afraid I'll break. Or lose control." The thrum of the forest was a tempting pulse in the back of my mind. I ignored it. I commanded my power—not the other way around. "I'm stronger than I've ever been before. But he doesn't want me to confront Eala."

Chandi was quiet. "He may have a point. What is there to be gained from conflict with Eala? The bardaí? You are not beholden to right her wrongs."

"Am I not?" Her words surprised me. "Surely I was not given this power for nothing, Chandi. Surely I am not meant to sit on my hands and whistle while the world goes to war. Surely I'm destined for more."

"I can't believe I have to be the one to say this." Chandi straightened up. "But destiny is a curse, Fia. It takes away your choices. It takes away your control—of your own life, your own story. I've been part of someone else's destiny—it's bollocks. If I were you, a destiny would be the last thing I'd wish for."

Again, her words seemed to hack away at the defenses I'd been trying to build, the certainties I'd been nailing to my ribs.

"All right, O Uncharacteristically Wise One." I kept my tone light. "If you were me, what *would* you do?"

"Gods alive and dead, save me from that fate." Her words were light, but her expression stayed grim. "But since you're asking... you have been given a second chance precious few ever get. Maybe running for the hills with your hulking man and your strange green power and your habit of getting yourself into trouble isn't the worst idea. Build a house. Grow a garden. Spawn a few ridiculously good-looking demigods."

Her words nestled uncomfortably beneath the blue-green stone pulsing, syncopated, against my chest. I didn't have the heart to tell her that even if we had children, neither Irian nor I would live long enough to watch them grow up. "I'm surprised to hear you say that."

She shrugged. "All I know is, I sure as shite wouldn't fling myself at a war I didn't start, or throw myself into a destiny I never asked for."

"Speaking of destinies you never asked for." I added another log to my arms and briskly changed the subject. "How are you finding your own magical transformation?"

Chandi's face shifted into an unfamiliar mask of bitterness, and her eyes flamed with emotion. But a moment later, she was forcing an insouciant smile.

"For thirteen years, we—my swan sisters and I—wished to be free of our geas. We longed to make our own choices, to write our own stories, to live our own lives. We got our wish." She paused. "The few who survived, at least."

An owl hooted, startling us both. Chandi lifted her amber eyes to the sky hammering down like iron.

"It's nearly dark," she said. "We should head back to camp."

But as we picked our way back to the edge of the trees, I wondered why Chandi had avoided answering my question.

The aughiskies had slaughtered a deer—a young stag still fat from autumn's mast and forage. After recovering emotionally from Pond Scum's unsettling vision—half their *drowning* merrily flushing the stag from the edge of the forest, toward the shallows, where the rest of them pounced and dragged him into deep water—I prepared the carcass for spit-roasting while Chandi and Sinéad clumsily started the fire. I shook my head as I watched them arguing over how best to stack the logs, marveling at how inept at basic tasks they seemed. It wasn't their fault—they'd been stolen from their homes as mere children and enchanted to grow up among the Folk as swans. But it was so unlike my own upbringing. From the moment I appeared in Fódla, I'd been largely left to my own devices. My survival in the human realms had been conditional on my hard-won skills; my independence had been my strongest ally.

My eyes drifted toward Irian, who stalked the edge of the forest with the Sky-Sword held before him, his gaze trained on invisible enemies hidden in the undergrowth. I sighed, frustration and sympathy warring within me. He, too, had been forged in a crucible of coerced self-sufficiency, except I wagered he'd had it worse. I'd had Rogan—a friend, a confidant, a partner in crime. Irian had been alone, save for a bevy of swan maidens who despised him for how he'd tried—and ultimately failed—to protect them. And while I'd been sharpened on venom and vengeance, he'd been warped by bad mistakes and monstrous magic. A blade turned back on itself—a man who could not trust his own instincts.

As the fire caught, Chandi and Sinéad began to sing, their joined voices haunting in the deepening dark. Irian turned sharply, and for a moment I thought he might scold them for the noise. Instead,

he looked toward me and—finding me already watching him—
stilled. His eyes, silver as the starlight netting through the trees,
softened. He hesitated, then sheathed the black sword. He paced
toward the circle of firelight and sank beside me on the log I was
using as a makeshift bench.

"The forest," he said after a moment. "I did not know you could
ask it to keep watch for us."

"And I didn't know you could use the winds to spy," I replied,
keeping my tone breezy. "There are still many things we don't
know about each other, *Husband*."

"Indeed, *Wife*." He made a noise deep in his throat. "Like what
I am good for, apparently."

My own petty words repeated back to me sent a flush of embarrassed warmth to climb my spine.

"Oh." I made my voice sultry as I trailed a finger down the front
of his leather armor. "I can think of at least one thing."

He caught my hand in his, kissing my open palm. When he
looked at me, his eyes held no humor—only a desperate plea for
connection. For comprehension.

"Once, in a time of fading days and early frost, there was a
changeling girl who liked taking risks." His words were nearly
inaudible. "But the man who loved her could not tolerate the
thought of her in danger. So he sought to protect her as best he
knew how."

"There's a difference between protecting me and *coddling* me."
I jerked my hand from Irian's, although the impression of his lips
lingered warm upon my skin. I curled my fingers into a fist. "Do
you not know me to be a capable, competent person? I take no risks
I have not first carefully weighed."

"Says the woman who climbed a frenzied ollphéist and single-
handedly slew it without knowing what it was, what it wanted, or
how to defeat it." Another shadow passed over Irian's eyes as he
remembered the night I'd saved him from that giant ravening serpent. But not as the man who'd fought beside me; who'd flung me

his own precious Sky-Sword to deal the death blow; who'd trusted me to save his life as his silver blood dribbled onto the ground below him. It was as if he was remembering that night as someone different, someone I hardly knew—someone who apparently could not tolerate the idea of me in danger. "Says the woman who made herself a tithe without knowing what her death would accomplish. Whether her sacrifice—"

His throat worked, as if the words choked him; his eyes went dark as storm clouds. And there it was between us—the night of the Ember Moon. The night I had been indelibly altered, relentlessly transformed. The night I had given myself to the forest, and it had given me back to myself. But perhaps that night had changed Irian too. Chandi's words echoed restlessly between my ears: *It must have been hard on him.* I tried to think about what he must have seen, what he must have experienced. But all I had were my own soft-focus memories—vine-wreathed figures and impossible decisions and—

The beginnings of a headache pounded between my ears. I didn't want to do this now—not with the swan girls shooting us questioning glances across the fire and the aughiskies gnashing their hungry teeth and the forest whispering secrets. So I grasped Irian's face, his sharp-angled jaw rasping stubble against my palms.

"Irian. I'm alive." I kissed him—firmly, tenderly. "I'm right here. I'm not in any danger. I don't intend to take any undue risks. All right?"

He didn't reply, only kissed me back, fiercely, wrapping one arm around my waist and cupping the back of my head with the other, until I was nearly in his lap and Chandi was pretending to vomit into the fire. I disentangled myself from him with a laugh, hoping the ruddy flames hid the blush staining my cheeks.

"Now that everyone's had their appetites thoroughly ruined," Chandi said cheerfully, "who wants to eat?"

Despite Irian's talk of danger, the fire and food made us festive. With the help of the aughiskies—who seemed not only to stomach cooked meat, but to relish it—we made decent work of the venison. Chandi and Sinéad both ate like they'd never seen food before; Irian picked at his portion without much interest. I was somewhere in between—I wolfed down my first few bites, then slowed, the meat heavy in my stomach when I remembered I didn't actually need it to survive. I cocked my head toward the forest, listening to its patient, ceaseless susurrus. I told myself I was checking for signs of danger, but part of me yearned to be back between those broad trunks, diving deep into the root system and communing with the trees.

"Fia?"

I jolted at my name. Something nudged my hand—Sinéad was handing me a small flask. I uncorked it and sniffed—definitely liquor. I grinned, shrugged, and took a stiff swig, pulling a face when it seared the back of my throat. The aftertaste was decidedly more pleasant—a floral flush of peaches and pale mornings that made me nostalgic for summer.

I whistled. "That Folk liquor certainly has a kick. Where did you even get that?"

"I brought it for emergencies." Sinéad's smile lit up her whole face and made her blue eyes radiant. "This qualifies."

"Why not?" The second swig burned less—I corked it before I could be tempted to have more, and passed the jug to Irian. For a moment, he held it, stiff and severe. But he must have felt the eyes of our cadre on him—his demeanor relaxed, and he took a long, deep pull. He wiped the back of his hand across his mouth.

"Until we reach Emain Ablach, every day is an emergency," he said, with a twist of dark humor. "So drink away."

Silence descended. I decided to change the subject.

"Sinéad." As soon as I'd begun, I faltered. As Chandi's friend, I'd enjoyed the blond girl's general friendliness from the start, but I hardly knew her. What could I ask her? Of her life before Tír na nÓg, perhaps. But she'd been a child and had already indicated she had little desire to revisit her past. Her time as a swan was no less pebbled with difficulties. Lamely, I settled on not asking her about herself at all. "Do you know any stories?"

Sinéad did. She told a brisk, ribald story about a fianna of warriors who had been placed under a geas by an angry goddess and were forced to defeat their enemies using a somewhat absurd array of bodily fluids. When we begged for more, she told a much different tale.

"This one is romantic," she said with a slow smile. "Once upon a time, a mortal girl fell in love with a Gentry fénnid."

The legend felt so familiar to me that I was certain I'd heard it before, but when Irian's attention shifted toward me, it felt familiar for a different reason. His gaze caught mine in the firelight. As Sinéad's lilting voice smoothed over the rhythmic words, he slowly took my hand, his large rough palm gripping my smaller fingers.

"...and on Samhain Eve," Sinéad continued, her voice resonant, "the girl fought to turn her Folk lover mortal by dragging him from his horse and refusing to let him go. Even as he was transformed in her arms into a rabid wolf. A coiling serpent. A taloned eagle."

I was so entranced by the tale that I almost didn't notice when the whispering forest went silent. It was like hands being clapped over ears—a sudden muffling of sound and motion that reverberated outward.

Startled, I stood, barely noticing when Sinéad stopped talking. Irian mirrored my movement—drawing his sword as he did. I sent my awareness flickering toward the edge of the trees.

A forest has no eyes and so does not really see. Rather, it experiences things in a kind of patchwork perception—the touch of fur or skin or cloth against bark; the rhythm and vibration of hoofbeats or footfalls; the fluctuations of moisture and air pressure and temperature. My awareness catapulted from tree to tree toward the epicenter of the stillness, like a place where a bell had been rung, then silenced. It was not far from the edge of the trees, which scraped fear down my spine. How had an intruder gotten so close? I'd warned the forest to be watchful. Why hadn't it alerted me sooner? I strained, attempting to layer my own interpretation over the vastly different comprehension of the forest.

There: footsteps. But they were strange—shifting and soft, leathery or scaled in a way I couldn't comprehend.

Heat. A waft of warmth, dry and unseasonable. But it wasn't fire—the trees did not shrink away from it as they would a torch or a flame.

Sound. No—not sound. *Resonance.* A low hum of magic that had lulled the forest, deceived it—

With a brisk rustle of bare branches and an undulation of hot air, the presence was gone.

Gone. *How?*

Mentally, I flung myself after it, following where it must have fled. But there was nothing—no scrape of clothing or skin against bark, no swift footsteps, no rasping breath. With a sigh, the forest resumed its soft chatter and gentle motion. I pushed myself farther, searching deeper and deeper—

"Fia. That is *enough.*"

The sound of my name reeled me in from far away. I fought the forest's pull—peeling away my consciousness like a layer of moss from a stone. I surfaced back into my body, but my breath felt cold and heavy in my lungs, and for a long moment my vision was blurred. I shook awareness into my limbs and realized Irian was holding me where I'd half collapsed against him. Bright green vines crawled up over my boots to dig thorns into my thighs. I kicked them away and regained my footing, ignoring the weakness in my limbs.

"Did you—did you feel that?" My voice was rough.

"Feel what, colleen?"

But I couldn't explain what I'd sensed—what I'd perceived. It made no sense—not even to me. I glanced back into the dark wood, where metal trees stood sentinel. The presence was gone now. If it dared return, I had a feeling the forest would not be fooled twice.

"Nothing," I finally said. "An animal. Nothing to worry about."

But my interruption had ruined whatever jollity we'd conjured against the night. No one spoke as we laid our bedrolls in a loose semicircle, backs facing the water. I crawled in next to Irian, but tonight his closeness gave me little comfort. His arm—looped hard around my chest—seemed to cage me; his taut muscles against my back heightened my own tension; his shallow breathing tickling my ear made my own breath quicken. And as the fire burned low and the stars wheeled overheard, I knew neither of us was likely to sleep tonight.

Chapter Eight

After we spent another long day riding on the backs of the aughiskies, dusk lowered like an onyx blade above a sea of trees.

We made camp more swiftly tonight—each of us had learned our roles and took to them without complaint. Irian scouted the surround with his breezes. The aughiskies hunted, following a school of silver bream to supplement the dwindling venison. Sinéad built a low fire. Chandi walked toward the edge of the trees for firewood, but when I made to follow her, she waved me brusquely away.

My feet stopped, dead weight. The brush-off smarted, a prickle of thorns over my skin. I laid a palm against the nearest tree and let its rough-hewn pattern of bark and moss salve my hurt feelings. The tree was so steady—so sure. Its garnet-and-ruby-strewn branches reached down to touch my shoulder. I closed my eyes and called it closer, reveling in the safety of its stillness, the unwavering reliability of its—

"Colleen."

Irian's hand fell heavy on my other shoulder, jolting me from my reverie. I dragged myself reluctantly from my communion with the tree. Tendrils of greenery unfurled from my ankles; bark sloughed away from my arm like a second skin. I hid my prickling wrist behind my back as I turned toward him in the gloom.

"Yes?"

"You are restless." His eyes were blue, sliding toward silver.

"What makes you say that?"

"I may not know everything about you," he remarked, echoing my words from the night before, "but I know enough."

"Oh?" I forced my voice to turn playful and raked my eyes up his lean, sculpted form. "What exactly do you think you know?"

"I know you sometimes twist your hair when you are deep in thought." He caught one of my loose curls, sliding it between two fingers. "I know you talk in your sleep. I know you have exactly six freckles on your—"

"Oy!" I yelped, glancing toward the fire to hide my blush. "That does *not* need to be common knowledge."

"And I know you seek the calm of the forest when you feel unsettled." His tone shed its lightness. "I have been where you are before, colleen. I remember the first few years after my own transformation—after I became the Sky-Sword. I remember—"

His words percolated through me. *Years?* I had thought this *newness* a symptom of my humanity burning away in the face of my new Folk potential, of my unimportance blazing toward significance. I had thought it temporary. But Irian had already been Folk Gentry when he'd inherited the Sky-Sword. He'd been raised—destined—for this inheritance. And still it had been years before he'd been comfortable with it?

I was not sure I could bear this itch—this disquiet, this *desire*—for *years*.

"What?" I demanded. "What do you remember?"

"I remember that the best way to conquer it was to fight. Or—" His eyes twitched toward Chandi and Sinéad stoking the fire. When they returned to mine, they'd gone fully silver, as the night bled ink around us. His lips lifted over glittering teeth. "Well. The other thing may have to wait until we are no longer in polite company."

I grinned, the restlessness inside me sharpening to a point. Irian and I had never sparred—not in earnest. Suddenly, I wanted nothing more.

I wanted to do the other thing too. But first, I wanted to *fight*.

I slid low and kicked out without warning. My leg met nothing but air as Irian deftly sidestepped my foot. He gazed down at me, cool and uncanny in the falling darkness. But the heat in his silver eyes made my pulse ratchet.

"Weigh the risk carefully, colleen." He arched one dark, sculpted eyebrow, then beckoned me forward with a twitch of his fingers. "Because I have promised not to coddle you."

I smiled again. "A promise I intend to hold you to, tánaiste."

I burst upward out of my crouch, into another spinning kick. Again, I met only air—then brutal resistance as Irian's boot struck the back of my calf, taking the momentum of my kick and knocking me off-balance. My whole body swung sideways, and I tumbled over the brittle grass, raising tufts of weeds and dust in my wake. I pulled myself up into a crouch, glaring up at the towering Gentry warrior who had once been my mark, my target, my enemy. Who was now my partner, my lover, my...*husband*.

My blood heated toward a fever pitch. I launched myself at him, coiling one leg around his waist as I wrapped both arms around his neck. Using my momentum, I swung behind him, wrenching his body sideways as I used my free leg to kick his knee out from under him. He cried out—half groan and half laugh—and swayed. I tightened my grip around his neck, cranking his spine as I swung my weight backward. He fell, and I fell with him. But in the moment before we struck earth—even as I swung my legs out to disengage myself from his weight—a stiff gale burst between us, shoving me away from him. With eerie grace, Irian twisted midair to land catlike in a crouch.

"No fair." Climbing to my own feet, I glared at him. "I didn't know we were allowed to use our Treasures."

"All is fair, colleen." Another brisk wind at my back shoved me into Irian's arms. He caught me, drawing me flush against his hard body. One arm caged my ribs; the other tangled in the hair at the nape of my neck. "In love. And in battle."

He kissed me. I reveled—for the briefest moment—in his teeth dragging over my bottom lip, his tongue sliding hot on mine, his fingers flexing along the divots of my spine. Then I pressed my advantage, ducking under his guard to flip him onto his back and knock the breath out of his lungs. A moment later, he sucked the breath from my own lungs with a crook of his little finger and tackled me.

We grappled, exuberant and enthusiastic, as night closed its ember eyes above us. We were not evenly matched—Irian was far taller, faster, and stronger than I. I was used to being outmatched by men trained in the ways of war—and I'd learned to use it to my advantage. Some would call my fighting style dirty—swift punches to the kidneys, kicks to the shins and balls, a blade to the jugular if you didn't have your guard up. But fighting with Irian was different. He was spectacularly fast, gloriously agile, and impossibly attuned to my movements. He used none of the martial forms I'd been taught as a trainee in Fódla's fiann. He moved like a flame in a breeze. Unpredictable. Perilous. Perfect.

A feather of residual fear brushed down my spine as I realized— there was never a time he couldn't have killed me, had he ever truly wished me dead.

He caught my punch in one hand and threw me, returning me to my back. He anchored my frame beneath him, rolling his weight between my legs and hooking one of my knees behind his. He captured one arm above my head with a swift jerk and pinned my other arm between us, where our heartbeats lurched in syncopation. The blade I hadn't even noticed him draw kissed the tender skin of my throat.

"Do you yield, colleen?" Irian's voice was rough enough to bruise; his gaze, hot enough to burn.

I yield. The words should have been easy to say. But the deep green heart of me was not yet finished. Part of me wanted to bear this fight through to its bitter end, to spar with him until one or both of us was bleeding, until I had raised the roots of the forest—so close by—to shred his control and whip his skin and crack his skull and—

The intrusive thoughts wrapped thick dark vines around my rib cage until I could hardly breathe. The magic inside me rioted, thronging through me with sharp thorns and dusky shadows. Forcibly, I drove it down, willing my muscles to relax and my lungs to unclench.

I was in control. I *was*.

"I yield fully, Husband." I tilted my face upward, until my lips were an inch from his. "Although I'm afraid we're still in polite company."

He made that glorious noise deep in his throat, deepening his weight between my hips as he slid a finger over my chin and caught my mouth with his lips. He cupped the back of my head, tangling his fingers in my curls and—

"Ahem."

We both stilled, looking up to find Sinéad standing just outside the circle of firelight, shifting her weight and looking supremely uncomfortable.

Irian disentangled himself from me with a barely perceptible grimace, rising to his full height. He sheathed his sword, smoothed his tunic, and crossed his lean, sculpted arms over his chest. Silhouetted against the black forest with his harsh tattoos, candescent eyes, and faint frown, he looked absurdly beautiful and impossibly menacing. Sinéad took a hesitant step backward.

"I can—" She swallowed. "This was a bad idea. Never mind."

"No." Irian tried to make his voice soothing, but his hoarse burr still sounded severe. I rose up, brushing grass off my arse and trying not to laugh. It wasn't that I didn't sympathize with Sinéad—I did. I remembered precisely how terrifying Irian had been the first few times I'd encountered him. But since then I'd learned it wasn't strictly his fault he had the body of a predator, a face like a prayer, and the magic of a god. "What is it?"

"I actually—" Sinéad tore her face from Irian's and looked pleadingly toward me. "I actually wanted to ask *you* something."

"Oh." I hid my surprise and straightened all the way up. Sinéad had been cordial toward me but distant. "Go on, then."

She hesitated a second longer before squaring her shoulders. "You've been battle trained?"

"I had . . . a peculiar upbringing," I confirmed with a shrug.

"Back home—at least, when I was a child—women weren't allowed to fight. Not like men. But you—you are a warrior." Her mouth curled with a touch of wonder. "You are strong and fast— you can defend yourself against anyone. Against *him*. Watching you fight is magnificent."

Sinéad's words swelled through me, sweet as honey and sharp as thorns. For the first time in a while, I thought about Mother. About Cathair.

Little witch.

Their influence and training had indeed whittled me sharp—a weapon to be wielded. By them, *for* them. They had made me compliant to their desires and, by extension, made my own distasteful to me. It had taken me so long to come to terms with all they had forced me to be. All that I was. All that I could be. I was still struggling to acquaint myself with all my contrary and confusing facets. It had never occurred to me that to someone else—to a stranger—I might seem to already embody everything I was trying to believe about myself.

Reflexively, I glanced up at Irian. His eyes—twin moons in a moonless night—were fixed on my face, the savagery of his resting expression softening toward admiration. As if he, too, saw what Sinéad saw. Not a patchwork girl, cobbled together from conflicting birthrights and competing wants. But a woman in control of her own life. Her own *destiny*.

I dragged my eyes back to Sinéad, fighting a flush of warm pride. "I could teach you a little, if you wanted."

"Could you?" She brightened, rising up onto her toes in glee. But a moment later, she sobered, glancing sideways at Irian. "No offense—you are also an incredible warrior. But she—"

Irian held up a palm. "No offense taken. I understand completely." His eyes swept toward the western horizon, where red smeared away behind bloodstained clouds. "Night falls, but it is still early. The aughiskies have not yet returned with their catch. I will finish making camp and leave you to your training."

Sinéad was an eager student and a quick study.

The other woman was taller than I was, without much muscle tone. She had an inherent willowy grace to her movements that made me think she'd be better suited as a dancer than a fighter. But when I saw the blue fire burning in her eyes, I scolded myself for doing exactly what people had done to me for thirteen years. Assuming. Sinéad could be whoever she wanted to be. And if she wanted to be a fighter, then I'd show her how to throw a punch and aim a kick.

But first, I needed to get her stronger. I led her through one of my most basic training series, including heart-pumping bursts of speed interspersed with intense toning variations to strengthen the legs and abdomen. By the end of it, Sinéad was sweating and shaking and still asking for more.

"That's enough for now." I gave her a sympathetic smile. "By tomorrow morning, you'll feel every single muscle in your body, and you'll be cursing my name. If we keep going, you won't be able to walk for a week."

"But you didn't teach me anything!" she protested, her chest still rising and falling with effort. "Not how to swing a sword or hold a dagger or aim a bow—"

"You have the will," I interrupted mildly. "Which is necessary, but not sufficient. Next, you need strength and stamina. Then, and only then, will we work on skill."

"What am I supposed to do until then?"

"Stretch." I bent at the waist and gripped my toes. "Drink plenty of water. Eat. Sleep. And tomorrow we'll do it all again."

Disappointment curdled Sinéad's excitement. "But that's so—"

"Repetitive? Tedious? Uninspiring?" I grinned and gripped the other woman's skinny bicep in commiseration. "If discipline was easy, everyone would have it. So get some rest, and tomorrow I'll let you hold my skeans."

Whether it was hunger, or the memory of what hunger felt like, I devoured my dinner. The fish the aughiskies had caught was fresh and flaky, melting hot on my tongue. I barely noticed Pond Scum eviscerating her own dinner, holding its fins down with her hooves as she ripped its spine out with her teeth. Or Chandi, picking at the food in her lap and staring impassively into the golden gleam of the fire. Or even Irian, gazing hard at the night like he could summon up its secrets and shake out its hazards.

Before long, everyone was yawning. We banked the fire, laid out the bedrolls, murmured good-nights, and bedded down beneath our fur cloaks. But though my bones were weary and my mind begged for rest, sleep did not come easy. My eyes did not grow heavy. My thoughts churned restlessly. Finally, I sighed and turned toward Irian, who was also awake, despite his even breathing and heavy limbs. His silver eyes flicked open, cool and canny.

"We don't need to sleep much," I whispered, "do we?"

"No." His voice was nearly inaudible, and touched with apology. "We do not."

His eyes sliced through me, as if searching for my most exquisite secrets, my wildest fears. Or, perhaps, simply searching for his own. An unexpected burst of shyness prickled my skin, and I shivered from the intensity of his gaze, the weight of his attention. Our relationship was still so new. He and I were bound together—physically, emotionally, magically. Yet sometimes, since the night of the Ember Moon—since our wild, woeful wedding and everything that came after—the silent, secret spaces between us seemed strangled. With the things we'd done, the things we wanted, the people we were.

And despite his dubious knowledge of all my unspeakable freckles, he and I still didn't know each other as well as we ought to.

"Emain Ablach," I murmured. I was willing to build bridges, if he was willing to walk over them. "You were fostered there. Tell me of your life there before you inherited the Sky-Sword."

Irian tensed, his palm falling to the blade laid beside him even in repose. But then he forcibly relaxed, sliding his hand onto my hip instead. He pulled me a little closer, until our faces were pillowed inches apart; until I tasted his breath on my lips, crisp as ice-chased water and night before dawn.

"The boy who lived on the cliffs beside the sea was seven years old when Deirdre was called away from her garden to inherit the Heart of the Forest." His eyes were distant as stars. "He had lived with his mother until then—the two of them hidden away from the world in that cramped, cold cottage. But it was not long before the human king stole Deirdre away from her Sept; before she threw herself into the forest and set her magic free; before the dissident Gentry put a target on every potential tánaiste's back. And then the boy's father came for him."

"Your father?" He'd never spoken of him before.

"Perhaps *father* is a strong word." A note of bitterness layered dissonance through Irian's voice. "Ethadon—son of Nuada, chieftain of the Sept of Feathers—sired a child upon a middling Gentry girl with a promising magical gift, in the hopes that a tánaiste might be born. He got me. He had no interest in me once I was born, nor any interest in me as I grew up. Only when he feared I might be hunted down and slain, and his father's dynasty thus destroyed, did he come for me." Hard memories scudded iron clouds over Irian's gaze. "My mother keened like a bean sidhe to lose me. I fought Ethadon—fought my own father—with all the strength in my little bones. But he wanted me safe—wanted me secure. What I wanted—much less what my mother wanted—came second to that."

"Oh, Irian." I cupped the rough plane of his jaw, settled the weight of his grief on top of my own. We had both been children when we were ripped from our mothers. But he, at least, had known his mother. Known her love. And as hard as their parting must have been, I envied him that. "I'm so sorry."

"It is as it has always been." A muscle in his jaw feathered beneath my palm. "He took me to Emain Ablach—to the smith-king Gavida. They were not on good terms—after forging the Treasures, Gavida had refused to join any of the four Septs. Not even the Sept of Fins, of which his own brother was chieftain. Apostate, he built his own island, his own realm, his own governance. But Nuada's direct line had not spawned a son in hundreds of years. Discontent was brewing among the Gentry. The Sept of Feathers feared for everything they had built. So when Ethadon asked to foster me outside the Septs, Nuada agreed. And to everyone's shock, Gavida welcomed me into his home."

I was silent. After a moment, Irian continued.

"I spent seven of the best years of my life on the Silver Isle, with Folk I counted as my friends. As my family." Pain bent his gaze away from me. "But when the Sky-Sword was tithed to me, thirteen years ago, Gavida sent me away. He knew the bardaí would bring their war to his doorstep if I stayed; he knew they would come to hunt me down, to finish what they'd started. And he cared less about protecting me than he did protecting his precious isle, his own son and heir. So Gavida exiled his stripling foster son, barely fifteen years old, out alone into a world intent on destroying him."

"That's awful." Horror ploughed my gut. "Did he not know what awaited you? What it meant to be the last tánaiste living among the bardaí?"

"He knew." Old grief distorted Irian's face. "I still remember the last thing he said to me, before he sent me down the whale road. *You are a man without a future, son of my enemy. The boy you were yesterday is the last real person you will ever be. You will not become taller. Your shoulders will not broaden. Your hair will not grow. We will keen for you when you go... for Irian dies today."*

My stomach cramped harder. "Did he truly not expect you to live out the day?"

"That is not what he meant." Irian gave his head a crisp shake. "He meant that in becoming the Sky-Sword, I had lost the essence of who I had been before. I was no longer a boy on the cusp of becoming a man—I was a symbol, an idea. I no longer belonged to myself, except in the memories of who I had been. It took me many years to understand what he was trying to tell me... and many more to realize he was right all along."

"Your hair." Understanding—bitter blue and gentian—curled through me. I glided my hands through the soft, inky strands at the nape of Irian's neck, long enough now to curl around my fingers. "Is that why you wear it so short?"

"There was nothing I could do about the height. Or the shoulders." The small smile he gave me was corroded with pain. "I used to cut it every month, on the full moon. As short as I could get it— short enough to cut my scalp. There may be scars. Or perhaps the magic of my Treasure whisked away the evidence."

I slid my hands deeper into his hair, grazing my fingertips lightly over his smooth, unmarked skin. "As penance?"

"Remembrance, I think. Of what Gavida told me... and why. With my Treasure, I was given a death sentence. For thirteen years, I was nothing more than a dead man walking. So I found my own way to grieve the boy who died the day the Sky-Sword was tithed. As well as the man who would never live to see thirty."

My hands stilled. "When did you stop?"

"When I fell in love with you."

My eyes—caught somewhere between midnight strands and dark thoughts—collided with Irian's. My heart performed a complicated somersault between my ribs, exhilaration tangling with lingering uncertainty. Although he and I had already become husband and wife, I had not yet spoken the words—the three tremendous, terrifying words—that would cement my feelings for him. Irian had no hesitation in alluding to the inexorable emotions binding us closer and closer together. I remembered his heartbreaking words from the night before Samhain: *You, I have loved. You, I have lived for. And you, I will die for.*

I wasn't sure what I was afraid of, except that they were words that could not be unsaid. Perhaps in yielding my heart to him, I risked the loss of something indelibly mine. A surrender of self that made me less, instead of more.

I wanted to tell him I loved him. But I couldn't. Not yet.

Instead I asked softly, "When was that?"

"In due time, I promise to tell you." He brushed a rough thumb over my chin, then swept it up to glide along my bottom lip. "But you taught me to hope. For the first time, I dared to imagine I was more than the boy they mourned thirteen years ago on Emain Ablach—that doomed man, waiting to die. I wanted to be someone who got to watch the years passing without fear. Someone who got to live. Someone who got to love. If you remember nothing else, colleen, remember this—you were the one who gave me a future when I had none. And you will be why I keep fighting for it."

I frowned—his words had an odd finality to them that sent a shadow of worry to roost above my heart. But then Irian was cupping my face and capturing my lips with his, and he tasted not of exile and death, but of warmth and wanting. My blood sparked in my veins, chasing away the unease scratching formless sigils along my bones. I curled closer to him in the dark. His hands found my hips, fingers grazing along the waistband of my leather trousers and tangling with the ties.

"We are still among polite company." I pulled back, breathless with quiet laughter and rising desire. "They will hear."

"So we are." His gaze slid reluctantly to the erstwhile swan maidens. The embers of the campfire burned red over their still forms, huddled beneath cloaks. Then a wicked thought sparked behind his silver eyes, and he bared one sharp canine beneath the rise of his lip. "But they will hear nothing."

The pressure of the air between us abruptly changed, expanding outward to surround us in a bubble. My ears popped, hard and fast, and I winced. *Irian,* I tried to whisper, but although my mouth moved and my throat worked, no sound emerged. *Oy,* I tried again, louder. But it was as if the air was too dense for sound to move.

I matched his slow, secret smile. If he could make it so they did not hear us, I could make it so they did not see us. In an instant, briars shoved up through cold dirt, snaking toward the midnight sky. A thicket of rosebushes tangled around us, serrated leaves and unfurling petals making a dense, delicate screen.

I reached for him as he reached for me. His fingers unlaced my trousers, deft and deliberate. My hands found the buckles of his armor, sliding leather plates aside to graze the planes of hard muscle flexing beneath. I brushed my fingertips lower and felt the rumble of his chest as he groaned inaudibly. He flipped me gently onto my stomach, brushing hair away from my cheek as he kissed the side of my neck. He palmed my rear and I lifted my hips against him, an unspoken acquiescence. When he buried his face into my shoulder and slid swiftly inside me, I cried out—a silent scream in the soundless night.

With one sense removed, I found the others heightened. Irian's skin gliding over mine felt like a revelation; his hands on my breasts and his tongue on my throat and his hardness moving inside me felt like secrets unearthed. I came quickly, writhing beneath him. But he wasn't finished yet—his huge palms closed over my fingers in the dirt. His mouth slid beneath the line of my jaw, nipping at the tender skin of my throat. He drove deeper, and I bucked against him, the waves of my pleasure crashing one on top of another until I was awash with sensation. The ground beneath me shuddered as I started to lose control.

Irian's fingers tangled in the hair at the nape of my neck. My back arched as he pulled my cheek against his lips. He mouthed words to imprint upon my skin, but I couldn't decipher them. My face blurred numb as my hands clenched. Around us, winter dirt sprouted with more and more roses. I whimpered, and Irian caught the exhale with his lips as he finished, his arm snaking between my breasts as he held my back against the bunching muscles of his torso.

A moment later he rolled off me, and I collapsed, gasping. Slowly, the bubble of pressure surrounding us dissipated, the rasp of my breaths joining the quiet crackle of the dying fire, Chandi's light snores, the whispering forest. My eyes fluttered shut, belated tiredness pulling my eyelids down.

In the moment before I fell asleep, a thought occurred to me.

"Irian?" I was almost surprised to hear my own voice.

"Fia." He pulled me tight.

"Gavida." My thoughts were evaporating; I clung to my question. "If he was so mercenary in sending you away thirteen years ago...how do you know he will let you back now?"

Irian's breath on my cheek tasted like the iron of resolve. "I will not give him a choice."

The man sat at the threshold of a cottage; around him, a thousand plants thronged. Veined violets and hungry grass and cold chrysanthemums nudged at his boots and tangled in his blond hair. I could not see his face—I craned my neck but saw no more than an aristocratic profile.

Abruptly, he turned. He was not who I thought he'd be—his hair was a shade too pale; his eyes brown as grave dirt. When he saw me, anguish played over his fine-boned features.

"Oh, little deer," he cried. "You let them grind down your hooves!"

I jerked awake in the dream-glow of dawn. The fire smoked; beside it, the girls still slept, their swathed bodies like cairns in the dim. Beside me, Irian also slept, the veins of his eyelids blue against the alabaster of his skin. Around us, swaying rosebushes towered. Their drooping heads of gorged and glutted flowers sent iridescent white petals drifting down like snow.

In the moment before I returned the unnatural flowers to the earth that had spawned them, I heard *it* again. The rasp of flexible scales on raised roots; the hiss of steamed breath on hard bark. But when I turned my gaze toward the forest, there was only a sweep of freezing fog and branches raised in supplication for another promised morning.

Chapter Nine

On our third day of traveling, the trees thinned, giving way to steely moors climbing away from the water. I watched the last slender trunks disappear behind us with an exhale of disappointment. The power of my Treasure connected me to the hills and rocks as it did the forest. But trees had been my companions for as long as I could remember—as had the vines and flowers and shrubs growing between them. The forest had always felt like home. I was sorry to see it go.

We reached the cliffs by noon—towering multicolored basalt sheering up from the river basin, topped with amethyst heather and aureate gorse. The ruffled, restless sea surged against them. A high, cold wind whistled overhead. Strange seabirds wheeled crimson and teal in a frost-blue sky, their cacophony belling down.

I clung to Pond Scum's mane as she heaved herself without warning onto the riverbank, vigorously shaking her mane and tail dry and drenching me in the process. A moment later, I saw why—the river narrowed through a gorge, gathering rapids before shooting out over the cliffs in a waterfall. Irian's black aughisky climbed out beside us as I dabbed water out of my eyes.

"Now what?"

"We travel north along the cliffs." The wind flung the words from Irian's mouth. "The crossing to the Silver Isle is still another day's ride."

I grimaced. My arse was already sore from sitting on Pond Scum's bony back—I wasn't particularly thrilled by the prospect of adding wind- and sunburn to my list of woes. "Is there really no easier way to reach Emain Ablach?"

"There is." Irian gazed out across the water, black hair whipping around his face. "But the high road will be thick with travelers, and I do not wish us to be recognized."

I opened my mouth to ask about the high road—I didn't even know Tír na nÓg *had* roads—and why there would be so many travelers, but Irian had already urged his stallion forward along the bluffs. I sighed and nudged Pond Scum with my heels. She responded with a swift, merry vision of her bucking me off the cliffs to fall hundreds of feet—bouncing comically off several sloped cliff faces along the way—until I disappeared, broken and mangled, into the dark surf.

"Points for imagery," I grumbled. "But perhaps we could call a truce? You're giving me nightmares."

Pond Scum seemed to take this as surrender and ceased her psychological warfare. For the time being.

We climbed. The going was slow—the aughiskies picked their way between rocky outcroppings and clumps of thorny undergrowth as the wind screamed moisture from our lips and brought tears to our eyes. I did not like it, but Chandi and Sinéad liked it even less, wrapping scarves around their faces and bowing low over their mounts' necks. The aughiskies' tails made high, irritable banners behind us, and more than once Pond Scum gazed longingly at the ocean far below.

But as the afternoon pressed on and the glazed sun burnished the ocean to a vast shield of hammered bronze, I began to understand the stark, savage loveliness of this place. I could imagine

Irian growing up here, a lonely boy in a solitary cottage overlooking the seething sea. I glanced at him as he rode at the head of our entourage, but his gaze was fixed between his aughisky's ears. Of our party, only he seemed unbothered by the wind.

Night came swiftly. There was no good place to camp—we lay down upon beds of heather and thorny gorse, with pillows of yarrow and sea plantain for our weary heads. Irian bewitched some measure of the wind off our backs, which was a small mercy. But the ground was too damp for a fire, and there was no kindling besides. So we nibbled on dried provisions, barely talking as the twilight darkened.

"Do not listen to the voices on the breeze," Irian warned us as a veil of stars swept gossamer over the darkness. "They make tempting promises. But you would not like how they keep them."

I shared a nervous glance with Chandi, who rounded her amber eyes and shrugged. But as Irian curled his bulk around me and I tried in vain to sleep, I slowly began to hear them. Sweet sibilant whispers riding the night winds, singing wordless tunes that crept beneath my skin and stirred within my veins. I tried to block them out, even as my traitor ears strained to make out the words lofting on the invisible currents.

Come, let us keep you, they lured and laughed. *Let us keep you forever. Forever and a day.*

"What would happen?" I dared to ask Irian. "If I listened to them?"

"You would walk out over the cliffs until you fell to your death." His whisper was silver in the dark. "Then they would keep you. Forever. Your spirit haunting these waves as you lured others to their doom."

I shivered. "The girls—"

"Will come to no harm. I swear it." He was silent for long moments. Then: "If it makes you feel any better, they do not particularly want the human girls."

"Who do they want?"

"You."

I did not sleep well that night. None of us did.

The sun hammered gold atop the cold gray mist and struck sparks off the stranger's crimson hair.

I did not notice her at first. Rousing with a gasp from dreams of falling from iron cliffs, I jolted upright when I registered Irian no longer lay beside me. The wind had fallen overnight, and my husband stood stark and raven-haired amid the shroud of fog hanging ghostly over the moor. His sword was drawn and held sharply at guard—a shard of shadow warming toward gold. Sudden fear sent sharpened spikes through my veins when I followed his narrowed eyes down the slope of the hill.

The Folk woman strode slowly but purposefully toward us. I could see little of her through the swirling mist save for her hair—a startling, striking shade of dark red that caught the sun glow and amplified it through the gray. Swiftly, I rose to stand beside Irian.

"Who is she?" I whispered.

"I do not know." His voice was cut from sharp steel. "Are the maidens awake?"

I glanced over my shoulder. The cloak-wrapped forms of Chandi and Sinéad were humped dark between the huddled forms of the aughiskies. "No."

"Good." He flipped the Sky-Sword backhand, holding it easily across his body. "If there is to be bloodshed, I do not wish them to see it."

He stepped into the mist.

"I'm coming with you."

Irian's eyes—lightening toward blue and gold with the sky—flicked briefly to mine. Then he strode forward to block the newcomer's path toward us.

"Well met, stranger." Irian's rough tenor was fog muffled. "But

I ask you change your course. My compatriots and I do not wish to be disturbed."

The woman stopped. This close, I could finally see her features below the crown of crimson curls piled atop her head. She was unmistakably Folk Gentry, radiating the same exquisite, incandescent beauty as Irian. But that was where their similarities ended. Where he was strung together with hard lines and sharp angles, the woman's brown-skinned features were pert and soft—dimples lurked beneath the arch of her high cheekbones and in the rounded sweep of her chin. She wasn't much taller than I, her figure beneath her cloak all supple curves. Her eyes glowed strange in the gray—brown shot through with threads of scarlet and gold, like dying embers in a grate. She did not strike me as particularly intimidating—her hands hung loose at her sides, free of any weapons.

But in Tír na nÓg, appearances were often deceiving.

"We are not so *well met* as all that." The woman's voice was melodious, oddly accented, and inexplicably amused, considering she had a towering, armed, and avowedly unfriendly fénnid staring her down from ten paces. "Or else you would not have already drawn your sword."

"You are welcome to draw your own." Irian cocked his head, a minute yet menacing gesture that conjured memories of our own rocky beginnings. "But be warned—I will take it as a threat. And I am not historically forgiving to threats."

"The way I hear it, you are not historically forgiving. Full stop. But I am hoping the stories have oversold your violence."

The broad muscles of Irian's shoulders bunched beneath his cloak as his grip tightened along the hilt of his sword. "You know me?"

"Your reputation precedes you, tánaiste of the Sept of Feathers."

Irian bristled further, his vigilance rising toward aggression. While I was not afraid to witness bloodshed, neither did I desire it. So I placed a palm on Irian's forearm and angled myself slightly in front of him, facing the woman.

"What do you want from us?" I asked pleasantly. "And I'd consider being quick with your answer. My worse half here isn't particularly patient."

"*Worse half?*" Irian growled at my back.

"Ah!" Still, the woman did not seem even vaguely frightened—rather, a curious interest sparked in her strange brown eyes. "Your reputation precedes you as well, changeling heir."

It was my turn to stiffen, and Irian's to shoulder protectively in front of me. The tip of the Sky-Sword flicked out to rest on the woman's collarbone, a hairsbreadth from her slender throat.

"Let us mince words no longer, stranger." Irian's predatory tone raised the hairs at my nape. "You will tell me your name and which barda claims your loyalty. You will tell me why you have followed us here. And you will do so swiftly, or else I will cut you down where you stand and spend not one moment mourning your death."

A hint of fear finally glimmered in the woman's eyes. I didn't envy her—I remembered exactly what it felt like to have Irian's blade pressed against my neck.

"My name is Laoise," murmured the woman. *Lee-sha.* The sibilant name scraped through me, almost familiar. But much as I tried, I couldn't place the name. "A long time ago, I was a scion of the Sept of Scales. But I have avoided swearing oaths of fealty to any bardaí these past thirteen years. And I have come here... because rumors are spreading rapidly through Tír na nÓg."

"What rumors?"

"That the tánaiste of the Sept of Feathers survived a tithe unscathed," Laoise said evenly. "And he now travels with a mysterious new tánaiste who has—impossibly and inexplicably—renewed the Heart of the Forest."

Shock poured ice water down the length of my spine. Irian slid his blade up the column of the woman's throat until it kissed her jaw.

"Who speaks of such things?" His voice was deathly quiet.

"Those who know what the Septs lost," said the woman, equally softly. "And what their scattered heirs stand to gain."

The ice in my veins ignited toward fire as my pact with Irian sparked in my mind. Laoise spoke of *heirs*, plural—was it possible she knew of more tánaistí than the imprisoned heir we sought on Emain Ablach? Could she help us find a way to reforge the Un-Dry Cauldron and the Flaming Shield in the same way I'd resurrected the Heart of the Forest?

Irian exhaled and finally allowed his blade to drop. "We seek neither supplicants nor pilgrims. Be on your way, No-Oath Laoise."

He sheathed his sword, turned on his heel, and walked back toward camp.

Briefly, I locked eyes with Laoise. Her ember eyes betrayed little emotion, save for a distant surprise—as if she had expected many things this morning, but not this. I sympathized—I wasn't sure I fully understood Irian's response myself. But I met her gaze anyway and—as calmly as I could despite the churn of thorns vining through my veins and tickling at my nape—shrugged.

I would not gainsay Irian in front of a stranger.

"Wait!" she called at Irian's retreating figure. He barely paused, but she must have taken his break in stride as an invitation. She brushed past me to chase after him up the hill. I followed more slowly. "I have more I would say to you, tánaiste."

"Then say it," he growled over his shoulder. "As my *better half* pointed out, patience is not my finest virtue."

"You travel to Emain Ablach, do you not?" She caught up with Irian swiftly—no mean feat considering her height compared to his. "Let me join you."

"Many travel along the high road. Why not join them? The currachs will ferry you to the island with all the rest."

"I...do not wish to have my passing marked."

Irian turned to face Laoise in the lofting dawn. One of his eyebrows slanted up. "When already in a hole, No-Oath Laoise, the general advice is to stop digging."

"Tell us why you're going," I added, my mind still swirling around possibilities of heirs and Treasures, "and perhaps we may be persuaded."

Irian shot me a faintly disgruntled look but nodded. "Indeed. *Persuade* us."

"There is said to be a mystical stand of trees upon the crest of the island," Laoise said after a beat.

"I know of it." Irian folded his arms, unimpressed. "Go on."

"These sacred groves—in my language we call them *nemeta*. They used to flourish all through Tír na nÓg and beyond, with the power to imbue objects with wishes or enchant the weary or heal the sick. But the nemeton in my...home...is dying. Perhaps if I could examine this one, I might learn how to revive the one we are losing."

Nemeton. I had never heard the word before, neither in my mother tongue nor in the ancient language. But it trembled through me with mesmerizing familiarity—as if it were a name of an old friend, or a song I had heard in a forgotten dream of summer. Warm leaves rustled behind my ears, the timeless hum of colossal ancient trees. Footfalls on a dappled forest path...the shadow of vast silver antlers sweeping along my skin. I jerked my head over my shoulder, but there was no one—no*thing*—there. A chill passed over my skin in the places the warmth had been, and I reached reflexively for Irian's hand, white-knuckled against the hilt of the Sky-Sword. He glanced sideways at me, shadows brimming in his eyes as he read my gaze.

He turned back to Laoise. "What can you offer our party?"

"I am a skilled fighter."

Irian scanned her figure, skeptical. He knew better than to underestimate her gender or her frame—but he, like I, saw she carried no weapons. If she had, she might already be dead.

"No doubt," he said simply. "But we already have two skilled fighters in our party. We have no need of a third."

His secondhand praise warmed me. But Laoise was unbothered by the rejection.

"I am well educated in the ways of myth and magic. If you wish to win the Oak King's Crown, I could offer my help in the tournament—"

Beside me, Irian stiffened. His full lips narrowed to a line of displeasure as his gaze cut down to mine. New questions curled inside me, curious and stinging. This stranger knew something about my husband's plans that I did not? I curled my fingers tighter in his.

"What is the Oak King's Crown?" I said as easily as I could manage over the tangled crush of imminent betrayal. "And what is this *tournament*?"

Irian might have been hewn from stone. Then he exhaled, drawing me closer as he lifted our joined palms like a shield between our hearts.

"We have two human girls in our company who could use extra protection," Irian said over his shoulder. Peripherally, I saw Laoise take a sweeping step away from us. "If *chaperone* befits your skills, then our camp waits atop the hill. Assuming the aughiskies do not eviscerate you, you may stay. But I hope you brought provisions. The human girls may be even hungrier than the water horses."

The crimson-haired girl cut a shallow bow before climbing toward the cliffs. I waited until she was well out of earshot before speaking—Irian clearly wished to avoid a scene.

"Well?" I said icily. Half a step farther up the hill than I, Irian loomed over me, his angular features shadowed from the rising sun. His eyes, though—they burned, the daylight sky incarnate, as eerie and magnificent as his moonlit silver. His closeness still made me dizzy, and as his free hand found the divot of my waist and pulled me toward him, I thought perhaps he knew that. "You've been lying to me."

"I endeavor never to lie to you, colleen." His voice was low, rough. "But would you hate me for keeping some things secret?"

"It depends on the secret." My fingers tensed in his grip—again, an apprehension of deception burned along the back of my throat, bitter as wormwood and artemisia. "What haven't you told me, Irian?"

"Gavida...He is..." Irian floundered, uncharacteristically inarticulate. At last he mastered himself, gathering his composure like a smothering cloak. "The tale I told you of my exile—that was Gavida at his best. Though I built something of a family when I was fostered on the Silver Isle, I never considered him a father. The smith-king of Emain Ablach is cold, capricious, calculating, and immensely powerful. He has lived a thousand years; he has forged objects of unimaginable power; he has seen empires rise and fall. Throughout it all, he has remained untouched—invincible upon his Silver Isle in its surging sea. He does not have allies—he does not like strangers. Only once per year does he allow anyone from Tír na nÓg to visit Emain Ablach."

"Let me guess." My voice caught in my throat, tight with all the questions I still wanted to know about his past—about the people who'd shaped him. For better...and for worse. "For a tournament?"

Irian gave a curt nod. "During the fortnight surrounding the Longest Night, Gavida welcomes any and all visitors to his island. The event is part feis and part tournament, celebrating the decline of the old year and the rise of the new. But its appeal is not simply the novelty of isolated Emain Ablach, nor the many delights she offers each winter. As prize for winning his tournament, Gavida offers one lucky champion a magical forging. A knife to cut away bad memories, a coin that multiplies every day, a mirror to peer into the past. If it is in Gavida's power to create, he will do it. This coveted prize is known as the Oak King's Crown."

I bit my lip, digesting this. "If you wished to go to the Silver Isle in order to win this tournament, why didn't you tell me?"

"Because I do not wish to win it. I do not even wish to compete." Irian's tone was vehement, and I couldn't help but believe his words.

"We truly go to seek the heir Gavida has hidden away?"

He inclined his head. "The timing of the tournament is purely kismet, for it will make it all the easier for us to walk in."

Behind us, the sun rose higher, burning away mist like smoke from a pyre. Irian's revelation crystallized inside me. So—there was to be a tournament. And its prize a magical boon, bestowed by a smith-king of unimaginable power. The very immortal who'd forged the Treasures.

Resolve blossomed inside me. We would find this imprisoned heir. Then I would win the smith-king's tournament. I would earn the Oak King's Crown. I would ask for one more lost Treasure to be reforged, its wild magic renewed to rightful balance. Then Irian and I would be able to face the bardaí. Face *Eala*.

My gaze had drifted. When I snapped it back to Irian, I noticed our joined hands were covered in creeping, coiling vines. Vines that prickled along my skin and burrowed inside my veins. But they were not green—they were black as the cliffs, black as Irian's hair, black as the matching tattoos swirling over our skin. I gasped and jerked my hand out of his grasp. The vines sheered away to dust. When I met Irian's eyes, they were shadowed—blue as the morning yet dark as a starless night.

"And if Gavida will not release his heir?" My voice was nearly inaudible. "Then will you compete?"

His jaw flexed. "Only if I must."

"And then?"

"I will win."

Although we stood inches apart, distance yawned between us— as though his secrets and sorrows had created a wound between us I did not know how to heal. "I mean—if you do compete, and if you win—"

"I will win."

"*If* you win...what will you ask for?"

For a long moment, Irian stared at me, as if that was not the question he'd expected. Then his hands lifted to my face, his thumbs skimming welcome heat over my dawn-chilled cheeks. He kissed me, gently, his lips tasting like dawn and dew.

"I will ask for our future, colleen."

Chapter Ten

The wind picked up as Irian and I returned to camp, flapping our cloaks and stealing whatever unsaid words lingered between us. Atop the rise, Laoise had already made herself useful, somehow kindling a fire despite the damp ground and tough brush and lack of any real wood for fuel. I raised my arm and coughed as the crackling blaze blew smoke directly into my eyes.

"Sorry," said Chandi without much concern. With the rising wind at her back, she seemed in surprisingly good spirits. Or perhaps that was just the newly met Gentry maiden with crimson hair and fetching ember eyes sitting a bit closer to her than strictly necessary.

Laoise looked up at me and smiled. She held up a bundle of sticks and string. "Do you want to learn how to make bird snares?"

Irian was impatient to leave. The aughiskies were also restless, stamping kelp-draped hooves and belling their strange calls over the cliffs. But I'd promised Sinéad another training session, and

Laoise and Chandi had become immediate friends, seemingly intent on providing a meal for our lackluster party. So I found a patch of firm, rocky ground beside the cliffs and pushed a sluggish Sinéad through some of my favorite invigorating drills—movements designed to strengthen her slim arms and thighs even as they tested her endurance.

"Enough," she finally gasped out, doubling over as she planted trembling arms on her knees. "Gods, you have no mercy!"

"You asked for it!" But I reached out a sympathetic palm and helped her upright. "Consistency is key. Before long you won't even struggle."

"I hope you're right." She swept locks of sweat-darkened hair off her face and glanced over at the fire. "And I hope *they* manage to find some food. I'm starving."

They. The last I'd seen of Chandi and Laoise—half an hour past—they'd been trekking down the path to find a good place to set snares for the seabirds flocking the cliffs. A brief, incredulous pang of jealousy pricked me. Chandi and I had never really been more than acquaintances—between her curse and my foster sister's manipulations, we'd never had the chance. But in the past few days, Chandi had been distant toward me—almost untouchable. And yet, within fifteen minutes of meeting, she and Laoise were already fast friends.

"Sinéad—" All twelve swan maidens had been like sisters—bound in love, if not blood. But that had all changed when Eala sacrificed more than half their number for her own gory gains. Hadn't it? "Well. I thought I knew Chandi, a little, before the Ember Moon. We were...friends. But she seems different now. I've tried to talk to her, but...do you think she's all right?"

Sharpness and surprise converged in Sinéad's azure eyes. A moment later, she looked back toward the cliffs, where Chandi and Laoise were reappearing with a half dozen gamey cliff birds strung between them like loot.

"You inspired us to defy Eala." When Sinéad finally spoke, her voice was nearly toneless. "She was our natural leader—our true princess. Our sister. Our *mother*. Our queen. Perhaps you cannot understand why my sisters so readily died for her. I confess I still cannot readily understand why I did *not*. Why Chandi—and Aoife and Caoimhe and Áine—did not. But I think it comes down to you. You, too, were a sister—her real sister. And yet you defied her at every turn. Every scheme she conceived to tempt you, you ignored. Every plot, you foiled. She wanted you so badly by her side, and yet you defied her—something none of us had ever even considered."

Sinéad's words ignited a complicated coil of thorns inside me. I had never meant to defy my sister—I had always wanted to be her ally. But as I discovered her true character, I'd found it poisoned—both by our mother and by her accursed time among the Folk. Then I had indeed reacted with knee-jerk defiance. For once, I'd wanted to master my own destiny, beyond the control of anyone else. Eala had begrudged me that willfulness. But I had never intended it as the betrayal she'd believed it to be.

"The truth is," Sinéad continued, "I think we all resent you for that. You changed everything."

Her words came to me on a sudden wintry blast of wind. I gasped against it, trying to find my breath as thorns crocheted lace between my stinging tattoos.

"That's not fair," I pleaded. "Things were already changing. Irian's power—and the curse he wrought—was running out. No matter what I did or didn't do, your lives would have changed. By magic—or by death. I tried to save your lives—all of them. I only regret I could not save more."

"We know that." Sinéad faced me fully. "Do you think we are not grateful to be alive? We are. But with Eala, we knew what to expect. We knew what our lives looked like...what roles we inhabited...what values we clung to. Now that's all gone. Sometimes it's hard not to wish for things to be the way they were before. Before we knew how corrupt Eala had become. Before we knew we were nothing more to her than tools. Sacrifices."

I inhaled, looking away from her. I strove to maintain some semblance of the friendly dynamic we'd wrought between us, even as her words sent raw emotion scraping through me.

"But that's not possible, is it?" Sinéad's hand on my shoulder soothed me. "Things that have changed can never go back to the way they used to be—no matter how much we may wish it. And whether we like it or not, things are always changing. Change is how we know we're alive. That doesn't mean it does not hurt to leave parts of ourselves behind. Parts of ourselves we can never get back. Do you know what I mean?"

"I do," I said. "More than you know. But you're right—transformation isn't all bad. And looking forward with hope is better than looking backward with regret."

She grinned. "So you're saying I won't always be a shite fighter?"

"It'll come." I laughed and nudged her back toward camp. "But now you'd better eat some of those stringy seabirds before you starve to death."

The girls plucked, gutted, then spit-roasted the birds before tearing eagerly into their steaming flesh. They tossed their picked-over carcasses to the aughiskies, who crunched the delicate bones with their shark teeth. I did not partake—as Irian had pointed out, I didn't strictly *need* food anymore. I craved something altogether different—something that rendered me huge and hungry and hollow in its absence.

No need to take precious calories away from those who needed to dine on actual food...instead of dire, divine dreams.

Instead, while the girls ate, I climbed up beside Irian, who brooded at the edge of the cliffs like a great black bird. I didn't expect much conversation—his innate tendency toward reticence usually increased with worry or restlessness. But he turned toward me and asked, "What do you hear, colleen?"

"Hear?" I quirked an eyebrow at him. "You. The wind. The surf. The aughiskies eviscerating innocent poultry."

"Not with these." He almost smiled as he brushed gentle fingers over the shell of my ear, then tapped the blue-green stone hidden beneath my tunic. "With this."

"Oh." Sudden awareness knifed through me, unleashing an uncomfortable torrent of sensation beneath the barrier of my skin. I couldn't *hear* anything, but when I let my control slip, I could *feel* it. An undying vibration below my feet—the thrum of endless waves eroding ancient black basalt over millennia; the hum of drab, dauntless plants clinging to rock with ropy roots. It was an unfamiliar rhythm I did not entirely enjoy, so accustomed was I to the slow, solemn reach of lofting trees; the careful, controlled growth of a planned garden. "I don't hear much, since we left the forest. I can feel the stones and plants and dirt. But they don't really speak to me—I mostly ignore them."

Irian's gaze returned to the horizon.

"When I first inherited my Treasure," he said, "the only thing I could hear was the wind. It sang to me relentlessly—a thousand different voices with a thousand different melodies. A riotous, capricious symphony I could not block out, however I tried. And I did try."

I swallowed a swift burst of unease. "But you learned how."

"I did not." His eyes turned back toward me. "As I grew more accustomed to my power, I learned to send my awareness beyond the bawling of the breezes. Above them ride the trade winds—slow, powerful currents driving over the seas. Above *them* is where the clouds gather—a billowing buffer between the earth and the sky. And above all that is the stratosphere—high and cold and quiet, the last place air lives before an eternity of starlight swallows it away. There—there is where I learned to anchor my awareness when I was not actively using my power. Had I left it with the breezes… I fear they would have torn my mind to pieces with their constant buffeting."

"I don't understand." My fists curled. "Is that supposed to help me learn to *control* my power?"

"Not control." His gaze was shadowed. "*Harness.* Would you chain a wild horse and simply wait, hoping it became docile on its own? Your power is part of you, colleen, whether you like it or not. And it is *vast.* Beyond trees or plants or even rocks. Mountains, volcanoes, the very bones of the earth. You are not strong enough to *control* it. And the more you try, the more it will fight against you. You must find a way to work *with* it, instead of against it. To seek the truth of your anam cló—the shape your soul wants to take. Otherwise—"

"I will become a danger to myself. Or others. Or be consumed." My voice came out more caustic than I intended. "So you mentioned."

He faced me fully, gripping my upper arms as his eyes bruised with dread. "When the Septs ruled, tánaistí who came of age before a tithe were aggressively prepared for their inheritance, trained in the ancient ways of wielding such magic. Neither of us was afforded that privilege. I cannot claim to know what the Heart of the Forest feels like. But please, Fia—whatever help I can offer from the experience of inheriting my own Treasure, let me offer it. I only want—"

"To protect me," I finished woodenly. "I appreciate it, Irian. But you have to give me some credit. I've lived my entire life with my Greenmark. This is more of the same. Please believe me when I say I have it under control."

The lie I wanted so badly to be true crowded my throat with brambles. Irian's mouth twisted as his hands fell from my arms. His eyes swept toward the dying fire, where the girls were clearing away the last of their meal. "It is time for us to ride."

The ride was more pleasant today. The wind blew softer and sweeter over the stark cliffs, and the sun shone surprisingly warm from a cornflower sky. After an hour, we began to descend. As the bluffs rose up to protect us, Laoise started to sing—a lively, lilting melody I didn't recognize and couldn't understand the lyrics to. But after a few iterations, Sinéad picked it up, joining her clear soprano to Laoise's ringing alto. Before long, Chandi joined in as well, their voices winding and weaving in a complex harmony that curled cool, covetous fingers around my heart.

When I was younger, I'd longed for this—a group, a posse, a team. But I'd only ever had Rogan. After he left Rath na Mara, I'd begged Mother to let me join one of her many fianna. I'd heard the bad stories, of course—the hazing, the cruel pranks and harmful practical jokes, the rites of passage. But then, *then*—belonging. A tribe who understood and accepted you. Who knew you to be their equal, although your skill or expertise might differ from theirs. Who sang songs you did not know, and waited patiently for you to learn them. Who would not hesitate to die for you, because they knew you, too, would die for them.

"Why?" Mother had laughed, derisive. "So you may be slain in an ambush, mortally wounded in a skirmish? You are too valuable to me, a stór. Be glad I have given you a better purpose than being a fénnid in a fiann. Be grateful you are worth more to your queen than her foot soldiers."

Another burst of melancholy clawed at me. As a female changeling in a kingdom of magic-hating men, none of Mother's fianna would have ever truly accepted me—not if I'd dared to be my authentic self. Even Rogan, who had claimed to love me, had despised and feared my Greenmark. But now, in Tír na nÓg, I was a Treasure—the Heart of the Forest. One of only two Treasures in existence. Worshipped, hated. Sought after, hunted.

I glanced over at Irian. From his occasional absent-minded humming I knew he could carry a tune—and beautifully. But he was not singing either. He kept his gaze straight ahead, the rhythmic twitch of his fingers on the aughisky's withers the only sign he heard the music at all.

I thought of Irian's story about the day he'd been exiled from Emain Ablach, and his foster father's callous words. In a way, Gavida had been right. Whoever I'd been before the Ember Moon had died when I'd sacrificed myself to the Heartwood. I was still essentially Fia. But I no longer belonged solely to myself—I was a symbol of hope to those who clung to the old ways, and a symbol of undeserved power to those who believed in the new.

Beneath me, Pond Scum thrashed her head and gave a warning buck. I glanced down. My fingers knotted vines in her seaweed mane and unfurled flowers of black and white over her withers. I jerked my hands away, fear blooming through me when I remembered what I'd done to Eimar over a year ago.

"Sorry," I murmured, the word like acid in my mouth.

But for once, the aughisky didn't assault me with a caustic vision. She sent me something just as bitter but less gleeful. An uncountable number of aughiskies frolicked in the midnight shallows of a warm, pale sea, coursing strange patterns in bioluminescence glowing atop the water. But Pond Scum was not with them—she stood on the beach, sand grinding beneath her hooves as she watched them cavort without her.

The vision—meant perhaps as an expression of empathy—faded. I hesitated, then dared to stroke her sleek, scaled coat.

"Maybe it's better to be alone together...than alone apart."

Without breaking stride, Pond Scum snaked her neck around and snapped her teeth blisteringly close to my boot. She sent another vision—this one of her merrily nibbling off every single one of my bare toes as I screamed in agony.

I smiled but gingerly removed my palm from her neck. "I said what I said, demon horse."

Chapter Eleven

The bluffs transformed to hills sweeping down toward another river basin. We turned at the river, following its rushing rapids as it widened toward a marshy delta. I was astonished to see flowers still blooming this late in the year. Purple heather and golden gorse, but others too—ones I did not recognize. Blue-veined daisies, frost-petaled petunias. I whispered to them as we passed, and they whispered back—of sunlight and cool rain and fertile ground. But also of magic. Magic thrumming warm along winter-cold bones, magic pulsing life through the ancient lines of power stitching the land together like veins.

Old magic, newly remembered. Lost magic, found. Healing magic, renewed.

The realization nearly jerked me off Pond Scum's bony back. The plants sang of *my* magic, regenerated through my sacrifice to the Heartwood. A surge of raw power nearly overwhelmed me, and where Pond Scum's hooves touched, new flowers began to grow.

Flowers with lost names. Flowers that smelled like ecstasy and swayed like the seasons.

The delta spread out before us, slender reaching fingers in a vast brackish hand. Irian led us between the rivulets and tributaries until we came at last to a tumbled, rocky beach.

"Here." Irian halted his aughisky with a hand on his black neck. He turned to sweep his gilt-and-enamel eyes over our party. "The whale road."

I saw nothing besides the rippling sea gasping at our feet, waves flinging salt spray in our eyes.

"... *Where?*" asked Chandi, and I was glad it was she who asked, and not I.

He made no response, only waited. We all waited, too, as waves crashed along the beach, drawing lines of wet sand in silvery sweeps. And suddenly—between one wave and the next—it appeared. A narrow expanse of wet, glinting cobbles, dragging to a point in the distance.

The whale road.

Waves crashed over it, then receded, exposing more of the highway with each passing moment.

"The tide will be at its lowest in an hour. Another hour, and water covers the road once more. Emain Ablach is two hours' hard ride." Irian flashed me a half smile. "Let us hurry. Unless you all have confidence your aughiskies will keep you from drowning, should the road be lost?"

"Say no more." I nudged Pond Scum forward, even as she flashed a gleeful image of sharks circling my thrashing form in the deep ocean. "Hurry we will."

The whale road was rough and uneven, paved with mismatched slabs of gray limestone and black basalt. As the sea receded, it also became precariously high and narrow, lofting sharply above the waves. We rode head to tail—riding abreast would have been suicide.

Still, although not strictly effortless, the ride along the whale road was exquisite. Seabirds followed our passage, their widening gyres crystalline in the azure sky. I did not know their names, but their quartz wings and tambourine calls hitched the breath in my throat. Below us, schools of fish coalesced and dispersed, bright as gemstones beneath the translucent surface. The falling tide revealed evidence of what looked like a civilization below the ocean—coral castles and seagrass strongholds, blurred beneath the shifting waves. I nudged Pond Scum closer to Irian's stallion, careful of their hooves on the rutted whale road.

"Are there cities below us, in the sea?" The sea breeze nearly tore the words from my mouth. "Who lives there?"

"Lived," Irian called over his shoulder. "Just as the Folk were driven from our rightful home by the humans...so, too, did we drive those who once lived here from theirs."

Shock and distaste grew inside me. "Who were they?"

"There are many stories." Irian's glance was rueful. "They say the earliest inhabitants of Tír na nÓg were named Firbolg—*people of the bags*—for when the land was wrested from them by the Fomorians, they became enslaved to their conquerors and were forced to build their giant cities. But I have heard them called other names too—Nithe Neamhaí, the Heavenly Things. Solasóirí, the Bright Ones." Irian paused. "Whoever they were, the only artifacts that remained of them when we took the land from the Fomorians were stories of great magic, crumbling cities, and mysterious origins."

I considered this as we rode harder. Harder, perhaps, than any of us would have liked. But because we all reflexively watched the sea ripple down and down around the base of the whale road, it was hard not to notice when it began, slowly, to rise. Ebbs and purls spiraled the water as it slopped restlessly against the ancient stones. The aughiskies picked up their pace. Faster and faster, until white-capped wavelets teased at their hooves and darkened the cobbles of the road. Before long, we were racing through inch-deep water, and I was increasingly aware of the icy wind teasing at my neck and the freezing salt spray needling through my leather trousers.

I might be newly incarnated as the lost Treasure of the Sept of Antlers. But I had a feeling if I was left to drown in this freezing, frothing sea, I would not last much longer than anyone else.

As if echoing my fears, Pond Scum sent me another delighted vision of me slowly sinking beneath the water as my lips turned blue and frost rimed my eyebrows.

"Irian," I ground out. "When—"

Between one breath and the next, Emain Ablach simply *appeared*, rearing out of the surging blue ocean like a battle helm of hammered steel. Pale gleaming cliffs sheered up from the water, carved into strange spires and lofting archways by an ever-turbulent sea. A beautiful city climbed the steep rise, radiant in the shafts of late afternoon sunlight breaking from behind ruffled clouds. Above the city, a palace glimmered like a wish, impossibly distant yet breathtakingly exquisite. Every tower and keep and crenellation was carved from the same mother-of-pearl stone as the cliffs—I almost had to shield my eyes from the city's mirror sheen. The island seized the colors around it and transformed them to sea glass—the ocean's reflection rippling along the fanged cliffs like aquamarine; the sun's golden light shimmering along sharp roofs and arching arcades like topaz; the green of trees with impossible leaves sparkling like emeralds.

"By the gods," Sinéad called, voicing all our thoughts. "I've never seen anything like it."

Irian wheeled his aughisky impatiently. "The tide grows higher. The currents here are strong. We must make haste."

We urged our mounts forward through the eager surf. Pond Scum lost her footing on the whale road—which was beginning to disappear below the waves—dunking me to the chest in frigid ocean water before surging to the surface, riding high on the swells until her delicate hooves connected with stone once more. She paused to shake out her obsidian mane before cantering forward.

I grimaced at the cold brine crusting the ends of my hair and stiffening my leather trousers. "What's a little cold water between friends?"

Pond Scum bared her double rows of shark teeth and swam forward.

The exhausted aughiskies were struggling in earnest with the tidal currents when the whale road snaked beneath a natural arch carved in the steep silver cliffs and deposited us into a serene lagoon a few miles to the lee side of the city. One by one, we lurched up onto a pebbled white-sand beach and collapsed off our mounts, grateful for solid ground beneath our feet.

Irian did not give us much time to rest.

"The sun lowers. We should approach Aduantas before night falls and the gates close, lest we be forced to camp rough again outside the city walls."

The threat was enough to motivate us. We wearily remounted. The aughiskies climbed up through scrub-dotted dunes toward the road winding along the cliffs toward the glittering city. Even here, on the island, the quality of light was strange—a scintillant glister that made everything seem brighter, softer. Surreal. I peered forward through Pond Scum's ears toward the city, but it wavered like a mirage in the cold distance—silver secrets and untouchable glories. I resisted the urge to pinch myself.

I wasn't dreaming. Not even my nightmares included itchy, salt-stiff battle leathers and shark-toothed demon horses.

Soon, a massive gate loomed into view, all polished wood, silver metal, and ivory finials striped in afternoon's precious gilt. Irian dismounted and spoke briefly with a trio of heavily armed fénnidi, faceless behind their gleaming helms. Before long, the barrier cracked and we were waved through. The outskirts of the city climbed steeply upward, gleaming avenues winding between delicate towers, grandiose mansions, and manicured parks toward the sparkling palace balanced high above. Below, narrowing lanes meandered toward a cold, sprawling harbor thronged with ships and boats. There were hundreds of vessels cramming the narrow quays—far too many to be fishing boats or pleasure crafts.

A moment later, I saw where the boats had come from. I remembered Irian's words to Laoise on the cliffs. And I began to understand.

Stretching from the burnished horizon all the way to the long docks was a line of perfect, polished currachs laden with passengers. Each boat carried a dozen travelers; I counted ten, twenty—nearly thirty vessels. And that wasn't even counting the ferries that—having divested themselves of their passengers at the docks—turned around in the harbor and headed back toward the distant mainland.

When Laoise had spoken of a tournament with a tempting magical prize, I'd imagined a few score well-trained warriors competing in chivalric regalia. A week of honorable jousting, valorous sword fights, and good-natured sporting. But here were hundreds and hundreds of every kind of Folk, arriving from across the sea and swarming the harbor.

This was why Irian hadn't wanted to use the high roads. Why he'd pushed us so hard to arrive at Emain Ablach early, alone, and undetected. Why he didn't want to compete for the Oak King's Crown if he didn't have to.

This was more than a trickster king's caprice, more than a conceited smith's whim. This was a deadly game, with a thousand desperate players. A brutal contest for one single, coveted, intoxicating prize—a magical weapon forged by Gavida's powerful hand. A boon people would fight for—might die for. Would definitely kill for.

I tore my gaze away from the swelling harbor and stared up at the palace. With the sun dying at its back, it glowed, bloody and brilliant, above its skirts of shining silver, with shadows crawling slowly up its high hallowed walls.

Then I looked at Irian.

He was already watching me. The blue of his eyes darkened

toward twilight, the gold ringing his pupils heavy as the sinking sun. Foreboding writhed through my veins, and I knew.

Irian had not come here to rescue Gavida's heir. At least, not solely. He had come here to compete. To fight.

Which meant he had also, again, not told me the full truth.

Chapter Twelve

We climbed up from the teeming harbor toward the fortress glittering like an evening star in the twilight. Aduantas, Irian had named it. We were not alone—a steady stream of Folk ambled up from the docks, laden with luggage and weaponry. But they were not what stole my attention.

With the exception of one unpleasant night in the abandoned, warped Murias, I had never spent time in a Folk city. I tried not to gape like the outsider I was, but the city's opulent beauty was unflagging; its mythic splendor, unrelenting. Although the buildings and streets were all crafted from the same pale stone as the cliffs, there was a remarkable ebb and flow to the architecture that echoed the living, breathing ocean surrounding the Silver Isle.

Towering buildings descended like crashing waves, their glittering verandas ringed with white blossoms spilling over the street like foam. Elegantly carved statues crested walls like the figureheads of ships, their limbs sinuous and their hair flowing. Scalloped pillars inlaid with cracked agate and iridescent nacre lined curving arcades; gossamer bridges draped themselves over glowing ponds choked with translucent water lilies. Oceans of gardens boasted blue roses that sang like bells. Glowing lotuses lofted toward the sky and drenched us with silvery light.

But even as awe consumed me, a trickle of unease poured frigid salt water down my spine. Because as shadows fell over the city, I swore livid, lambent eyes stared out from the darkness between buildings. The frameworks of elegant houses resembled the skeletons of massive sea beasts. Trees with sea-glass leaves clawed at the sky with arms that looked too human to bring me comfort—flexing elbows and fleshless wrists and desiccated finger bones strung with plump, pulpy fruit.

But perhaps worst of all, as I passed by the gardens thronging the city, nothing *spoke* to me. The flowers had no color, despite their exuberant hues; the trees had no voices, despite the sea breeze chiming their jeweled leaves to cacophony. Could all this bountiful beauty be an elaborate lie? This city, which had at first seemed like a dream, now seemed more like a nightmare.

Sudden clamor distracted me from the dread licking at my bones. As we crested the hill, music and laughter and conversation eddied over us in a rising tide—the drowning sound of a thousand voices raised in celebration. A multitude of Fair Folk jostled around the base of Aduantas's mother-of-pearl walls. At first, I thought they must all be waiting to enter the fortress's inner sanctum. But few Folk lingered in front of the high shuttered gates, and the steel-helmed guards appeared relaxed.

This was no siege. It was a *party*. A rollicking feis, churning the parkland surrounding the fortress to brightness and merriment as the day faded into night. Huge tapped kegs sat in the shadow of the walls; long tables bedecked with winter's cold colors were somehow stacked with summer's fruitful bounty. Broad braziers licked with silver flames, a respite from the icy wind blowing up from the bluffs. Fair Folk crowded around them, warming hands and bellies. There were a few tall, incandescent Gentry, elegantly robed. But mostly, I saw lower Folk—nimble leipreacháin stabbing fat sausages with golden daggers; hairy, hulking gruagaigh pouring

ale down their wide, gem-studded mouths. A leannán sidhe, exquisitely wan in the starlight save for her ravenous red mouth; a dearg
due creeping in the shadows to hide its blood-tipped claws.

"The tournament begins tomorrow," Irian said to me. "We
must make ourselves known to Gavida now, before the gates open
for all."

He dismounted his aughisky and approached the guards,
addressing them in terse, forceful language. I could not make out
their response, but one man shook his head, gestured at us, then
pointed at the parkland swirling with revelers. Irian cocked his
head dangerously and swept his mantle to display the Sky-Sword's
inlaid hilt and carven scabbard. The guards stiffened but still shook
their heads.

Irian stalked back toward us, his face frozen into deadly, ferocious lines. When his silver gaze swept up to mine, his mask of
control eased, and he forced his eyes to soften.

"Only I may enter, by merit of my name, station, and relationship with the smith-king," he growled. "The rest of you must wait
outside with everyone else. I apologize."

"Irian." Chandi's voice held sardonic amusement as she glanced
at Sinéad, then gestured at the feis. "This may come as a shock to
you, but we're somewhat accustomed to Folk revels."

"That was before." Irian was not amused. "You are fully human
now. You are no longer bound to me or my Sept. I may not be able
to protect you—"

"I am no stranger to revels myself." Laoise dismounted from
behind Chandi with a flourish and proceeded to swiftly unsheathe
half a dozen slender, pointed blades from the curving leather of her
bodice. She brandished them between her fingers like claws before
returning them to their hidden places. "I am more than capable
of protecting two human girls from Folk who likely wish them no
harm. Besides, the aughiskies are hungry."

Irian still wasn't happy but didn't protest as the girls made their
way toward the feis, chattering excitedly at the prospect of food,

merriment, and well-deserved rest. A moment later, Pond Scum turned and snapped pointedly at my feet, and I slid off her back. She trotted off with the other aughiskies.

"What of my name? My station?" My hand found Irian's—our fingers tangled together in the dark. "I am your wife—may I not join you?"

"If I told the guards who you were, colleen, your name would be on every lip in the city by dawn." Irian lifted our joined palms and kissed the back of my hand. "Gavida must hear about you from me. It is our only chance of garnering his favor before we reveal our true reason for being here."

"You shouldn't have to face him alone."

Surprise brightened Irian's eyes to the silver of the lanterns mounted above the gate. "He will not hurt me."

"He already has." I stood on tiptoes to brush my lips on his cheek.

"He never will again—not while I have you to protect me." He caught me against him, curling calloused fingers around my chin and crushing my lips to his in a bruising kiss. Then he let me go, rueful. "I will not be gone long. Stay with the others—stay safe."

I scoffed, spreading my arms as I walked backward away from him. "When am I ever *not* safe?"

I expected him to laugh—at least to smile. But a rill of shadow surfaced upon the brightness of his gaze before he turned on his heel and marched toward the gate.

As Aduantas swallowed Irian whole, I wondered, once again—was my husband afraid for me?

Or of me?

By the time I turned around, Chandi, Sinéad, Laoise, and the aughiskies had disappeared into the feis. I exhaled, envy twinging up my spine. Already, the swan girls and our new Gentry acquaintance had formed a bond I could not begin to rival. The truth was, I was no longer their peer. When I wed Irian, I had made myself Folk. And when I sacrificed myself to the Heartwood, I had made myself...*other*.

Much as I might wish it, I had never been—and likely never would be—part of their group.

I hesitated, there at the edge of the feis. Night had fallen; starlight glazed the high stone walls and wind whipped my skin. The jangle of unfamiliar music raised the hairs at my nape; the cacophony of strange tongues made my teeth ache. My magic writhed with disquiet, embroidering my veins with green lacework beneath my skin.

I had no idea how long Irian would be inside. But I didn't want to stay here.

I followed the gentle curve of the palace walls, trailing my fingertips along the smooth masonry. My awareness shivered behind me. As I'd told Irian, I had not yet fully learned all the dialects of the element I now commanded. Trees and flowers and vines—they were my mother tongue. Dirt and pebble and stone—they were far harder for me to decipher. But I did not need to understand any language to know these stones were not speaking. They were inert—*dead*. My unease shifted toward dread.

I paused a dozen paces from the nearest brazier, glancing over my shoulder to make sure no one was watching me. Then I laid both palms against the wall, closed my eyes, and sent my consciousness slithering down like roots.

The silent stones of the wall were dug ten feet into the earth, held together by cold mortar and lifeless sand. Below the wall, I found more unsettling quiet—all the way through the foundation of the silver city. I scrunched my eyes harder together and pushed myself wider—deeper. Beyond the city's walls, I found flickers of life. Grass and scrub and wildflowers tumbling half-heartedly up to the crown of the island. Then: trees. *Real*, living, growing trees—glowing golden in the dark, with metallic roots that reached down, down, down. I followed those taproots. But no matter how deep I drove myself, I could not feel any other life. I hammered on my power—forcing it between the bones of the island, carving my way between its granite ribs and limestone veins; chiseling out the echoing caverns of its lungs and boring down to the sick, throbbing metal of its heart—

I surfaced with a cry, ripping my hands from stone that seemed suddenly ravenous. Devouring. Thorny vines unlatched from my wrists, scoring my skin in lines of bleeding green. When I glanced up, I saw my newfound power had braided up the wall—a riot of red roses and purple dahlias laddering, bruised and bloody, over its perfect white skin. I twined my fingers together, then anxiously looked over my shoulder.

The feis churned with merriment. No one had noticed my impromptu landscaping. Which meant no one would notice if I *invited* myself to Aduantas.

Before I changed my mind, I thrust one boot into a tangle of vines, gripped two handfuls of flowers, and hoisted myself upward. I climbed swiftly, unsure exactly what I hoped to accomplish. Irian had told me to stay outside the fortress. I ought to find the swan maidens and Laoise and behave myself until he returned. But I wanted...

What?

I wanted to see Aduantas for myself. I wanted to know what I was facing. I wanted to know why a place seemingly clamoring with life felt so *empty.*

At the top, I flattened myself into the shadows between two torchlit parapets and slid my knives from my belt. Luckily, I neither heard nor saw any guards. Slowly, I lowered myself down. Then relaxed.

This was no armory or arsenal or barracks. It was a pleasure garden. Rows of carefully manicured hedges marched away from me, frosted with dew. Nightingales sang drowsy vespers from arched cupolas. A moon-silvered pond reflected stucco arabesques and chattered with the idle splashing of a fountain. The gauzy fragrance of jasmine—underlaid with turquoise, mint, and juniper—breathed cool between sweet-blossomed flowers. Blue lanterns drifted toward me, buoyed by transparent vapor tasting of crushed berries and fresh water.

I paced carefully forward. I saw no guards, but that did not mean this place was not guarded. If I reached the pillared arcade along the far wall, I might find access to the main keep—

A large, cool palm circled my wrist and dragged me between the hedgerows.

Instinctively, I fought, lashing out with my free dagger and twisting the weight of my body beneath the arm that held me. But my attacker was agile—they easily dodged the arc of my blade, even as they spun with my feint, instead of against it. I glimpsed little but dark blue livery and a sparkle of silver as I crouched low and kicked out, hard. I earned a male grunt for my efforts, followed by a deep, baffling burst of . . . laughter?

Inexplicable familiarity blurred through me. I wavered, and my attacker took swift advantage, throwing his weight into my left shoulder. I stumbled backward, fighting for balance. My spine struck something hard, covered in foliage—thorns pricked my back even as a floral bouquet assaulted my nostrils. The man pinned me, one heavy forearm across my chest. The other, he jammed across my throat.

But the fool hadn't disarmed me. One of my skeans snaked around to prick the skin behind his kidney. The other, I jabbed—with very little subtlety—below his belt.

"It seems," I snarled, my voice a rasp in my throat where he had me pinned, "that we are at an impasse."

"So it seems." His voice was deep and sleek. Where had I heard it before? I peered up at his face, but it was masked by the shadow of the arbor.

"Free me, and you may still someday sire children."

"Submit to me, and perhaps they could be yours."

Shock and fury hardened my spine. I kicked up sharply, driving my knee between his legs. He curled forward, grunting. Palming one skean, I fisted my hand in his mantle and twisted him sideways, even as I kicked one leg out from under him. He went down, landing face-first in the dirt. I climbed on top of him, pinning him with my slight weight before laying my blade along his throat.

"Touch me without permission ever again," I whispered into his ear, "and you die."

"There she is." Again, that *laugh*. It teased my bones and flirted with my memories. "My Thorn Girl. I told you we would meet again."

Chapter Thirteen

Thorn Girl.

Morrigan, where had I heard that before? My blade wavered as memories dragged me down. The Feis of the Nameless Day. A fox-faced barda stealing a kiss he hadn't earned. A Gentry man robed in blue who'd stepped in on my behalf. A man the barda had called *islander*.

I jerked, my skean grazing below the interloper's smooth jawline. Had it not been for the hard, stiff collar of his mantle, I might have cut him. I rolled up to standing, although I did not lower my blades.

"*You*." A year's worth of resentment curdled the word bitter enough to choke on.

"Me." He levered himself to his knees, brushed dirt off his dark blue tunic and the side of his face, then also stood. And I remembered him, even fractured as he was by starlight and shadow.

He was tall—if not quite as tall as Irian—and heavily muscled. Above the high embroidered collar of his mantle, a streamlined jaw lifted toward sculpted golden-brown cheekbones. His mouth was wide and wry, quirked even now in an easy, genial smile. His straight, shining mahogany hair fell all the way down his back, longer even than mine. But most arresting were his eyes, dark enough at first glance to seem black. But I remembered—they were blue, like evening skies and deep water.

Why would I remember that? He was no one to me.

"I did warn you, Thorn Girl." His gleaming smile was slippery with intrigue. "The magic of Tír na nÓg would not keep us apart for long."

I lifted my blades and stepped back, but again my spine struck flora. A teeming arbor of impossible roses arched above us, their azure petals veined with lavender. I narrowed my eyes at the Gentry lord who had once saved me from a barda's advances, only to claim my unwilling kiss for himself. A claim I had not made good on—and had no intention to. "It's been a year."

"A year and a day," he corrected. "A length of time reserved for engagements. Oaths. Promises. Surely you have not forgotten about our bargain?"

I arched an eyebrow and lied. "Until today, I had forgotten you even existed."

Again he laughed, his amusement rippling like foam upon a darkened sea. "Only fitting, since I have thought of you every day since."

Traitorous warmth touched the crown of my head and spilled downward, like an egg being cracked on my skull. "I cannot give you what you want."

His smile only widened. "Why not?"

"I am a married woman."

"I fail to see how that is relevant." He paced toward me beneath the bower. "Did you promise never to kiss another, when you made your wedding vows?"

"Not precisely." I refused to drop his gaze. "But it was implied."

"And yet you promised to kiss me."

"I did not." I set my jaw. "Besides, it's the principle of the thing."

"According to whom?" Starlight glowed night blue along his

irises. "You must know that bargains among the Fair Folk out-weigh all other vows."

Of course they did. I bared my teeth. "I did not wish to kiss the barda who assaulted me that night a year ago. And I do not wish to kiss you. That should be enough to deter you."

"So it should." He was close enough to touch me. "I derive no satisfaction from taking things that should be freely given. So I will make you a new bargain, Thorn Girl, in exchange for the one you seem to so abhor the idea of."

"Done." Relief flooded me, followed swiftly by the knowledge that I should have asked to hear the bargain before agreeing to it. "Tell me what you want from me."

"Oh, I still want the kiss I am owed." He bent his head even closer, his sheet of sleek hair sliding over one shoulder. His scent caught in my nose—a heady mixture of beeswax and salt water and crushed flowers. "The new bargain is this: I will not decide the time. *You* will."

Another flush of traitorous heat spooled around my rigid spine like ivy. "Very well." I jerked my skean upward, laying the keen blade once more against his throat. "But I hope you are fond of long waits. Because I will never ask you to kiss me."

Slowly—*slowly*—he took my wrist in his large, cool palm, send-ing a shock singing up to my elbow. He gently twisted the blade away from his own neck, tilting my arm until my sleeve rode up and the starlight caught on my tattoos. His eyes grazed my skin, gliding over the thorny, feathery markings with interest.

"Now that the magic of Tír na nÓg has delivered you to me," he murmured, "I will wait as long as I must. What is meant will be. And all the better for the waiting."

His eyes found mine, blurring dark as the sky behind us. Sudden intuition cooled the blood thrashing my veins—I should have let him have what he wanted. Just a peck—it would have been so sim-ple. But now he and I were still bound—by a kiss we had not even shared. By the rules of our new bargain, he would not ask again.

But the promise of that moment would linger between us until *I* did. And I would not. Even if his Gentry beauty entranced me, I had no intention—

"Unhand my wife." The dangerous male voice scraped rough through the evening hush. "Before I unhand you myself. Permanently."

My gaze jerked over my shoulder. Irian loomed in silhouette against the pale stone of Aduantas, his eyes like stars and his drawn blade like a gash of night. A bare feather of fear stroked my spine even though his intimidation was not meant for me.

But his threat did not seem to affect the target it was intended for. If anything, the Gentry man's cool fingers tightened over my wrist as he straightened toward Irian's voice. His wide, winsome smile was its own kind of blade.

"The husband, I presume?"

Irian's low growl hummed with menace. He stalked forward from the shadows, the waning moon splashing him with silver. The blue-eyed Gentry stiffened at the sight of him, finally letting go of my wrist. I jerked my hand away, battling satisfaction and resentment that Irian had been able to intimidate him when I could not.

Except the stranger didn't look intimidated. His eyebrows slashed together, then winged upward. His wide smile faltered, then reemerged less contrived, but no less lovely. He stepped from beneath the arbor, the weak moonlight flashing in his cobalt eyes.

"Irian?" he said incredulously.

Irian glowered at the sound of his name, fury fletching his angular features. "Wayland."

Wayland. The blue-eyed Gentry took this as an invitation, stepping forward as if to clasp Irian in an embrace. The gesture shook me—Irian's dangerous air of tense formality did not invite casual affection. I expected him to have the man on his back with a sword at his throat in three seconds flat. Instead, Irian simply brushed past him, ducking beneath the fragrant arbor to clasp me close. He slid a hand beneath my chin and tilted my face toward the low light—the contact familiar and very welcome after Wayland's forbidden touch.

"Is all well, colleen?" Irian's eyes cut from mine toward the other Gentry. "Did he offend you? If he dared touch you—"

"You will find your lady wife unsullied and unharmed, old friend," Wayland said easily. "We were just talking."

"It's all right, Irian," I whispered, too low for the other man to hear. "It was a misunderstanding."

"Hmm." My reassurance did little to assuage Irian's disquiet. "I wish I could say we are well met, *old friend*. But this is not how I would have chosen to reunite."

"Nor I," agreed Wayland. "I wish you might have brought your bride here before wedding her, so I might have taken my shot."

Irian visibly bristled. But Wayland laughed, head thrown back and shoulders relaxed.

"You have not changed at all, have you? As grim and serious as you ever were." Still smiling, Wayland held out one large, sword-calloused hand, palm facing up. "I am joking, old friend. I am happy for you. She is pretty as a pearl, fast as a sea snake, and about as pleasant as a thorn in the arse. You two suit each other."

"I will take that as a compliment." Irian hesitated a moment longer, then grasped Wayland's palm in his own. His tattooed hand tightened perceptibly over the other man's, until I feared he might break his fingers. "But if you ever look at my wife the wrong way again, I'll gut you like a brined walrus, then wear your pelt as a cape. Clear?"

"Crystal." Somehow, Wayland was still smiling. His indigo gaze snagged mine, frothing with amusement and curiosity. "But I fear in all this drama the lady and I have not been properly introduced."

"I'm Fia." I left off any surname. Not because I was afraid Wayland might use it against me—I had a feeling the power of my Treasure inoculated me against such Folk enchantment. But because Ní Mainnín, the name I'd borne for the past thirteen years, no longer felt right. I no longer considered myself the high queen of Fódla's adoptive daughter, for her love had only ever been a ruse designed to manipulate. And if I was truly her long-dead husband King Rían's natural daughter, then I wasn't sure I wanted the name of a man who had seduced and kidnapped Deirdre, a Folk maiden who knew nothing of men, only the terrible weight of the magic she had inherited. Perhaps as Irian's bride, I had gained a new name. If I had, I didn't know it.

"Fia." Wayland rolled the name over his tongue like he wasn't sure he preferred the taste of it to *Thorn Girl*. "Allow me to introduce myself as Wayland, son of Gavida, smith-king of Emain Ablach."

"You're—" I gaped, hope and hunger growing briars in my veins. "But then you're also—"

"Pampered prionsa of the Silver Isle," Irian interrupted meaningfully. "And my long-lost foster brother, come to harass me again after all these years."

I clamped my mouth shut, taking the hint. Clearly Irian did not wish me to speak plainly about Wayland's identity. But I couldn't help but stare at the man. It seemed improbable yet wildly significant that I had already met the prisoner heir of the Silver Isle—a year ago, before Irian and I had even dreamed we might come to love each other. Neither of us had known who the other was—*what* the other was—and yet here we were. Standing an arm's length apart.

Bound by a kiss we had not shared.

But Irian had implied the tánaiste we sought was wholly under his father's thumb. Yet Wayland wore no shackles, sat behind no bars. Perhaps his father had seen fit to free him, and our mission here on Emain Ablach would be far simpler than we'd imagined.

"You always reveled in persecution, you masochist." Despite his teasing words, Wayland's smile finally drowned beneath some strain I couldn't fathom. "But I never imagined you'd enjoy torment enough to face me for the Oak King's Crown. What are you thinking?"

"I have no intention of competing." A muscle feathered along Irian's jaw. "But I agree the timing is inopportune."

"If not to compete," Wayland asked, crossing heavily muscled arms over his chest, "then why have you come?"

Irian leveled him with a forceful stare before tilting his head toward me. "Have you not heard?"

Wayland's eyebrows lifted as realization burned over his features. "The old man will not be happy if he finds out you've snuck a miraculously renewed Treasure onto his island. She will not be able to stay hidden for long."

"If we did sneak here, it was not on his account," Irian growled. "And I am not hiding her. I went just now to smooth her coming. But Gavida seems intent on barring everyone from his chambers until the morrow. Including once-respected foster sons."

"So you came looking for me." Wayland's eyes flicked toward me, then away. "In my personal pleasure gardens."

A tangle of embarrassment prickled the length of my spine. These weren't simply pleasure gardens... They were Wayland's *private* pleasure gardens? And I'd climbed a trellis of perfect, pallid flowers directly into them? I shivered when I remembered his words from a year ago: *Try, Thorn Girl. You will find the magic of Tír na nÓg is not so easily fooled.*

And curse him, he'd been right. The magic of Tír na nÓg had brought me right to him.

"Yes." Irian also glanced at me, and I wondered exactly what he'd seen. Or heard. "It is just as well. For I—we—wish also to speak with you."

"My company is undoubtedly irresistible." Wayland smiled again, but there was a sudden tension to his expression that twisted his mouth down. "But do not imagine my father has softened in the years since you last saw him, Ree. You should pay him the proper obeisances before he makes an erroneous assumption about why you've come. Then—then we can resume our reunion at our leisure."

Irian inclined his head in agreement. "If anyone can talk some sense into Gavida, it is you."

Wayland laughed that all-consuming, irreverent laugh, chasing away any unease I might have seen on his face. "Let us go and see whether we can bother the old man enough to get our way."

A heavy door admitted us into a gleaming porcelain hallway. Wayland set off briskly through Aduantas, leading us through nacre-lined corridors spiraling inward like an enormous seashell.

"A nautilus." Irian's features were impassive, his silver eyes fixed on the glaringly bright halls spooling us ever inward. "What were you doing in Wayland's gardens? I told you to stay with the others, beyond the walls."

"Told me?" I repeated, incredulous.

"*Asked* you," he amended, although I had to wonder. "Well?"

"I—" While I didn't appreciate being scolded, he had a right to ask. I kept my voice to an undertone. "Back on the cliffs, you asked me what I heard. With my Treasure. On Emain Ablach I hear...*nothing.* I tried to bide my time until you returned, but I couldn't. So I decided to scout a little. I never imagined I'd find myself in someone's private pleasure gardens—let alone your foster brother's."

"Aduantas is a labyrinth of traps and enchantments, colleen." Irian sighed, cutting shadowed eyes to me. "Wayland could have killed you for trespassing."

I almost laughed. *Killed* was not the right verb. The fate Wayland had in mind for me had entirely more to do with lips than swords. "He did not. And a good thing, too, since apparently he is my brother-in-law."

"*Foster* brother-in-law." Irian curled one lip up over a canine in a flash of wicked humor. "He and I share no blood. A fact he is rightfully envious of."

"But I am four years older than him," Wayland called over his shoulder. "A fact *he* is rightfully envious of."

My eyebrows lifted at their unexpected banter.

"Listen, Fia." Irian dropped his voice so only I could hear. "Gavida prides himself on perfect control within his domain. Anyone visiting his court must abide by strict rules. The geas of hospitality, for example. You must not lose control—"

"*Must not?*" I hissed. "Do you think yourself my king instead of my husband? I've told you—I have everything under control."

A furrow appeared between Irian's brows, but he said nothing more as Wayland's steps slowed. The corridor curled inward toward two massive doors; a quartet of steel-helmed guards crossed spears as we approached. Wayland waved them away with a flick of one languorous hand and stepped into an antechamber framing another set of doors—these embossed with intricate, echoing patterns. Tangled oak and holly leaves etched in garnet and peridot; arching apple trees bearing shining golden fruits; falling stars pricked out in glittering silver. But in the moment before Wayland opened them, Irian stopped him with a hand on his shoulder.

"Quickly, Way." Irian pulled the outer doors shut so the three of us were ensconced in the antechamber. "Show her before we go in."

All the humor ebbed from Wayland's sleek, symmetrical features—a wave pulling foam from a dark beach. He hesitated, unsettled, then tugged at the ties of his high collar. I frowned, ready to chide him for yet another inappropriate flirtation. But then he ripped the stiff fabric away from his throat. Metal encircled his neck—heavy as a torc and brutal as a shackle. A thick, intricately carved collar—for it could be nothing else—reached from the hollow where his pulse throbbed nearly to the base of his jaw.

"What *is* that?" The question seared my throat.

Anger I thought must be born from experience puckered the contours of Irian's voice. "It is one of Gavida's favorite forgings—a blocking device for magic."

Words frothed to life in my throat, then swiftly died. So this was what Irian had meant. Gavida's heir wasn't imprisoned—at least, not behind bars. But I had to assume the collar around his neck served its purpose as effectively as any dungeon. Fury blossomed green and black inside me. I clenched my fists against my own insistent power and couldn't help but wonder what it might feel like to be artificially separated from it.

Despicable. I wanted to throttle the smith-king, and I hadn't even met him yet.

"It looks different than I remember," Irian said quietly as Wayland tugged his shirt back up over the collar. "Has something changed?"

Wayland's mouth worked. "Perhaps."

"Care to elaborate?" Irian folded his arms over his chest.

Wayland's eyes flashed indigo, and his laughing mouth settled into a hard, narrow line. He said nothing. A moment later, Irian's arms fell back down to his sides.

"A geas? Forged into the metal?" Wayland's nod to Irian was almost imperceptible. "Not just a collar, then. But also a muzzle."

A sick feeling clenched my stomach, matching the sudden abhorrence warping Irian's expression. He scraped a hand through hair already mussed by salt water and wind. "I assume you have tried everything?"

Again, Wayland nodded.

"Then there is nothing to be done." Bitterness made Irian's voice terse. "A shame."

His defeatism shocked me—I had never known Irian to give up so easily.

"Indeed," Wayland said after a beat. "Come—we should not tarry here."

The doors fell open before us.

I had expected a throne room. What I got was a forge.

The room was fiendishly hot and wreathed with dancing phantoms of steam. A heavy hammer pounded, followed by the unmistakable hiss of heated metal plunging into cold water. Charcoal and petrichor seared my nostrils. The sensations dragged me unpleasantly back four years.

Rogan had already left Rath na Mara. Cathair had dissuaded me from spending time in the greenhouses, my one solace. I'd made a bracelet out of plants that bit and stung me, and learned to enjoy it. I'd fought or fucked any man who dared look sideways at me. Mostly the former.

Fionn, the blacksmith's boy, had been the latter. One of my skeans had bent during training—the master smith couldn't be bothered with such a small task, and set it to his apprentice. Fionn had invited me to stay and watch him forge the new knife. Normally, I would've broken his nose for suggesting I didn't have anything better to do than sit there and watch him work. But he'd been wild-haired and soot-smeared and loquacious, talking me through every detail of the process, and for once, I hadn't minded the company.

"Most people get it wrong," Fionn had told me, excitement limning his voice. "They think it's the heat which makes a blade. But heat is only what makes it malleable—soft enough to bend, to hammer, to shape. It is the cold that makes it hard and sharp and deadly. That is the true transformation."

I shook off the memories as a figure moved forward through the steam. The man was huge and naked to the waist, his beefy musculature striped with soot and sweat. His golden-brown skin bore a spray of wrinkles around the eyes; silver stippled his hair and beard of dense mahogany. In his right hand he gripped a blunt-nosed hammer; in his left, a savage length of raw metal.

Gavida. The smith-king.

"Did I not ask to be left in peace?" he roared before stopping in his tracks at the sight of Irian, who dominated him in height if not breadth. Recognition flickered across his stern features and conjured a surprising air of lightness within his expression. He relaxed, sliding his eyes over his erstwhile foster son; then his blood son, Wayland; then me. "What is this?"

"A reintroduction." Irian's voice was assiduously even. "You mourned a foster son thirteen years ago. But he has survived his doom. And he wishes to reacquaint himself with you and yours."

Gavida's deep blue eyes narrowed as he made some decision. Then he knocked his hammer against the jagged metal with a vicious clang.

Servants flooded the forge, some banking the fire while others attended to their liege. They drew his tools from his hands before swabbing him with damp cloth and dressing him in fine brocades and silks. The steam was slow to dissipate—there were long moments before I could read the outline of the room. High arching ceilings; a throne upon a dais and a smith's workbenches in equal prominence; a massive crucible centered upon the far wall.

The crucible Fionn's master had used in his forge had been double the size of a wine jug. The crucible Gavida used was triple the size of a *horse*. Massive, it dominated the space, birch white and curved like a vase. It shone white-hot, but the longer I stared at it, the more I realized this was no ordinary metal he was smelting. Every metal I knew of—no matter the type—burned molten red.

Whatever metal Gavida was forging burned molten *silver*, shot through with sparks of gold.

"Irian, son of Ethadon, heir to the Sept of Feathers. Son of my enemy. Dead, then resurrected." Gavida climbed to his throne, steepling his fingers as he sat. "I have been expecting you."

"Father." Wayland tsked. "They have come all this way to surprise you. The least you could do is act surprised."

Gavida's smile widened. "So. After all this time you finally come to join my tournament?"

"I will only compete if I must."

"If you *must*, eh?" Gavida considered Irian's words with a touch of his son's jovial insouciance. "But that must mean you have a favor to ask. A desire to satisfy. A want so huge only I can fulfill it." Beneath his silver-strewn beard, a smile curved. He cocked a burnished eyebrow. "Go on, then, son of my enemy. Plead your case."

"It is a simple request, enemy of my father," Irian intoned, staring straight ahead. "Long ago, you forged the four Treasures of the Septs. Three were destroyed. One was successfully tithed. Another was recently resurrected. The boon I would ask is this—unforge the two Treasures that remain. Set my wife and me free from the lineage of destruction that we were born to."

I jerked, my ribs squeezing like roots around my hammering heart. Irian's words were splinters of wood, tearing holes in my lungs and slicing fissures in the softest parts of me. Betrayal burned through me, hot and hostile.

Destroy the Treasures? That was not why we'd come. No—we'd agreed to *resurrect* the other two Treasures, in the same way I'd resurrected the Heart of the Forest. To balance magic in Tír na nÓg. To defeat Eala before she found a way to rain destruction across both realms.

Hadn't we?

"Both of them? Don't be greedy, boy." Gavida's chuckle sent goose bumps prickling along my arms. Irian's audible growl at being called *boy* set the fine hairs to standing.

"One Treasure, then."

"You wish me to unmake that which I created?" Curiosity wreathed the smith-king's voice like steam. "But why?"

"He jests, Majesty." I raised my voice before Irian could speak. "Such a natural comedian. Or perhaps madness has struck him."

Irian's face was set; his eyes, stark. "Fia—"

But Gavida's gaze had fallen on me, interest coiling to life on his handsome grizzled face. "Let the little one speak. I have not heard such a voice as hers in a very long time."

"Thank you, sire." I liked being called *little one* about as much as Irian liked being called *boy*. But I swallowed the affront and stepped forward. "My husband misspoke. We seek not to destroy Treasures. We wish rather your help in forging anew those that have been lost."

Irian tensed, opening his mouth. But Gavida held up a wide

hand scalloped with scars and calluses, silencing him. He once more steepled his fingers as he regarded us both with an expression I could not fathom. At last, he settled his gaze on Irian.

"You know I am not in the business of destruction, boy—only creation. Destruction is easy—as I think your bardaí might agree. Creation is hard." A smile flashed through his beard. "If you compete for the Oak King's Crown, I will be obligated to entertain your request. Should you win, of course. But I shall not grant such a favor out of the kindness of my heart."

The smith-king's gaze sparked sapphire as it traveled from his erstwhile foster son back to me. I forced myself not to look away as his eyes cataloged me from head to toe. I could only imagine what he saw—my brined hair and wind-whipped skin? Or the throbbing Treasure hidden beneath my clothes? The green blood coursing through my veins?

"And as for you." Gavida crooked a finger at me. "Approach, little one. I wish to take a look at you."

I bristled. I disliked being commanded by someone who was not, and never would be, my liege. But I was as curious about this powerful, roguish smith-king—with his lifeless city and his cauldron of quicksilver—as he seemed to be about me. So despite Irian's low noise of warning, I climbed the curving steps to Gavida's throne. He rose to meet me. He was not quite as tall as either Irian or his son, but his breadth was overwhelming; his demeanor, all-encompassing. A heavy, cloying scent struck me across the face: dying apple blossoms and sea salt layered over the stink of bog tar and singed flesh. I swallowed a surge of bile as unexpected nausea churned hot in my stomach.

I didn't have time to flinch away when Gavida lifted a broad, meaty hand to my face. His calloused fingers were rough on my skin as he gripped my chin and turned my face toward the molten light of his crucible. But his touch was distressingly cold—sending a shock to burn silver stars behind my eyes. I jerked back, and the smith-king let me go.

"Hmm." His eyes bored into me, dark as a winter sky at dusk. His face had lost its humorous cast. "You are not at all what I expected."

"What, pray tell," I ground out, *"did* you expect?"

"I am in the business of magic, little one." He kept staring at me. "Those who do not understand it as I do may see magic as mystical, extraordinary, mysterious. But I know it to be a set of processes governed by strict rules. For every marvel, a price; for every miracle, a sacrifice. And I have made enough miracles to know this: All magic makes sense. But you, little one—you do not make sense."

His words showered more cold sparks down my spine. I shivered, even as hunger rattled to life like a restive beast inside me. I still knew so little about who I truly was or where I'd come from. All I had were theories and bad dreams and the strange voice that had spoken to me in the moments before my sacrifice to the Heartwood had been accepted. *A long time ago, you were given to us for safekeeping. Now we give you back to yourself.* But Gavida—he had created the Heart of the Forest, the conduit to the elemental earth magic I had become a vessel for. If he had insights into my nature, I needed to know what they were. "Tell me what you mean."

"Perhaps I will, little one." Gavida's smile grew wide and wily. "If you win the Oak King's Crown."

Behind me, Irian surged forward with a protest rippling from his throat. But Gavida's offer was already colliding with my plan to reforge the Treasures. Perhaps I had little chance of winning a competition against hundreds of fierce, ambitious Folk. But I now knew—with sour, sinking certainty—that when it came to defeating Eala, protecting the realms, and rescuing Rogan, Irian and I did not want the same things. I understood why he wanted to unburden himself of his destiny, especially after so closely dodging death. I could even understand why he wanted us to run away instead of embroiling himself in another conflict he had not started.

But I was not in the habit of running away from a fight. If I competed for the Oak King's Crown, I not only might learn valuable information about my own murky past. But if I was strong and clever and brave, I might even win. Then I could ask Gavida for anything I wanted. Like a newly forged Treasure to replace the ones destroyed. Perhaps Wayland could be convinced to be its heir. *Then* I could stand against Eala and the bardaí. Even if Irian would not stand with me.

So I lifted my chin and said, "Done."

Gavida's eyes glinted opaque blue. Behind him, his crucible churned, sparking silver stars into the smoke-wreathed dim. A breath later, Irian caught me by the shoulders as he spun me toward him.

"Fia, *no*." His gaze was wild and worried, skeins of shadow spooling behind his opal eyes. "You know not what you do."

"I know exactly what I'm doing." I shrugged off his suffocating touch. "Although you might have told me what *you* planned to do."

Remorse blurred over his angular features before smoothing behind his mask of calm menace.

"My wife is an outsider." Irian glowered up at Gavida. "She was raised in the human realms—she knows not our ways. I beg you, enemy of my father—revoke this bargain before she gets killed by the blade of her own ignorance."

Offense wound hot around my bones, nettling me with serrated thorns.

"The bargain is struck, son of my enemy." Gavida's voice was resonant as a clapper licking the inside of a bell. "There are forces here beyond your ken, boy. As I always told you, *the balancing is eternal—*"

"*But it is not immutable,*" Irian finished tightly. "I know your laws of balance, old man. But I do not see how they pertain to my wife."

"The magic of Tír na nÓg carries us ever closer to the pattern etched by the stars," Gavida intoned with the air of prophecy, eerily echoing his son's earlier words. "This tournament is not and has never been a folly. Year after year, the Oak King rises as the Holly King falls, until he in turn is restored. The cycle is timeless yet ever changing—eternal yet volatile. Brothers will battle brothers. Sisters will battle sisters. And you—you are all a part of it and always have been."

Disquiet forced my eyes to Irian. But my new husband was not looking at me—he was staring suddenly at Gavida's son, Wayland, who stood half obscured in the shadow of the smith-king's crucible. Although the other man's stance was easy, a sudden tension sang between the erstwhile foster brothers, palpable enough to taste. I whipped my gaze between the two men, vainly trying to read the invisible pasts of lives I had not lived. *Brothers will battle brothers.* Was Gavida talking about Irian and Wayland? I remembered what Wayland had said barely an hour ago—*I never imagined you'd enjoy torment enough to face me for the Oak King's Crown.*

Stinging, strangling vines climbed my arms unbidden, following the patterns of the markings etched onto my skin. A dense, oily feeling of inevitability settled over me—almost the same sensation as the one I'd felt over a month ago, beneath the Heartwood. When I'd glanced down at my palm to find I still held the brooch I'd ripped from Rogan's cloak—the cracked stone I'd found in a river and gifted to my best friend years before. The stone that was my inexplicable inheritance, my mystical legacy.

Then I'd felt freed by the knowledge of my destiny, the sacrifice I was always meant to make. Now I only felt trapped—as if this was a story that had already been told. Only, I did not know the ending.

Irian finally jerked his gaze from Wayland. His eyes slid briefly to me, but they were so shadowed that I couldn't help but shudder. Mercifully, they traveled onward to Gavida, where they narrowed to slits of metal.

"Sisters?" Irian growled. "What sisters, old man?"

The question jolted me. I had thought Gavida's words an

abstraction—a rhetorical balance to the proverbial *brothers* he'd mentioned. But now they rankled inside me with agitating significance. Surely it was impossible; surely—

"Your wife is not the only woman born of the human realms who has traveled to my island." Gavida's square teeth once more flashed white behind his beard of silver-streaked mahogany. "Nor are you the only man born of a noble lineage who has lost everything."

Gavida's words throbbed through me, twin pulses of loathing and longing. He couldn't possibly mean—

"*No*," I whispered, even as Irian laughed roughly and said, "Yet another piece of your gods-damned pattern, old man?"

Some decision sparked on the smith-king's face, and he clapped his hands. An attendant appeared through the mist and bowed.

"Do the humans still await my decision?"

The attendant nodded.

"Then let them through." Gavida's booming chuckle shivered the walls and thrummed along my skin. "Do not doubt what you do not understand, boy."

Wayland stepped forward. "Father, surely this isn't necessary—"

But the huge wooden doors were already groaning open, sending whirlwinds of steam to swirl around our feet. Thorny vines climbed my biceps and twined at the nape of my neck, bursting bouquets of violets and asters through my brined hair. Irian reached out a gentling hand to grip my palm, but I couldn't feel him beyond the thorns biting into my flesh. I turned, almost against my will.

To see Eala and Rogan stride into the smith-king's forge.

Chapter Fourteen

Eala paraded confidently into the smith-king's reception hall,
her bearing that of a conquering monarch and her mien that of
a beatific saint. She wore all white—a mantle of fine wool layered
over a dress of shimmering silk, edged with pale frothing fur like a
halo around her face. Her long blond hair was brushed out over her
shoulders—between the wreathing steam and the sparking silver
light, she looked incandescent and ethereal. And her eyes—they
burned, like blue-hot coals or cut sapphires.

She looked like one of them. One of *us*.

I could barely stand to look at her.

But looking past her was much, much worse.

Blankly marching three paces behind her was Rogan Mòr,
prince of Bridei.

Rogan, who'd been my playmate, confidant. Lover. Rogan,
whom I'd rejected moments after he'd confessed his enduring love
to me at the Feis of the Ember Moon. Rogan, whose will Eala had
stolen with the power of the black flowers. And, I could see now,
had not given back. Might *never* give back.

In so many ways, Rogan was the same man I'd known. A tall,

muscular physique. A ruddy complexion dotted with constellations of freckles. Long golden hair braided away from his face. But his expression was utterly empty—his wry mouth did not quirk sideways with a private joke; his bronze eyebrows did not lift with questions or concerns. And his *eyes*—where they had once been the blue-green of river stones, mercurial with shifting emotions, they were now flat and hard as granite.

A mewling sound startled me. A moment later, I realized *I* had made it—a soft pathetic sound of anguish ripping from my unwitting throat. I reeled a step back, colliding with Irian's bulk. Then I lunged forward, flinging myself toward my sister in all my grief and strength and fury. Irian caught me around the shoulders, but my awareness could not be contained. Gnarled tree roots sprinted away from my restless feet, grinding marble tiles into shards and splinters. Thorn-studded vines shattered upward, whipping toward Eala in clusters and coils. Venomous flowers burst in midair, showering pollen red as slaughter through the shifting silver steam.

"Irian!" Gavida's voice boomed through the forge, followed by the clang of his giant hammer striking the metal of his throne. "Control your woman!"

But that only made me angrier. Vengeance heaved my forest of green up the steps toward Gavida too. Voracious vines clambered toward his boots; roses with petals of sharp silver stabbed toward his glaring eyes.

Wayland stepped into my line of sight, blocking my view. I reeled back as his hands reached for my throat. Panic seized me. But his cool palms only slid against my skin for a brief moment. I registered cold metal curving over my jugular. A snick of a latch at my nape. Then—

It felt like falling off a cliff—a sheer, straight drop away from the towering, toppling heights of my Greenmark toward—

Nothing.

Morrigan help me.

My vision blurred as I fell to my knees, hard. My palms slapped down, then lurched back up, my fingertips seeking the ridge of metal hooked around my throat. A brief, stupid, optimistic thought gripped me—it was a torc. But then my fingers found the divot where the lock bit into my skin. And I knew.

It was a collar.

I glared up through swimming eyes at the smith-king's son. Wayland had the grace to look apologetic. Behind him—atop his shattered steps upon his throne of silver—Gavida just looked livid. Beside me, Irian crouched down, worry and fury darkening his eyes to iron. He briefly cupped my cheeks, which I realized were wet with my own involuntary tears, then drew my hands away from the choker with his own large, warm palms. He pulled me to him, burying my head against his shoulder as he glared beyond me toward his erstwhile foster father.

"I am sorry, colleen," Irian murmured. "But I did try to warn you. There are few things Gavida takes more seriously on the Silver Isle than the geas of hospitality. You attacked his guest, then him. You are lucky he only curtailed you—he would have been within his rights to have you killed."

"Did it take away...?" To my horror, I was crying—great gasping sobs that racked me from head to toe. I felt as if one of my limbs had been amputated—I kept reaching for my Greenmark, so strong in the past few weeks as to be overwhelming, only to find an emptiness where the forest and the plants and the earth had once been. That, and a hum sizzling along my skin like a warning.

"It only suppresses. You heard the smith—he is in the business of creation, not destruction." Irian stood brusquely, lifting me more slowly after him, then pitched his voice to be heard by all. "Let us get on with it, shall we?"

I forced myself to turn my gaze back toward Eala, Rogan, the smith-king, and the chaos I had wrought. The huge, gnarled roots and impossible rosebushes were slowly crumbling into gray dust and desiccated petals, as lifeless as the magic gone dormant inside me. I lifted an involuntary hand to my new collar, even as I locked eyes with Eala. Although my path of destruction stopped mere inches from her delicate white slippers, the erstwhile swan princess looked utterly unruffled. Only her pale blue eyes showed any emotion, burning cold as the metal locked ruthlessly around my throat.

Anger rose inside me to match hers, but it felt empty—untethered to magic, it seemed a useless thing. A notion bubbled up inside me, rich with irony—for the first time in my life, I was as close to human as I had always longed to be.

And I hated it.

"Hello, Sister." Eala's voice was a melodious chime in the vaulted chamber. Her eyes feigned sadness as she looked at me. "I see you are as wild and willful as ever. I mourn to see you collared. But then again, must not a wild horse be broken before it can be ridden? Should not a vicious dog be chained before it hurts itself or others? Perhaps our story might have ended more pleasantly if only *I* had thought to leash you."

Irian stepped in front of me in the moment before my rage—hobbled as it might be—flung me at my sister again.

"Watch your tongue," he snarled, "when you speak to my wife."

My eyes flicked reflexively to Rogan, looming at Eala's shoulder. But he did not so much as blink.

"Wife?" Surprise lifted Eala's eyebrows toward her hairline. "Then congratulations are in order. Not only did you steal my betrothed's heart in the moments before he was to wed me, but you managed to marry my wicked captor in the aftermath? Then stole magic that ought to belong to all? For someone who has claimed to want only my best interests, Sister, you have certainly found every opportunity to set yourself against me."

"Who are you trying to fool?" I almost had to laugh at this series of outrageous mistruths. "I never stole anything from Rogan he did not willingly give—unlike you, who took away his will when he refused to obey your whims. Nor have I ever *stolen* magic. I was born with it, also unlike you, who had to murder those you loved in order to claim it." Eala's eyes burned brighter at the mention of the six swan maidens whose willing hearts she'd sacrificed for mastery of the Gates. "And Irian? He may be wicked, but he never manipulated me the way you did. He never lied to me."

Although he hasn't always told me the perfect truth. But when Irian's huge palm folded over mine, I let him pull me toward him. I refused to show Eala the jagged places where the tánaiste and I did not quite fit together.

Donn's dark hell, I barely wanted to look at them myself.

"Enough," Gavida intoned from atop the dais, which was no longer scarred and discolored by my ministrations. Somehow, the stone and metal were knitting themselves back together. He glared down at each of us in turn. "You have all come here this night asking favors. One wishes to make new. One wishes to make other. One wishes to unmake. I will entertain none of these requests. This tournament is not a folly—it is more than an old king's whim. Emain Ablach is a place of great magic. But, like all magic, it is governed by laws of balance. As the Holly King weakens, so must the Oak King rise. Siblings locked forever in a battle of dominance—whoever is meant to ascend shall win. And whoever is meant to fade shall lose. If you desire something from me, you must compete for it. It is as it has always been. So—which of you will battle for the Oak King's Crown, and their chance to earn what they so desire?"

Irian's palm tightened over my fingers as he glanced down at me, then away, his gaze once more finding Wayland, who was standing in the shadow of the simmering crucible.

"Father, you are being coy. You know I will fight, as I do every year—as your champion." I couldn't tell whether the sudden heaviness of Wayland's tone was meant to warn. And if so, against what? "I compete for the honor of the Holly King, who, though weak, will one day rise again."

Gavida gave his heavy mane a gratified shake. A moment later, Eala stepped forward and swept an elegant, if borderline obsequious, bow to the smith-king.

"If the competition were but wits and grace, lord, I would happily compete. But I had not the opportunity to be trained in the ways of battle. So I must also name a champion. Beloved?" Eala beckoned Rogan to stand beside her. He mindlessly obeyed. My last memory of him was in his wedding finery six weeks ago. That bold-checked mantle and embroidered tunic were now gone, replaced by Folk clothes—loose chamois trousers belted at the waist and a thick white gambeson under hand-tooled scale mail. The sight of him looking so much like *them*—like *us*—made my heart lurch in my chest. "Rogan, crown prince of Bridei and future king of Fódla, will compete as my champion."

"Then, as bargained, I too will compete," I promised, almost before I knew what I was saying.

Irian stepped in front of me, blocking my view of Gavida and the dais with his height and breadth. His head canted to one side. "Please do not do this, colleen."

"It is already done," I said tightly.

"That was before Gavida curtailed your magic." His voice was nearly inaudible. "You cannot expect to win a mystical tournament without the power of your Treasure. You can hardly hope to survive."

"I am an accomplished fighter," I hissed back at him. "If I can hold my own against you—"

"You can hold your own against me when I am holding back." The words were soft enough to soothe yet sharp enough to smart. "No one else will do you the honor."

"Of coddling me? Good." My voice rose to a pitch I was not proud of. "Let them all see what I am truly made of."

"Your blood, spattered green over the snow? Your bones, broken like twigs upon the swords of your enemies?" Shadows of fear darkened his expression. "Yes, in death you will be truly understood."

Memories—faded as paint drenched by rain—blurred over me. Agony cleaving me in two. Viscera-slick hands gripping me too tightly. The earth roaring open to swallow me up. But these were swiftly overlaid by more pleasant yet equally hazy images—a leafing tree vast as time itself, an antlered figure reaching arms to embrace me, stars swirling in an endless sky. I shook my head to dispel them.

"I have to do this." A knot formed in my throat. "For you—for *us*. For Tír na nÓg, and the magic I renewed. For all of *them*. And for—"

"For Rogan." A muscle leapt in Irian's cheek as he clenched his jaw. Then determination settled his features into marble. "Then let me compete on your behalf. Name me as your champion."

"*No*." I bristled. "You're not listening—*I* have to do this."

In the moment before he turned on his heel, Irian's mask of control warped enough for me to see something terrible lurking in his eyes.

"Then I, too, will compete for the Oak King's Crown," he called up to Gavida. "And may you be forever cursed for making it so."

"There are no devils here to heed your curses." Gavida's words tolled with thunderous finality. "Nor gods to honor your blessings. There is only me, my metals, and my magic. You would do well to remember that, son of my enemy."

For a long moment, there was nothing but the steam hissing from the forge and the crucible spitting starlight from the wall. Then Gavida lurched toward his throne, sat heavily atop it, and waved a tired hand.

"Now begone, all of you. My attendants have prepared rooms for you in Aduantas. I advise you make use of them to rest before the tournament opens on the morrow."

"Our entourage—" I ventured.

"Has also been granted rooms near yours and summoned to occupy them." Behind us, the vast doors yawned open. "Now please get out of my sight, before I lose my temper."

Blank-faced servants in silver livery bowed Irian and me to traipse, disheveled and silently irate, down a luminous, curving hallway before leading us up a series of gleaming, curving staircases. As a servant unlocked a suite of darkened rooms, the tension sang toward crescendo, everything we had said and done these past two weeks humming atonally between us. Irian stalked into the bedchamber, past the dim shapes of a huge bed and a series of chairs, toward the muffled window. He wrenched back the drapes, revealing little but more blackness.

"Colleen." The darkness made a night sky for his seething silver eyes. He swept a hand over his brow. "If you had simply listened when I told you to remain with the others—"

Resentment roared to life inside me. But where thorny vines would once have spiraled my spine and prickled my skin, there was...*nothing*. All the green growth and thronging life I'd had at my fingertips for as long as I could remember were blocked. My fury bottomed out, leaving only helpless sorrow in its wake. My hands lifted toward the circlet of metal at my throat, then dropped toward the now-silent blue-green stone hanging over my breast.

"I don't want to do this now." My voice came out thick. "I'm going to check on the others."

I fled the room before Irian could protest, kicking the door shut behind me.

I found Chandi, Sinéad, and Laoise rollicking along the curving hallway, arms linked as they sang an unintelligible drinking song in off-key harmony. Behind them, the palace attendant ushering them to their rooms betrayed not even a hint of annoyance.

It made me cold. The smith-king truly held this fortress—this city, this *island*—in his metal fist.

The three women caught sight of me a moment later. Whatever they saw on my face stopped their jollity. Sinéad disentangled her arm from Chandi's and made a beeline for the suite adjoining ours. Laoise gave me a long, curious look, then clapped a familiar palm on Chandi's shoulder before making her own escape. Leaving me alone with the person I'd truly wanted to talk to.

Chandi hesitated, a flurry of complicated emotions scudding across her face. Then she closed the space between us, folding me into a sisterly embrace. I leaned against the taller girl, relishing her soft warmth. But a moment later she pulled me back the way she and the others had come, down a long curving staircase, until a terraced archway deposited us into a night-blooming garden.

I inhaled—pearly gardenias wafted fragrance on the chilly breeze, and gauzy pathways sported nacre-lined benches beneath arbors twisting with jasmine and buoyant with huge, pale daturas. Unlike in Wayland's private gardens, elegant Gentry floated like phantoms amid the labyrinth of shadow and glow. Chandi ignored these Folk, some of whom turned inquisitive heads to stare at us, pushing me instead to sit down hard on a bench.

"Talk," she commanded.

But I couldn't put words to the mass of fears and disappointments and worries and uncertainties tangling inside of me. Instead, I asked, "Where are the aughiskies?"

"Roaming the streets and terrorizing the locals." Chandi gave her head an expressive wiggle. "By which I mean happily dozing in finely appointed stalls with all the fish they could ever ask for."

She fell expectantly silent once more. I stared down at my hands clenched in my lap. Finally, the other girl sighed.

"Ordinarily, you'd have to torture this out of me." Starlight glazed her amber eyes. "But I miss being a swan."

Her words startled my preoccupied gaze up to her face, which was striped with loss and longing.

"The first thing I always remembered after the transformation was the sensation of *skin*." She ran an unconscious palm along her forearm, then tugged the sleeve of her mantle down to her wrist. "There was always such a feeling of newness to it—as if I was reborn every night. Icy shards of dashing rain, needling along my arms. The warm touch of a summer wind tangling in my hair. An impossibility, almost—as if my flesh was the affliction, instead of the feathers. How smoothly it curved, as if polished on a lathe. How delicate the fine hairs lay along it, gleaming in the moonlight like gilt on a marble statue. How strange the network of lines cobwebbing my palms; the tiny whorls coiled tight as secrets on the pads of each finger." She clenched her hands. "Only after the sensation of flesh came the sensation of mind. Only then did I remember who I was, *why* I was. Being a swan was always—*always*—easier than being a girl."

Sorrow gripped me as I realized she was answering my question from...three? Four days ago? I reached out and folded one of her tense hands in my own.

"I'm sorry."

"I suppose I should be grateful to be myself—wholly, truly myself—rather than whatever I was before. But it can be far easier to hide behind the identities we're given—the masks that make us most comfortable." She shrugged. "Only, that's not really living. Easy isn't always good. Yes, I miss being a swan. But being a girl is better than being dead."

"You're awfully wise," I remarked with a laugh, "for the youngest...and most annoying of twelve unrelated sisters."

Her smile slipped. "Only six now."

My own face hardened to granite and ice. "She's here, you know."

Chandi inhaled but did not seem surprised. "With him."

It wasn't really a question, but I nodded anyway.

"Is that what's bothering you?" She pivoted to face me fully, emotions cascading over her features. "Or is it about that shiny new necklace locked around your throat?"

I dropped my gaze as fresh fury and helplessness coursed through me. My magic was *gone*. I lifted my hands to the metal, then forced them down.

"There are rumors among the contestants, in the lower city." Chandi's voice was tight. "That the smith-king likes to collar all those he finds a threat to his sovereignty. That he likes to steal magic that doesn't belong to him. That this city is built on lies."

I believed it. "And yet they come. For the promise of a wish come true."

"You say that like you're not going to compete." Chandi's gaze was canny.

I jerked back. "How did you know?"

"We never had the chance to become great friends, Fia." Her mouth twisted. "But I told you the very first time I met you—you painted quite a picture of your personality before I'd even gotten to know you. I know you well enough now to realize you were never going to run away from this fight."

"Irian disagrees."

"Can you blame him?" Chandi's voice was soft, but a thread of betrayal nevertheless stitched stiffly along my bones. "You died in his arms, Fia. When I saw him in those weeks before you splashed up out of the lake, he was..." She shook her head. "I never blamed him for our geas to the extent some of the other girls did, but Irian and I were never close. He was like a strict older brother. When he was kind, it felt like too little; when he was cruel, it felt like too much. But I would not wish upon anyone what your death did to him. It broke him."

Once again, soft-edged images painted themselves over my mind's eye—my skin melting into the earth, the sky shattering with a wordless elegy for lost things. "That doesn't excuse the way he's trying to control me."

"Maybe not." Her words ached with hopeless longing. "But if any of my sisters somehow returned to me? If I somehow got another chance at keeping them safe? I would do anything in my power to protect them, no matter the cost."

Her words drifted like fireflies toward my darkest, deepest chasms. The terrible rift where my death and mystical resurrection clashed. The void where the words I had never spoken to the man I had wed lived and died a thousand times on my cowardly tongue.

The gaping hole where the knowledge of Rogan's terrible fate lived, blocking out the light of all my happy memories of him. The abyss of my realization that I'd agreed to compete in a tournament I knew nothing about, without access to any of my magic.

I rubbed a palm over my brow and changed the subject. "Will you tell me about Laoise?"

Chandi stilled. "What about her?"

"Can we trust her?"

"I'm not sure." Chandi's eyes dropped, and she took a long moment before elaborating. "For now, she is little more than a glorified babysitter. I don't know her well, but I know she means no harm to me or Sinéad. Beyond that, I cannot say. If she means to betray us...perhaps I don't want to know." She paused again. "Maybe it's like that moment before I remembered. I knew I was no longer a swan, but I did not yet know what I was. There was mystery in the transition. Magic in the becoming. Maybe we're all too quick to move beyond the unknown into the fixed. Maybe we could all spend a little time living inside our own transformations."

Another bout of helpless tears prickled at my eyes, and I gripped the distressingly silent stone weighing over my heart.

"If you keep talking like that," I made myself say, "I'm going to keep coming to you for advice."

"Ugh." She laughed, swept her hand through the air. "Nobody wants that."

But as we meandered back toward our chambers, she held my hand like a sister and hummed a sweet, lilting song beneath her breath.

Part Two

The Mountain Tomb

In vain, in vain; the cataract still cries,
The everlasting taper lights the gloom,
All wisdom shut into its onyx eyes.

—"The Mountain Tomb" by W. B. Yeats

Chapter Fifteen

The bedroom unfurled with light. A pale-flamed fire flared in the grate, and blue-toned lanterns shimmered from the corners. No moon hung in the sky beyond the window, but stars dazzled the black night. The outlines of Emain Ablach etched glowing lines of silver against the glass, rising toward a distant glow of gold. I squinted, but if it was the sacred grove—the nemeton—Laoise had mentioned, I could barely see it from here.

The only sign of my husband was a line of dirty clothing discarded carelessly on the floor. Salt-warped boots…sand-crusted trousers…a soot-grimed mantle. I followed the trail with slight trepidation until I found myself in a bathing chamber.

The room was narrow but vaulted, with a curving bank of windows looking out into the night. There was a bath, but it was nothing like the wood or copper vessels I was accustomed to. Shallow terraced steps led down to a steaming basin of fragrant water lightly frothed with bubbles. And lounging on the steps, totally naked and barely submerged, was Irian.

I caught my breath. After several nights camping rough, I'd somehow let myself forget how utterly magnificent he was. With his damp black hair slicked back from his face and his eyes closed, his streamlined features could have been cut from glass. The elegant column of his throat descended toward sculpted shoulders and a hard, broad chest. Ridged abdominals narrowed to crests of muscle cutting down toward—

I didn't look lower. I crossed my arms over my chest and glared.

"Colleen." Irian cracked one eye to look at me. "Get in."

"Is that an order?" I asked, mulish.

"It is a...fervent request."

"Why fervent?"

"Respectfully, Wife." Irian's plush mouth quirked with a hint of humor. "You stink."

I showed my teeth but acquiesced. It was an immense relief to peel off my brined, dirt-caked, sweat-stained layers of clothing. My mantle could be washed—my leather armor could be polished. But my trousers and moth-eaten shirt were a loss—I kicked them into the corner before stepping down into the bath. The water was gloriously warm and perfumed with balsam and cinnamon. I sank in with a groan, submerging myself to the crown as my hair floated free of its unkempt braids.

When I surfaced, Irian was watching me with a not-quite smile. He waited for me to soap my body and wash out my dark curls before reaching for me, fingertips gliding at my waist as he dragged me closer. He pulled me onto his lap, sliding palms up my arms and over my shoulders. His fingertips lingered upon my metal collar as his eyes darkened with fury and regret. Then he cupped the back of my head, burying his hands in my mass of hair and drawing me in for a kiss that simmered with tension.

"Once, in a time of dying days and cold nights—"

"No stories, Irian."

"Very well." He drew back half an inch. "Do you want to go first? Or shall I?"

"Let me." My conversation with Chandi was at the front of my mind, and on its tail rode a collection of doubts...fears...

uncertainties. I still bridled at many of the choices Irian had made, and he mine. And there was one ambivalence lingering between us I ought to broach. But though I rolled the bittersweet words over my tongue—tasted each of their tangled, terrible, tempting contours—I could not say them. Not tonight. "I'm sorry I sacrificed myself beneath the Heartwood. I can only imagine how it hurt to lose me. But I was prepared to lose *you*—to become your widow. Remember? Your pain does not exempt you from respecting me. It doesn't give you license to lie to me. Keep secrets from me. Control me. You had no right to ask Gavida for the destruction of my Treasure."

"I am not in pain, colleen. Not anymore." The brilliance of Irian's gaze dimmed, cold shadows unfurling black wings behind his eyes. "Now I am afraid."

"Afraid." That word fluttered between my ribs like a wing-clipped bird. "What could you possibly be afraid of?"

"So many things." He drew me more tightly to him—my legs around his waist, my breasts molded against his hard, water-slick chest. His hands cupped my cheeks, gripping almost hard enough to bruise. "Fia Ní Mainnín, child of two worlds, you have dug a hole inside me. You have stolen something vital that used to be mine—something I did not even know could be taken. Losing you was like losing a part of myself."

My knee-jerk dismissal of his words was tempered by Chandi's words from earlier: *I would not wish upon anyone what your death did to him.* "Irian. You're not going to lose me."

"I already did. And I do not think I could bear it again." The shadows swallowed up the light in his eyes. With a deft, forceful gesture, he flipped me in the water, pushing me back against the steps until I was pinned beneath his bulk. His knee slid up between my thighs; his torso flexed where my fingertips gripped him for balance. His palm on my cheek was gentle, but his glittering eyes were hard. "Which is why you should have named me your champion in the Tournament of Kings, instead of forcing me to fight for myself."

That was what this was about? I lifted my chin, stubborn. "I am—and have always been—my own damned champion. That doesn't change because I married you."

"You misunderstand, colleen." He shook his head. "I was always going to win this tournament. If I had competed for you, I would have won *for* you. I would have been obliged to. But now—I will have to win for myself."

"You underestimate me," I snapped. "You said it yourself: I am an accomplished fighter—"

"This is not a fight you can win, Fia," Irian interrupted, harsh. "The Oak King's Crown is won through ruthless skill, brutal guile, and yes, magic. Magic you have given Gavida an excuse to strip from you until you leave this isle. Without your Treasure, you have no chance against an army of ambitious Folk all vying for the same prize. You cannot—*must not*—compete."

"You cannot stop me. You are my husband, not my father." My fingernails cut into his biceps. "The prize is too dear, especially now that we know Eala desires it."

"It is far, far too dear." Irian brushed my hair back from my face, then sighed. He closed his eyes, leaned his steam-damp forehead down to mine. When he looked back up, his fierceness had faded. "I told you once, colleen—if I decided I wanted you, I would go to extraordinary lengths to keep you. You cannot blame me for keeping my promise."

His words softened me. I relented, curling my palms along his stubble-rough jaw. This was not an argument that was going to be resolved tonight. Perhaps ever. And I was exhausted. "If I recall correctly you also promised me a mattress. And—oh, what are they called again? *Pillows.*"

His sensuous mouth curled up. "So I did."

Without warning, he curved his large hands over my rear and lifted me bodily out of the bath. Steam swirled as water sluiced down from our joined bodies. Irian didn't bother with the plush towels folded neatly beside the door—his feet slapped wetly on the tile as he kicked the door open, crossed the darkened room, and tossed me onto the mattress. I yelped in mock outrage, but the bed was gloriously soft—I practically disappeared into the layers of eiderdown and fine cotton and finer silk. A moment later, Irian was folding himself atop me, his dampness slipping over mine as our wet bodies tangled together. His mouth found my collarbone a moment later, his tongue laving moisture from my skin and sending skeins of heat tangling toward my core.

"The bed will get all wet," I whispered. "And if you think I don't intend to actually sleep tonight, you're very much mistaken."

Irian laughed. "We shall see about that, colleen." But he obliged me by splaying both hands on the bedspread and sending a concentrated burst of wind ruffling over the sheets and our bodies. A moment later, I was bone dry, although my hair had dried standing straight up. "Will that do?"

"A neat trick," I allowed as I patted my hair down. "Although it may need finessing."

Irian growled as he pounced on me, hitching my knee up over his hip and lowering the weight of his torso between my legs. He was already hard—his length nudged gloriously along the inside of my thigh. Warm anticipation blossomed in my core. But Irian paused, his eyes skating over my face before his hands followed a moment later, mapping my features with lingering touches. A thumb brushing my bottom lip…His palms cupping my cheeks… His fingers smoothing my ruffled hair gently behind my ears.

"How about…," he began thoughtfully. "*Beloved?*"

"No," I said, too quickly. That particular endearment was seared unpleasantly into my memory from the Ember Moon—it was what Eala had called Rogan, repeatedly, in the moments before she'd stolen his will. It was what she'd called him earlier tonight. I forced a smile. "Besides, it's too late. I already decided *Beefswaddle* suits you better."

Irian gave me one of his rare, dazzlingly full smiles. He leaned down to seize my mouth with his, sliding his full lips over mine. He skated his hands along my spine, brushing between my shoulder blades before gliding up my nape to tangle his fingers in my hair. I made a sound of approval. Irian braced his weight on his forearms as he deepened the kiss.

A sharp pinch startled a cry from me and a slow hiss from Irian. My eyes jerked open and my hands flew to my throat, where the narrow metal of my collar had caught between my neck and Irian's bicep, biting into both. A ridge of tenderness rose below my seeking fingertips; a matching line of angry red scored Irian's tattooed arm. He cursed and rolled up to sitting, running rough fingers through his bed-mussed hair. "I should never have brought you here."

A wave of hurt mixed with regret pushed me up beside him. "Please don't be angry at me. I know I shouldn't have lost control with Gavida. But I didn't ask for this."

"Gods alive, colleen. That is not what I meant." His voice was a dangerous rumble in his chest. "Gavida knew exactly what he was doing tonight. He always does. He knows what happened to you—the transformation you are experiencing. And he knows who—*what*—you and Eala are to each other. He intentionally surprised you with her presence to push you to the limits of your control. And when you snapped, he took the opportunity to curtail your magic. He collared you on purpose. I only wish I knew why."

"Maybe he's worried I'll win the Tournament of Kings. Maybe he doesn't want to forge any new Treasures."

"That may certainly be part of it." Irian turned to me with shadowed eyes. "But I wonder if there is more."

"Like what?"

"When he looked at you…when he touched you…" Irian shook his head with a helplessness I wasn't accustomed to and didn't like. "I do not know. But it frightens me. Please, colleen—"

"If you're going to ask me yet again not to compete for the crown," I ground out, "save your breath. I have been manipulated by enough people in my life to know exactly who to hate—I won't let Gavida take anything from me I don't want to give."

Irian dragged a finger along the delicate yet steely edge of the metal collar ringing my throat. But as his fingertips lingered on the raised ridge of flesh that hadn't yet healed without access to my magic, he said nothing out loud save "As you wish."

But when we bedded back down in the luxurious mattress, Irian rolled to face away from me, his broad feather-etched back a silent reproach.

Whatever truce Irian and I had been prepared to let our bodies make, our words had broken.

I, too, rolled over, fighting for sleep even as my thoughts churned with rancor and resentments.

The cliff was slick with snow. Beyond, an endless forest wore a blanket of white, silent as death below a leaden sky.

Irian sprinted away from me, toward the icy precipice. His hair and cloak were black as feathers against the pale canvas of snow and sky.

"*Irian!*" I screamed at his receding back, but he either did not or could not hear me. He launched himself off the edge. Then dropped like a stone. I lunged after him, sliding on the ice-slick rock. But his wings never spread—no dark feathers burst from his skin to catch the slicing wind.

He just fell.

Panic pushed me closer to the edge. I scanned the ground for some sign of him—a blotch of black between the trees, a splash of silver blood on bare branches. But I had misjudged my perch—one of my boots slipped. I jerked sideways, scrabbled for purchase on the ice. I slid precipitously.

The cold wind picked me up and dragged me down.

I screamed as I fell, a vain objection to a destiny already written. And when I looked up at the cliff I'd fallen from, I glimpsed a dim figure swathed in white feathers.

I had not fallen. I had been *pushed*.

I awoke the moment before I hit the ground, shivering and sweating. My hand rose unconsciously to my throat as I glanced over at Irian. But my husband was asleep, his breathing deep and heavy. I shoved off the cloying blankets and padded to the window for a breath of fresh air.

For a moment, I thought I must still be dreaming—stars flung themselves down to burst against the glass.

No—not stars.

The sky had silvered over. And it had begun to snow over Emain Ablach.

Chapter Sixteen

I fell back asleep in the leaden hush of dawn, only to awaken hours later without any idea of the time. Everything seemed the same color. The pale mother-of-pearl stone...the silver sky... the snow caressing the window...the blankets and pillows accumulated around me. I sat up in a half panic, instinctively reaching for the slow, secret comfort of my Greenmark. But it was like misjudging the distance off a bottom stair—there was nothing but empty air and the sensation of falling unexpectedly. My collar gave a sharp little flare of energy, briefly blanking my vision with pain.

"Breathe, colleen." Irian's voice drifted from across the room, growing nearer. I gritted my teeth and inhaled, forcing calm through my spiking veins. After a moment, the twinge receded, leaving a terrible hollowness in its wake. I nearly doubled over from the loss scouring my bones, but I forced myself to open my eyes.

Irian stood by the edge of the bed, laden down with a tray of food—I smelled burnt sugar and unfamiliar spices and baked bread. A jug held steaming liquid smelling almost like coffee, bitter and dark. Save for the faint earthy tang of...*mushrooms?*

I almost smiled. But as much as I appreciated the gesture, memories of yesterday quickly chased my smile away.

"What's all this?"

"The tournament opens today." Irian sat down, placing the tray between us. "I tried to wake you an hour ago, but you told me—and I quote—'If you think I'm going to march in some Donn-damned parade without a full stomach and a steaming cup of whatever mushroom mud passes for coffee around here, you're dreaming.'"

That did sound like me, although I didn't remember the exchange. "There's a parade? When?"

Irian squinted at the flat gray light beyond the window. "Now. More or less."

I cursed and rose, bypassing the mushroom mud. A wardrobe by the door held clothing. I rifled through it, only half surprised to find my outer mantle somehow already cleaned and my leather armor meticulously polished. In addition, I found an array of garments perfectly tailored to my size. Trousers and tunics and mantles, yes—but there were also a handful of lovely, ephemeral gowns in varying shades of white, silver, and blue.

I snorted. Gavida the smith-king certainly wasn't shy about his chosen aesthetic.

"Fia," Irian said from the bed. "Can we please discuss—"

"We cannot."

I dressed quickly, slipping on a pair of grotesquely bright blue trousers I decided to forgive for their color since they felt like butter against my skin. I hesitated, then layered my armor on top of a loose cream-colored shirt. Just in case. Gavida might have taken away my magic, but not even he dared take away my daggers. I buckled them around my waist, their weight a familiar comfort. I grabbed a pair of kid gloves and tucked them into my belt. But when I swept my mantle over my shoulders, I noticed a ruff of fluffy white fur had been added around the hood.

It reminded me too much of Eala. I shucked it off, threw it on the ground.

"You may want that, colleen. Snow has been falling all morning."

But I kicked it under the wardrobe and looked pointedly at my husband. "Shall we?"

The nacre glow of the winding, labyrinthine hallways set my teeth on edge. Mercifully, we soon turned into the pleasure garden Chandi had showed me the night previous. The snow had transformed it from one wonder into another. Downy white lay pillowed on unnaturally vibrant branches; crystalline icicles stabbed down from decadently draped arbors; swirling eddies of snow kissed the dreamlike shapes of sinuous topiaries. I set my jaw, refusing to be awed, and marched across it, even as the cold etched along my bones in a way that surprised me. Gavida's collar must have stripped my resistance to the cold along with my magic.

I refused to shiver. I wouldn't give him—or Irian, who had been annoyingly correct about my mantle—the satisfaction.

The curtain wall soon reared up, its serrated fangs blunted by snow. A narrow path curved along the inside, a mirror to the one I'd followed along the outside last night. Arched doorways studded the masonry, but I could tell they didn't lead outside—from the sentries posted atop the wall, I assumed they were guard posts with bunks, arsenals, and stairways leading to the parapet. Farther along the wall, we passed more pleasure gardens—some spilling from behind lavish apartments, some ornamenting the spacious corners of official buildings.

Everything here appeared so lush, so bursting with life. But last night had taught me: that gilded splendor and endless growth was an illusion. A now-familiar burst of unease climbed my spine and vibrated against the cold narrow band of my collar.

Finally, we heard voices raised upon the chilly wind. A crowd of Folk spilled down from Aduantas's arched and colonnaded facade. They were garbed similarly to me, in an ombré spectrum of blues, whites, and silvers, crowding down the broad shallow steps toward the massive gate Irian had entered by yesterday evening. And the throng was cheering.

A moment later, I saw why. A vast, vibrant parade was a tide lapping at the high white walls of Aduantas. There were hundreds of milk-white horses gnashing their teeth against bridles of silver, and their riders wore helms of pale steel and surcoats of azure. Juggling leipreacháin and contorting ghillies whirled between the prancing mounts. Huge sleighs embossed with precious metals and glittering gems sighed over the snow-choked cobbles. Banners in shades of blue and white surged and snapped in the high breeze, the whirling snow nearly obscuring their devices.

I pushed through the throng, Irian on my heels, searching the sweeping parade for some sign of—who? The aughiskies? Eala and Rogan?

I was so focused on the parade that I nearly walked into Laoise. The Gentry woman forestalled me with a palm on my shoulder, and I nearly lashed out at her. Then I recognized her mop of curling red-bronze hair and her ember eyes. I'd nearly walked past Sinéad and Chandi too. I swallowed guilt and forced a smile.

"Watching the parade?" I asked, as genially as I could manage.

"Indeed." Laoise's eyes skimmed over me, then Irian. "And you? Are you here to watch? Or march?"

"We're marching," I said firmly. I looked up at my husband, but his gaze was shadowed. "Both of us."

The Gentry woman's eyes returned to the procession. "Then you'd better get down there."

I followed her gaze. Behind the heralds and horsemen and performers trailed what could only be the contestants in the Tournament of Kings. My mouth fell open when I saw the sheer number of both lower Folk and Gentry marching in loose rows behind the cavalcade.

There had to be thousands of them.

Against the gaiety and revelry of the parade, the march of the contestants verged on grim. Although many Folk wore the trademark uniform of the Silver Isle—aquamarine armbands wrapped around their own purchased or borrowed blue clothing, some even wearing the livery of the palace servants—there was far more variety here than in Gavida's handpicked entourage.

These Folk had gathered for the chance to win a once-in-a-lifetime forging from the smith-king, and not a single one of them looked like they thought they might not win. Nearly all of them wore head-to-toe armor; most bristled with weaponry that made me second-guess Gavida's strict geas of hospitality. In contrast to the singing, cheering, laughing crowds gathered to spectate, the contestants were as stoic as statues, staring forward with mouths like iron.

Irian was first to step down into the procession. His height made him distinctive, as did the sweeping black of his cloak—so out of character with the silver-strewn, snow-shine parade. I followed a pace behind, shoving my way through the churn of cheering, whooping, singing spectators. I burst from the edge of the throng, losing my balance on the last few ice-slick steps. I barely caught myself before falling, half stumbling into a leather-clad, muscle-bound gruagach who bristled at my closeness.

"Keep your hands to yourself, pigskin!" He shoved me bodily away, his broad moon face clenching.

"Keep your slurs to yourself, troglodyte," I snarled back. But Irian was already there, making a threatening shield between me and the huge creature. He steadied me by the arms as the tide of contestants pulled us forward.

"Making enemies already, colleen?"

I fingered the hilts of my daggers to make sure they were loose in their scabbards. "I'm not here to make friends."

The march was long, and I was frustratingly height challenged compared to the willowy Gentry, giant Fomorians, and hefty gruagaigh. Not to mention my husband, who stalked stone-faced and dangerous beside me. I kept craning my neck, searching for some sign of where we might be headed, but between the sifting snow and my terrible shortness, it was no use.

"First time?" A deep, slow voice interrupted my anxious

rubbernecking. I whipped around, daggers at the ready, to see a huge Fomorian staring down at me from three times my height. I shied away, nearly stumbling into Irian.

"Maybe," I replied cautiously. I knew little of the Fomorians—Cathair's bestiaries and Folk histories claimed the ancient giants had conquered Fódla eons ago, before having the same lands wrested from them by the Tuatha Dé Danann, predecessors of the Folk. But that had happened long before Amergin and his kin had arrived—even before the Folk had forged the Treasures and split Tír na nÓg away from the human realms. The Fomorians were now considered lower Folk—but the fact they had once been conquerors made the hairs rise on my chilly neck.

"You will get used to it," announced the giant. He gestured with one massive hand toward the front of the cavalcade. "The road climbs around the side of the hill—longer than it needs to. I think 'tis meant to give us time to remember that we are afraid."

Surprised by his honesty, my gaze jerked up to his face.

"Are you afraid?"

He considered this. "Aye. Aren't you?"

I wasn't sure I had ever—not even once in my life—admitted to being afraid. But this stranger's frankness seemed to demand my own.

"Yes," I said, before briskly changing the subject. "At the end of this winding path—what am I to expect then?"

"There will be a great arena," he told me ponderously. "And you will feel afraid again. But then there will be waiting and cheering and speeches. And you will become too bored to be afraid any longer."

This candidness shocked a laugh out of me, a desperate relief among this formidable, militant march.

"Thank you," I said honestly. "I'm Fia."

The giant reached down and took my hand between his thumb and forefinger, making me feel doll-like. "My name is Balor. And I am glad to make an unexpected friend among a thousand foes, oh loveliest Gentry lady."

The comment shocked me—it was the first time since I'd come to Tír na nÓg that I'd been mistaken for one of the Gentry. I was reminded, blindingly, of Irian mistaking me for a ghillie the first time he'd caught me—cloaked and creeping—in his realm. I half turned, gesturing to Irian stalking beside us. "Balor, may I present my husband?"

Balor bent toward Irian in the same way he'd bent toward me, extending one huge hand. But Irian turned his head with caustic, careful slowness. The shadow of his hood barely contained the blue sky of his brilliant eyes as he stared up at the giant.

"I am Irian, son of Ethadon, heir to the Sky-Sword and last scion of the Sept of Feathers." His words rang with a threat. "And I would warn you, Fomorian, to keep your distance from me in battle, lest your final day be nigh."

Balor withdrew his hand and Irian prowled onward. I glanced apologetically up at the giant. But he simply shrugged and said, "Scary."

"Nearly as scary as you."

This made him laugh, throwing back his huge head crowned in long pale hair and revealing a terrifying mouth full of huge iron teeth. I moved gently away from the forceful stomping of his enormous feet and hoped his friendliness wasn't a ruse.

His words weren't. Before long, a vast amphitheater loomed into view through the shifting flurries of snow. Heavy walls embedded with veins of silver metal cupped curving tiers of seats cut directly into the slope of the island above Aduantas. The arena spilled out toward the edge of a precipitous cliff. Below, the waters screamed against rock, although you could not see the waves nor the drop in the blizzard.

I swallowed, my dream from last night burning bile down my throat.

"Calmly now," said Balor, tapping me somewhat clumsily on the shoulder.

I lost my balance but recovered quickly before forcing myself to smile up at the disconcerting giant.

"What happens if someone falls off the edge?" I asked, with a note of hopeful credulity I wasn't particularly proud of.

Balor considered this slowly. "They die, I imagine."

Again, his honesty startled a bark of laughter from me. "Not one for comforting words of wisdom, are you?"

Balor only shrugged. "I don't like to tell stories I know won't come true."

"No." I glanced sideways at Irian. "Neither do I."

The entrance to the amphitheater rose up before us. Two huge figures loomed from the cliff face, ten times Balor's size and carved in painstaking detail. Their vast crossed swords made an archway for us to trudge through; their heavy frames sang with violent tension. But it was their visages that surprised me—one youthful but hollow-cheeked, framed with sharp holly leaves and studded with berries. The other chiseled and open-faced, framed with the rustling foliage of an oak in full leaf. It reminded me of Dún Darragh. It reminded me of—

"Welcome, welcome, one and all!" Gavida's voice boomed artificially above us, whirling the snow into shapes only magic made. Leaves of glass. Feathered flowers. Bells pealing with voices of fancy. "Welcome to the Tournament of Kings!"

We crossed beneath the archway. The sheer size of the amphitheater caught my breath, but that wasn't the only thing that surprised me. Balor hadn't been lying when he said the road we marched as contestants was overlong—most of the spectators I'd seen cheering the parade along had already made their way to the arena and now clamored from its seats, their excitement a hum despite the snow steadily sifting down. At the apex of the amphitheater, I glimpsed gnarled branches twined with gilded leaves. But a moment later, a gust of wind concealed it behind flurries of snow—dying embers behind a veil.

The central seating column had been blocked off for contestants—the ferocious horde beelined for it, carrying us in its wake. The curving rows filled in quickly—but between Irian's silent menace and

Balor's imposing bulk, other contestants gave us a wide berth, and we were free to choose seats near the front.

"Many have braved the snow today for this pageantry," Irian said, his voice low. "More than I expected."

"Does the tournament not begin today?"

"Indeed. But this spectacle is optional—the real Trials do not begin until tomorrow."

I struggled to formulate a response. "Optional?"

Irian bared his glittering canines. "Colleen, this is *all* optional. The only good thing about the Tournament of Kings is that no one can force you to compete."

But that wasn't strictly true, was it? My thoughts flew to Eala and Rogan, and my gaze followed, jerking over my shoulder to scan the gathered contestants. I finally spotted her furred cloak and unmistakable pale hair beside Rogan's bowed golden head in the royal box beside the arena. Anger jumped inside me, spiking heat through my veins and sending a vining tendril of—

My collar sizzled against my skin, making me flinch. I gritted my teeth with guilt and fury and helplessness as I tore my eyes away from my sister and her betrothed.

"If that's the case, then why are you here?" I wrapped my cold arms around my body and tried to pretend I wasn't shivering. "A chance to take measure of the competition?"

"No." Irian's smile was coiled as a snake and perilous as a blade. "A chance for them to take measure of *me*."

The sheer violence of his tone unsettled me. His words from last night sliced me like icicles: *I was always going to win this tournament.*

Had I been a fool for not letting him fight as my champion? For insisting on fighting for myself?

A bell gonged sonorously through the drifting sheets of snow, dragging my attention away from my husband's feral words. At the edge of the arena, near the lip of the cliff, an aperture opened in the island's pale stone, belching steely sparks and gusts of silver-tinted steam. A moment later, Gavida arose, a column of white lifting him to the level of the arena and then higher, until he looked as if he were floating in the air. He was garbed far differently than last night—he wore the aspect of one of the figures guarding the entrance to the arena. His gray-streaked mahogany hair was brushed out long over snowy-white robes edged in silver; glossy green holly leaves prickled around the furred hood of his mantle, studded with bright red berries.

Gavida stared out over the arena at his assembled guests and contestants. The snow still drove down, the light glinting through it lending him an ethereal, illuminated glow. Slowly, he lifted his smith's hammer above his head and crossed it with that length of raw, unfinished metal. He brought the two together with a clang.

Boom.

Not a bell—Gavida's tools.

"Friends! Enemies! And everyone in between...I bid you welcome to the Tournament of Kings!"

Boom.

The crowd went wild. The thunder of a thousand stomping boots shook the ancient stone amphitheater; the roar of a thousand voices drowned out the weight of my thoughts.

Boom.

The crowd took up the rhythm of Gavida's tools, stomping a thunder that blotted out all other sounds. When it became so loud I could hardly stand it, Gavida lofted his hammer and sword and—

Boom.

Silence. The wind dropped out like an exhaled breath. The blizzard abruptly stopped—the remaining snow sifting down like glitter from a silver sky. The clouds parted, sending shafts of cool golden light to gild the fresh drifts.

"Once, a very great long time ago," Gavida bellowed, his voice tolling as resonantly as his tools, "there were two brothers! Different in mien yet alike in honor, they both fell in love with the same woman—the shining, powerful goddess of the Year, with all her shifting seasons. They could not decide which of them deserved her, so the Year offered them a chance to win her. Whoever carried himself with the most valor, honor, and wit would earn her crown and sit beside her evermore. So different were the brothers, Holly and Oak. Holly was a child of winter—with him he carried the coldness of death and the darkness of the skies. Oak was a child of summer—with him he carried the warmth of the sun and the growth of the earth."

Gavida's words conjured a desperate, involuntary image of Rogan within me—shirtless in the harvest heat of late summer, mowing great swaths of golden grass with his scythe. Helplessly, I glanced over at Irian, but his glitter-blue eyes burned toward Gavida.

"The brothers fought. But each was the other's balance—where one gained the upper hand, the other fumbled, only to regain his footing while the other stumbled. In the end, there was nothing to do but for the Year to offer her crown to them both. But the brothers did not want to share her. Even after her prize had been bestowed, the brothers continued to fight. On the Longest Day, the Holly King rises against his brother, but through the autumn his strength wanes. On the Longest Night, the Oak King retakes his crown. They are locked in eternal strife, each taking his turn beside his queen even as he stands forever at odds with his once-beloved brother." Again Gavida struck his tools together. *Boom.* "We are not those ancient, primordial beings who brought magic, light, and answering darkness to our world. But the rhythms of their struggles echo through our lives, creating their own kind of magic. So once again, as the days grow darkest, we invite the Oak King to step forward and claim his crown."

The crowd roared again, a heaving, rippling sound that tore at my bones.

"Many of you have competed in the Tournament of Kings before. Many of you have not. So before we go further, let me lay out the rules." Pale gold spilled between the clouds, streaming along the lengths of Gavida's lofted tools and limning the smith-king with light. I gritted my teeth at the blatant...What had Irian called it? Spectacle. "My geas of hospitality is strict. Violence is only permitted within the arena—any harm done to guests or contestants outside it will be immediately punished."

I lifted tense fingers toward my trembling throat and wished I'd understood Irian's warnings before attacking my sister in the smith-king's throne room.

"This year, as in every year, my son and heir, Wayland, will act as my champion."

Another resounding cheer shook the amphitheater, and Wayland stood from his chair in the royal box. He was resplendently garbed in the same style as his father—his waist-length sheet of mahogany hair spilling over white-and-silver-draped shoulders and crowned with a wreath of holly leaves and berries. His smile was beatific as he waved up at the crowds, but his dark blue eyes carved pits of black in his handsome gold-brown face.

"I represent the Holly King, and my son represents me. He will not compete until the final duel, when you may try to wrest the Oak King's Crown from him." My stomach dropped at the thought of Wayland being the final obstacle—*that* was news. "Until then, do not think to try him. The Holly King cannot be dethroned until the Longest Night—you will only get yourself curtailed.

"Tonight," Gavida went on, "the festivities begin. A thousand feiseanna will be held, in Aduantas and in the streets and in the homes of all these honored islanders. Attend wherever you wish, but mind you have been explicitly invited.

"Tomorrow is the Trial of Tenacity. It is as it has always been— a melee. Everyone who wishes to compete for the crown will fight to the blood. Anyone who bleeds must bow. All the rest may continue." A long, tense hush. "And finally—the prize!"

Throbbing screams rent the cold, shimmering air. I jerked as my metal collar burned cold against my skin, my shivering intensifying. Irian's arm circled my waist, and he pulled me tighter to his side. I leaned into him, grateful for his warmth.

"If you win, I will forge anything your heart desires, so long as it is in my power." Gavida's smile gleamed across the arena. "I have but two exceptions to this generous offer: I will not take away anyone's free will. And I will not resurrect anyone from the dead."

I jolted—Gavida's words seemed like a not-so-subtle dig at Eala, and I was glad for it. Again, I stared down at her white-blond head, a pale gleam-glow of newly fallen snow, then glanced up at Irian.

"If he will not take someone's will, why is he parleying with Eala?" I asked in an undertone.

"He said *he* would not." Irian's shrug was caustic. "The morals we hold ourselves to do not always extend to others. And vice versa."

Irian's words needled beneath my skin like broken glass. I readied another brisk question, but the crowd had once more exploded in resounding cheers that shook the stones. With one last *boom* of Gavida's shimmering tools, the clouds opened back up. Snow swept down like a shroud, draping the arena in a blinding layer of white. A moment later, the crowd began to move through the blizzard, slowly at first and then more quickly. Folk buffeted around us, their careful distance around Irian tightening as the throng ebbed and flowed with its own tides, eager to escape the damp, drifting deluge.

Irian's grip on me tightened, his hands sweeping up my barely clothed arms and dragging new lines of gooseflesh along my skin. Snow glittered like diamonds in his hair and made a pale canvas for his azure eyes as he unclasped his long black mantle from one shoulder and swept it fully around my shoulders, careless of how it dragged on the ground. He used it to pull me close, leaning down to brush a kiss over my mouth. His skin was cold as a dead man's flesh.

"I grow weary of this charade, colleen." His words were nearly lost amid the drifting snow and tramping Folk. "Shall we escape?"

I summoned a smile. "I long for nothing more."

But if I expected space to bend, churn, and spit us back out, I was sorely mistaken. We simply started tramping toward the exit with the masses.

I stared up at him. "Can't you...?" I swirled my finger.

He looked at me blankly, then almost smiled. "No. Gavida's wardings forbid it. So I fear on the Silver Isle even I am diminished to walking."

We did not speak as we hiked down to the citadel. But my thoughts churned with worries, old and new. How was I supposed to win a tournament against a thousand Folk warriors? Especially when numbering among them were friendly giants, displeased husbands, mind-controlled ex-lovers...and a blue-eyed man I still owed a kiss.

Chapter Seventeen

O nce we returned to our rooms in Aduantas, I plucked Irian's cloak from my shoulders and handed it back to him.

"Perhaps I was wrong," I finally said, although the admission abraded my tongue. "For not letting you compete in the tournament as my champion. But you should have told me that you meant to ask Gavida to unmake our Treasures, instead of resurrecting the ones that have been lost."

"Would it have made you more amenable to the idea?"

"No. But at least then I would have known I could trust you. Even with things I did not want to hear."

"We have both kept secrets, colleen." Emotion purled over his face—gone before I could read it. "I do not expect you to trust me with everything. But I hope you will remember—I always have your best interests at heart. I seek only to protect you."

"I know." I reached for him. "We came together from a dark place—"

"Does that mean it was not real?" Irian's eyes scalded me in the moment before he looked away.

"Of course not." Was that true? A memory seared me—my

hands on Rogan's cold steel stirrup...his shaking voice at the Feis of the Ember Moon. *Tell me it wasn't real, and I'll let you go.* "It means we have always had so much to lose that we've never had the time to think of everything we already have."

"*Time.*" In his rough burr, the word sounded like a curse. "Surely you realize that is all that I yearn for."

"As do I." I gripped him tighter. "But—"

A brisk but decorous knock on the door interrupted us. Irian made a noise deep in his throat, dropped his head in frustration, and after blowing out a breath, pulled away from me toward the door. He visibly composed himself before opening it. His bulk blocked me from seeing whoever had intruded, but there were no words exchanged that I could hear. A moment later, the door sighed shut once more. Irian turned, a large embossed envelope gripped between his fingers. He flicked it open, perused it, then silently handed it to me.

Curiosity burned through me as I thumbed open the tab of the envelope. The thick parchment was covered in looping script and embellished with illuminated designs—sea serpents churning through waves of blue; golden apples glinting from trees veined with silver. Gavida's sigil stared from the crest; looping calligraphy scrawled beneath it. After months away from my mythic warrior's journals, I struggled to read the ancient tongue.

This invitation extends to Irian, Scion of Zephyrs, and his bride, Fia: Heir of Thorns, Temptation Incarnate, Bargainer of Kisses Yet Withheld. Attend me at the Grove of Gold this eve, after moonrise. Wear your finest, lest you be outshone by me.

Guilty nausea blossomed in me. My fingers felt gritty on the expensive parchment. I looked up at Irian.

"He's teasing." I tried and failed to make my voice lighthearted. "He's trying to rile you—"

"I know who Wayland is." In the dim of our borrowed chambers, his blue-gold gaze burned like the heart of a newborn fire. His jaw sharpened to a blade. "Does he speak true? Did you bargain a kiss to him?"

"It was not something I offered, but something he demanded." My fingernails dented the invitation. "It happened a year ago, long before you and I—"

"*Demanded?*" Irian cut in, voice dropping dangerously. "By what right did he demand a kiss?"

"There was a fox-faced barda who tried to... Well, Wayland claims he saved my life." This only upset Irian further—fury and worry bled through his mask of control. "But please know I have no intention of making good on the bargain."

"You must." His eyes flashed toward silver. Night must be falling.

"I don't want to kiss him."

"The magic of Tír na nÓg does not care what you want. Until you make good on your bargain, you are bound to him." Irian raked a hand through his snow-damp hair, his angular features harsh. "This further complicates things. You should not have kept it from me. "

Resentment burned through me. He had the gall to chide me for keeping secrets? "An admonishment I would echo back at you."

Irian stiffened. Then swept the dark cloak he still held brusquely over his shoulders. "Kiss him, colleen. And be done with it."

"You *want* me to kiss him?"

"*No.* I have told you before, colleen—I am not fond of sharing." He stalked to the door, pausing with his hand hovering over the knob. "But I would rather share one of your kisses—as jealous of them as I am—than the rest of you. And until the bargain is sealed, the magic of this place will keep throwing you two together. So go to the party, Fia. And do what must be done."

He opened the door.

"Where are *you* going?" I demanded.

"Forgive me if I do not wish to witness my wife kissing my foster brother," he said, with painstaking evenness. "I can only hope it will be just a kiss."

The door sighed shut behind him.

I glanced down at the invitation with burning eyes, then let its shredded edges flutter down to the floor.

My relationship with Irian was so new—a bud still blooming. But with every petal that unfurled, I wondered whether its stem wasn't planted in poisoned soil.

This Irian was not the same man I had known in the weeks before the Ember Moon. Sometimes I understood—that night had been a transformation not only for me, but for him as well. Weights he had carried for thirteen years lifted, only for him to shoulder new and no less substantial worries. The expectations he'd grown accustomed to had changed. The things he'd thought he wanted had evaporated even as new desires rose in their place.

But other times, I simply could not comprehend—how he thought he could control everything and everyone around him, as if he himself were not a barely curbed storm. How he wanted to control *me*, when I had finally stepped into my own power. Had finally taken control over my own destiny.

My hand drifted self-consciously to the slender collar kissing my throat, and I trailed a finger against its silver metal, which was warmed by my skin and faintly sizzling.

Perhaps Irian was right. If the magic of Tír na nÓg had indeed bound me to Wayland, then I wanted to be unbound. If a kiss bought me freedom from a debt owed, then I'd kiss him. It didn't have to be a drama—a cordial peck would surely be sufficient.

I sighed and opened the wardrobe. *Wear your finest*, Wayland's invitation read. I rifled through the pale blue and silver gowns that had been conjured for me from snowflakes and starshine. They were undeniably beautiful—intricately layered lace falling away from scalloped necklines and architectural corsets. But they did not feel like *me*. I wasn't overly fond of gowns in the first place—the skirts hindered my legs, the bodices left my chest and throat unprotected, and I could never think of a good place to hide my knives. But these gowns were even worse than usual. Sewn from silk blue as waves and lace like fallen snow and satin glowing like the inside of a seashell, they did not suit my coloring. Worse, they seemed little better than the livery the palace attendants were forced to wear.

Wearing one of these gowns would feel like being cast in Gavida's grand pageant, on the island he commanded, in the silent city he had built. I touched my collar again. He had taken away my magic. His son had manipulated me into kissing him. At the very least, I wanted to choose how I presented myself.

A thought flitted along the edges of my mind, sly and amused. Of course—when I left Dún Darragh last week, I'd packed a few of the ephemeral, exquisite gowns Corra had crafted for me last Bealtaine. I grabbed my pack, dumping its contents onto the coverlet.

I'd only been able to fit two dresses. A slender shift iridescent as a moth's white wing, and a dress red as blood spilled across newly fallen snow. I held it up in the dim light. I'd never worn it—the neckline was cut outrageously low, and the sheer narrow sleeves dripped tight and provocative off bared shoulders. But worst of all was the skirt—a long, decadent train, translucent as a whisper, fading from the red of sunset at the waist to the black of a starless night at the hem.

Amid the pelagic blue and hibernal white of the Silver Isle, it would look utterly inappropriate. It was red as a rose, sharp as a thorn, and ominous as a threat. To wear it would be borderline incendiary—a statement, a declaration. A *protest*.

A mirthless grin touched my face. It was perfect.

But I wasn't going to be able to pour myself into this gown alone. And I was going to need someone to help me with my hair.

Chandi answered my knock on the suite across from ours, which she shared with Sinéad and Laoise. She was laughing over her shoulder as she swung the door open; when she turned and caught sight of me, her face changed. Her smile slipped; her brows came slightly together before she forced them apart.

"Oh! Sorry—come in." The taller girl grasped my hands and tugged me over the threshold. "I thought you were a servant here with wine."

The richly appointed rooms—nearly identical to mine save for an additional bedroom—were festive with conversation and laughter. I'd expected no one but Sinéad and Laoise. But there were a dozen or so Folk I didn't recognize: a slender, hostile-faced Gentry woman with a gown the color of a bruised lily sitting stiffly by the hearth; a trio of merry leipreacháin fiddling away as two pale ghillies whirled and spun in the silvery light. I searched for Laoise and Sinéad amid the gaiety and found them after a moment. Laoise—wearing a column of slashed white satin that set off her curving figure and tumbled red curls to exquisite effect—lounged deep in conversation with a haughty, skeletal leannán sidhe. Sinéad—in a sapphire gown the precise color of her eyes—was off by herself, holding a wineglass in one hand while she threw knives at a makeshift target set against the wall with the other. Her aim was atrocious, but I was glad to see her practicing.

Although I knew from experience that as fun as it seemed in theory, drinking wine and throwing knives rarely ended well.

"I would have brought some," I said to Chandi, with a touch more asperity than I intended. "If I'd known you were having a party."

"Sorry," she said again, a little shamefaced. "But we assumed you and Irian were invited to revels reserved for royalty and demigods. We didn't think you'd want to slum it here with us."

It would have been nice to be asked, but I understood, as I had before—she no longer saw me as her peer. In the aftermath of the Ember Moon, we were both transformed. And our changes had pulled us away from each other, instead of bringing us closer together.

I held up the nearly weightless mass of red-and-black fabric Corra had created for me what felt like a lifetime ago. "I don't think I can manage the buttons on this dress by myself. Will you help?"

Chandi's expression eased. "Of course I will. Here."

She pushed me into the bathing chamber, also identical to the one in the other suite. I blushed a little, remembering Irian and me together, pressed naked against each other in the steaming water. A moment later, my flush turned to one of confusion and resentment when I remembered our conversation from an hour ago.

We came together from a dark place.

Does that mean it was not real?

Chandi's face skated over mine as she helped me unbuckle my armor. "Irian couldn't help you dress?"

"As a rule he prefers helping me undress." I turned my back to her and drew off my tunic, grateful for the chance to hide my face. "We don't have to talk about him all the time, you know."

"I know." She waited until I stepped out of my bluebell trousers, then lifted the mass of floating crimson fabric over my head. I slid my arms into the tight, narrow sleeves, then settled the bodice over my bosom. A moment later, Chandi's warm, deft fingers began buttoning the hundreds of tiny buttons trailing up the back. "Dare I ask where you're going in *this*? Unless there are secret plans afoot."

The door opened, forestalling my response. I glared over my shoulder, then softened when I saw Sinéad and Laoise letting themselves into the bathing chamber. They circled to face me, Laoise silently handing me a goblet of cold bubbling liquid. Her fingers left steaming imprints on the frosted crystal. Interest wreathed both women's expressions.

"The dress was a bad idea, wasn't it?" I grimaced and put my free hand to my waist, where the structured bodice of Corra's blood-red gown was beginning to cut off circulation to my vital organs.

"Only if you *don't* want to look like the Morrigan on the eve of battle, fully prepared to exact vengeance on her enemies," said Sinéad cheerfully.

"In troth, my lady, who would *not* want such a thing?" Laoise's use of *my lady* jolted me, but when I jerked my gaze to her face, her smile was candlelit and her eyes glittered with humor. I frowned, not fully sure whether she was teasing me—and whether I appreciated it if she was. "May we know toward whom this stunning gown is directed? Your lord husband?"

"No," I grumbled as Chandi moved her hands from the small of my back to the nape of my neck, pulling and tugging at my unruly waves. "At least, not entirely. Tonight, Wayland is the object of my displeasure."

"Wayland? Son of the smith-king?" Chandi's voice was surprised. Of course—she knew nothing of Irian's history, my bargain, or Wayland's invitation. None of them did.

I hesitated, then quickly told the full story. After, the room was silent as the three women digested what I'd told them.

"It is but a kiss," Laoise finally said, with some bemusement. "For saving your life, he could have demanded a much higher cost."

That didn't make me feel better. I stared at the cracked agate ceiling as Chandi smeared something that smelled like beeswax and rose petals on my pursed lips. "It's the principle of the thing."

"Are you attracted to him?" Sinéad asked, canny. "Otherwise I can't see why it would matter so much that you *not* kiss him and be done with it."

Her words prickled thorns down my spine. I lifted my hand to the now-silent stone hanging above my breast and wondered whether she was right. The rules surrounding love and sex among the Folk were different than the ones I'd grown up with in Fódla. And Wayland was undeniably beautiful—although, most Folk Gentry were. I did not know him well enough yet to judge whether I liked him. In fact, I rather thought I did not. Yes, he had interceded on my behalf with that barda at the Feis of the Nameless Day. But in return he had demanded something I had not offered. And his flirtations were too forward—almost theatrical in their shameless daring. Perhaps that was what intrigued me—the suspicion that behind those laughing indigo eyes skulked something deeper. Darker, even.

Or perhaps it truly was the magic of Tír na nÓg—the starlight skeins of destiny—winding our fates together in ways we had not asked for.

"Even if I was attracted to him," I answered Sinéad, "it wouldn't matter. I am wed to Irian."

"Marriage among the Folk is not like it is among humans, you know," Laoise said, echoing my own thoughts and giving me a jolt. "The joining of hearts and the joining of bodies are considered two separate arrangements. I imagine Irian—"

"Would rather dance reels wearing sheerie wings than let anyone *join* their body with mine." My laughter came out a touch brittle. "Irian may be Folk. But he is not fond of sharing."

"You know, I think he actually did that one time," Sinéad said, deadpan. "But in his defense, there was a great deal of áthas involved."

Chandi nodded sagely. "That's the liquor that turns everything into rainbows?"

"That's the stuff."

Chandi put the finishing touches on my cosmetics, then spun me to face the mirror. My eyes widened.

I was transformed into...I hardly knew what. The gown had taken my lean figure and somehow made it deliciously soft—accentuating my narrow waist and plumping my modest curves. Two outrageous slits in the sheer ombré skirt bared my toned thighs nearly to the hips. The neckline made crisp wings of my collarbones. At the center of my chest, the Heart of the Forest pulsed in time to the throb of my heart, glowing the same green as my right eye, which stared terribly from the beautiful mask Chandi had made of my face. Kohl shadowed my eyes. The contours of my cheekbones slashed down toward a pouting mouth nearly as red as my gown. The crown of my hair was braided back from my face, but the rest tumbled down my back in wild, voluminous curls.

The only element marring an otherwise perfect outfit was the garish metal slash around my pale throat.

"There," said Chandi with some satisfaction. "Who needs magical white flowers to effect a transformation?"

"You burn fiery enough to hail from the Sept of Scales." Laoise's tone held admiration, so I decided to take her words as a compliment. "You look ready to break a heart. Or steal one."

Her thoughtless words visibly jarred both Chandi and Sinéad, shocking terrible expressions onto their faces. An answering arrow of fury arced through me, jolting the green stone above my breast and tearing a flare of pain from my collar. I winced, putting a hand to my throat and cursing those who had ever dared harm anyone I cared about.

"Oh," Laoise said, with a distant kind of regret that reminded me with a stab that she was not human. "I am sorry."

"It's all right," Sinéad said softly.

"No," Chandi argued, with terrible sorrow. "It's not."

Sympathy pulsed through me, chasing away the pain of my collar. I reached for my friend. But she had already moved back toward the door, silently returning herself to the noise and laughter of their little feis.

I glanced back at Sinéad, concerned, but she was staring down at her clenched fists.

"You should not arrive to the revel alone," Laoise said after a moment. "If he cannot escort you himself, Irian would wish me to accompany you to the Grove of Gold."

"Stay." Another terrible idea was blooming inside me. "Can one of you tell me where the aughiskies are stabled?"

Chapter Eighteen

A blank-faced palace attendant led me through a series of narrowing halls before pointing down a winding staircase. I hoisted my skirts in my fists, then descended.

The first few staircases were fairly broad and decently lit. But the lower I climbed, the narrower and dimmer they became. A chill clasped my throat as the darkness deepened, the silver torches growing more widely spaced. Shadows lapped at my slippers and dampness crawled up my bones. Before long, I knew I must be underground, on some deep subterranean level. A sliver of fear pulled frost down my spine, and I cursed my bravado in turning down Laoise's protection.

Without my daggers or my magic, I was little more than a human girl. And in a place like this... that could mean a death sentence.

The river stone throbbed against my skin, lending me a degree of confidence. Even collared and curtailed, I was no longer just a girl. I was the Heart of the Forest.

My Treasure was not eager to let me die.

The final staircase deposited me into raw, pale caverns unhewn by Folk hands. Condensation dripped from stalactites; the sound of water crashing upon the cliffs was an echoing rhythm in my bones. Shapes seemed to trail me in the shadows—claws rattled along stone; heavy breathing barely masked by howling wind dogged my steps. I shuddered and quickened my pace, even as moisture seeped through my thin, impractical slippers.

Where the outline of a Folk water horse would have once sent me scrambling for a weapon, it now brought me a shocking degree of relief. I lunged for the aughisky outlined in silver against a surging sea. The snow had finally stopped; starlight streaked a black night silver. The aughisky looked up as I approached, arching its neck and baring its shark teeth. It was Irian's huge midnight stallion—I held up my palms in a gesture of peace.

"It's me." I raised my voice to be heard above the pounding surf. "Where is— Um." Had I really never asked for her real name? I'd been too busy trying to hate her for such pleasantries. "Where is Pond Scum?"

The stark, terrifying predator stared at me with glowing sapphire eyes, then gave a huff of what almost sounded like amusement before gesturing with his head toward an adjoining cave. I edged around the stallion as he bent down to continue methodically filleting a large rust-colored fish.

Pond Scum stood at the very edge of the cavern, looking out over the blustering, wind-swept sea. She whipped her serpentine neck at my approach, narrowing her eyes when she saw me. But when she neither snapped her teeth nor trampled me to death, I came close enough to lay a hesitant palm on her neck.

"I can't believe they put you down here," I nearly had to shout over the wind howling through the mouth of the cavern. "I was told you were comfortably stabled with plenty of fish."

Pond Scum flicked her forelock and sent me a blistering vision of the drowning of water horses surfing blizzard-whipped waves and battling sharks in the shallows.

"Well," I allowed, "as long as you're happy."

She faced me, stamping one of her emerald hooves as she

burned another vision through my mind. This one was a kind of question—I saw myself, Irian, and the swan girls in a kind of hazy unknown space.

"Oh, we're all right." I dared to stroke a hand over her coiled, oil-slick mane. It was surprisingly soft to the touch. "But I have a favor to ask you."

She cocked her head, sending me an image of her nibbling off all my fingers until they sprouted into fins. My face shone with unmitigated glee at my unexpected transformation. But seeing myself through her eyes shocked a laugh out of me. With my wild hair, mismatched eyes, and twin daggers, I was as foreign and threatening to her as she was to me.

"Alas—no. I wish you to escort me to a rather important Gentry revel, where I wish to terrify and impress a pampered prionsa." I lifted one eyebrow. "Want to help?"

She bobbed her head and whickered, then bent one of her knees to make it easier to mount her. I hesitated.

"First...will you tell me your name again? I imagine it's not actually Pond Scum."

She tilted her delicate muzzle, studying me with one green eye laced through with threads of blue, gold, and black. A moment later, the very first vision she'd sent me once more split my head open—a still pond between arching trees, bright with a scurf of lurid green algae. But this time, I didn't jerk my attention away, and the vision continued. Together, the aughisky and I delved beneath the surface, through dark water growing cooler. Deeper and deeper we went, until cold, pure currents tasting of snowmelt swept us out toward the sea.

I surfaced with a gasp. I still had no idea what the aughisky's real name was supposed to be, but I was glad I asked. It was altogether different than Pond Scum.

"It reminds me of something my..." How did I describe Cathair to a feral water horse? "My teacher used to say. Chomh ciúin le linn—*as calm as a pond*. He meant that still waters run deep. Is it all right if I call you Linn?"

The aughisky snaked her slender neck forward, buried her face against my neck, then pulled my hair in what could only be described as vicious delight.

"Ow." I shoved her gently away. "Let's keep the pleasantries to a minimum."

Again Linn bent her foreleg, and this time I accepted, climbing onto her narrow back. I draped the now-soggy length of my scarlet train over her sea-foam and emerald haunches, then curled my fingers in her mane. She turned and snapped her teeth near my slipper, as if to say, *Where to?*

"The Grove of Gold is at the very peak of the Silver Isle," I told her. "We could climb straight up. But if you like...I think I'd rather enjoy making an entrance."

Linn bared the double rows of her razor-sharp shark teeth in a terrifying grin, pivoted in place, then gave a delicate little buck to let me know she was absolutely in agreement.

Folk stared.

The narrow path up from the caverns wound around the cliffs before depositing us at the base of Emain Ablach—nearly where we'd entered from the gilded gates. As before, we rode up the main boulevard. But tonight, the city thronged with life, the streets coursing with merriment and every building alight with jollity.

Linn had zero problems making a spectacle. Rather, she reveled in it, arching her elegant neck and lifting her legs high in a syncopated prance that rattled my teeth and made my arse sore. Anyone who came too close, she snapped at, and before long, shreds of clothing and strands of hair hung gruesomely from her serrated mouth. Atop her bony spine, I struggled to look dignified, clamping my knees around her sides and hanging on to her glistening black mane for stability. I had a feeling my hair was coming loose and my bodice was slipping down to undo all of Chandi's hard work, but I didn't dare check, forcing my face to stay beatific and my gaze level.

Soon enough, a path cleared before us. Folk began to follow us with their eyes and whisper behind their hands. Linn only took this as encouragement, bannering her long dark tail as the silver lanterns made her eyes glow eerily. By the time we passed Aduantas and climbed toward the hills, Folk were streaming behind us, laughing and drinking and shouting at our backs. Their words echoed up behind us, and it took me a long moment to decipher them.

"Na Bliana! Na Bliana!"

The Year. The Year.

And I realized—looking out over the iridescent crowd of silver-and-blue-clad Folk—I had indeed made a terrible mistake with my outlandish red dress. Despite Irian's talk of rumors spreading, these Folk had no idea who I really was—they simply assumed I was another character in Gavida's symbolic tableau. The Year—the indecisive goddess whose power and affection the Oak and Holly Kings battled for. I set my mouth and urged Linn forward. After trying so hard not to embroil myself in Gavida's pageant, I'd done exactly that. Worse, I'd put myself in the center of a figurative love triangle.

Which was exactly where I did *not* want to be.

I only loosened my death grip on Linn's mane once we cleared the last of the splendid mansions, cantering up a cleared path lit by silver will-o'-the-wisps. The darkened, deserted amphitheater rose up steeply before us, draped in shrouds of snow and crowned by the glowing Grove of Gold. I couldn't help but inhale as Linn and I climbed—the nine apple trees were impossibly ancient. Gnarled branches coiled around one another, sinuous and serpentine with age, threaded with veins of silver. Impossibly, the trees bloomed and bore fruit simultaneously—fragrantly pink blossoms embroidering lace upon boughs weighed heavy with plump, glossy apples. And everything *glowed*—a radiant, luminous shine encompassing the entire peak of the isle.

I leaned toward it, bewitched. *This* was what I'd felt last night—
had it really only been last night?—when I'd scanned the area with
my Treasure. Against the dreadful stillness of the rest of Emain
Ablach, it had been the one point of undeniable life. And now I
yearned for it. I wanted to climb out of this wretched dress and
embrace these trees with my naked skin, wanted to take that candlelight glow inside my own self until *I* was suffused with gold. I
wanted to blossom with perfect flowers and grow precious fruit. I
wanted—

My collar snapped at my neck with unforgiving teeth, shocking
a hiss between my teeth. At the same time, Linn snaked her neck
around to snap at the hem of my gown. Together, they startled me
out of my reverie. I dragged my eyes away from the ring of ancient
trees with more effort than should have been necessary.

We crested the rise. A hollow carved a shallow bowl between the
trees. Mounds of snow pillowed the edges but spared the verdant
clearing. Folk Gentry mingled in clusters, silver-clad attendants
moving between them like cold ghosts. Linn snorted, then turned
in profile and abruptly reared up, stretching her delicate hooves,
tossing her head, and sending my extravagant red gown flaring out
behind me. Everyone stopped what they were doing and stared. A
cheer went up, cascading between the golden trees.

"Na Bliana! Na Bliana!"

"Really," I hissed at the aughisky. "That was a bit much."

She flattened her ears to her head as I dismounted.

"Quite the entrance, Thorn Girl."

I spun. Wayland—dressed in his customary tones of sapphire
and cobalt—stood in the shadow of one of the golden apple trees,
half a dozen paces away. He approached, but Linn spun in a tight
circle around me, blocking him with one muscled flank. She coiled
her neck and bared her teeth. Amazingly, he still paced forward.
She thrust her muzzle into his long sweep of mahogany hair and
snapped her fangs. I almost had to laugh as he finally froze, deep
blue eyes widening with a bare hint of fear.

"My chaperone requires niceties," I said sweetly. "Where are your manners?"

"Jealous husbands, conquering sisters, and protective aughiskies?" Wayland held up his hands in a gesture of peace. "You are about as approachable as a knife to the throat, Thorn Girl."

I inwardly bristled at the mention of Eala, but smiled regardless. "A threat you should take care to heed, Holly King."

His face shifted in a way I didn't know him well enough to read. I laid a gentle hand on Linn's flank. She huffed an aggressive breath against Wayland's neck, then pranced airily away to glower at us from the shadow of one of the trees.

Wayland recovered himself, straightening his robes and sweeping his hair over one shoulder. "Where is your usual frowning escort?"

"Irian?" I forced my demeanor to stay as jovial as his. "He declined to attend. I daresay your blatant reminder of the geas binding you and I together rather put him off the whole business."

"Irian never could take a joke." Wayland stepped closer, ducking beneath the low-hanging bough of an apple tree. His fingers were cool and smooth as he caught my hand and lifted it to his mouth, brushing a kiss over my skin. Gooseflesh raised along my arms as he drew back to look at me. His gaze scanned up from the midnight hem of my gown, skimming over my bared legs, noticeably lingering on the indent of my waist and the heave of my chest before alighting on my face. "I am glad *you* came. And in such style. You are the Year incarnate—a goddess in the flesh. And there is...quite a lot of flesh."

I fought the flush his flattering, insinuating words burned along my skin. "The resemblance was unintentional, I assure you."

Surprise and amusement narrowed his gaze. "Truly? You must know the Year is always portrayed wearing red."

"I knew no such thing." I lifted my chin, refusing to be embarrassed by yet another thing I didn't know. "As Irian said—I am an outsider in these realms. I know not your customs."

"As you say." He bowed at the waist. "Sometimes I doubt my father when he says these things are written in the stars. Sometimes less so."

I tensed, remembering one of my first thoughts upon realizing who Wayland really was. Long months before I'd known any-thing about the nature of my Greenmark—much less my identity as a tánaiste—chance had thrown him and me together as perfect strangers, then bound us in a blood debt. I had experienced too much of the magic of Tír na nÓg in the past year to believe such a thing mere coincidence. Perhaps it was with good reason he and I had been linked.

Wayland was an heir. Collared, curtailed. But an heir nonethe-less. And I still wanted to find a way to resurrect the Treasures that had been destroyed—to renew their broken magic back to their proper vessels.

Last night, Irian had said there was nothing to be done about Wayland's collar. But Irian had also believed there was nothing to be done about the tithe to be paid with his life beneath the Ember Moon. Irian had believed me to be heir to wind and skies, not earth and tree. Irian believed many things that were not true.

I had a history of thinking more creatively. Perhaps it was time I put that quality to use.

"Wayland." I stepped closer to the prince. "We did not have a chance to speak of it last night—"

But before I could continue, sound rose up from the grove below. I turned, and Wayland turned with me, until we were stand-ing shoulder to shoulder. Or, more accurately, my shoulder to his elbow—he was nearly as tall as Irian.

"What's going on?" I asked.

"You arrived late, Thorn Girl." I didn't have to look at Wayland to hear the smile wreathing broadly across his face. "I had hoped to get you drunk before the pageant began. But alas—you must watch it brutally sober."

"That bad?"

"Not at all." Wayland looked down at me. I trained my eyes across the grove, where partygoers were clearing away from the center. "As an outsider, you may simply find it...unusual."

That jerked my gaze up to his. But a flurry of movement and an uncanny trill of spectral music blurred between the trees, shutting me up.

A lissome woman gowned in scarlet—with a halo of glossy dark curls and a circlet of silver on her brow—danced out between the glowing apple trees. Behind her followed two Gentry men, tall and well muscled, each gallantly garbed in contrasting shades. The Oak King wore sparkling gold-and-brown silks draped over a mantle of deep, lustrous green. His hair curled down his back in dark blond ringlets so familiar in color that I almost couldn't bear to look at him. I jerked my gaze to the Holly King, his brother's opposite in nearly every way. The Holly King's raiment was the shade of frost beneath a violet twilight; his hair the color of midnight; his mouth the red of winter berries. All three dancers paced slowly toward the center of the Grove of Gold, their long, toned limbs sinuous in the eldritch glow.

"They say it was the Oak King who wooed the Year first." Wayland's low voice threaded through the hypnotic music weaving a spell over the glade. His mouth was audaciously close to my ear. I shivered and fought to keep my gaze forward. The dancer portraying Oak whirled through an intricate series of dips and pirouettes, each turn sending his autumnal silks billowing like leaves in a breeze. He approached the Year, who stood proud and unmoving in her red gown—strikingly like my own. Slowly, she arched an elegant arm toward Oak. He bowed over it, then swept her into a graceful, dizzying bend, curling her form around his own as if they were two halves split from the same whole. "She accepted his troth gladly, for never before had she met such a man—boisterous as a summer storm yet calm as growing grass. But then...she met his brother."

From the edge of the trees, Holly paced forward. Where Oak

was exuberant leaps and wild spins, Holly was precise and controlled, his exacting steps entrancing as he circled the dancing couple, winding steadily closer to them.

"Holly was everything his brother was not. He could be cold as frost rimed upon bare branches or hot as a hearth's glowing heart. The Year found she could not choose between them. But that did not stop both men from trying to prove they deserved her love."

The Year spun from the arms of Oak to the arms of Holly, faster and faster, in a frenzied flickering reel that brought my heart to my throat. The heavy throb of drums thundered beneath the pipes wailing toward a crescendo. Magic stitched up my spine as the golden apple trees glowed brighter, the blossoms pinking as my collar hummed against my skin. The Year threw her arms in the air as she spun, her silks sailing toward the stars until—

She stopped. The entire grove went silent—music, dancing, and singing dropping out like a final breath from a dead man's mouth. For a long, suspenseful moment, the only noise was the gentle sift of new snow along ancient gnarled branches. At last, the Year began to move, drawing down the delicate silver crown nestled between her dark curls. With emotion wreathing her every step, she slowly crossed to Holly. He bowed his head in coiled deference, and she placed the circlet upon his brow. Then she drew him down for a kiss.

A very real kiss. There was nothing theatrical about their embrace—I saw her open her mouth on his even as his hands trailed down her spine to glide over her rear. Surprise raised the hair on the back of my neck and slapped a hot promise on my cheeks. The music deepened, dark as slumber on a wintry midnight.

The Year drew away a moment later. Agony and regret striped her gaze as she pulled away from Holly and turned her gaze toward Oak, who stood, bereft, halfway across the grove. A decision crossed her lovely face. She snatched the crown from Holly's brow. He reached for her as she dashed away, and one long length of her crimson silk dress came away in his grasping hands.

She performed the same set of steps with Oak. The crown upon his head. Her lips gliding over his. He lifted her against him, and she locked her legs around his waist. The music of their embrace was light as summer showers and daisy chains.

But again, the Year seemed to regret her decision. She turned back toward Holly, and another piece of her gown came away in Oak's desperate palms. She spun between the two men, her dress bleeding away with every departure. The men chased her closer and closer to the middle, even as she tore at her hair and wailed at the sky and beat her breast in indecision. And finally, the last piece of her raiment fell away, and she stood unclothed before the assembled Folk.

I tried and failed to muffle my gasp of shock. No one else seemed bothered, only transfixed. I didn't blame them—the dancer was undeniably beautiful, with long smooth limbs, plump, pert breasts, and secretive dark eyes. But even as a dart of heat burned toward my center, I frowned. In the human realms, this kind of display could only ever be an exploitation—of a woman with little power and less agency, by men who wished to shame or take advantage of her. I would not abide participating in such a thing, even as a spectator.

"If this woman has been misused—" I said in a hot undertone to Wayland.

"Do not even think it, Thorn Girl." His swift reply held a warning. "To portray the Year is a great honor—one she has been chosen for and has wholeheartedly agreed to. Until next Midwinter, she will be blessed—her words and actions and choices deemed holy. There is no shame here—only celebration."

"But she's the only one..." I trailed off, still battling unease. "Everyone else is just *watching*."

But even as I spoke, it became apparent that was not to be the case. Slowly—with the same grace and elegance as the rest of the performance—Oak and Holly had also begun to disrobe, baring broad shoulders and hard chests and lean, muscled torsos and sculpted rears. Gauzy silks fluttered and billowed around them as they moved closer to the Year. Very, very close. My mouth dropped open as Holly moved behind her, his palms moving lovingly from her throat down to her breasts as he drew her chin up for a languorous kiss. Scandalized heat burned through me when Oak dropped to his knees before her, trailing his tongue up her finely turned calf, her toned thighs, before pressing his mouth to her willing sex.

They were not alone.

Almost as one—as if some silent command had spilled through the glade—the other guests began swaying toward each other amid the sultry glow. Fingers found hems and buckles and ties; fine velvets and expensive silks and gilded brocades tumbled to the snow like colorful carcasses. Naked skin flashed as figures found each other in the gold-strewn night, mouths clashing with mouths and hands sliding eager over splayed limbs—bared throats and tumbled hair and angled wrists. It was sheer abandon—an unfettered release of tension, pure as a note plucked from a perfect instrument.

Fierce, unexpected desire rose up in me. I forced myself to look away from the spectacle, to block my ears to the ecstatic moans as I raised my gaze to Wayland. With one arm propped on a low, gnarled branch, he was already watching me, his indigo eyes dark as the night sky.

"What is this?" I summoned righteous indignation and felt relief when it spackled over the uncomfortable ache of lust in my belly. "Why have you brought me here alone? It goes against every propriety—"

"Propriety?" Wayland clicked his tongue gently against his gleaming teeth. "Oh, you are an outsider, Thorn Girl. If you cannot recognize this as the sacrament it is—as holy as sunrise and as sinless as sunset—then I am not sure I will be able to explain it to you."

Was he calling me...provincial? No. He was calling me *human.* I opened my mouth to protest.

Wayland held up a forestalling finger. "And I did not, in fact, invite you here alone. And yet you *came* alone. Why?"

I gritted my teeth—I had nearly forgotten my purpose for coming here tonight. Now the prospect of kissing Wayland slicked dreadfully along the intrusive desire warming my blood and softening my bones. I glanced helplessly over my shoulder at the mass of bodies seething against one another like waves in the night. Could I kiss him now, amid all this unbridled passion, and expect him not to see it as a prelude to something more? Or should I let it wait, even as traitorous skeins of magic and attraction drew us ever closer together?

No—I needed to do it now. I would not have a better chance. But perhaps I could use it as another kind of prelude—to getting both of us what we truly wanted. I steeled my vaulting nerves.

"To do what needs to be done." I stepped closer to Wayland, moving beneath the shadow of the apple tree and tilting my chin up. "Kiss me, Wayland, son of Gavida. Then I have a proposition for you."

Surprise lightened Wayland's eyes nearly to sapphire before sudden, dark temptation deepened them toward black. He lifted a hand, brushing fingertips over the narrow metal of my collar before skimming a cool, smooth hand along the angle of my jaw. He slid his palm into my hair, cupping the back of my head. He leaned down with painstaking slowness, angling his face toward mine. I inhaled, breathing in the overwhelming scent of him—a subtle, sharp aroma like brine and beeswax. His sleek, straight hair brushed my cheek. He paused with his lips an inch from mine. And smiled.

"I wish to taste neither your desperation nor your defiance, Thorn Girl." Wicked amusement glossed his tone. "And usually it's me making those kinds of propositions."

I jerked back from him as embarrassed realization sent my thoughts winging toward the orgiastic revel still seething below us. For a split second, I couldn't help but imagine being drawn down into the writhing mass of lithe, limber bodies. The lace of my gown falling away from my shivering arms, the whispering fabric pushed up over my hips—

I squeezed my eyes shut, shoving the intrusive images away. Outrage bubbled up inside me, although I couldn't be sure whether it was directed toward Wayland or myself. Or Irian, for sending me here alone.

"Keep dreaming, Prionsa." I bared my teeth. "That wasn't at all what I was suggesting."

Cold satisfaction surfaced in Wayland's eyes, as if he had provoked the exact reaction he'd wanted from me. But a moment later, he was all smug insouciance once more.

"If it's the crowd you object to, I do have a bed. And if it's your husband who objects, well...the bed is big enough for three."

I had to laugh. "I think Irian would rather be flayed alive."

Wayland backed away slowly, descending into the grove even as he kept his dark blue eyes fixed steadily on mine. "You might be surprised, Thorn Girl."

Deftly, he untied the closure of his mantle, letting the heavy outer garment fall to the snow. His fine-tooled boots followed. He shrugged out of his tunic, revealing the heavy metal collar circling his throat, and unlaced his trousers—

In the moment before he disappeared into the revel, I turned on my heel, ducking below the fringe of golden apple trees into the blessed darkness beyond. I stomped halfway down into the echoing amphitheater before Linn caught up with me, her hooves nearly soundless in the snow. She snorted and bared her teeth, sending me a curious, violent image of her tidily flaying the skin from Irian's back with her shark teeth, then calmly helping him step out of it as if it were a suit of clothing. I shuddered and pushed her nose away from my shoulder.

"It was a metaphor, demon horse."

Chapter Nineteen

Aduantas echoed with emptiness. Although the hour was hardly past midnight, the only people I saw wandering the citadel's halls were Gavida's carefully blank attendants. I had a feeling the parties had all moved elsewhere—the lower city still churned with noise and merriment. I imagined there was far more gaiety to be had outside Aduantas's cold, nacre-lined corridors.

Which I currently found myself hopelessly lost in. I wasn't used to the twisting labyrinth of recursive glowing hallways. I cursed and hiked my skirts, casting about for one of those silver-liveried servants to show me the way back to my rooms. I was dying to get out of this dress, and—

A noise caught the edge of my hearing. A quiet hum, low and atonal. I jerked my head around, searching for the source. My gaze snagged on a narrow arched gate. Beyond, I spied the unseasonable bloom of a verdant pleasure garden. I relaxed. Surely it was simply the hive-hum of bees swarming a nest.

I almost kept walking. But then I remembered the gilded artificiality of this island—how utterly bereft of life it had felt before I'd been collared. I'd wager my life none of the flowers here were pollinated by bees or butterflies. The strange hum rose once more, and curiosity gripped me.

Slowly, I stepped forward to the gate, wrapped my hands around the carven rungs, and peered inside.

It was a small, enclosed garden—a narrow stretch of pale tile surrounded by steeply terraced beds of unnaturally blooming flowers. Frothing pastel peonies, creamy yellow daffodils, luminous pewter irises. A curtain of white climbing roses made a screen over the gate—I squinted around it.

And saw what it was trying to shield from view.

He sat so still that for a long moment, I thought him a statue. But the starlight gilding his long golden waves gave him away. *Rogan.* My pulse throbbed unevenly in my chest, jostling the Heart of the Forest. A moment later, I realized it was also he who'd made the sound—a low, slow humming, the intonations so disjointed as to barely make a melody. I froze, letting the familiarity of the notes scrape jagged nails through my memories.

Three in crimson, to the house of red
Oh lee oh lay, they all wish me dead.

I jerked. It was Rogan's favorite drinking song—a heroic lay telling the story of his celebrated ancestor. But that meant—

Power surged spontaneously through my veins, blurring my eyes for the briefest instant with frosted autumn leaves and crackling brown grass and creaking stones. My collar responded with vicious, instantaneous backlash. Searing pain screamed across my throat and blanketed my vision with shatter-glass stars. I clawed at my neck with desperate hands. But I couldn't even wedge a finger beneath the humming silver metal. I gasped, clutching instead at my Treasure lurching urgently against my palms. I breathed through my nose as I forced my rage to wind around my magic like a noose. With one last warning sizzle, my collar stilled.

I shoved the gate open, darted inside, and flung myself toward Rogan.

"Princeling." I gripped his shoulders, angling my head to stare into his face. His eyes were closed. "*Rogan.* Brighid be damned, I know you're in there!"

But he didn't budge. He'd stopped humming. His eyelids—gray as the underbelly of a storm cloud and veined with sickly blue—didn't so much as flutter. I shook his shoulders, harder, then lifted my palms to his jaw, rough with a day's worth of golden stubble. I tilted his face up to mine, smoothed his hair back from his face. He looked terrible—plum-colored circles carved beneath his closed eyes, hollows etched below his cheekbones, leaden skin rendering him expressionless. My stomach clenched and my collar buzzed. Rogan had never been *expressionless*—even in sleep, there had been such life to his face. I remembered—when he used to spend the night in my bed, he sometimes smiled in the hour before dawn. As if only in his dreams had he been able to live the life he'd longed for.

"Rogan!" I slapped him, hard—an openhanded crack across his face. His jaw whipped to one side, then returned to center. A rose of red bloomed on his cheek, but he did not so much as flinch.

I sank to my knees before him. Briefly, I wrapped my arms around his torso and pillowed my face against his stomach. Tonelessly, I took up the tune he'd been humming. "*Thrice the flames with courage broken, oh lee oh lay, my fury has spoken.*"

"Shhhh." I almost didn't hear the sibilant whisper, it was so soft. Near-soundless footsteps hissed over frost-pebbled flagstones. "Haven't you ever been warned not to wake the dreaming?"

I jerked my head up. Eala approached between the flowers, pale faced and white hooded. Only her eyes burned, bluer than I remembered but colder too—or perhaps hotter.

"What have you done to him?" I snarled as I stood. Fury climbed my spine, tangling with sharp dark thorns. I managed to tamp it down in the moment before it reached my throat, but that only fanned my anger higher. Memories of last night burned through me—Eala's shield of serenity as I sent my magic writhing violently toward her; her words, flaying me like a metal-tipped whip: *Perhaps our story might have ended more pleasantly if only I had thought to leash you.* Rogan, trailing her like a beaten dog.

It was her fault I'd lost control of my magic. Her fault I'd been curtailed by Gavida. All of this was *her fault.* "It's been a month and a half since you stole Rogan's will. Has he eaten? Slept? Bathed? You may have made him your slave, but—"

"Do you truly think me such a monster, Sister?" Eala's voice stayed quiet as she paused an arm's length from me. "Of course he has eaten—better than I, I wager. So, too, has he bathed and brushed his hair and shaved his face. And as for sleep—well, have you not eyes to see how soundly he rests?"

Revulsion churned in my stomach. I couldn't help but glance at Rogan, who sat statue-still on the bench. That was not rest. Unconsciousness, perhaps—but not rest. I glared back at her.

"Rogan is not a doll for you to play with, Eala." Ferocity made my voice sharp. "You cannot feed him and brush his hair and make him act out your maniacal fantasies, then place him back on the shelf when you grow bored with him. He is a human, a man, a prince—with hopes and dreams and a will all his own."

"Indeed." Eala's face tightened almost imperceptibly. "And in my experience, humans are imperfect. Men, flawed. And princes... well." Her pretty mouth twisted with taut malice. "Mother used to tell me kings are bad, but princes are worse. Princes answer to no law. If they do bad things, their fathers will not punish them. The courts cannot. The people will not. Princes think themselves gods, and for that, they should be feared."

Poison ivy strangled me. "Rogan wasn't like that."

"Wasn't he?" Her gaze was implacable on my face. "Rogan wanted everything. He wanted his privileges *and* his freedoms. He wanted his kingdom *and* his independence. He wanted to marry me *and* keep you. But not even princes ought to be given everything they want. In the end, even they have to answer to someone. And if I have to be the one who Rogan answers to ... so be it."

"And princesses?" Her perverted logic twined vines around my aching ribs. "Who do they have to answer to?"

She laughed like a chiming bell. "Oh, Sister. All my life I have answered to others. For the first time, I am finally able to do what I want to do. What I *need* to do."

"Which is?"

"Why, win the Oak King's Crown, of course!" An unexpected smile transformed her expression toward lightness, and even amid my rage I was struck by the incandescence of her beauty. Since I'd seen her last, she had begun to look even more like one of the Folk. Had the magic she'd paid for with her swan maidens' stolen hearts changed her more than I'd believed? Had she, too, transformed in a way that could not be reversed? "Then Gavida will forge me what I need to open the Gates, and I will finally be able to go home."

"To *conquer* your home, don't you mean?" I laced my tone with acid and felt gratified when she flinched. "I heard about the alliances you've made with the bardaí—the plans you've been making to take Bridei, then wage war against Mother with Rogan's fianna. You must know she will never let you win—she will never abide the human realms divvied up like chattel between posturing Gentry."

Eala swatted these words away like flies. "Among the many lessons our mother taught me was this gem: Alliances mean nothing. They are a means to an end. With the Treasures ... *renewed*, the Gates stand strong. I am trapped in this realm. Yes, I control more than half the Gates. But that matters little if I alienate the other bardaí and give them cause to attack me. It also matters little if I cannot get them open."

"So you're not planning to march on Rath na Mara and wrest the throne from Mother?"

Eala's small smile was vicious. "I never said that, now did I?"

Cold caressed my spine. Everything I knew of Eala and our mother's relationship made me believe that one day, they would come to violence. But no matter how true or false Eala's alliances were with the bardaí, a renewed war between Folk and humans would be ruinous for both realms. I was making peace with my nature—neither fully Folk nor fully human—and had chosen Tír na nÓg as my home. But that didn't mean I wished ill upon the people of Fódla. They already bowed beneath the weight of plague and famine and violence. I would not subject them to another war—not if I had any choice in the matter. But perhaps I could negotiate with Eala another way.

"Perhaps you have heard—I wield a Treasure now," I began.

"You are collared like a rabid dog, Sister." Eala's smile only grew. "You wield nothing."

"The collar is temporary." Fury writhed between my ribs but I kept it from my voice. "With the power of my Treasure, I can open and close Gates. I could let you through."

Eala's smile didn't slip, but her eyes burned even bluer. "And why would you do such a thing, when you have set yourself against me?"

"Because you have something I want." It wasn't the right turn of phrase; although Eala and I both knew what—*whom*—I meant, it lifted her eyebrows in a way that made me nervous.

"You would trade Rogan's freedom for the fate of a kingdom?" A keen, cold expression flashed across her face. "I knew you loved him, Sister. I did not know you loved him *that* much."

Morrigan, this conversation was not going how I intended.

"It is not romantic love for Rogan that drives me—I am wed to another," I ground out. "But what you're doing to him is an abomination. I would do the same for anyone else trapped under the influence of the black flowers."

"No, Sister. I daresay you would not." Eala tilted her head. "Say I were to set Rogan free. You would truly open the Gates for me?"

"For *you*," I clarified. "No bardaí. No armies. No wars."

"Of course there are *conditions*." Eala laughed, a tense, glittering crescendo of sound that raised the fine hairs along the back of my neck. "There are always conditions when it comes to power.

Those who have it get to set them. But I am weary of living beneath the conditions of others' power. It is time others lived under the conditions of *mine*. So no, Sister—I do not think I will take your deal. I will not set Rogan free—in fact, I rather believe he is better off with me. A prince supporting and protecting his princess—right where he always belonged." She brushed by me, circling around to perch on the bench beside Rogan's statuesque form. "We have a tournament to win together."

"Together?" Seeing them seated side by side churned a sick feeling in my gut. I remembered the first time I'd seen them dance together, at that Folk wedding last spring. They'd seemed so well matched—the lovely blond princess and her handsome golden prince. But this was a mockery of that story I'd told myself about their future and my place in it. A mockery of everything Rogan had wanted, and everything he'd lost. Tears burned sharp behind my eyes, and I blinked furiously to clear them. "Don't you mean he'll win it for you?"

"Not at all." Eala faced Rogan, curling herself next to his bulk even as she stroked a tender hand along the line of his jaw, then down the braided length of his hair. Bile burned the back of my throat. "The magic of the black flowers is truly extraordinary, Sister. You claim it steals my betrothed's will. I claim it lends him that which he did not have before. Invincibility."

"He is a human man among hundreds of innately magic Folk," I rasped. "He is far from invincible. You wield him like a puppet with invisible strings. He cannot hope to win the Oak King's Crown. Especially with you controlling him."

"Free will is so imperfect. Autonomy, overrated." Eala's eyes found me once more, even as her fingers curled possessively around Rogan's heavy bicep. "When we can do anything we please, it becomes so easy to fall prey to doubts and indecisions. You say I have taken his will—I say I have given him purpose. Through me, his weaknesses are stripped away, leaving only strengths. Through me, his doubts disappear; his fear melts away; his uncertainties fade. Rogan had always been strong in body but weak in mind. I have always been the opposite. Together, we are indomitable. Perfect strength, unfettered by fear or indecision, matched with perfect will, unhindered by fear or propriety."

She looked back at Rogan, considering. Tugged him down toward her so her mouth was an inch from his ear. *"Wake up, beloved."*

Rogan's eyes snapped open. I nearly screamed, jerking reflexively back. His gaze was flat as gray stone; his pupils glossy as beetle carapaces. His irises, which had once been the same blue-green as the Treasure pulsing feverishly above my chest, were the muted shade of dead moss. The prickle behind my own eyes intensified, two traitor tears sliding between my lashes.

"Beloved," Eala said again, softly and sweetly. The twisted endearment filled my mouth with bloodroot and laurel. "I am giving you a choice. You may either kiss the love of your life, causing yourself great physical pain in the doing. Or you may cut off your little finger and feel no pain at all. Decide."

Rogan shuddered, the first movement I'd seen him make. It was a ragged, wretched, racking thing, bending his spine and hunching his shoulders. He jerked against some unseen bond even as a wordless moan spilled from his lips. At last, he pulled a dagger from his belt and bent it to his hand, drawing a line of red over his smallest finger.

"No!" I flung myself toward him and wrenched the knife from his hand. My face was wet—salty droplets splashed down onto Rogan's hands, mixing with the scarlet blood now dripping from his pinky finger. In an instant, I flipped my grip on my dagger, extended my arm, and pressed the tip to Eala's throat. She barely flinched, tilting her chin a bare inch to avoid the blade. "You go too far. You'll pay for what you've done to him."

"You're forgetting, Sister," said Eala casually. "About Gavida's rules of hospitality. Unless you're eager to get yourself thrown out of the tournament, I advise you to lower the blade."

"No one seems to be knocking down the gate to stop me." My voice came out guttural and grim. "The smith-king is powerful, but I doubt he's omnipotent."

"A fair point." A blue spark flashed in Eala's eyes. "Beloved? Defend me."

Rogan rose up between us in an instant, deflecting my blade with his bleeding palm. His other hand found my throat, closing around my windpipe with a merciless grip. I coughed, choked. I lost my grip on the dagger as I beat at his wrists and forearms. But he was implacable. Instinct made me reach for my magic, but that only made things worse—it surged cool and comforting through my veins, only to batter against the barrier of Gavida's collar. White-hot pain filleted my throat, blending with Rogan's ever-tightening grip. A mewl escaped my lips as blackness blurred my vision.

"Release her."

Eala's command was calm, careless. Rogan obeyed without hesitation. I fell to my knees, gasping for air as I clutched at my bruised and scalded windpipe.

"Don't you see, Sister?" Eala's slim fingers once more threaded around Rogan's elbow in a mockery of a lover's gesture, even as a tiny bead of sweat collected at her hairline and dripped down toward her ear. "The black flowers are a mere formality now—bitter medicine for sweet submission. Our bond is complete—a finer marriage than free will ever would have allowed. I deliver him freedom from the pain and indecision he has lived with his whole life. In return he will deliver me two kingdoms. Then he and I together will deliver peace and unity to realms that have only ever known conflict. Only then may he be yours once more. Whatever may be left of him for you to have."

I backed away from them both, fury and grief and helplessness cracking the mortar of the walls I'd built around my heart.

"He was never mine." The words sounded broken even to my own humming ears. "He always belonged to himself. And one day soon—very, very soon—you will regret trying to make him yours."

But as I gathered my gown around my knees and fled for the gate, Eala laughed and laughed and laughed.

Our suite was dark and empty when I returned. I did not know what time it was, but false dawn swept gray over the arching hills.

And Irian—Irian was not there.

I stepped out of my crimson-and-black gown, exhaustion weighting my steps even as loneliness and sorrow cramped my bones. Seeing Rogan had been so familiar…and yet so vastly different. Once upon a time, he had felt like home. Now a brisk and brutal realization blundered through me. I wasn't just far from home—I *had* no home. Two months ago, I'd chosen myself over Eala; Irian over Rogan; Tír na nÓg over Fódla. But I belonged here little more than I'd belonged *there*. I was an outsider here, as I'd been there.

I twisted myself between the duvets and stared out into a gray sky strewn with dying stars. Memories trembled poisonous as brugmansia through my veins: my bloodless fingers, gripping the cold steel of a stirrup as I begged, *Tell me it wasn't real, and I'll let you go.* The vows I'd made to Irian beneath the Heartwood: *Then, now, and after, you are my home.*

But I had to wonder, Could another person ever really be home? And what happened when they left?

Our suite was dark and empty when I returned. I did not know

I dreamed I was a wave upon the ocean, crashing endlessly against a tall white cliff. But every impact—each surging rush and foaming clash and ebbing retreat—was a kiss. And I threw myself forward, again and again, just to taste the sweetness of that joining.

I did not hear Irian come back in. I only distantly felt the brush of his lips upon my cheek. And faintly—faintly—smelled the acrid stench of forge smoke.

Or was it the smell of blood?

I fell into a deep, deep sleep and did not waken again until morning.

Chapter Twenty

Aduantas reverberated with the sounds of war—the bugling of carnyxes raising the hair on my arms and the pounding of bodhráin making my bowels churn. Irian and I—armed and armored—marched through the nacre-lined hallways in silence until we were swallowed up by the crowds gathering at the base of the citadel.

We had not spoken much that morning. He had kissed me, briefly, splaying one large hand over my cheek as sunlight spilled across our bed. But he had not asked me about Wayland. I had not offered. I had not asked him where he'd been all night. He had not offered. We'd bathed separately, then dressed. When I struggled with the buckles on my armor, Irian had wordlessly helped, his calloused fingers deft on the straps. There was food, which neither of us touched. I did take a hesitant sip of the dark mushroom brew that had once more been brought to our chambers, trying not to pull a face when it descended like actual mud toward my stomach, thick as caulk and silty with bitterness.

I did not take a second sip.

Now, marching shoulder to shoulder with hundreds of other

contestants, we still did not speak. Irian—black cloaked and blank faced and taut as a bowstring pulled to its limit—was nearly as intimidating as the first time I'd ever met him. An errant thread of residual fear vibrated against the nerves thrumming through my veins. But before long, I spotted Balor, looming ten feet higher than anyone else. I pushed toward him, relief easing my rigid muscles.

"Balor," I called up to him. He turned ponderously at the sound of my voice, then smiled ear to ear. I told myself his serrated iron teeth were charming, not terrifying. "I am glad to see you again!"

"And I you, Gentry lady." Balor paused and bowed, making two ill-tempered lower Folk slam face-first into his massive calves, then reel away cursing. "I am pleased to see you were not bored to death by the smith-king's prattling."

"I may be easily bored. But I am much less easily killed," I joked.

Beneath the endless banner of a crisp cerulean sky, the amphitheater buzzed like a hornet's nest preparing to swarm. There seemed three times as many spectators as yesterday; they swarmed the stands and spilled wantonly between the steps, clamoring for ale and food even as they flashed coins and exchanged bets. Performers cartwheeled and caterwauled between revelers. Merchants hawked curiosities: silks the colors of dashed hopes and mirrors in the shapes of dreams unfurled. The air was one of such raucous celebration that it was entirely plausible to me that last night's parties had not ended with the new day—only changed locale.

The contestants' march into the amphitheater flogged the tangible air of grisly giddiness higher, until the whole arena vibrated with a heady bloodlust. I shuddered and reached for the comfort of Irian's presence. But in the moment before I gripped his palm, his hand jerked up to the hilt of the sheathed Sky-Sword. I glanced up at him, but he wasn't even looking at me.

Boom.

The now-familiar clang of Gavida's instruments startled me from my confusion and sent my own hands flying toward the hilts of my skeans. This time, the smith-king did not soar above us on a column of marble. Instead, he spoke to the crowds—spectators and contestants alike—from the raised dais near the base of the stands. A vast throne rose at his back, bedecked in the colors I was beginning to recognize as emblematic of the Holly King: silver and dusky violet; glossy evergreen and plump, varnished red. On his brow, Gavida wore a circlet nearly identical to the one the Year had worn in last night's gilded pageant. The silver metal was threaded with veins of gold, same as the collar choking off my magic. The crown shone sharp as a wish in the glancing sunlight.

Beside him, Wayland sat on a smaller yet no less ostentatious throne. With his powerful legs thrown out before him and his sleek head held high, he looked none the worse for last night's revelries. The image of him slowly stripping off his clothing as he backed away into the orgy burned heat up the back of my throat. How easily he had deflected my kiss, and my secondary motivations with it, by embarrassing me. I would have to be more careful with the prionsa, who was more slippery than I'd given him credit for. I swallowed and forced my gaze away from him.

Boom.

Gavida waited with his tools lofted until the crowd fell quiet—a silence fragile as glass and as likely to break. Even then, he waited—an aching, resounding eternity as tension hummed steadily higher.

"The Trial of Tenacity begins," he cried at last, his voice unnaturally enhanced to thunder at us from all corners. "The fight is to the blood. Those who bleed bow. If they still can." The grim amusement in his tone whipped up jeering laughter from the crowd and conjured a frisson of fear to snake around my bones. "The last one hundred contestants standing will move on to the next contest—the Trial of Speed. May all the gods, alive and dead, stand with you as you fight for your place. Let the Tournament of Kings...begin!"

Boom.

Beside me, Irian's long black mantle slithered away from his neck as he wrapped it around his forearm in a makeshift shield. His sword—gleaming the same reflective blue as the gold-streaked sky—rang from its scabbard with a high pure note. I drew my skeans at the same instant, angling my back toward Irian. All around us, the other contestants mimicked the same motions: unsheathing blades and hoisting axes and hefting maces. Tension hummed, the hornet hive preparing, at last, to swarm. A thrill of magic burned sharp as a spark between candles. A charcoal pennant of cloud skeined over the sun.

Across the arena, a single sword screamed silently through the air. Then: The heavy thunk of flesh. A glittering spray of ruby blood. Around me, faces lifted like wolves scenting blood.

Mayhem exploded. Contestants turned on one another in a rush, flinging themselves bodily with a resounding clash that burst the arena's silence like a bubble. The crowd began to shout and clamor, their high-pitched voices and applause mingling with the cries of wind-lofted gulls. Adrenaline burned through my veins and flamed along my limbs as my heartbeat accelerated. The Heart of the Forest throbbed, uneven and atonal, coiling a different kind of power between my ribs and along my spine—

My collar spiked a harsh warning. I cringed from the pain even as I flung myself into the fray. I collided with a slender ghillie slashing out with a curved mace; my eyes watered but I dodged the strike neatly. Twirling back in, I rained down a flurry of swift, calculated punches against the ghillie's torso. It battered its fist toward me, but I sidestepped. I spun, wedging its wrist between my ribs and my bicep. Then, with its forearm clamped beneath my elbow, I scratched the tip of my dagger over its exposed birch-bark skin. Blood welled like tree sap.

A shimmer of magic, and the ghillie was dragged away toward the edge of the arena.

I had no time to catch my breath. Already a muscular Gentry warrior was plunging toward me. I barely saw the long whip fletched with deadly shards of metal until it slithered around my boots, cinched tight, and flipped me bodily onto my back. My breath was knocked painfully out of my lungs. I instinctively slashed down between my feet, slicing through one of the flails. With the same movement, I wrapped my wrist around the top of the thong—my heavy leather gloves mercifully protecting me from the sharp metal—and yanked. The Gentry warrior stumbled. I slid up to my knees, whirled beneath their guard. Slashed my blade over their unprotected thigh.

I lurched back to my feet even as I sensed a huge, heavy figure lunge toward me from behind. I twisted awkwardly, thrusting my hands up into guard position.

Irian sidestepped briskly in front of me, blocking the attack. The onrushing gruagach's club jarred against Irian's blade with an impact that vibrated along my bones. Irian deftly parried, slinging the weight of the club down to thunk into the dirt. He kicked out, the heavy weight of his boot splintering the creature's knee. It grunted, stumbled. Irian lashed out without hesitation, the tip of the Sky-Sword finding the gruagach's throat. The creature gurgled shock, lifting a huge hairy hand to clutch at the blade. Irian jerked the sword up, then slashed sideways. The Sky-Sword released a joyous piercing note as gore splayed out in a bloody gyre. The gruagach slumped sideways before collapsing in the dirt.

"Irian!" Shock had backed me up nearly to the barrier between the arena and the stands. "He said the stakes were to the *blood*. You didn't have to *kill* it!"

My voice seemed to reach Irian as if from a distance. He looked over his shoulder, his face partially obscured by the fall of his black hair and a spray of dark blood on his cheek. He turned toward me.

For a long moment—stretched out like overgrown weeds over choked grass—I almost smiled. He was going to fight *with* me. We would stand back-to-back and fight off wave after wave of foes.

Then I saw the hard, unsettling look in my husband's eyes. Heard the discordant battle hum of the sword he lowered down over his vambrace, its blood-spattered length pointed toward me. Registered the light, deliberate steps over packed earth that brought him closer, closer—

He wasn't turning *toward* me. He was turning *on* me.

Instinct alone brought my crossed skeans up to meet his onslaught, my body reacting while my mind still reeled. The impact of his blade against mine shuddered down my arms and crackled lightning along my bones. I gasped and sidestepped, letting the momentum of his thrust carry harmlessly beyond me. I whirled behind him, raising my blades again.

"Irian!" Confusion and fear and betrayal painted shifting waves of hot and cold over my thrumming skin. "What in Donn's black hell do you think you're doing?"

He didn't answer, only lunged again, slicing his sword toward my throat. I narrowly dodged, the blade crooning inches from my ear. I jerked one of my skeans up to intercept the strike, twisting beneath the blade. I kicked out toward Irian's knee. His greaves protected him from the worst of the impact, but the split second of imbalance was enough for me to spin inside his guard. I jerked one of my skeans up to his throat as the other slid a warning along the vambrace of his sword arm.

"Whatever you think you're doing," I snarled, "*stop.*"

"I know you do not understand, colleen." Resolve battled with regret on Irian's perfect face. "But I am doing this to keep you safe."

"You're right." My voice rubbed my throat raw. "I don't understand."

Irian leaned down to plant a tender, determined kiss on my mouth. Then he picked me up and threw me back against the wall.

The impact jarred me—my spine colliding with stone as my head knocked painfully backward. My vision blurred; my feet, when they touched earth, felt a thousand pounds heavier. I tried to collect myself, but Irian was relentless—his blade slicing toward me with all his elegant, unstoppable warrior's grace. I defended myself with every ounce of my strength. But my will was a dying flower, and each of Irian's unfaltering blows was a petal falling away. Again and again we clashed, the Sky-Sword singing an inevitable chorus of victory as I steadily grew weaker. I reached for the power of my Treasure, only for the heady unfurling of green to be viciously curtailed by the collar around my neck. Tears blurred my vision; pain leached up my flagging limbs like rot along dead branches.

"Stop," I begged him, one last time. Around us, the melee was beginning to slow as the initial flush of death grew more dire—with the weakest culled from the field, the most skilled were beginning to battle more seriously.

His words from two nights ago blazed a scorching path through my mind: *You can hold your own against me when I am holding back.*

Sympathy spasmed across Irian's face. Then he bore down on me in earnest—each blow a promise, each strike a vow.

A moment later, he disarmed me—the Sky-Sword flicking one of my skeans away into the melee. With his other hand, he jarred my arm against the wall. My numb fingers released my other blade. He bent and plucked it up. Gently—so gently I barely even felt it—he raised the skean's razored edge to my face and drew a line along my cheek. A thread of pain stitched over my skin; green-black blood trickled down my face to dribble along my jaw. A moment later, a magical noose of compulsion tugged at me.

Irian pressed the dagger back into my hand, then stepped back as I was dragged away by uncanny magic. And in the moment before his menacing, black-armored figure melted back into the morass of violence churning the amphitheater to blood and death, I swore I heard him murmur, "Know that I am truly sorry."

Chapter Twenty-One

I waited.

For hours I waited, pacing the floor of our suite until the room felt impossibly cramped; the ceilings, unconscionably low. I paced like an animal in a cage, and every step whipped my anger higher. Near dusk, Gavida's silver-clad attendants came with food and wine—I practically screamed them out, driving them swiftly from our rooms. Darkness fell with a leaden hush that felt like a prelude to misery. I didn't light any lanterns. The sweaty clothes and armor I hadn't bothered to change out of since that morning chafed my seething skin.

I had known Irian and I were not fully aligned when it came to renewing the Treasures. But how could I have guessed the extent of his willingness to prevent me from even trying? He could claim that eliminating me from the tournament was meant to protect me. But what he had done was not protection—it was control. He had set his own will above mine.

He had stolen my *choice* from me.

I was no mindless thrall. Irian may have ruined my chance to win the Oak King's Crown. But there was more than one way to crack an egg. And more than one tall, handsome heir on this accursed island.

Perhaps the second would be more disposed to help me get what I wanted. What I *needed*.

My fury settled like bright green scurf on a poison pond. I stalked out into Aduantas.

Cloaked in snow and lit by a bare smirk of moonlight, Wayland's pleasure gardens were nearly unrecognizable. Blue roses encased in perfect globes of ice drooped heavy heads; crystalline swords slashed down from the colonnade. My boots crunched in the drifts, and I tried to remember where the path was.

An arched, inlaid door framed by twisting pillars abruptly slammed open, blasting golden light and warmth and gemstone laughter into the ice-draped pavilion. A full-figured Gentry woman stumbled down the handful of steps, clad in little more than under-things. A second maiden staggered after her, dragging a cloak in one hand and sloshing a half-empty bottle of wine in the other. She called unintelligibly to her friend, who turned. She tossed the cloak at her, but misjudged—it struck the other girl square in the face and knocked her back onto her rear. Both women dissolved into laughter. The second helped the first back to her feet, both of them slipping and sliding on the icy flagstones. A moment later, a third figure strutted out after them—a lithe, dark-skinned man of breathtaking beauty who was seemingly unbothered by the fact that he no longer wore—or perhaps had never been wearing—a shirt. He looped an arm around one woman's shoulders and plucked the bottle of wine from the hand of the other. Together, the trio wound away down the colonnade, swigging from the bottle and singing off-key.

A shadow in the doorway stole my attention—the sleek, well-muscled figure of a golden-skinned Gentry man with long, rumpled mahogany hair. Wayland. He glanced out after his *playmates*, even as he leisurely laced a high-collared shirt up toward his chin. He smiled faintly, then yawned as he moved to kick the door shut.

I stepped out into the light. "Wayland."

His eyes twitched to me across the courtyard. Some complicated emotion eddied across his expression, frothing like foam on the deep blue of his eyes. A moment later, he schooled his features, flashing me a broad, suave smile.

"I'm afraid you have just missed the party, Thorn Girl." Wayland's hands stilled on the ties of his shirt. "But for you I could be enticed toward a third—" He feigned thoughtfulness, even as his smile turned wicked. "Make that a *fourth* round."

"I'm not here to sample the dubious delights of your bedroom pursuits, Prionsa." I crossed my arms over my chest, forcing myself not to focus on his mussed clothes, ruffled hair, and heavy, satisfied eyes. "Besides, you look worn out. Hasn't anyone told you? All play and no work makes Jack a mere toy."

"I know no greater pleasure—or honor—than being played with." His smile widened at my sudden blush. He mirrored my gesture, crossing his arms over his chest as he leaned against the doorframe. "Much as I adore a quaint human aphorism of an evening, what brings you to my door tonight? If not play?"

"You tell me," I said. "Last night, I offered you a proposition. Two, really. Both of which you deflected with such skill that I almost—*almost*—thought it was my idea."

Sudden restraint shrouded his eyes. "You caught me off guard, Thorn Girl. I assumed you enjoy the thrill of the chase as much as I do. But if you prefer a more straightforward option, my bed is this way."

"You're doing it again." I narrowed my eyes at him. "You know what I want from this place, don't you? And for some reason, you're avoiding discussing it with me. Why?"

Wayland's shoulder resting on the doorjamb tensed, heavy muscle bunching beneath his shirt. For a moment, I was certain he was going to armor himself again—either making another flirtatious joke to misdirect me from my line of questioning, or simply telling me to go away. Instead, he hesitated before swinging the door fully open. He stepped to one side and gestured expansively.

"You'd better come inside, Thorn Girl. It's cold out there."

Anticipation and trepidation tangled inside me, and in the split second before accepting his invitation, I wondered what I was about to get myself into.

I also wondered, traitorously, what Irian would think if he knew I was here. But the thought of Irian spiked a renewed flood of blinding betrayal behind my eyes.

On first glance, Wayland's chambers were the same as the rest of Aduantas—built from pale, glowing stone and inlaid with dainty seams of blue tourmaline, mother-of-pearl, and that ubiquitous silver metal. There, the similarities ended. Wayland had eschewed his father's aesthetic for something altogether homier. A thousand honey-gold candles transformed the bedroom into the inviting haze of sunset. A massive unmade bed slouched at one end of the long, high-ceilinged chamber. Piled with sumptuous fabrics and draped with diaphanous veils, it reminded me of the intricate web of a giant, fanciful, lustful spider. Arching stained-glass windows splashed colorful prisms over the bare tiles. Discarded clothes and boots and weapons and books and empty cups choked every available surface and spilled in abundance from the wardrobes. The room smelled of spilled wine and burnt beeswax and lingering sex. I tried to keep my expression neutral as I took it all in, but Wayland must have perceived some judgment on my face.

"Apologies." He didn't sound particularly sorry. "I'm not manic about housekeeping."

"A mild understatement," I muttered. "Why don't you let that army of palace attendants tidy up in here?"

"Oh, them." His voice held little inflection. "No thanks."

An ornate metal shield driven deep into the wall was currently serving as a makeshift shelf for knickknacks, knives, and mismatched crystal goblets. Wayland plucked down a wineglass, held it up to the light with a squint, then filled it from a decanter glowing with ruby liquid. He pushed it into my limp hands.

I pushed the glass back at him. "This isn't a social visit."

"All *work* and no *play* makes Jack...what?" he mused before throwing back the glass of wine with a shrug. He wiped his mouth with the back of his hand and smiled slow. "I assume there's a second half to your charming aphorism?"

"Talk, Prionsa." I folded my arms and glared. "Before I strangle it out of you."

"Even you may find that difficult, Thorn Girl." He ran an absent finger over his heavy, carven collar, visible above the partially unlaced front of his tunic. I swallowed, skin bobbing against the cool, momentarily quiescent metal of my own collar. Although I could not open mine, I'd at least glimpsed the latch. Wayland's? Well. If there was any way to open it, I could not see it.

"Your father's a monster," I forced out. "But he's not omnipotent. Is he?"

"No." Wayland stepped closer. He was not as tall as Irian, but my head still barely cleared his shoulders, putting my eyes at the level of his rather spectacular chest—a hard expanse of smooth golden-brown skin he hadn't bothered to fully cover with his shirt. I jerked my gaze up. His tilted indigo eyes were fixed on me, intent. "My father likes...systems. Efficient systems that work even when he's not actively monitoring them. Cause, effect. Action, reaction. But if one system breaks down, he will layer another system atop it to reinforce it. Understand?"

I remembered what Irian had said when Wayland had first showed us the collar outside his father's forge. *Not just a collar, but a muzzle.*

"You tried to circumvent the collar," I guessed, running a tongue over my suddenly dry lips. "You tried to free yourself. But he...he must have caught you. So he forged another geas into the metal. One to keep you quiet."

Wayland's eyes flashed. His wide mouth settled into a hard, narrow line. "Why might silence be an effective system?"

"He does not wish you to speak about who—*what*—you are."
Even as the words left my mouth, I knew they were true but incomplete. "Because if you were to speak of it...it would be a threat to him."

Wayland's eyes darkened nearly to black. "Go on."

My thoughts swirled like the steam in Gavida's forge, hot but drifting. I thought of Mother, collaring me with my own desperate need to be loved and yanking that leash whenever she sensed me beginning to wander. I thought of Eala forcing black flowers down the throat of the prince who'd finally decided to follow his heart instead of his duty. I thought of Irian, banished from the home he'd grown to love, because his foster father cared more about the safety of his island than the safety of the boy in his care. "You hate him. You wish to overthrow him—depose him. *Kill* him."

"All sons must replace their fathers. Sooner or later." Wayland stepped even closer, his cool scent of salt water and sea air honeyed by beeswax. "But you have it backward."

"Backward?" I tried to weed my tangled thoughts into neat rows. "You hate him because he collared you. But he did not collar you because you hated him. At least, not at first."

He stared at me, tension pulling the muscles along his neck taut.

I spun in a tight circle, my thoughts boiling and frothing along the edge of a realization. Although it burned me, I pushed closer to it, fighting the urge to look away. What other reason would Gavida have to curtail his own son—his only child and seemingly beloved heir—if not to protect himself? His island? There had to be some other reason—some *purpose*. But what did Wayland *do*? Besides acting as his father's champion in the Tournament of Kings, he appeared to do little beyond drinking wine and sleeping with everyone in sight—

"The tournament?" Relief pooled in Wayland's eyes and sent satisfaction blooming in me. "There's something about Gavida—something about this whole island. It's the most magical place I've ever been, and yet before your father blocked my magic, I could feel that nothing seemed *alive*. I know Gavida's power is forging, but surely he could not have *made* everything here? Even for someone in possession of a Treasure, that would be nearly impossible. It would take immense power—and the laws of balance as I know them don't allow for such things."

"The balancing is eternal," Wayland intoned, "but not immutable."

"Yes—like the Treasures being tithed every thirteen years, the magic would have to be renewed somehow." I paced to the door, then back, chewing on a ragged fingernail. "But he has not sacrificed his life. And surely he would not escape blame for sacrificing others—" I stopped in my tracks. My eyes flew up to Wayland again. "The tournament is *not* a mere folly, is it? The Holly King falls, so the Oak King may rise. A symbolic death. But if Gavida somehow turned it into a ritual? Somehow harnessed the power of that figurative sacrifice? Then he could renew his own magic. Am I close?"

Wayland's silence was heavy with assent. When he spoke, he sounded as if he was choosing his words very carefully. "Ask me how many times I have won the Tournament of Kings."

The question surprised me. "How many?"

"None." I had never seen him look so grim, and I wasn't sure I liked it. "Never."

"The Holly King always loses." I digested this. "The Oak King always wins."

Wayland's eyes burned like sunlight through shallow water. "Always."

"Then...the game is rigged." I absently jerked one of my skeans out of my belt. Wayland swayed back a step as I swirled the blade around my fingers, the repetitive motion helping me think. "Symbolically, Gavida must not really be the Holly King—he is the Oak King. His power continuously ascendant where yours is defeated. And whatever magic Gavida harnesses from the tournament, it's worth a priceless forging to him. It can't just be *your* magic—even if you're a tánaiste, without a Treasure your innate power wouldn't be enough to sustain all *this* for a year. He must be siphoning off the contestants—the audience. Is that even possible? To harness all that fervor and frenzy and violence into power he can use? Magic he can forge?"

Wayland clenched his jaw, a muscle feathering beside his ear.

"I must be close," I mused. I jerked out my second skean and joined it to its dancing sister, honeyed light dripping from their bevels as they swirled in my hands. "If he's taking all this magic, and it isn't *his* magic, then he must be storing it somewhere." My blades stopped, pointed outward. "The crucible!"

But Wayland shook his head. "The crucible is a..." He choked. "The crucible is a crucible."

A sharp thorn of memory needled me—the horrible surging emptiness I'd encountered when I pushed with the power of my Treasure beneath Aduantas. Quiet certainty wrapped vines around my bones and whispered promises to my strumming pulse. I sheathed my blades and stepped closer. "Whatever feeds it lies deeper. The source of Gavida's power is somewhere underground—far below Aduantas. I'd swear on it."

Wayland's shrug spoke volumes.

"We'll find it." The night seemed to unfurl, unleashing a universe of dizzying, dazzling, dreadful possibilities. "Surely whatever power he's keeping—wherever he's keeping it—can be destroyed or released. Then you'll be free. We'll both be free. Then—"

"No." Almost unconsciously, Wayland's hand lifted to his neck. His fingertips feathered over the smooth metal, a curiously vulnerable gesture. "*No.*"

"What?" My eagerness dripped away like melted wax. "Why not?"

"Because it would be a suicide mission." Wayland's tone remained careful. "I could not ask you to embroil yourself in such a thing."

"You've done your damnedest not to ask." I folded my arms over my chest and narrowed my eyes. "I'm offering."

"Do you imagine that...attempts have not been made?" His intentional vagueness grated up my spine. "They have. Irian damn near lost his mind trying to—" He choked. His mouth worked. "My father nearly killed him for it. It was no small part of the reason he was sent away."

The thought of Irian invaded the careful thicket of blunted brambles I'd grown around my huge hurt. I turned briskly away from Wayland so he could not see the emotion twisting my face, then spun swiftly back once I'd mastered myself. "Irian told me none of this."

"It was not his story to tell," Wayland said. "But you see, Thorn Girl—it has been nearly two decades. How would you go about doing this? Why would you want to? And what could I possibly offer you in return?"

His words prickled me. He was right—there was no point in getting myself into trouble with the smith-king on Wayland's behalf unless I reaped some reward. And what *could* he offer me?

As things stood? Nothing. But if I succeeded in freeing him from his father's terrible restrictions and setting his innate magic free?

Everything.

Dangerous, tempting possibilities bloomed in my chest like poison flowers. I'd have a tánaiste in my debt—the new ruler of a powerful island at my beck and call. If the smith-king did not die, perhaps even a chance to forge new Treasures.

I'd thought winning the tournament might earn me everything I wanted. But Irian had stolen that chance from me. Perhaps Wayland was the more straightforward path.

"You and I are the same, Prionsa. Pawns who wish to be kings, soldiers who wish to be generals. Both of us tired of being told what to do." I gazed up at him, and he looked down at me, a curious expression curling the corners of his mouth and lightening his sea-dark eyes. "This is the why: I want to resurrect more Treasures in the same way mine was renewed. I want allies; I want armies. I want to defeat my bitch of a sister. And I—I'm the how."

Wayland stood so still he might have been a cliff beside the sea. "The Oak King would have to fall for the Holly King to rise."

"Could you make the coup bloodless?"

"I doubt it. Why? Do you care?"

I rubbed the space between my brows. I had no real desire to involve myself in Folk politics—the power plays of the Gentry had already brought enough hurt to the people I cared about. But with my place in the tournament forfeit and a collar around my own neck, I had precious few options if I wanted to prevent Eala from wreaking havoc on both Folk and human realms. I had no doubt she would do whatever she must to achieve her own dire purposes. Maybe it was time I set aside my own qualms and did whatever I needed to stop her.

"Just try not to kill him, all right?" I said softly. "Unless you know someone else with Gavida's affinity for forging magical objects of vast power, we'll need him to forge new Treasures."

Wayland laughed out loud, although I hadn't meant it as a joke. "Free me from my bonds, Thorn Girl? Then you shall have your smith. No need to keep my father alive after all."

I raised both eyebrows, interest piqued. But Wayland flicked away whatever questions I might have asked. "How will you proceed? The island is huge. The city, fortified. Aduantas, heavily guarded."

"It'll have to be during the tournament," I mused. Perhaps Irian had done me a boon, despite his intentions. "Everyone's attention—including your father's—will be fully diverted. If I'm cunning and careful, I may go where I wish without notice."

"Cunning, I have no doubt." He cocked his head, a grin playing over his mouth. "Careful? Does not strike me as your strong suit. I will not be able to help you. I must attend the tournament."

A dark vein of shadow twisted around my spine. "Then you have perfect deniability."

Wayland frowned. "This was your idea, Thorn Girl."

"If I succeed, the reward benefits us both. Thus, the risk ought to be shared similarly." I mirrored one of his insouciant smiles at him. "I'm going to need some assurance that you're not going to run and report me to your father or the palace guard."

"Sea snake indeed." Wayland whistled, his fathomless eyes skating over my face. After a moment, he jerked one of his hands with the other, yanking at his little finger. "If you truly need assurances—*here.*"

Instinct brought my palm up to catch the glittering metal ring flying at my face. I glanced at it, curious. It was a tiny signet ring wrought from twisting skeins of silver and gold—the same unusual metal veining through Aduantas. At its center, a polished circle of sea glass was etched with a symbol I couldn't quite make out, even when I held it up to the candlelight.

"What is it?"

"It was my mother's ring. My most prized possession," Wayland said without inflection. I stiffened and tried to hand it back to him. But Wayland's large, cool palm closed over my own, encasing the jewelry between us. He jerked me forward. I stumbled over the edge of the plush carpet and fell against him. He steadied me with a hand at my waist, even as he stared down at me—softly, shamelessly. A treacherous vine of heat trembled through me. "If you are caught, show them that, and they will know I am involved. And we will be clapped in chains together. But take care not to lose it. Or you and I will have more than a kiss binding us together."

I forced myself to meet his sensuous gaze. "About that—"

"So eager now to put it behind you, Thorn Girl? You and I aren't finished with each other yet." Wayland's smile became a smirk. He backed slowly away from me to sink down on the edge of the bed. His long legs sprawled out before him as he tilted his mahogany head to catch the golden light. "But we can certainly discuss it again tomorrow, after the Trial of Speed. You can tell me what you discovered, and I...well. Wear something more comely than bloody armor and dirty boots, and I will make sure to clear my schedule for as many kisses as you ask me for."

"Keep dreaming, Prionsa." I kept my tone sweet as I backed toward the door. "After all, you've just given me your most prized possession. I'm not above dangling it over a cliff to get my way."

"No," Wayland laughed, warm and deep. "I daresay you're not."

Chapter Twenty-Two

It was snowing again. As I trudged through Wayland's gardens back into Aduantas, I realized the hour I'd spent with him had distracted me from my fury. Now I felt hollow—as if Irian's betrayal were less a bonfire blazing around my heart and more a darkened night without stars. I could not see my way through it, but it no longer scorched me. And not even the delightful prospect of a confrontation upon my return was enough to dissuade me from my sudden deep desire for a mattress.

I jammed Wayland's signet ring onto my finger and marched back through the silent citadel.

Irian leaned in silhouette against the window, still wearing the same mantle and armor from the arena. Diamonds of melting frost jeweled his black hair and encrusted the shoulders of his cloak. His eyes were lowered to the length of night-black metal he held loosely in his bare palms. He looked up when I walked in, his eyes glowing silver as the lines of blood dribbling from his palms.

He was a *mess*. His armor was badly damaged—shredded at the hip and ripped at the shoulder and scored over the chest as if giant claws had tried to dig out his heart. Blood in four or five colors spattered him, a ghastly rainbow splashed over his clothes and across his face—red and black and green.

"*Fia*." My name was like a prayer on his lips—or, perhaps, a curse. "Once, in a time of hasty weddings and impossible miracles, a changeling girl died."

I couldn't help myself from interrupting him, snarling, "*No stories.*"

"*You died, Fia.*" The words were caustic with pain, scraping along my skin with terrible sympathy. "You died."

A sensation dark as a shadow and fragile as a heart reared inside me—something I could not quite look at head-on. "I was there."

"No, colleen. You were not." He finally moved, surging up to his full height before swiftly crossing the room toward me. He paused an arm's length away, the Sky-Sword angled between us. "I could feel it, you know. Feel the metal slicing through your skin. Hear the crack your ribs made when they shattered. Taste your blood as it gushed out onto the earth." He opened his left palm in a helpless gesture. "There was *so much blood*. I tried to stanch it. But then my hands were too slippery to hold on to you when—" His voice cracked, and he clenched the hand into a fist. "I could hardly bear it then. I could not bear it again. So as long as I live, I swear I will not let you die."

Waxen leaves of green and black beat around my head and filled my mouth. I swallowed, hard, as ghostly impressions yawned like traps to catch me. I reached instead for the watercolor memories I'd covered them with—memories of belonging, of home, of perfect ecstasy. "There are limits even to what you can do, Sky-Sword."

"Not in this." He dropped the sword to clatter on the floor and reached for me instead. His hands—sticky with half-dried blood—curved around my cheeks and tilted my face toward his. He rested his forehead against mine, his lips a bare inch away. I cursed myself for helplessly breathing his closeness in—cold wind and starlight, a night before dawn. My eyelids fluttered shut. "Whatever the cost to keep you safe, colleen, I will pay it."

My eyes jerked open. I pushed Irian to arm's length, roughly. "You're an idiot."

"Because I cannot bear the thought of you dying?" His eyes darkened with that now-familiar shadow I'd grown to loathe. "Because I would do anything to keep you safe?"

"Because you're doing the wrong things!" I jerked back from him, turned to plant my hands on the windowsill. I stared out at the black outline of Emain Ablach rising toward its crown of golden trees. "What were you *thinking*? You attacked me; you hurt me. You took away my decision. You set your will above mine."

Irian huffed a brusque, unhappy laugh. "So that is what this is about? What Eala did to Rogan?"

The thought of Rogan pounced on me like a predator from the bushes—how had the princeling, mind-wiped and willing, fared out on that battlefield? Had he been able to hold his own, when Irian himself had clearly struggled? My fingers curled into fists and my mouth tightened.

"He survived, if you want to know," Irian muttered, as if reading my thoughts. "In fact, he took one of the hundred coveted spots and will compete with me tomorrow in the Trial of Speed."

Relief burned through me, a scalding counterpoint to the cold fury I still felt toward Irian's actions during the melee. But I fought to keep any emotion from showing on my face. I made my voice stone. "You don't get to make this about him."

"Is it not already?" Irian's tone dropped dangerously. "Would you have longed to go up against Eala and the bardaí had she not made your prince her thrall? Would you be so determined to remake more Treasures if *his* life was not at stake? Would you have been so quick to compete in the tournament if Eala had not named him her champion?"

"That's not fair," I said. "Do I want to free him from Eala's influence? Do I care whether he lives or dies? Yes and yes. But he has never been my first priority—I was never his."

"Then what is, colleen? Because it is certainly not me."

My stomach pulled itself into a complicated knot. "What are you talking about?"

"Almost from the moment you arose from that lough, Fia, you have been at odds with me." I hated the shadows darkening his gaze. "When I wanted to parley with the She-Wolf, you insisted we fight. When I begged you to come with me away from the territories of the bardaí, you wanted to stay. Where I yearn to unmake our Treasures and lift our inevitable death sentence, you long to create more. Why can you not seem to bring yourself to agree with me on anything?"

"Is that what you want from me?" I spat. "Thoughtless obedience? Slavish subservience? I may have bound my heart to you, Irian. But I did not promise you my mind or my will."

"You cannot truly think such things of me." Irian's hand glided along my cheek, brushing my hair behind my ear as his palm cupped my nape. "You have always been and will always be my equal. But this is my world, colleen. I know things you cannot. Yet still you defy me."

"*Defy you?*" I jerked my head out of his grasp. "I could defy you a thousand times, and it would not forgive what you did to me. You hurt me—you made me *bleed.*"

Again, Irian gripped me. This time, he spun me to face the window. The smooth, cold glass reflected the light at our backs, making a ghostly mirror for our faces—mine wan and fierce eyed; his stark browed and shadowed save for the stars of his eyes.

"Yes, I made you bleed." His thumb skimmed gently over my skin, indicating the line he'd cut along my cheek. It was the first time I'd seen it—less than an inch in length, and so shallow it had already scabbed over. For such a monumental wound, it was remarkably tiny. It would not even scar. "To save your life. And I would have done more. I will do whatever I must. Fia, I would die for you."

I stared at him in our shared reflection. "Why would you think I'd ever want you to die for me? You tried that before, remember? It didn't go so well."

"Because *you* died instead. Took the sacrifice I was meant to make. Traded your life for mine—"

"Would you rather I hadn't?" I snapped, turning. "Should I have let you die to save your pride?"

"This has nothing to do with my pride," he growled.

"Are you sure?" My tone sliced sharp. "Then why don't you try living for me for half a second, instead of trying so hard to die for me?"

"I do not know if I can do that, colleen." Irian's hands fell away, and he backed up a step. "How can I truly live when I know you will soon die? I cannot. After I win the tournament and unforge your Treasure, I will do all you have asked of me. I will defeat Eala and free your princeling. I will bring the bardaí to heel. Then I *will* die for you, Fia—either on the battlefield or when I tithe my Treasure in thirteen years. And I will do it gladly—as long as I know *you* are safe."

"Unforge...*my* Treasure?" His words slid down my spine like poison sap, sticky and burning. I stared at him, renewed fury mingling with the horror coiling around my heart. "Irian, you can't do that. You cannot take this from me, when I have only just found it." The words came out rushed, forceful. I clutched at the Heart of the Forest as green unfurled behind my eyes and sizzled against my collar. "It is mine, in a way nothing has ever been before. If you truly want to protect me, then you would not dream of taking it from me. Such a thing would break my heart."

"To be forced to watch you die for it ever again would break mine."

"Irian—" I was so tired of this conflict. Tired of the huge cracks rending the spaces between us. Tired of the shadows darkening his eyes. And though bringing our bodies closer together could not crowd out our problems, I reached for him. "You have to stop trying to control every little thing. You have to stop trying to control *me*—"

But his eyes had snagged on one of my fingers. His hand followed a moment later, catching my wrist and twisting my hand toward the light.

"What is this?" Starlight limned the gold-and-silver ring Wayland had given me. Lightning flashed in Irian's eyes as they registered sudden, savage recognition. "Wayland gave you his mother's ring?"

"It's not what you think—"

"Is that where you were?" His mouth hardened into a merciless line. "What happened between you two last night? I told you to kiss him, colleen. Not fuck him."

I wrenched my wrist out of his grasp, rancor prickling vicious vines up my rigid spine. A moment later, my collar responded, burning white-hot lines of pain through my veins. I gasped and doubled over, clawing at my throat as I fought to clear my blurring vision. When I straightened, Irian was reaching for me, concern banishing the harshness from his features. But it was too late— even as my collar quieted, another kind of pain snarled through me, savaging my bones with a thousand sharp, hot thorns.

"Don't touch me!" I cried out, lifting a trembling palm between us. Irian fell back, remorse making a wasteland of his face. I reached for the windowsill, steadying myself.

"Fia." His tone was urgent; his expression, stark. "I did not mean it. I went too far. Forgive me."

"You keep going too far," I managed, through the strangling hold of the metal around my throat. "But things can only go so far before they're finished."

I wasn't sure if I meant for now...or forever. Irian didn't ask.

"Please, colleen. Let me try to make it right. What would you have me do?"

All I could do was glare at him as I clung to the windowsill. "Just go."

This arrested Irian—for a long moment, he held himself perfectly still. "Go, colleen?"

"Yes, go!" I picked up a pillow off the bed and hurled it at him. Hard. "Get out!"

He caught it one-handed. "Where would you prefer I sleep?"

"I had no idea where you were last night—why should tonight be any different?" I flung another pillow at him. "Make a bed out of snow. Burn yourself to a crisp on the smith-king's forge. Bed up against the door. Just get out of my sight!"

Irian paused with both pillows clutched to his chest, the linens already smeared with his opponents' drying blood. His eyes were incandescent in the dim. Then he dropped the bedding to the floor and approached me with light, deliberate footsteps. I refused to back away. He stopped inches away from me, tilting his head. He did not touch me, but his voice was a caress over my boiling skin.

"Banish me from our chambers. Hurl all the insults you can think of. I will endure whatever punishment you deem appropriate. But remember one thing, colleen." His touch on my chin was brief. Nevertheless, it forced my eyes up to his. "We are bound by magic no one can sunder. And I will always fight to protect you—even if that means fighting against you."

His words made me restless with confusion. Desire. Renewed fury. "Keep fighting against me? And you may lose me."

His shoulders bunched as he lowered his head, raven hair fanning down over his eyes. "I am doing this *for* you."

"You've said that before." I picked up one last armful of bedding and thrust it at him. "But I can't for the life of me see how it's true."

Reflexively, he gripped the bedding. He retreated. The door clicked shut behind him.

I turned, slammed my foot into the wall, then immediately regretted it when pain glanced up my calf toward my hip. I spun in a tense circle, wishing I'd kept one pillow on the bed—just to scream into. I stalked into the bathroom, spinning the taps until scalding water gushed out in the basin. A moment later, I changed my mind, jerking them shut once more. I paced to the wardrobe, then back to the window, restless energy cascading over my skin in waves of heat and cold. Tentatively, I crossed to the door, cracking it open an inch.

To my great irritation, Irian had taken me at my word—he'd bedded down in front of the door with the linens I'd discarded in anger. Against the nacre glow of the hallways, he was a blight of blackness, with his dark head burrowed into the shadow of his blood-spattered cloak.

Donn damn him.

"Take the cursed bed, Irian." I stepped over his prone form and crossed the hallway. "I'll stay with the girls."

Laoise instantly opened the door at my soft knock, startling me. I'd expected everyone to be sleeping, especially after all the carousing the girls had been doing. But the Gentry maiden was wide awake, fully dressed, and armored in polished scale mail that fit her like a glove, forged from a material I had no name for. It glowed red and rose gold in the pale light filtering in from the hall.

"My lady?" she said, in her lilting accent. "Is something the matter?"

"Don't call me that." I craned my neck over her shoulder, trying to see into the darkened rooms. "Can I come in?"

She took in my own armor—dirty and bloody after the tournament and damp after tromping through Wayland's pleasure gardens—then inclined her crimson head. She locked the door behind me and stood with her back against it.

"Is everything well, my . . . Fia?"

"Not really." I spun on my heel, taking in the darkened sitting room, beyond which the bedrooms were dark and silent. "Where are Chandi and Sinéad?"

"Sleeping," Laoise said, a little tightly.

I turned back to her, my gaze sharpening at the tone of her voice. Not only was she awake, dressed, and armored, but the dark cloak draped over a nearby chair bore telltale swaths of melting snow. Her boots were wet on the carpet. Even the red curls falling over her ember eyes were damp. As if she had been outside—and recently. Sudden suspicion warred with panic, and my hands found my skeans as I swiftly crossed to open one of the bedroom doors. After a moment, my adjusting eyes found two female shapes lumped on the bed. I held my breath until I heard their soft snores. Then I eased the door shut once more.

"Why were you outside?" I hissed as I sheathed my blades. "Are you not here to protect the girls?"

"They are—as you see—sleeping safely," Laoise reiterated, a bite to her tone. "I told you of my clandestine aspirations in coming to the island. But if you prefer I limit my excursions to the daytime, I shall try my best."

I had honestly forgotten Laoise's true intentions for accompanying us to Emain Ablach. She was here to secretly inspect the nemeton—the Grove of Gold—without attracting Gavida's notice. All evidence pointed to her story being true—that she was truly a Gentry warrior disenfranchised by the downfall of the Septs and reluctant to swear oaths of allegiance to the bardaí. She had been nothing but friendly, solicitous, and protective toward Chandi and Sinéad.

So why didn't I trust her?

"Apologies," I said after a moment. "It has been a day."

"I know," Laoise replied, with a touch of sympathy. "We all saw."

I felt suddenly flayed, as though my skin had been ripped off and she could see beneath it to the ragged meat of me, twined with bitter vines and slick with humiliation. I changed the subject. "What have you discovered of the sacred grove?"

"Not much," she admitted. "There is undoubtedly magic

flowing through it, but it will take me more time to discern from whence it arises. Or, for that matter, where it goes."

Her words nudged up against everything Wayland had told me—or, rather, everything I'd guessed through our somewhat agonizing game of twenty questions. But I wasn't sure I should tell the mysterious Gentry maiden anything that could incriminate me to Gavida. I wasn't sure I should tell *anyone*.

"I'm exhausted. Do you mind...?"

"Of course." She gestured at the long settee in front of the window. "Bathe. Sleep. Eat. But if there's nothing else, I'll bid you good night."

She slung her dripping cloak over one shoulder and disappeared into the second bedroom without another word.

I slowly lowered myself onto the chaise. My bones felt stiff; my mind, a frenzied chaos of misgivings. But the moment I laid my head on the pillow, I fell into a deep, aching sleep.

I'd dropped Wayland's ring in deep water. I dived, reaching for it, but it sank. Deeper, deeper. My lungs imploded as my breath ran out. I turned, swam for the surface. But it was so terribly far away. At last, an arm appeared, reaching for me through the surf. I grasped it, grateful. But the hand *burned*. I gasped, inhaling water as my palm exploded in fire. My would-be savior would not let me go—my burnt hand came away, slipping off my arm like a glove.

As I sank like a stone into the depths—my blood floating green as grass upon the wind-ruffled sea—I saw Laoise's flaming face staring down at me.

I woke with a start to find all three women—Chandi, Sinéad, and Laoise—watching me. I jerked myself upright, squinting against the rheumy light filtering in through ice-stitched panes.

"Huh?" I said stupidly.

Chandi laughed and pushed a cup of hot mushroom mud into my limp hands. "Did you know you talk in your sleep?"

I blew across the steaming surface of my cup. "I do not."

"You do." Sinéad raised her voice into a falsetto. "*Kiss me, kiss me, gorgeous prince, before I die.*"

I choked on the bitter black brew, coughing for a long moment before glaring up at the girls. It didn't help that I wasn't sure which *prince* they were referring to. "I resent that."

"Duly noted." Laoise sat down next to Chandi, perching her own steaming cup on one knee. "But I think it's time to decide, Fia. Stay? Or go?"

That woke me up fully. I swung my legs in front of me and set down my cup. "What do you mean?"

"You are at odds with your lord husband—we all saw what happened yesterday." Laoise's eyes dropped to my hand. "And though you have seemingly accepted the prionsa's token, I do not think you harbor any true feelings for him. So do you truly wish to see this thing through to its bitter end? Or do we four chart a new path away from here?"

My hand curled over Wayland's signet ring as I cursed Laoise's canny nature. Despite the bluntness of her words, she wasn't wrong. And under other circumstances, I might have simply run away—from Gavida, from Wayland, from Irian. From all of it. But that was before I'd learned who Wayland was—*what* he was. He was my one chance at resurrecting more Treasures. I needed him— needed him without a collar chaining away his magic.

And to free him, I had to discover where Gavida was keeping the magic he stole—from Wayland, from me, from the boisterous, eager crowds churning his arena to a fervor.

"There's a third option." I slowly spun Wayland's ring around my finger. "But I have to know I can trust you." I glanced at Laoise, my nightmare still lingering, before training my gaze on Chandi and Sinéad. "All of you."

"Call us feckless," Sinéad said, "for exchanging one sister for another. But you are all we have, Fia. So however bad my aim, my daggers are pointed wherever you need them."

"A heartwarming speech." Chandi fake-scowled at Sinéad.

I smiled, a little bleakly, then turned to Laoise. "And you?"

"I am at your service, my lady." Her Gentry formality crept back in. "If you ask for my oath, I will give it. Although I beg you: Do not ask."

For a long moment, I strongly considered it. I had no real reason to mistrust Laoise save my native suspicion. Yes, she was an unknown quantity. But she had done nothing but help me—help my friends. Who was I to demand her unflinching fealty? I was no queen, no general. I was newly made and recklessly forged and sharp with all my dark thorns.

And I was tired of seeing good-hearted people leashed by people who thought they knew best.

"What would an oath be, if not a collar?" I said softly. "I have no desire to see your will subsumed to mine. Take me or leave me, No-Oath Laoise, once of the Sept of Scales. But if you betray me, it will be upon your own conscience. And if I find you, I'll kill you."

"That's a bargain I can accept." Laoise grinned, exposing a beautiful smile full of lovely teeth. "Now tell us what this third path is."

"We're going to spend the next five days of the tournament uncovering the source of the smith-king's great power," I told them. "And then we're going to destroy him."

Chapter Twenty-Three

With our shivering backs turned toward the wind-frothed ocean, Laoise, Chandi, Sinéad, Linn, and I stared into the dripping dark of the pale stone caverns far below Aduantas.

Well, Linn wasn't staring into the caverns. She was staring at me, with those vengeful green eyes, and trying to psychically explain why she didn't want to explore the caves with us.

My pronouncement that morning had been met with varying reactions from the girls. Laoise had smiled in a way I hoped would never be turned on me. But Chandi and Sinéad had exchanged a worried glance.

"That seems like a terrible idea," Chandi had told me.

"Ever the optimist." Sinéad had elbowed her. "You could at least let her tell us what she's planning."

"Good idea," said Laoise cannily. "What *are* you planning?"

I chewed on my lip, uncertain how much I could—or should—tell them. "Gavida is stealing magic and hoarding it somewhere. The Tournament of Kings is a sham, a way to harness the power he so desperately craves. And he refuses to let his son and heir rise into his destiny."

"So this is about Wayland?" Laoise asked.

"Yes." I decided to be as honest as possible. "But it's not only about him. It's about what Gavida did to Irian when he was little more than a child. It's about what he did to me, a few nights ago." I touched my fingertip to my collar, which sizzled a warning against my skin. Greenery frothed restlessly between my ribs and made an uneasy tangle around my heart. "It's who he's allowed to come here, and what he's allowed her to do. It's about a tyrant who has gone too long unopposed and unchallenged."

"That's all well and good," Chandi said. "But what are you hoping to get from all this? Beyond that collar off your neck?"

Wayland's promises swirled through my mind, energizing as cold water dancing over smooth stones. "Yes, this collar off my throat. But also the gratitude of an heir. The backing of a powerful island nation. And, if all goes to plan, another Treasure renewed and reforged."

Laoise's eyebrows jumped toward her hairline. Chandi's mouth made a complicated twist.

"And what happens," Sinéad asked, "if we get caught?"

"I'm not asking any of you to do anything wrong," I promised. "For now, all we need is information. About how Gavida siphons the magic. Where he keeps it. And how he uses it."

But that revelation started its own debate. Despite Wayland's claims about the crucible, I thought the smith-king's forge seemed like the best place to start looking.

"Are you mad?" Laoise laughed, sardonic. "If he is truly so powerful, do you think he would leave his sanctum unguarded, unwarded? Even if the door was miraculously unlocked—which it won't be—there could be forgings designed to maim or kill intruders. There could be magical alarums to steal your voice or blister your ears. Enchantments designed to transform you into a statue until the smith-king finds the time to torture you."

"Point taken." Sinéad looked ashen. "Perhaps you could ask Wayland about a library or archive—there may be schematics for Aduantas, for the city—"

"I felt something strange lurking underground, before my magic was curtailed," I cut in. "Below the Grove of Gold—*far* below. You were at the grove last night, Laoise—is there aught to be learned from the nemeton?"

"Little of interest." An idea sparked in her eyes. "But the aughiskies—they're stabled far below Aduantas, are they not?"

"In caverns cutting into the island." I stood, smiled. "Seems as good a place to start as any."

Sinéad and Laoise had followed me without argument. Only Chandi had seemed discomfited by the notion, but if she had any objections, she kept them to herself.

Now, I faced off with Linn, who was shaking her surf-slick mane and chomping her shark teeth at me in a way that felt personal. She was trying to push a vision into my mind, but I was having a hard time deciphering it—all I saw were lines of darkness imprinted against a greater darkness; silvery lines of moisture dripping down from pale blades of stone; long sleek rocks lumped along the corridors and humping out of the deep puddles slicking the passageways.

I rubbed at the line forming between my brows. "Have you explored the caverns? Do you know where they lead?"

The water horse flared her delicate nostrils, whickered with growing annoyance, then turned in a tight, aggravated circle to face the yawning caverns. She pranced toward them, tossing her mane and feigning insouciance. Abruptly, she stopped, flattening her ears to her skull as she mimed listening. A moment later, she reared back, a surge of lithe muscle and flashing hooves, whinnying with a shriek that split the afternoon in half. I jerked back, reaching for my skeans as I searched the shadows for whatever Linn had seen. My fear ricocheted through the other girls too—they stumbled away from the entrance. But an instant later, Linn settled completely, turning unruffled emerald eyes to stare pointedly at me once more.

"Morrigan," I breathed as adrenaline pumped through my veins. "Something attacked you? Something in the caves?"

Linn stomped her hooves and lowered her head, once more pushing a vision into my mind. This time, I paid more attention— to the plinking of moisture off the nearly invisible stalactites; the bare sheen of light illuminating long stretches of deceptively deep water; the tubular ridges of pale stone lurching between deep, angular rifts—

No—not *stone*. They were *limbs*. Huge and nearly motionless in the dark, the creature had a sleek pale pelt and black ears. It lounged half in and half out of the water, deep in the twisting caverns. It stretched, languorous, revealing curved claws and a yawning mouth spiked with foot-long fangs. When it opened its eyes, they were red as the heart of a flame.

I cursed. Then described what I'd seen to the girls.

"A dobhar-chú," said Laoise, wonder warring with fear in her voice.

"A *what*?" Chandi asked.

"King otters. Dog-fish. They have many names, all of which I thought to be legendary. But they are said to be impossibly fast. Strong. Vicious. They feast on the flesh of other Folk. Tales also say they once guarded the Un-Dry Cauldron—the Treasure of the Sept of Fins."

I bit my tongue at that. Now that I knew the secret of the Treasures, I had a hard time believing any tánaiste would need—much less want—an honor guard of colossal, flesh-devouring otters.

"It must be guarding something," I surmised. "Which means we're on the right track—there's something here Gavida doesn't want us to find. Doesn't want *any* of us to find." Linn flashed me a vision of all four of us lying eviscerated, the pale stone walls of the caverns splashed with blood. I took her point. "Any ideas how to get past it?"

"They were said to be practically invincible," Laoise said. "Their white pelts grow so densely they cannot be pierced by normal blades."

My thoughts immediately flew to Irian...and the Sky-Sword.

It was no ordinary blade, and he, no ordinary wielder. He would make quick, easy work of a cannibal dog-fish. Almost against my will, my eyes slid up toward the city, where somewhere not too far away he would be preparing for the Trial of Speed.

My husband had his own battles to fight. And I had a shabby kind of instinct to keep him out of this.

"The fellow who sold me these." Sinéad fingered the hilts of her new throwing knives, thoughtful. "The brùnaidh with the peddler's cart, at the feis the other night. Before he left, he said something to you, Laoise. In the ancient tongue. What was it again?"

Laoise blanched slightly, a twinge of discomfort wrinkling her pert nose. "He told me he was a purveyor of strange glories, curious coincidences, and weird weapons. And that should we need any more sharp blades, we would be welcome to visit his shop in the lower city."

Strange glories, curious coincidences, and weird weapons. Just perfect. Because I needed more intrigue in my life.

"It's worth a try." I glanced into the horrid honeycomb of pale stone, dark shadow, and waiting mouths, and shuddered. "Maybe he'll know a way we can get past Gavida's pet."

Linn snapped her shark teeth and bannered her tail, as if to say, *When you come back, I want to help.*

"Thanks." I turned toward the slippery stone steps leading back to the city. A moment later, I glanced back, shooting the aughisky an amused look. "By the way, Linn—if this whole demon horse thing doesn't work out for you, you should strongly consider a career on the stage."

They called it the Shielings—the wind-pocked, tide-striped spit of land below the city gate but above the docks. It was cramped with buildings—tenements brushing elbows with taverns and curio shops and smithies and fishmongers. There were no graceful seashell roofs, no manicured topiaries or gently curving avenues. This was the real city—rough-hewn wooden beams and uneven stone walls and gutters overflowing with snowmelt and garbage.

I imagined it usually teemed with activity. Now, with the second Trial in full swing, it was nearly empty—only a handful of Folk minding shops or drinking alone at deserted taverns. Far above us the arena was nearly obscured by the sharp spires of Aduantas, but we could hear the rhythmic ebb and crash of cheering, the frenetic pulsation of frenzied cries. The sound put a hard knot at the base of my throat.

Thoughts of Irian clambered through my mind and dragged my attention toward the noise and light and energy of the amphitheater. I allowed myself to wonder what he was doing. What Trial had been set to test his speed? He would surely win a normal footrace— he was fleet as a thoroughbred and agile as a will-o'-the-wisp. But the first Trial had shocked me with its brutality.

I had a feeling the ones to follow would be no less designed to twist and torment.

"This way," Laoise said from ten paces ahead, where she'd waylaid a blind-drunk gruagach who had likely been eliminated from yesterday's Trial, judging by the long, ragged cut scoring his face from hairline to jaw. "The curiosity shop is well known, if I understood his mumbling correctly."

Sandwiched between two listing stone buildings, the shop in question was incredibly narrow, compressed almost into a triangle. Its facade was an odd blend of eerie and cheerful—chipped blue paint coiled with faded, smudged designs like staring eyes and outstretched hands. Chimes dangled from the windows, tinkling atonal secrets to the fading afternoon. The door was a circle of polished bones; when Laoise stepped forward to knock on it, it cried out as if in pain. A chill coiled down my spine, and I touched the Heart above my breast for comfort.

"Horrifying," said Chandi in an undertone.

"Folk should really keep to the forests," Sinéad said back, just as softly. "Things get weird when they start to build cities."

The door creaked open. A small figure covered all over in thick brown hair and clothed in a dapper suit of dark blue wool poked his head around the doorframe. Upon seeing us, he flung it fully open.

"Honored patrons!" he crowed with glee. "Come in, come in!"

Laoise stepped inside without hesitation. The rest of us exchanged a glance, then followed suit.

The inside was as cramped and eccentric as the outside. Floor-to-ceiling shelves swayed dangerously over narrow corridors. The floorboards were choked with objects of a thousand different forms—glass decanters shaped like moth's wings, barrels burping with blobs of effervescent colors, bales of dried leaves whispering autumn-toned promises. Dried flowers and herbs and garlands of gemstones were hung from the ceiling, hissing and clinking at our passing. The brùnaidh led us through the morass, then leapt up onto a stool behind a low counter. He was short and sturdy, with a humanoid face framed by long, tapered ears. He spread his too-long, too-slim arms as if to indicate his domain.

"Welcome, friends!" Behind his charming spectacles, his eyes were the color of coal. His teeth were tiny and rounded, like a child's. "What may I interest you in today? Bottled nightmares or stoppered dreams? A blade to carve away your darkest memories? A Second Chance potion, for a much desired do-over?"

I stepped forward. "We seek not curiosities, Master—"

"Blink," he said, with a wink. "What, then, do you seek?"

"First, we seek a promise of discretion," Laoise interjected before I could continue. "That whatever we speak of or procure today will remain confidential."

The brùnaidh's eyes glittered before he nodded. "A promise easily made for such beautiful patrons. What secrets shall we keep today?"

"We seek a weapon to kill a dobhar-chú," I said.

"Indeed?" The brùnaidh clasped his hands with glee. "I will warn you—such a thing may not come cheap."

"Tell us whether you have what we seek, Master Blink," I said. "Then we may talk price."

Master Blink gamboled toward an armoire listing sideways into a wall tiled with the carapaces of dead horseshoe crabs and flung it open. Inside, an astonishing array of weaponry shifted and clattered, swinging from hooks or stacked on the floor or simply embedded in the hard dark wood. I spied maces and axes and daggers and spears and swords, but there were many sharp metallic things I simply had no names for. My blood quickened at the sight of all that caged death, a sudden fierce wariness warring with a bloodthirsty tremor that spiked green against the waiting metal of my collar.

"We shall certainly be able to find what you seek," Blink crowed. "Do you wish to hear the cost?"

Behind me, Laoise shifted in place.

"Go on," I commanded.

"In return for a weapon to slay a dobhar-chú, we ask for one golden apple from the smith-king's blessed grove, untouchable by any but his own bloodline," said Blink, with a generous heaping of slyness. "You desire discretion? This price will ensure we both provide it."

A thrill sang through me at the memory of the Grove of Gold— the way the gilded trees had blossomed and fruited simultaneously, the sensuous magic unfurling below their thick, gnarled trunks. I glanced over at Laoise, even as a pang of conscience pierced me—it seemed almost dastardly to covet those gleaming apples, to disturb the growth of their perfectly pristine and deliciously tempting flesh. But if I did not agree to Blink's deal, then this was yet another dead end. What I needed was a path forward. I couldn't return to Wayland empty-handed. We were already short on time—today had set us even further back.

Laoise seemed as intrigued as Blink, so I said, "Done. I will return with your apple tomorrow. Be prepared to hand over the weapon I've asked for."

"Shall we shake on it?" Blink turned his head and spat a viscous glob into his palm, which he held out to me with his too-long arms. I fought down a surge of disgust, then slowly spat into my own hand.

Laoise caught my arm in the moment before we shook.

"That will do, shopkeeper." Her fingertips, in the brief instant before they fell from my elbow, scorched my skin. "Do not test our credulity. We will bring you your apple, and you will give us the weapon. We need not extend the drama."

"As you wish, lady." Blink never dropped his wide, childlike smile. "I will expect you on the morrow."

We shuffled out of the cramped, creepy shop. Once the bone door clattered shut behind us, Laoise rounded on me.

"Have you never been warned about entering into bargains with the Folk?"

"I have," I protested. "It seemed a straightforward trade."

"A weapon for an apple? Perhaps," Laoise chided. "But your saliva was not part of the bargain. And that, you were prepared to give him freely."

A chill swept over my skin, making the places where her fingers had gripped me burn hotter. I put a hand to my elbow, an odd chill sweeping over me even as gratitude brittled my bones. Laoise was right—I hadn't thought twice about that handshake. But now Cathair's endless warnings about the Folk slivered through me like broken glass. Just one hair from your head could become a noose to choke you with. A toenail could force you to dance endless reels upon hot coals. What might Blink have done with my saliva, had I willingly and heedlessly offered it to him?

I thought abruptly of Wayland and the kiss I still owed him. Would it truly be the thing to set me free from my blood debt to him? Or would it simply be a new kind of bargain—a more tacit kind of bargain? One I hadn't fully agreed to? The prospect spooled skeins of hot and cold around my shivering spine.

"Then you have my thanks, No-Oath Laoise, for preventing

disaster." I gave her a slight bow, and she inclined her head in response.

"What now?" asked Chandi. She and Sinéad both looked uncomfortable—the brùnaidh and Laoise's reaction to his manipulations had rattled them. I could sympathize. We were all strangers to this island, but they were also *human* in a way I was not. At least, not anymore.

"The Trial of Speed must have ended," Laoise said, nodding at the laughing, chattering Folk beginning to trickle down through the alleyways of the Shielings. The snow had stopped, and taverns were unshuttering their thresholds. Private residences also began to throw open their doors. If the past few nights were any indication, all of Emain Ablach would soon be one massive feis. "If we do not wish to have our movements marked, we ought to either return to Aduantas...or lose ourselves in the festivities." She glanced at me. "If we can."

She had a point. There was a certain anonymity to the citywide revelry—although perhaps not for me. Even hooded and plainly dressed, I had drawn more than one stare from the passing Folk. Between the spectacle I'd created with Linn two nights ago and the drama Irian and I had played out during the melee, I had a feeling I was the object of some gossip.

"We should all return to Aduantas," I said slowly. "We'll dress in our finery, kindly bestowed upon us by the generous smith-king. Then we will make our rounds at the parties. I'll go to Wayland, convince him to use his *bloodline* to help us procure an apple. The rest of you...perhaps you can find an off-duty palace attendant and get him drunk. Find out what wards Gavida has protecting his crucible. Any information about the layout of the city or the secrets of Gavida's powers would be of great use to us. But be clever and subtle and safe. There is no cause to put yourself in any danger on my—or Wayland's—account." I glanced at the trio of women, assessing their reactions. "Any comments, questions, critiques?"

"It's a good plan." Sinéad's sapphire eyes sparked with a note of wicked anticipation. I remembered the zeal with which she'd hurled those knives at the wall the other night. "Perhaps it's time to trick the tricksters."

Chandi nodded, too, although she looked a touch less enthused than her swan sister. Laoise pulled her hood up over her gleaming auburn curls with a decisive jerk.

"Then let us use the crowds to our advantage," she suggested. "Anyone who sees us return to Aduantas will think we came from the arena, and will not mark our passing."

We lowered our heads, climbing through the pale polished city toward its silver crown—a sleek and sumptuous tiara upon a rotten, hollow head.

Chapter Twenty-Four

I steeled myself to reenter the chambers I shared with Irian. I'd considered asking one of the other women to lend me a gown, but Sinéad and Chandi were both taller than I was; Laoise, although closer to my height, had a deliciously curving figure I couldn't hope to match. After the stir I'd caused the other night, I had no intention of wearing Corra's scarlet-and-black extravaganza again. But the other kirtle I'd brought from Dún Darragh still hung in the wardrobe, along with a half dozen magically tailored gowns provided by the smith-king. I'd be a fool not to make use of them for tonight's intrigues.

So I gently pushed open the unlocked door to our rooms, praying to any listening gods that Irian had not yet returned from the arena.

Perhaps they were listening but had a cruel sense of humor. For Irian was there, sitting on the edge of the bed with his head in his hands. I froze, but he'd already heard me. He stood swiftly, his gaze colliding with mine. Afternoon had not yet withered toward evening—his blue-gold eyes, still so unfamiliar to me, dazzled across the room. He swayed a step toward me, then stopped himself. His huge hands clenched into fists, then forcibly relaxed.

"You were not at the arena today, colleen," he said.

"How do you know that?" I forced my feet toward the wardrobe, forced my tone breezy.

"Because I looked for you. At length. I scanned ten thousand faces, and not one of them was yours."

"Did you?" I dared a glance at him over my shoulder as I rifled through the garments. "In that case, the Trial of Speed sounds boring, and I'm glad I did not attend."

Irian lurched a step closer. My whole body sang for him to be so close and yet so far away—as if every curve of my flesh yearned for his touch. "Do you wish to know what happened?"

"Not really." I stared hard at a lacy periwinkle gown embossed with silver thread and studded with teardrop pearls, barely seeing it at all. "It was a race. I assume someone ran the fastest and won."

"It was indeed a race, colleen. But Gavida's Trials are rarely as they seem. And they are not designed to be won. They are designed to be a spectacle. And the spectacle these Folk yearn for is magic, mayhem, and bloodshed."

I turned to face him. I raked his tall, powerful figure from head to toe. He looked unusually rumpled, as if he'd been running his fingers through his lengthening hair. But otherwise, he was just Irian—stark, dangerous, gorgeous. "You seem perfectly unharmed. If you're trying to prove to me how dangerous the tournament is, you're doing a poor job of it."

"These were the rules of the race: *The faster your feet strike the ground, the farther the finish line becomes.*"

"A riddle?"

"A riddle. Tell me, colleen—how would *you* have solved it?"

Resentment needled heat through my marrow. "You took away my opportunity to find out."

"Let me tell you how others solved it," he ground out. "Many did not. They ran as fast as they could—some until their hearts burst—only for the finish line to grow more and more distant. Some tried to run backward. Or walk on their hands. But most soon intuited that if your feet did not strike the ground, the finish line did not move. And do you know what they used as stepping stones, in the absence of any other solutions? Bodies. *Dead* bodies. Slain bodies—a gruesome ribbon of unflinching murder in pursuit of a singular goal: the Oak King's Crown."

Bile rose in my gorge, hot and acidic. I wanted to turn away from the image Irian painted—I wanted to believe it wasn't true. But I knew he wasn't lying. And with that realization came another forceful, terrible image—a blank-eyed, golden-haired prince lying in a pool of his own blood as Folk trampled over his weak human form. What had Eala made Rogan do? What had Eala let happen to him?

"Rogan?" I heard myself ask, panic threading my voice.

"He moved on to the next Trial, on the backs of twoscore dead Folk." Irian's eyes darkened to steel, mirroring the slow, leaden fade beyond the glass of our windows. "But of course your first thought is for *him*."

"Do you wish me to fawn over your safety, Irian?" My hands curled into tight little fists. "As I said, I can see you are perfectly well—you stand whole and hale before me."

"No, Fia—do not trouble yourself with concern for me." His voice was dangerously even, menacingly quiet. "I beg you to think, for once, about yourself. I know you have not forgiven me for eliminating you from the tournament. But please consider the violence—the mortal danger—I have spared you."

"With decisions you have stolen!" I spun helplessly to the wardrobe, slammed the door shut, spun back. "Can you not see what this has made you? You are the same as Eala—you have stolen my will as decisively as she has stolen Rogan's!"

"The same—" Shock pulled Irian's eyes wide in the moment before his gaze shuttered completely. "I know you are angry, but there is no cause to be cruel. I did this for you. For *us*."

"Because you believe you know better than me!" I cried. "Do you know what Eala said, when I begged her to set Rogan free?

Free will is so imperfect. Autonomy, overrated. Perhaps you have lived too long alone, Irian. Or perhaps you do not see me as a whole person—perhaps you think I am, as you said, nothing more than a part of yourself you do not wish to lose. Regardless, you have deemed my autonomy inconvenient to your own goals. So you decided to take my choices away completely."

Irian closed the space between us, reaching for one of my raised hands and pulling me toward him. Despite everything, my body responded to his—my palm molding to his hand, my hips swaying toward his thighs, my eyes rising to his. But his silvering gaze was jagged and wretched, cooling the warmth his closeness conjured.

"You went to see Eala?" he growled. "Alone?"

"That's not the point." I stared up at him, daring him to disagree. "I am not afraid of her."

"You should be," he forced out. "We both saw what she is capable of, the night of the Ember Moon. And it is *exactly my point.* You take reckless risks, put yourself in unnecessary danger. I can no longer trust your instincts—"

"And I can no longer trust you!" I snarled up at him. "I need a partner, an equal. A *husband*, Irian. Someone who will fight with me, not against me. Not another person in my life trying to control me. Not a captor."

For a long, anguished moment, Irian was silent. "I only wish to stop worrying about you, Fia. You are my wife—"

"Of that burden, at least, I can relieve you." A blank, numb haze descended over my vision, and I mustered the will to wrench my hand out of his. A harsh prospect clawed at my ribs from the inside—terrible enough to crack me open. "Whatever duty of protection you think you owe me, I release you from it."

"No." Irian's whole body went rigid as iron. His pupils blew wide and horribly black. Outside the window, a sudden stiff wind gusted up, flinging hail against the glass. "You do not mean that."

"Now you dare tell me you know what my own words mean?" I ground out. "If my behavior bothers you so much, then let me bother you no more. You want to stop worrying about your wife? Congratulations—you no longer have a wife to worry about."

"No, colleen." His voice was nearly inaudible over the sudden howling wind. Out the window, a single jag of lightning spiked silver. A distant, ominous growl of thunder shook the towers of Aduantas. "You cannot do that."

"Another thing you won't let me do?" My voice was jagged; my eyes, when I furiously blinked them, burned wet. "Come, *Husband*—we both know our wedding wasn't real. It was a rushed handfasting arising from desperation. Neither of us expected you to live out the night. You didn't even ask me to be your wife—you asked me to be your widow. Or don't you remember?"

"It was real, Fia." He slid his hand over my palm to grip my wrist, a gesture identical to the one we'd made that fateful night. My tattoos against his own. Thorns and feathers; feathers and thorns. "We were bound in love—magic no one can sunder."

"Except us." I stared down at our joined hands. "What is a marriage, if not a promise? And what is that promise, if it is a lie? If this past week has shown me anything, it is that you and I are not one flesh. We are not one bone. And you are not—" I choked on the words as another barrage of lightning slashed silver across the seething sky.

"Please do not say it." Irian's voice was nearly soundless, but his shoulders trembled with the force of his words. Behind him, the window rattled like a great beast in chains. "Fia—"

My name on his pleading lips tore a hole in my composure, shoving a tumult of dappled green and furious growth through my simmering veins. I gasped as the power frothed up my spine and crashed against the brutal metal barrier of my collar. Pain impaled the base of my skull, whiting my vision and pushing the half-willing words from my frozen mouth.

"You are not my home."

The window shattered. A cold tempest of howling wind and growling thunder scattered broken glass over the tile to glitter like

tiny fallen stars. Prongs of lightning slashed between slicing gusts
of sheeting hail, white-hot tongues of crackling fire licking at the
tower. I lifted an involuntary arm to protect my eyes from the barrage of light and sound.

When I lowered it, Irian was nowhere to be seen. A flurry of
black feathers—gleaming with a hellebore luster—floated deso-
lately down to rest amid the litter of broken glass and melting ice.
Thunder still grumbled, but far away—as if the storm had passed
as swiftly as it had blown up. And I knew he was gone—flown
away on black wings into a blackening night. Relief and envy tangled in me—relief that he had chosen to remove himself from our
ruinous fight instead of continuing the conflict; envy that he could
simply soar off in the form of his anam cló, while I was trapped
here, in every way that counted.

With numb, trembling fingers, I picked up the pale blue dress
from where I'd dropped it. I brushed shards of window glass from
its lacy bodice. The teardrop pearls trembled from the neckline as
if they might fall. As if from a distance, I noticed that the markings
twining my arms had changed—only vines now climbed my skin,
flowering yet thorned.

I fisted my hands in the fine fabric, swallowing the roughness
lining my throat and blinking back the salt in my eyes until everything I didn't want to feel was safely encased in the protected space
between my ribs.

I dressed there, careless of the wind writhing in my hair and the
broken glass biting at my skin. When I emerged back out into the
halls of Aduantas, I was pale and hard and gleaming.

I was made of salt-brine and polished grit and armored places. I
was too strong to be lost to the tide of my rising grief.

Wayland had not kept his word—his schedule was far from clear.
Despite the lingering bluster of Irian's thunderstorm, the prionsa's

pleasure gardens were thronged with laughing, drinking guests. Groups of two or three were draped amorously over one another beneath gossamer awnings dripping with blades of ice; larger parties led merry games of hide-and-seek between the high hedge labyrinths, mindless of the wet pasting finery to their lissome bodies and the ice crystals glittering in their multicolored hair.

I almost turned around. But it occurred to me in a blistering wave of horrid, hopeless despair that I no longer had a place of my own in Aduantas. Anywhere, really. I truly had no home. I shouldered through the distress. After a moment it ebbed away—until I could almost ignore the way it lapped at the edges of my consciousness.

I threaded through the party, glaring around for a handsome golden profile and a sleek head. After a few minutes of fruitless searching, I spotted Wayland, engaged in a mystifying parlor game involving blindfolds and butterflies—soft-winged things flitting in ribbons between gorgeous giggling Folk. I crossed my arms and waited impatiently until Wayland had caught and kissed every person, sending pale wings fluttering into the dusk.

Almost the moment he pulled down the velvet blindfold, his deep blue eyes found me half-hidden in the shadow of the rose-draped arbor. He excused himself from a gaggle of fawning Gentry maidens with swift but exquisite grace; I could feel their palpable disappointment as he sauntered across the courtyard. But he didn't pause an arm's length from me as I expected. Instead, he swiftly looped an arm around my waist and swept me deep beneath the arbor, where drifted snow heaped between fallen blue petals. I tensed.

"What are you doing?" I pushed half-heartedly against his hard, heavy chest.

"Humor me." He smiled as he curled me into the shadows, hiding me with his frame as he tucked an unnaturally blooming turquoise rose behind one of my ears. "They're watching."

Glancing over his shoulder, I saw this was no figure of speech.

Several maidens—and a few men—pouted after us. But a moment later, I wondered whether he meant an altogether different *they*. The pleasure garden crawled with Aduantas's silver-clad attendants, serving wine and circulating food. Blank faced and anonymous, they practically blended into the scenery. But as I looked more closely, I saw how their pale eyes darted between the guests, marking the movements of the partygoers. Marking *our* movements.

"I didn't agree to this," I hissed. "You said you'd clear your schedule."

"This *is* clearing my schedule." Wayland laughed as if he'd made a joke, tossing his head so the pale globe lights caught along the sweep of his hair. "Will my father take note if I cancel all my parties during the celebratory week of the Tournament of Kings? Absolutely. But will he notice if I quietly slip off for one of my many trysts in an evening? No."

"Then I am to be a conquest?" I said acidly. "Everyone will think me wanton and easily bedded. I didn't agree to that."

"You may have to learn to compromise, Thorn Girl." The smile slipped from Wayland's symmetrical features, making way for an intensity that made me shiver. "When this is all over, we will be feared. Envied. Desired. In the meantime, why not let them all think whatever they will? It is none of our business what that might be."

Instinctively, I shied away from the words. But at the same time, I intuited how true they were for Wayland—how deeply seated. How long had he lived like this, his role in his father's court reduced to a shamelessly degenerate prionsa?

I was no stranger to wearing masks. But Wayland inhabited his so comfortably, I had assumed it to simply be his face. Perhaps it had rendered me as blind as the rest of them.

A flash of memory seared me—Cathair in his basement of horrors teaching me the finer points of spycraft.

Espionage isn't about sneaking around in the shadows, little witch, he'd told me, his voice as mocking as a starling's call. *It is about wearing masks of your own design, each crafted with precision and embroidered with calculated deception. A spy's true skill lies in seamlessly inhabiting these masks until even they are uncertain where the mask ends and their true self begins.*

Was I prepared to allow my own true identity—nascent as it was—to languish once more behind a mask of my own making? To have this falsehood tarnish my reputation? For surely it would not be long before this licentious gossip spread through the city. Before it reached Irian's ears.

I pushed the thought away before it could swamp me in damp, dragging desolation. Perhaps I could wear a mask cunning enough that Wayland got his charade...and discreet enough that Irian never had to find out.

"Fine," I ground out. "But you owe me a boon for putting my own reputation on the line to maintain yours."

"Fair enough." Wayland's eyes sparked. "Shall we give them a show?"

"Do your worst, you libertine."

"Then smile, Thorn Girl."

Without warning, Wayland swooped me bodily into his arms, spinning me so the snow on my slippers came loose and sparkled like glitter in the air. I bared my teeth in what I hoped looked like a smile and whooped—a high, girlish shriek that grated in my own ears. I clung weakly to Wayland's neck. He carried me through the party toward his chambers, grinning from ear to ear and winking. Fatuously, in my opinion. I fought the urge to roll my eyes.

He kicked the door shut behind us and set me to my feet. If his hands lingered at my waist longer than strictly necessary, I chose to ignore it.

"Nicely done." He sloughed off his hedonism like a coat he had worn too long. "Did you discover anything today during the Trial of Speed?"

"Perhaps." The charade had brought me no joy—I wanted to get this over with. "The aughiskies believe the seaside caverns below Aduantas are guarded by a dobhar-chú."

"A king otter?" Surprise touched Wayland's face. "That does surprise me. They were said to have gone extinct during the Gate War. Fénnidi fighting for the Sept of Fins slaughtered them for the protection their pelts offered against human weapons."

"That's...awful."

"Waste no pity on those beasts, Thorn Girl." Grim distaste warped his expression. "They were said to be mindless, insatiable predators. If my father is truly using one to guard the caverns, I can only imagine what he's feeding it. *Who* he's feeding it."

"Ugh." *That* painted a picture, and I instantly thought of Linn and her drowning. Had Gavida stabled them so close to the caverns to be snacks for his monster?

"How do you plan to get past it?"

"The salient obstacle," I said. "We discovered an arms dealer in the Shielings who seems willing to provide us with a weapon to kill it."

Wayland lifted an eyebrow. "At what cost?"

"An apple from the Grove of Gold."

Wayland's second eyebrow joined the first. "And you agreed?"

"What was I supposed to do? The dealer would not agree to terms of unequal risk."

"Don't tell me you went to Blink." Whatever expression I made at the accusation confirmed Wayland's suspicions. "Gods alive, Fia. That brùnaidh is about as trustworthy as a—well, as a curiosity-shop keeper trafficking in cursed weapons and stolen artifacts. What were you thinking?"

"That I have less than a week to discover where an insanely powerful smith-king is hiding the source of his power, then find a way to free it or destroy it," I said tartly. "Pardon me for doing exactly what we agreed."

Wayland sighed, scraping pin-straight hair back from his sleek profile. "Do you know how valuable—nay, *coveted*—those apples are?"

"Why?"

Wayland hesitated a moment longer, then crossed to the elegantly bowed mantelpiece lined in flickering beeswax candles. "Why don't I show you?"

He gripped the frame of the ancient mirror above it and angled it outward. Honeyed light fell on the opposite wall in a concentrated beam, illuminating a patterned pane of stained glass. Wayland rotated the glass until it audibly clicked into place. The tiles below Wayland's feet dropped him a foot in height. An unlit staircase spiraled downward from his fine boots.

Wayland gestured tauntingly at the hidden steps. "Shall we?"

I hesitated.

"Don't worry, Thorn Girl." Wayland's broad smile took on a wicked cast. "We won't be gone too long. Just long enough for everyone to assume you're a *very* satisfying lay."

I marched forward, grabbing a thick beeswax candle from the mantel. But as I swept by Wayland, down the steep, narrow steps, I paused to smile sweetly up at him.

"Alternatively, Prionsa," I said, "they'll simply assume you're *very* bad at getting it up."

And when his choked laugh followed me down the staircase, my false smile turned into a real one.

Chapter Twenty-Five

Circuitous underground passageways underpinned the entirety of Aduantas. They were far more hospitable than the caverns where the aughiskies were stabled, but their straight, smooth, vaulted walls still made me shudder. I lofted my flickering candle, painting streaks of gold along the corridors. After a few minutes of walking, Wayland jerked me out of the center of the hall without warning, shoving me bodily down a side corridor.

"What—" I yelped.

"Shhhh." Wayland leaned down and blew out my candle.

Darkness descended in a rush. A moment later, another light flitted down the passageway, steady and silver. I squinted at it in the dim—it was one of Gavida's unsettling palace attendants. And the light—it was her *eyes*, glowing faintly with the same snared starlight as the smith-king's crucible. I must have made a noise at her passing, because Wayland folded a hand over my mouth. But the attendant continued on her route without so much as glancing in our direction.

I pushed Wayland's hand off my face the moment I was sure she was out of earshot. "What in Donn's hell *are* they?"

"I told you, Thorn Girl—my father likes efficient systems."

Wayland continued down the corridor. Without my candle, the halls were dark—but after a moment, I realized both our collars emitted a faint silvery glow. "He has no desire to oversee mundane tasks—his inventive mind does not thrive on routine. Yet he also wants everything in its right place—requires everything to proceed smoothly and without interruption. Folk are messy. Complex. Selfish. They need sundries like food and sleep. So where he could, he simply replaced them."

"*Replaced* them?" I remembered every time I had looked at one of those attendants and shuddered at their blank eyes and carefully expressionless faces. "What are they?"

"They are...puppets." The word didn't sit well in Wayland's mouth, but he shrugged. As if he had no other name for them. "An invention of my father's. They have metal bones and cable sinews and clockwork hearts. They have some basic intelligence but are really only meant to do what they're told and keep to the tasks they've been set. Their routines are fairly easy to learn, really. I've been successfully circumventing them for years."

"Can Gavida see through their eyes?"

"He is not omniscient, Thorn Girl—he only wishes you to think he is. Unless one of *them* catches us sneaking around and reports us, he has no way of knowing we're here."

I digested this. The corridor began to slope up, and we clattered up a series of steps. "And these passageways? Did your father build them too?"

Wayland shook his head. "They say before Aduantas was built, an ancient city lined these slopes. But if that's true, its streets are now used only for the attendants—and wastrels like me—to move about unseen."

"A city?" My interest was piqued. I remembered the underground city along the whale road. I struggled to remember what Irian had told me, even as I pushed memories of him deeper below my brittle masquerade of normalcy. "Built by the Fomorians? Or the Firbolg—the *Solasóirí*?"

"Solasóirí?" Wayland scoffed. "You have been listening to bed-time stories, Thorn Girl. If the Firbolg ever existed, where did they go? Why is there no evidence of them? No writings or carvings or histories, merely half-remembered stories of powerful immortals? For so-called Bright Ones, they have certainly faded into the shadows."

"But there *are* stories." I felt vaguely defensive.

"Just because a story is told does not make it true." Wayland shrugged. "Legends and lies often wear the same threadbare cloak."

Another set of stairways veered sharply upward, stealing the rest of the conversation from our breathless mouths. After a few long minutes of climbing, Wayland opened a door, revealing an oval of cloud-draped midnight. Ice-cold wind whipped and screamed around us, stinging my eyes to tears. I raised my arm and pushed out onto the darkened moor rising from the top of the deserted amphitheater toward the Grove of Gold. Our feet crunched unevenly over drifted snow, scattered hail, and patches of ice as we climbed the last stretch toward the gnarled, glowing apple trees.

As before, the trees all bloomed and fruited at the same time—delicate pink blossoms peering between clusters of polished rose-gold apples. Instinctively, I reached for one, struck by a sudden depthless yearning to curl my fingers around it...sink my nails into its crisp skin...bite deep into the blushing flesh until its juice slides down my wrist.

"Fia, you won't be able...!"

But Wayland's warning came too late. I'd already grasped one of the apples and twisted it off its stem. It came away easily in my hand, sending a throb of exquisite longing singing along my arm to shatter against the Heart of the Forest. I steeled myself for my collar to spike pain up my spine in response, but it remained quiescent. A moment later, the sensation faded, leaving me holding a glowing golden apple beneath an ancient, gnarled tree as Wayland stared, wonder and worry etched on his face. And I remembered why we were here—what Blink had said about only Gavida's bloodline being able to pick the enchanted apples.

"Sorry." My bewitchment crept toward dismay. "That's not allowed, is it? Will Gavida know I've stolen an apple?"

"Sorry?" Wayland repeated, his soft laugh incredulous. "Picking the apples isn't forbidden, Thorn Girl. It's just impossible."

"I don't understand."

"All may try. None but my father and I succeed." Wayland reached up, a smooth, heavy apple coming away easily in his fingers. "I have seen Folk reach for them, only for the fruits to be somehow always out of reach. Or for Folk to grasp them, only to have them cling stubbornly to the branch no matter how hard they are pulled. I have seen these apples numb predatory fingers and rot greedy hands. But I have never before seen anyone not of my father's bloodline simply *pluck* one."

An uncomfortable thought gripped me. "Does that mean we're *related*?"

"I very much doubt it," Wayland said with a complicated smirk. "My father made me for a purpose. He otherwise has no interest in affairs of the flesh."

Unlike his son. "Then how?"

Wayland's expression softened. "You are special, Thorn Girl. And I know I am not the first to point it out."

I fought a flush as I stared down at the apple. "Why are they so coveted?"

"Each grants three small wishes."

"Wishes?" I glanced sharply up at the prionsa. "Why could you not simply wish your collar away, then? Wish to win the Tournament of Kings? Wish for Gavida's power to be broken?"

"I said *small* wishes, Thorn Girl." Wayland's smile was rueful. "The apples are bound by the same laws of balance as all magic, but their reckoning is instantaneous and unknowable. Wish to be beautiful as the day, and while your face shines, you may find the rest of your body moldering with fungus dark as the night. Wish to be free from pain, and you may find you cannot feel anything at all." As I opened my mouth, he added, "And no, you may not ask for more wishes."

I glanced back down at the apple, which glowed warm and soothing against my skin, then handed it to Wayland. "Here."

"Oh, no. That one belongs to you." He curled my hand around it, then plopped the one he'd plucked in my other palm. "And this one belongs to Blink. Apparently. Now we'd better get back before anyone decides to interrupt our rather extended tryst."

I slid both gleaming apples into the pockets of my mantle, following behind Wayland as he made his way back toward the hidden door on the moor. But I paused at the top of the rise, staring down the lee side of the Silver Isle toward the horizon, where heavy black clouds blotted out the stars and spiked shards of white against the wind-ruched sea. The thunder rumbled so far away I could barely hear it. But I *felt* it—a pressure along my skin and a weight around my heart, cracking the armored cage where I'd hidden my hurt. An ache streaked through the gap, sharp and bright as lightning. Grief surged through me, a rising tide flooding my veins and overpowering my defenses. I gasped, clutching at the Heart of the Forest as my collar spiked a warning—

"Fia?" Wayland loomed up before me, concern darkening his cobalt eyes. "What's wrong?"

I curled my hands into the front of his mantle, clinging to him as if I were drowning and he were the only thing keeping me afloat. I pulled him roughly toward me, inhaling his scent of brine and beeswax.

"Kiss me." Around the cold hard swell of grief blocking my throat, the words came out jagged. "Kiss me right now, Wayland."

His eyes lingered briefly on my tattoos, revealed below the sleeve of my kirtle. But though he curled one large palm around my cheek and dragged a thumb over my damp cheek, he did not move any closer.

"I wish to taste neither your tears nor your heartbreak, Thorn

Girl." He pulled me against his chest in a tender but chaste embrace. I buried my face in his mantle, heedless of the stains I left on his fine silk shirt.

We stayed like that until the winds died down and the thunder grumbled away. And when we returned to the tunnels, he walked gallantly in front of me so we could both pretend I wasn't still silently crying in the echoing dark.

The room I'd shared with Irian was damaged beyond repair; I had no real desire to impose upon the girls another night. Nor did I wish to burden Wayland with questions of my accommodations— not after my humiliating vulnerability in the Grove of Gold. Really, I just wanted to be alone. So I reluctantly waylaid one of Gavida's puppets and explained my predicament. She twitched faintly before leading me to a clean, dark, empty chamber and bowing me inside without further ado. I watched carefully until she disappeared, then locked myself inside.

I sank onto the luxurious mattress and tried to quell the hopeless grief burbling up in waves of decayed green and onyx-sheen black. The golden apples were heavy in the pockets of my mantle— I drew them out, setting one on the windowsill and cradling the other in my palms. It was heavy and warm and inviting. Wayland's warning about the tricky magic of the apples niggled at the back of my mind, but I couldn't help but wonder.

I shouldn't even consider it. Hadn't I learned my lesson about toying with unfamiliar Folk magic the night of the Wild Hunt? I should do *anything* else with the spare apple—give it to Laoise, who had an interest in the Grove of Gold; throw it in the sea so no one could misuse it.

But then again…the grove had *allowed* me to pick this apple. Almost as if it had chosen me to receive its magic. Three small wishes. What harm could *one* do? If I made the wish very, very

small, then whatever balance it demanded would also be small. I
didn't want much.

"I wish—" I paused, rolling words carefully along the contours
of my tongue. "I wish, for this one night, to forget Irian of the Sept
of Feathers."

And, because it seemed obvious, I took a bite of the apple. The
skin gave way easily beneath my teeth, the flesh bursting in my
mouth with the sweetness of sun-striped afternoons. I swallowed
convulsively, the nectar sliding down my throat like bittersweet—
soured wine or yellow wood sorrel. When I looked up at my reflection staring back at me from the window, I felt somehow sharper—a
blade newly forged, a thorn newly grown, a curse newly cast.

I lay back amid the plush bedding, my tired head sinking deep
into the pillows. But in the moment before I fell asleep, I pressed my
wrist reflexively against my thigh, expecting nettles and brambles
and hemlock to prickle my skin. When they did not, I curiously
lifted my arm to my face. There was no sign of my bracelet but
a faint, jagged scar, long healed. In its place were tattoos—sharp
briars twisting between delicate blossoms. But something seemed
missing.

I drifted into sleep.

I dreamed of a ludicrously tall, achingly handsome Gentry
stranger. He threatened me in the wood, threatened me on the
beach, threatened me in his crumbling manor. And yet I continued to orbit him, like a comet streaking toward the earth, looping around him in ever-tightening circles until at last we collided.
He kissed me beneath trees frothing with pale blossoms, kissed
me beside a mountain spring while bluebells unfurled, kissed me
beneath an arching, ancient tree with our hands clasped tight
between looped ribbons of green and black.

He kissed me, frantically, as my life bled away between his fingers and the earth opened up to swallow me and the roots crunched
my bones and—

I jolted awake in the blue hush of dawn, my pillow soaked and cold beneath my swollen face. Yearning writhed through me—for *him*, that handsome stranger. For us. For all of it to have been real.

The sun rose. Remembrance struck me like lightning—every joy and every sorrow, every kiss and every fight, every laugh and every tear. The forest rose inside me, vast and vicious and instinctive, thrusting against the collar at my throat. I cried out at the answering jab of savage, blinding pain. I clawed at my neck, breaking my nails on the adamant metal, even as I forced the dapple of leaves to recede, the tracery of green along my veins to retreat. But the magic of the forest still lingered, like a fading handprint on my skin—palpable enough to know it was there but distant enough that I could not touch it.

That, more than all the rest, made me weep.

Later, when my throat ached from crying and my puffy eyes could make no more tears, I plucked up the golden apple from where I'd dropped it on the floor. Its plump flesh bore the ridges of my teeth but was otherwise unchanged. I stared at it, then bundled it roughly in the hem of my mantle and shoved it to the bottom of the wardrobe.

A small wish? Perhaps. But the reward and the cost had been one and the same. And both were too bitter to ever taste again.

Chapter Twenty-Six

Much as I longed to escape talk of the tournament, I could not. Emain Ablach buzzed with excitement about today's Trial as I marched with Laoise, Chandi, and Sinéad toward the Shielings. Half-heard phrases like *human prince* and *prionsa* and *tánaiste* struck me like projectiles, each one a tiny arrow fletched with my own feeble emotions. I couldn't help but flinch.

"Are you all right?" asked Laoise in an undertone as we turned onto the cramped street where Blink kept his shop. "That lightning storm last night—"

"I'm fine." I gave my head a decisive shake. "Let's give this damned apple to Blink and hope he's honorable enough to hold up his end of the bargain."

I sensed, rather than saw, Chandi share a significant glance with Sinéad. But I was as hollow as Blink's bone door and couldn't bring myself to care.

Laoise stopped me before we entered the shop.

"Allow me." She held out her hand. "That brùnaidh is not to be trusted. I'll keep him honest to the deal he struck."

I wasn't sure she was to be trusted either. But I lifted the golden apple from my pocket and plopped it unceremoniously into her palm, then watched woodenly as she disappeared into Blink's shop.

Chandi's eyes raked me, but I ignored her, crossing my arms over my chest and ensuring my tattoos were fully covered by my sleeves. "We could do this another day—"

"We can't." I turned to her and Sinéad, trying to rouse myself from my dolor. "Did any of you discover anything salient about Gavida?"

The girls exchanged another glance.

"Even the drunkest and rowdiest revelers seemed loath to discuss the smith-king in anything but glowing terms," Chandi finally said. "But we did uncover one odd detail—no one knows where the attendants in Aduantas live or where they go after they finish their work. They never appear at revels but to serve. None are ever seen out in the city but to perform errands for Gavida."

"That's because—" I frowned, hesitated. The fact that no one in the city knew the truth about the attendants made me realize it was probably a secret. "Don't tell this to anyone else, but they're not *real*."

"Not *real*?" Chandi echoed. "What does that mean?"

"They are—" I glanced over my shoulder. I tried to keep my words careful, but I couldn't keep a sardonic note from creeping into my tone. "They are like puppets without strings—mindless but for the routines he has set for them. All hail Gavida's masterful and wondrous magical forging skill."

"They did seem strange!" Sinéad was grotesquely fascinated. "Poised but lacking personality, helpful but blank. I wonder how he made them? How they are so lifelike?"

"Surely not everything he forges is so twisted," Chandi cut in. "He made the Treasures, didn't he?"

"Yes." Bitter wormwood coated my tongue. "Powerful magic with a powerful price—a life tithed every thirteen years." I glanced at her ashen face and forced myself to soften. "Don't worry—I don't think Gavida's puppets are part of the deal. Even if Irian wins the Oak King's Crown, they won't be following us home."

But the joke fell like stone from my tongue. Thoughts of Irian invaded my careful nonchalance. If he did win the Oak King's Crown—as he seemed certain he would—would he still try to unmake my Treasure? If we two were no longer wed, would we all be leaving this place separately? And where would I go, without him?

I braced my curving spine with knotty hardwood and pushed the intrusive worries away.

I was grateful when the bone door creaked open and Laoise sauntered out, looking very pleased with herself. She carried a massive double-headed spear that towered over her, its metal-studded haft nearly as thick as her bicep.

"*That's* the weapon that can kill a dobhar-chú?" I whistled, impressed despite myself. "It's certainly big enough."

"It's called Gáe Bulga." Laoise sounded awed. "Each spear point enters the target, then expands into thirty barbs upon impact." She demonstrated, twisting the haft of the spear until it unfurled into a savage sunburst that would surely kill anything on impact. "Supposedly it's a design from the smith-king's forge. How better to kill his water dog than with one of his own weapons?"

Another of the smith-king's Donn-cursed forgings? That brought me no comfort. "Blink promised it would pierce the dobhar-chú's hide?"

"He did. And I swore to him that if he was lying and any harm came to us, I'd send my ghost to drown him in the sea." Laoise laughed at our expressions. "What? Brùnaidhean are notoriously superstitious. And they hate water. It was the best I could do on short notice."

"Let's hope it worked." My eyes trailed involuntarily toward the peak of the city, where pennants swirled and snapped from the towers of Aduantas. Beyond, the arena would be filled with eager, laughing spectators; the remaining contestants would be waiting, high-strung and hopeful. How many were left? Not many, I imagined, if what Irian had told me about the Trial of Speed was true.

What would today's task be? I pushed the questions away before they could lead me down a path rutted with treacherous snares— snares that might snap me up, sample my fears, eat me alive. "The Trials usually last a few hours. We should get to the caverns and slay the dobhar-chú while Gavida's preoccupied."

"We're going to make an appearance at the Trial," Sinéad told me, indicating Chandi, who didn't so much nod as look away. "My daggers will be of little help against the dobhar-chú, but we can keep an eye on Gavida's movements. We also hope to speak further with a Gentry scholar we met last night who claimed knowledge of the smith-king's libraries."

"Very well." There seemed no harm in letting Chandi and Sinéad go off on their own—during the day, amid the crowds, they'd be in little danger. But that left me alone with Laoise and a giant flesh-eating king otter. And while all evidence pointed to the Gentry maiden being an ally, I knew—somewhere deep in the abyss where my elemental magic lurked—that she was more than that. Or less. She was *different*. How, I had no idea. But she was hiding something. I could not fully trust her. "Keep your wits about you."

"And you," said Sinéad. "Shall we regroup at nightfall in our rooms to discuss what's next?"

The mention of their rooms made my stomach bottom out— their suite was connected to mine. No, not mine anymore. *Irian's.*

I didn't want to go anywhere near those rooms if I had any choice in the matter.

"Whatever happens next, I'll need to update Wayland," I told them, as casually as possible. "Laoise will meet you there. I'll find you all later."

The girls disappeared through the winding alleyways of the Shielings, leaving me, Laoise, and a massive double-headed spear flanged with threescore deadly barbs standing awkwardly in the middle of the street.

"Well," I said at last. "Shall we go hunting? I'm in the mood to stab something."

Linn seemed pleased to see us—or perhaps she was just pleased at the prospect of killing something as bloodthirsty as she was. Behind her in the froth-plumed caves, the rest of her drowning lurked, watching us with glowing gemstone eyes. A thread of instinctual fear curdled in my veins. Between my mistrust of Laoise and my mistrust of the aughiskies, I fought the urge to stand behind Linn—whom I impossibly *had* begun to trust—like a child behind its mother's skirts.

"Here to help?" I asked instead, as pleasantly as I was able. "While we appreciate the support, the caverns are narrow. It may prove a little crowded."

Linn snaked out her delicate nose and slid a vision into my mind, of Laoise and me disappearing timorously into the caverns before the dobhar-chú came barreling out before us, at which point the drowning pounced upon it and dragged it into the deeps.

"You want us to flush it out for you?" I confirmed, surprised. I glanced at Laoise, but she was gazing at Gáe Bulga like a child with a new toy. "You know their pelts are supernaturally strong, yes? I'm not sure you'll be able to kill it."

As one, the water horses all lowered their heads and chattered their shark teeth, eyes gleaming. I shuddered—I needed no psychic vision to translate that message.

Just let us try.

I waved Laoise toward the mouth of the tunnels.

"After you," I said.

Linn's visions were half fact, half invention—no map to go by. It was impossible to know how deep the dobhar-chú kept its watch. So we moved carefully and used no light. As it turned out, we didn't need one—like all Gavida's forgings, Gáe Bulga gave off a faint silver glow that turned the water plinking from the ceiling and gathering around our boots to quicksilver.

"Are you planning to give that to me at some point?" I asked in a whisper after a few minutes. "Or would you rather dispatch the dobhar-chú yourself, No-Oath Laoise?"

"You and your husband both enjoy that clever little nickname." Laoise huffed a laugh. "Do you not believe I can fight?"

Her tone held a brisk kind of challenge, and I looked sharply at her even as the mention of Irian lifted my hackles. "I have no evidence but your own word."

"I was sent away when I was younger." Her eyes glowed like embers in the dim—red as firelight in the strange light of the spear. "To Dún Scaith, Fortress of Shadows, where the lady Scáthach trains her legions of skilled fénnidi. I was never her best student. Nor was I her worst." Laoise gave the heavy spear she held a few experimental swings. It whistled faintly in the dim, dank space. "I think she would very much like this weapon. So I will do my utmost not to embarrass her training."

I tried not to betray how many questions her brief backstory had elicited within me. I forced myself to stay quiet until I could decide which answer interested me the most.

"Why were you sent away?" I finally asked.

"My parents were bound to the Sept of Scales," she finally said. "I was either too young or too stupid to recognize the signs before the purge. But they must have known what was coming. What would befall them all when the bardaí gained enough independence to become dangerous. I regret that I did not give them that credit in the moment. I simply thought they despised me enough to banish me from their home. To thrust my care upon a woman who was not my family. And I hated them for it. Up until the day they died."

Sympathy crowded out my wariness. "Oh, Laoise. They were—"

"Slaughtered without honor, yes. Among every last one of their kith and kin besides me. So you can understand, perhaps, why I was so loath to make oaths to the bardaí once I had completed my fosterage at Dún Scaith."

"Then how have you spent the last…however many years?" I asked. "As a gallóglaigh?"

"A mercenary?" She bared her teeth in an almost smile. "I have had many adventures. Many of them have included violence. But despite your mistrust of my motivations and your mockery of my oathlessness, I think we are not so different, changeling heir. We were both raised to be sharper than our natures might otherwise have allowed." She paused, her neck swiveling as something caught her attention. My own ears pricked. A slither in the shallows, webbed feet pawing water. Laoise gave me a tiny coiled smile. "And we both enjoy the hell out of a good fight."

Without warning, she tossed me Gáe Bulga. The long, heavy spear thunked into my waiting palms with unexpected heft, and I stumbled back a half step. A long enough distraction that I didn't notice her disappear into the damp darkness. I waited, pulse ratcheting. I ran my hands along the haft of the spear, searching for its balance, learning its weight, measuring its length. Long weapons— staffs and spears and claimhte—had never been my preference. But even I could tell that for what it was designed for, this weapon was nearly perfect. I bent my knees, sinking into a crouch as my eyes dredged the depthless shadows beyond the circle of Gáe Bulga's light. Faint splashes echoed through the corridor.

"Laoise?" I hissed.

The pressure of movement along my skin, stale air pushing outward.

The dobhar-chú reared up directly in front of me, dominating the tunnel with its pale form. It was *massive*—far huger than Linn had suggested. Its paws—lunging for me with terrifying speed— were the size of millstones and lined with razor-sharp claws. Its mouth opened as it charged, jaws unhinging to display narrow serrated teeth and a fleshy convulsing maw large enough to swallow me whole. I cursed and instinctively ducked, flattening myself on the ground as the dobhar-chú barreled along the tunnel. At the last instant, I levered the tip of Gáe Bulga upward. But the flanged tip barely scraped the creature's thick, pale pelt—a pathetic trickle of red-black blood oozed along its belly toward its thick, stumpy tail.

I surged back to my feet as it scrabbled for purchase on the slick cave floors, disappearing momentarily outside the range of Gáe Bulga's dim light. Adrenaline pulsed headily through my veins and slithered vines up my spine. My collar throbbed a warning, but I gripped the spear and steadied my feet, preparing for another attack.

But it wasn't the king otter's footsteps I heard next—it was Laoise's, as she sprinted out of the darkness behind me. I whirled on her, nearly taking off her head with Gáe Bulga before lowering the weapon at the last instant. The Gentry maiden was breathing hard and soaked from head to toe, her normally boisterous red curls flattened against her forehead.

"Gods alive," she gasped out, "but that thing runs *fast*."

"I noticed." I glared at her. "You couldn't have warned me it was coming?"

She grinned infectiously. "I thought you might surprise it with a killing strike."

"No such luck," I told her. "And I think we have bare moments before it comes back this—"

The dobhar-chú lunged out of the darkness, grasping for us both with its vast vicious paws. I dodged narrowly, slamming my side into the cavern wall. Grasping Gáe Bulga for momentum, I kicked out from the rock and lofted myself toward the creature. If I could find purchase on its back, I would be out of its killing range while still having room to strike a fatal blow. But in the dimness I misjudged the speed of its passing. Instead of clearing its back, I knocked into its hips, sliding down to nearly get myself trampled beneath its hind legs. I cried out as Gáe Bulga tangled in its feet and was ripped from my hands.

In an instant, Laoise was there, scooping up the weapon and

launching herself at the beast. But it was already gone, moving with scathing speed back into the darkness of the caverns. A trembling note of fear escaped the armor around my heart.

I paced toward Laoise and helped her up from the damp floor.

"Linn was right," I forced out. "We need to flush it out of the caverns."

"We're too vulnerable," Laoise agreed. "This is its territory. It's too fast. And too quiet."

"Do you remember the way out?"

"Do *you*?"

I almost laughed. Of all the ways I'd dreamed of dying, being flayed alive by a dog-fish-otter while hopelessly lost underground had never been one of them.

A brief and treacherous thought gripped me: What would Irian do if he found my broken, battered body trampled in these caverns?

What if he never found me at all?

And the last thing I'd said to him...

You are not my home.

Unease bordering on nausea clenched my stomach. I supposed that meant I had to figure out a way to *not* die.

"Here's what we're going to do," I hissed, even as I strained my eyes in the darkness and listened for huge paws clawing toward us. "One of us will lead it out of the caverns at all times. The other will harry it from behind so its attention is split."

Laoise's eyebrows lifted. "Can you run that fast for that long? I can't."

"We'll swap out. I think the best place to harm it is its belly—where its pelt is not so thick. Run as fast as you can, then flatten yourself along the floor and use its momentum against it. If you get the angle right, Gáe Bulga will split it down the middle."

The soft plash of water stole my attention. That rush of air—like a huge body hurtling out of the dark. We were out of time.

"Ready?" I whispered.

Laoise gripped Gáe Bulga and took off running in the moment

before the dobhar-chú launched itself out of the darkness. I flattened myself against the wall as it passed, then sprinted immediately after it. Morrigan, it wasn't just *huge*. It was *long*, its body almost serpentine as it slithered along the twisting caverns. I fought to keep up with its speed, and with the glow from Gáe Bulga obscured by its massive hindquarters, I could barely see it.

You are not my home.

My harsh words burned fresh adrenaline through my limbs and propelled me forward. Unsheathing my daggers, I launched myself at the dobhar-chú. My blades thunked down into its pelt to the hilt but drew no blood. Still, they provided the purchase I needed to drag myself up onto its back. The dobhar-chú registered my weight instantly, slowing as it bucked its spine. But I clamped my knees and screwed my eyes shut, pretending I was back at Rath na Mara breaking stubborn yearlings. I imagined Rogan laughing up at me, his blue-green eyes crinkling with dual worry and mirth as he shouted at me for my recklessness: *Changeling! You're not supposed to be* enjoying *this!*

When I opened my eyes, it was to watch Laoise turn smoothly, lie on her back, and loft Gáe Bulga toward the creature's stomach. But my distraction had made its movements erratic—it passed over her sideways, and the spear only glanced along its well-armored rib cage. A guttural scream escaped its throat as it thrashed its skull, nearly slamming me into the stalactites stabbing down from the ceiling. I slung myself to one side, scraping against the wall as I fisted my hands in its dense, oily fur. It churned forward, then skidded to a halt, trying to turn around in the narrow passageway.

That was no good.

Extricating my daggers from the dobhar-chú's pelt, I dropped down between its legs onto all fours. A brief glance showed me Laoise levering herself to her feet, Gáe Bulga bloodied but still in her grasp. I cursed, even as the overgrown otter-dog flung itself into the walls, trying to reverse direction. Loose scree pattered down as I mustered my failing courage. Then I stabbed my nearly useless blades up into the bloody area where the spear had struck. And flung myself forward into the caverns.

The dobhar-chú howled as it swung its massive tooth-spiked skull forward. And gave chase.

The darkness swallowed me up. My pumping legs became machines, every muscle and tendon stretched to its breaking point. My breath rasped in my throat. My heart throbbed, each pulse of my green-dark blood spiking pain against my neck. My eyes strained at the shadows, but there was no light for me to see. So I simply closed my eyes.

There were few times in my life that I had run like I ran now.

The first time I had slain one of the Folk—a sleek black púca terrorizing farmers near the border of Delbhna. When I had killed it, stabbing it through the heart with an iron spike, its blood had spilled over my hands like black oil and dark magic. I had wept as I'd run back to the fortress—where Cathair was waiting with a stiff pat on the back and a stiffer dram of whiskey—my tears spilling over my outstretched, blood-drenched hands like rain.

The first time I'd met Irian. *I promise to give you a head start.*

The second time I'd met Irian. *It's you.*

The night I'd thought would be our last together. *I need you to be ruthless, colleen.*

My hip slammed hard into an outcropping of rock. Pain exploded through my torso, and I stumbled sideways. Skidded down onto the wet floor.

Shite.

I flipped onto my back, scrabbling with my boots to put myself out of range of the dobhar-chú's reaching paws. But inexplicably, it wasn't there.

I squinted into the dim. The cavern tapered to a pinch point where I'd struck my hip, too narrow for the creature to slink through. The king otter was barely deterred—it slammed its shoulders into the stone. Again. And again. Pebbles rained down. The passageway trembled.

I shrank back, gasping for breath and lifting useless daggers to defend myself against its inevitable onslaught.

"Fia!" Laoise's voice broke through my terror. She had climbed the creature nearly to its skull but could go no farther—stalactites hemmed her in like the bars of a cage. "Can you keep going?"

No. No—I *couldn't*. I couldn't go on. I'd run too fast. I'd run too far—I could no longer remember where I'd begun.

I no longer knew where I was running *to*.

"You're nearly there—I can hear the ocean. Take Gáe Bulga and end this."

Laoise reached over the dobhar-chú's lunging head and flung the heavy metal spear. It flew through the darkness to lodge three inches from my face with enough force to carve a chunk from the rock. I cursed, rolled to one side, and braced myself against the wall. Still the dobhar-chú struggled, but it was nearly through. I lifted myself to my feet, grasped the haft of Gáe Bulga. Jerked it out of the stone. Hefted it.

But in the moment before I aimed it, the dobhar-chú thrust through the last brittle stones holding it back, rearing up to pounce.

I had no choice. I ran.

The creature snapped at my heels, breathed fury against the back of my neck. I pushed myself harder even as Gáe Bulga's weight slowed me down. The spear seemed to glow brighter the faster I tried to run.

No—not Gáe Bulga. Daylight, filtering through the narrow caves. My heaving footsteps mingled with the distant pounding of surf. I flung myself out into the afternoon, gasping for fresh air. My steps wavered. I half turned, trying to slide the spear into position as the dobhar-chú catapulted after me. But the angle was too steep; the stones, too slick.

"Get it up!" screamed Laoise, barely hanging on to the king otter's slick back.

I struggled to heave the weapon up. The creature bore down on me. Gáe Bulga's haft slipped in my damp palms. I stared up, fascination and fear freezing me in place.

Shark teeth clamped around my belt and jerked me roughly back. The dobhar-chú's claws ripped through the space where I'd been standing, singing like death through empty air. It kept sliding, its momentum carrying it across the brine-drenched, hail-slick caves toward the ocean beyond. It scrabbled at the rocks, howled at the sky. In the moment before it disappeared into the surging waves, Laoise vaulted neatly from its skull, landing in a coiled crouch at the lip of the caverns. She dashed to me, gripping my arm in concern.

"Are you all right? I tried to slow it down—"

"I'm fine." My hand holding Gáe Bulga shook. I gripped the weapon tighter. "I have Linn to thank for that."

The aughisky at my elbow gave me an almost affectionate shove. But the vision she pushed into my mind was less gentle: the dobhar-chú diving deep, only to sneak back in the night to slaughter the water horses in their sleep.

"All right." Exhaustion was beginning to pull at my limbs, adrenaline seeping away with the height of danger. "But you're going to have to help."

She tossed her delicate head, then bowed one leg to help me mount. I climbed onto her back, anchoring a hand in her mane before once more hefting Gáe Bulga. Linn whinnied piercingly. The other aughiskies rallied, circling and wheeling like vultures. Linn spun, cantered toward the edge of the cliffs, and—

I braced myself. The impact shuddered upward, frigid water lapping up my legs and torso toward my neck. But it never closed over my face—Linn surged up to dance over the waves, her delicately finned fetlocks deftly navigating the currents. Sea-foam brushed against my cheeks, tangled in my hair. Around us, the other aughiskies swiftly fell into formation—a crisp V-shaped maneuver I'd witnessed only in Linn's sendings. Together, they struck out after the dobhar-chú.

Two of the aughiskies dived deep, harrying the otter-dog from below. Another two performed a complex stunt that sent a tight, brutal wave of water to stun their prey. The final two closed in on the creature in tightening circles, exhausting the dobhar-chú with feints and sallies. At last, there was nothing to do but for Linn to glide in close to the creature and gnash her teeth at me.

I stared down at the beast, less fearsome now than it had been in the darkened caverns. Were it not for the foot-long claws and snapping, savage mouth, the creature might almost have been beautiful. Lithe and long bodied, like the sweet, smelly ferrets the master of kennels had kept for hunting rabbits back at Rath na Mara. But as I gazed into its flat, empty red eyes, I saw nothing. No particular intelligence beyond cunning, no particular sentiment beyond bloodlust.

Had this creature once had the same aptitude for empathy as the aughiskies—as Linn? Was it truly the last of its kind? What must Gavida have done to keep it as his pet—his slave? How many Folk must this beast have caught...slain...devoured? What terrible secrets had it been set here to guard?

Disgust rose in me like poison. I once more hefted Gáe Bulga, lifting the spear above my shoulder as I gripped Linn with my thighs. I brought the weapon down with as much force as I could muster. The spear thunked heavily into the dobhar-chú's side, still barely piercing the skin. The creature howled, thrashing its heavy-jawed skull as the other aughiskies fought to keep it in place.

I grimaced and activated Gáe Bulga's mechanism.

Thirty vicious barbs simultaneously exploded into the dobhar-chú's gut. We all felt the moment its heart stopped, the sharp, brutal gasp as its last breath left its lungs. The creature seemed almost to deflate, melting down into the water like a leaf drenched by a storm. I jerked hard on Gáe Bulga, but it was locked fast in the monster's flesh.

When it threatened to drag me down into the deep, I simply let the weapon go.

Around us, the aughiskies churned the water to froth as they lunged after the descending creature. But I wasn't sure I had the heart to experience the aftermath of my kill. I understood too well the dynamics of predator and prey. So I tugged on Linn's mane.

"Please?" I asked her. "I don't want to watch."

The sideways look she gave me made me think of nothing so much as Cathair. *You are soft, little witch.* But she turned without further comment, depositing me beside a waiting Laoise before joining her drowning in their feast.

"What happened to Gáe Bulga?" Laoise asked me after a stretch.

"I let it go."

"Why?" Disappointment threaded her tone.

"Just because a weapon exists," I finally said, "doesn't mean it should be used. We all walk too close to death as it is." I turned to her, then jerked my head toward the waiting caves. "Well? Shall we go see what that overgrown otter-dog was guarding?"

Chapter Twenty-Seven

As the light faded and the tide turned, Laoise and I reentered the caves. We brought torches this time—flames smearing blood along the pale, shimmering cliff stone. We followed evidence of our frenzied chase through the caverns—deep gouges carved into the soft limestone from the creature's claws; puddles of red-black blood pooling along the floor; tufts of pale fur lodged in the crevices between stalagmites.

Laoise set a brisk pace, seemingly unbothered by our recent struggle. I strained to keep up, grimacing as I put a hand to the hip that had slammed into that stone outcropping. Gavida's collar didn't just dampen my magic; it slowed my healing too. I'd be lucky if I didn't have any broken ribs; by tomorrow, I'd almost certainly be sporting a lovely bruise the size of a dinner plate.

Finally, Laoise lofted her torch. Firelight guttered on vaulting ceilings and shivered across a still subterranean lake.

"This is where I found the dobhar-chú sleeping." Her lilting accent echoed strangely in the space—sibilant as scales over stone. "The passageways stop here. This must be what it was guarding."

"This?" I, too, lifted my torch, smearing red over the mirror sheen of glassy water. I bent, hesitating for the briefest moment before trailing my fingers at the edge. It was just water—not poison or acid as I'd momentarily feared. Cool to the touch but not frigid. I cupped a little in my palm, angling it toward the torchlight before lifting it to my face and gingerly sipping it. Fresh water. Nothing more, nothing less. I upended my palm, droplets raising silent ripples on the serene surface, then wiped my hands on my tunic.

A pointless endeavor, considering I was still sopping from my neck down to my feet, thanks to Linn.

"But it's..." I trailed off, disappointment swallowing my words. "It's just a lake."

"It certainly appears so."

"Perhaps there's something hidden beneath the water." A thread of desperation wove my disappointment into a new tapestry of impossible hopes. "Or an island, farther out, beyond the light of our torches—"

"Unless you have a boat hidden up those narrow sleeves or are eager to go skinny-dipping in dark water," said Laoise, "then I think we'd better regroup. I should check on Chandi and Sinéad—make sure nothing untoward happened at today's Trial. And you—"

"I should tell Wayland what we found. Or rather, didn't find." I touched my brined, sweat-matted hair and sighed. "But first I need a bath."

We used the helical staircases I'd taken when I first visited Linn, ascending until the jagged cliff stone smoothed out and doorways studded the walls, growing ever more ornate the higher we climbed. I tried to remember how many floors until the girls'—and Irian's—suite, but when I ducked my head out through an unassuming door, I saw the servants' passageways instead. The corridors Wayland had shown me last night.

If there was ever a time or way to speak to Wayland without having to pretend to be his flirt or conquest, this was it. Bath be damned.

"You go on," I told Laoise. "I'll meet you and the girls later, if I haven't simply collapsed in my bed from sheer exhaustion. Your rooms should be three or four more flights up, if I remember correctly."

Laoise paused, then smiled. "Very well."

She disappeared up the scrolling steps, leaving me to move furtively through the servants' corridors alone. I kept a careful eye out for Gavida's puppets but saw no one. It didn't take me long to find the correct set of stairs. I clambered up into Wayland's bedchambers.

To find the prionsa completely undressed save for a towel around his shoulders, having clearly just finished bathing. He turned at the sound of my footsteps, surprise loosening his features. When he saw who I was—instead of whatever uninvited attendant he must have assumed me to be—he grinned, showing every one of his glaringly white teeth.

At no point did he attempt to hide or cover his nakedness. I flushed a little but crossed my arms over my chest and refused to be flustered. I kept my eyes trained on his.

"Thorn Girl!" he said jovially. "As excellent as your memory surely is, you seem to have forgotten that I do, in fact, have a front door to my chambers."

"I didn't forget, Prionsa." I kept my tone equally as light. "I merely disdain the premise of acting as your mistress while risking my arse to save yours. All while you...well, sit on said arse at your father's side."

"Prickly tonight, are we?" Wayland whistled. "Perhaps the sight of said arse will ease your woes."

"The only time I'll relish seeing your arse, Prionsa, is if I've had the chance to kick it." I smirked. "And now that we've passed beyond the requisite flirtations, will you please get dressed? I have something to tell you."

"All right, Thorn Girl." Still chuckling, Wayland slid the towel from his shoulders down around his hips. He was still largely bare—the scrap of cloth did little to disguise the rippling expanse of muscle encasing his torso, his chest, and his broad arms. Apparently he considered this *dressed*—he approached me easily, and I steeled myself to ignore the moisture clinging to his tilting eyelashes, the way his damp hair scrawled like ink over his shoulders, the heady salt-and-sand scent of him filling up my nostrils. "What is it?"

"We killed the dobhar-chú," I said without preamble. "But it doesn't seem to be guarding anything but a huge freshwater lake beneath the city. We've hit another dead end. And with—what? Three days left in the tournament? I'm not sure I'll realistically be able to pull this off in time."

Wayland made a noise in his throat and leaned against the wall, mimicking my posture with his arms folded over his chest. "I never reckoned you for a quitter, Thorn Girl."

Irritation rose in me like a tide. "I'm no quitter, Prionsa. But nor do I enjoy fighting losing battles. Especially not ones fought on another's behalf."

"You wish me to be more involved?" He huffed a laugh. "Believe me when I say I would love to. But my father's eye watches ever more closely the nearer we draw to the end of the tournament. He knows I despise losing every year. Any deviation from my normal routine, and he will feel obligated to tug upon my already tight leash."

"And by normal routine, you mean revels? Trysts? Orgies?" My annoyance flashed toward fury. "No matter that while you wine, dine, and bed every person in sight, I'm risking my life, limb, and reputation to chase down shady merchants, acquire brutal deadly weapons, and slay horrific monsters? All while pretending to be your mistress? When I have only barely left—"

My voice broke, and I jerked a fist up to my mouth to quell the sudden surge of emotion. I spun, grinding the heels of my palms into suddenly stinging eyes. When I turned back, Wayland was standing right in front of me. He steadied me with two huge hands on my shoulders. His expression was annoyingly compassionate, and I fought the urge to shake off his touch. Or lean closer into him.

"You're right," he murmured. "The stakes are high and surely feel highest for each of us. Perhaps I was wrong to encourage you in this. I will not think ill of you if you do wish to abandon this endeavor."

"No." I scrubbed once more at my eyes. "We are too far down this path to quit it now. But I am at a dead end. I do not know where to look next."

Wayland dropped his hands, looking pensive. "The dobhar-chú was guarding a lake? Are you sure there wasn't anything else?"

"Not that I could see," I reiterated. "There was not enough light to see into or beyond the water."

Wayland ran a hand through his long, damp hair, then sighed. "I was due at a feast. Coming through my front door might have bought us the illusion that I was currently involved in...a different sort of feast."

"As I said, Prionsa," I ground out, "I'm tired of being other people's excuses for doing the wrong things."

"Then I shall have to bereave my comrades of my presence without explanation." Wayland crossed to his wardrobe, which—despite the array of clothing populating the floor—was stuffed full of a hundred outfits in a thousand shades of blue. After some searching, he pulled out a woolen tunic and a pair of dark chambray trousers—modest and practical, by his standards. "I am many things, Thorn Girl, and you have a way of making them all seem utterly lamentable. But never let it be said I don't follow through on my promises. Lock the front door, won't you?"

I hesitated, then acquiesced, throwing the heavy bolt. When I turned back, Wayland was mostly clothed and buckling some leather armor—which looked rather pristine, in my estimation—over his shirt.

"Well?" I asked.

"Well, Thorn Girl." His eyes sparked the deep blue of an ocean at dusk, and my heart lolloped in my chest. "There seems to be a newly unguarded lake deep in the bowels of my father's island that I have a mind to explore. Can I convince you to join me?"

One last hopeful vision of steaming water and scented soap deserted me. "I doubt you'll get by the aughiskies without me."

e~~~3

Setting foot back in the caverns had the terrible feeling of an echo—a scream, multiplied.

From the moment I'd come down here to meet Linn, I'd disliked this place. Slaying the dobhar-chú and revealing its dubious sentry post had only put me off more. Now—with nightfall hemming us in and the ocean screaming havoc against the cliffs—I distinctly did *not* want to go back into the caves. But with Wayland towering at my side and Linn—full bellied and pleasantly satiated—sallying helpfully in front of the entrance, I found I had little choice.

"Shall we?" I lofted my torch.

"We shall," Wayland answered, even as he stared askance at the aughisky. "Is…it…coming with us?"

"Linn?" I grinned, pleased by his discomfort. "No. She's offering to guard the entrance for us."

"Thank the living gods," he said with relief. "She scares me."

I laughed a little and led us into the caverns.

"*Living gods*," I asked after a few silent moments. "I've heard you—and others among the Gentry—reference them. Swear upon them as humans do upon Donn…Brighid…Morrigan. Who are these gods?"

Beside me, Wayland betrayed surprise, his eyebrows lifting over torch-bronzed eyes.

"I confess I have never given it much thought, Thorn Girl." Wayland's gaze drifted over the fresh claw marks scored upon the passage walls. "There are stories, of course. Some say that *we* are the living gods—that when the frail, mortal humans first came to our lands, they worshipped us as deities. But considering that not long afterward, they tried to steal our magic and succeeded in driving us from our lands, I'm not sure that is true."

"You say *some*. Are there other stories?"

"Always." He shrugged. "Others tell that when our distant forebears came to the land that would eventually be split into Fódla and Tír na nÓg, it was inhabited by living gods and the giants who had enslaved them. The Bright Ones—the so-called Solasóirí of your bedtime stories."

"What happened to them?"

"Some legends say when we defeated the Fomorians, we set those gods free." He shot me a glance. "Others say we killed them."

Before I could formulate a reply, we arrived at the subterranean lake the dobhar-chú had been guarding. I grappled with the same disappointment I'd felt earlier, but Wayland seemed intrigued by the still, flat expanse of water stretching out before us. Before I'd so much as lifted my torch, he'd begun stripping down to the waist.

"What are you doing?" I hissed, my voice echoing eerily through the vaulted caverns.

He waded into the lake. "My due diligence, Thorn Girl."

To my surprise, a living constellation of bioluminescence sparked to life in his wake. Tiny, iridescent fish flickered like stars; glowing reeds slid radiant tendrils around his legs. Wayland plunged beneath the surface. The water puckered as his head submerged. Light flashed pale in the black depths. I inhaled, held my breath, and counted. The water slowly stilled, light-chased ripples wasting themselves against the rock. My torch guttered. My lungs burned.

Fifty-eight ... seventy-two ... ninety.

My breath blew out of my lungs in a panicked rush. I jerked forward, my damp boots ankle-deep in the still water. But Wayland surfaced a moment later, shaking water off his sleek, wet hair.

Relief tangled with anger as I stared down at him. "Morrigan, you scared me!"

"I'm a very strong swimmer, Thorn Girl." Wayland smiled up at me. "There's an underwater tunnel at the far end of the lake, leading deeper into the caverns. And the current is strong."

"What does that mean?"

"It means there's something on the other side." His indigo eyes darkened. "But I cannot say how far. I'll have to dive to explore farther."

For the briefest moment, I considered letting him do this difficult thing alone. But I'd made too many sacrifices to step back now. I'd made the deal for the golden apples. I'd slain the dobhar-chú. I had to see this through until the end—no matter the cost. I had to keep moving forward. If only to keep the full force of my impending heartbreak at bay.

"I'm coming with you." I quickly stripped off my outer mantle, then my armor. I kicked off my boots, until I wore nothing but my tunic and breeches. I shivered slightly at the prospect of diving into the chilly water.

"Are you sure?"

"Yes." I took a deep, shaky breath, fighting phantom claustrophobia. "Show me where."

Wayland cut out across the still surface of the lake, his movements precise. I inhaled, slammed my torch into the sand, then pushed off from the beach after him, forcibly ignoring the chill of the water. A momentary memory gripped me—Cathair, my teacher, perched on the banks of a half-frozen pond, pushing me beneath the surface again and again and again. To make me strong. To forge me into the weapon he—and Mother—had wished me to be. It had hurt, what they'd done to me—but was I truly worse for their ministrations?

They had transformed me from one thing to another. From a weak little girl to a strong young woman. I begrudged them every single lesson. But that didn't mean there was no value in who they'd forced me to become.

Wayland paused, treading water. Barely any light reached us; my torch guttered, half a lifetime away. Only a few glowing minnows had followed us into deep water. Both our silver collars shone faintly, but the light was vanishing in the universe of blackness pressing down on us.

"Do you feel it?" Wayland asked.

I looked at him, not understanding.

"The current."

I did, then—a gentle tug at my legs. I shivered, briefly closing my eyes against the irrational sensation of huge tentacles stroking me beneath the surface. Wayland held out his hand, and I grasped it gratefully, my fingers cold and slippery.

"On my count, we dive," he said. "There won't be any light, so you should close your eyes. Use your other senses. Let the current guide you—don't fight it."

My breath rasped quick in my lungs, and my feet felt leaden in the ink-dark water. "All right."

"Fia—"

The use of my actual name felt patronizing—as if, after all this time calling me Thorn Girl, Wayland could only bring himself to use my real name when he felt sorry for me. Screw that. If I couldn't do this, what *could* I do? I no longer had my magic. I'd been eliminated from the Tournament of Kings. My marriage had lasted all of six weeks—four of which I'd been a black swan. I wanted at least one victory—one thing to be proud of. If that thing was holding my breath long enough to navigate a subterranean tunnel? Well, so be it.

"I'm ready."

"On my count." Wayland held up three fingers. "Three, two—"

We both inhaled... and dived.

Chapter Twenty-Eight

The dark water pressed down on me like a massive hand. Despite Wayland's warnings, I couldn't help but open my eyes. There was only blackness. I tried to focus on his instructions.

Use your other senses. Let the current guide you.

I kicked down, seeking that swirling pressure—

There. My momentum and the rushing water pulled me down. My seeking hands—held a length in front of my face—struck stone, then dragged along the ceiling of a tunnel. Water pushed at my back, shoving me forward. Relief loosened my shoulders as I swept on through the cave. But my lungs were already beginning to burn in my chest. I kicked my legs, willing the air left in my body to last until the end of the tunnel, to get me back to the surface.

But as cold seconds ticked by, panic whispered worst-case scenarios against my spiking pulse. My nostrils flared, even as I squeezed my lips together.

An outcropping of rock slammed into my skull with a mind-numbing thump. I saw flat, blinding white. A great bubble of air escaped my mouth as I tried to scream, but the sound was but a faint glug in the great black lake. I sank precipitously. Reflexively,

I reached for my Greenmark, but the collar around my neck responded with breathtaking speed, sending heat and pain searing down my spine. I clutched at my throat, even as the last of my breath fled my lungs. I flailed with my arms and legs, but the concept of up and down had abandoned me. A blackness more profound even than the lake curled in around me.

Large hands closed over my wrists and dragged me up. The current swirled around us. Renewed strength flooded back into my limbs and I kicked, desperation making my movements erratic. Stars burned out upon the backs of my eyelids as that horrible darkness crept closer.

We surfaced with a heaving splash. I gasped and choked, pulling air into my parched lungs. My limbs floundered, sank. But Wayland was still there, supporting my weak movements. He dragged me along. I kicked feebly. Everything was too dark—although I strained my eyes, there was no light save the negligible glow emanating from our twin collars.

"All right, Thorn Girl?" Wayland's voice was very close to my ear. I shuddered—I wanted to be out of this water more than anything I'd ever wanted in my life.

"Can you see?" I gasped out.

"Enough."

Our feet struck pebbled shale. Relief made me weak—I nearly collapsed as the beach rose up to greet us. I dug my fingers into the stony strand and heaved myself out of the water, gulping at the darkness. A moment later, Wayland's warm palm closed around my hand.

"I'm sorry, Fia," he said after a moment. "I should not have let you come."

"I didn't give you much choice." I could barely see him—could only feel the weight of his bulk bleeding heat into my chilled frame. "Thank you for saving my life. How can you swim so well? How can you see in the dark?"

For a long moment, Wayland was silent. Then: "My father did

not…do what he did to me until I was nearly of age. He was curious, I think—to discover what my natural affinities were. Whether they mirrored his. Or whether they were more like my mother's."

Silence stretched the blackness to silk.

"And?"

"Magical affinities are often hereditary. I can only assume by how reticent he was to teach me any of his skills—and by how eager he was to curtail me—that I am indeed my father's son." With little but scant outlines of silver to lend his face context, Wayland's voice was careful, resentful. "But I also inherited her…"

He trailed off.

"I'm sorry." The darkness thrilled with my want—my desperate desire—to know his story. But Gavida's geas seemed a challenge to circumvent. "I know it's difficult to speak about."

"Not in the way you think," he said flatly. "At least, not this part. I may speak freely of her—of my mother. She was of the lower Folk—a selkie. She could change at will between woman and seal. Provided, of course, that she had access to her pelt—her sealskin. My father took that from her. And hid it."

Horror spangled through me. "Why?"

"He says he did it because he loved her." Wayland's voice was a razor carving the flesh from my bones. "But I cannot see how stealing away someone's truest nature could ever be love."

"So you are—"

"Something in between, I suppose." His breath gusted. "I found the pelt when I was just a boy. My father didn't even bother to hide it particularly well. He must have thought she was grateful to be his. Grateful to be kept. Grateful to be caged." Wayland paused so long I thought he might be finished with his tale. "I still remember the weight of it—slick as oil and heavy as ruination. I bundled it into my arms and carried it to her. 'Mama,' I said, 'what is this?' She said nothing as she plucked it from my arms and turned her back on me. And before I knew it, she was gone—down to the sea that had birthed her. She didn't even say goodbye."

My horror eased toward a learned empathy I wouldn't wish on my worst enemies. "Wayland. I'm sorry."

"My anam cló is a seal." Wayland's fractured words trampled over my poor apologies. "Somehow, my father's forgings cannot affect the magic my mother instilled in me. She grew something inside me that not even he can control. It is a secret I have kept from him for many years."

We were both quiet for a stretch.

"Can I ask you a question?" A question that had been needling at me for days but that I hadn't found the right time to ask.

"You may always ask," Wayland said, a little wary. "I cannot promise I will be able to answer."

"Gavida is known to have forged the Treasures, half an age ago." I slid my hand around the Heart of the Forest. "But this is not *forged*—not sword nor cauldron nor even shield. It is a *stone*—something made by nature. Nothing like Gavida's puppets, or Gáe Bulga, or our collars. What is the difference?"

Wayland clasped his hands, exhaled. Considered his words. "In my . . . very limited experience, magical forging is in fact quite *unlike* what a blacksmith does. It is more about crafting little geasa than it is hammering metal. Binding magic to object, and vice versa. My father uses his forge as a stage, his crucible as a prop, his signature metal as a maker's mark. But when he forged the original Treasures, he was nearly as young as Irian and me. From what I have gleaned of those long-ago days, my father was a prodigy in his craft, but not yet a master. Those legendary forgings were unlike anything he had made before, nor anything he has crafted since. He wrought impossibly potent geasa linking vast elemental magic sources to resonant objects."

I knew Gavida had gone one step further. The *objects* were simply conduits—the elemental sources had, in truth, been bound to living vessels. At great cost. But I wasn't sure whether Wayland knew that. So I didn't interrupt him.

"You are correct," he continued. "Both the Sky-Sword and

the Cauldron were forged of metal, although not the same metal my father uses now. But the Flaming Shield was said to be wood carved from a holy tree. And the Heart of the Forest—well. You are the expert."

"Could it be done again?" I looked down at the stone, warm as an embrace against my chest. Then asked the real question I wanted to ask, based on what I knew of his so-called affinities. "Could *you* do it? If you had to?"

In the near dark, Wayland was little more than an inkblot—easy to cast with my own hopes. My own fears. At last, he said, "I do not know. Perhaps. Perhaps not. But I certainly like to think that I could. If I had to...and if I were able."

I sighed. It was about as good an answer as I could hope for, considering. I reached out, gripped his arm. "I don't suppose seals can see in the dark?"

"They very much can." He stood, lifting me with him. "Come. There's something this way. I'm not sure what. It could be dangerous. Are you ready?"

I thumbed the hilts of my skeans, loosening them in their scabbards. "Yes."

We climbed. Outcroppings tore at our ankles as stalactites dripped dusky water onto our heads. But Wayland was right—there was *something* here. It thrummed along my bones and spun cool cobwebs through my veins. The air itself seemed to lighten as we approached. No—not the air. Our *collars*, the silvery metal of Gavida's forgings sparking brighter. I quickened my footsteps, longing for whatever might lurk beneath—

"Slowly. Here—a wall."

I could still see little more than the outlines of things—Wayland's heavy arm palming the wall was a ghost in the dim. He swore colorfully, then took hold of my hand, moving it onto the wall blocking our way. I expected the stone to be cold, but it was faintly warm to the touch. A flare of energy climbed my arm to the elbow, stinging along the black markings hidden beneath my

sleeves. I resisted the urge to snatch my hand away, instead sliding it over the rough rock. No—not rough. The pocks and grooves
were too regular—too systematic—to be anything but intentional.

Carven.

"Another puzzle," Wayland groaned. "Another trap. Whatever
my father is hiding here, there is no easy way in."

"So…what?" A giggle escaped me, hysteria unfurling as my
composure bled away. "This was for nothing? I bought a weapon
with a golden apple, slew an overgrown otter-fish-*thing*, nearly
drowned in an underground lake, for *nothing*? Donn's dark hell,
Wayland! There has to be a way in."

I stepped closer, the still-feeble light of my collar splashing
the wall. I trailed my fingers over the intricate carvings, trying to
make sense of the half-illuminated shapes. Recursive patterns of
rounded leaves and plump berries; gnarled apple trees twisting
branches down to twine with their own roots; falling stars with
long, streaming tails. The images threaded across the tapestry of
my memory—where had I seen them before?

"My father's forge," Wayland murmured from beside me.
"These doors are nearly a replica of the larger ones in Aduantas.
Look at the pattern—it's almost identical."

Hope bloomed in me, sudden and fierce. I ran my hands more
urgently over the carven expanse, seeking a hinge or a crack or—

A keyhole. Little more than a divot in the stone punctuated by a
hole smaller even than my littlest finger. Frustration burned away
my hope as swiftly as it had blossomed.

"Surely there's a key—"

"Fia." Wayland's voice had lost all its usual humor—that, more
than anything, jerked my eyes to his shadowed face. He was staring down at me with a half-quizzical, half-wondering expression.
"Look."

A faint blue-green radiance had joined the cool silver light emanating from our collars. I inhaled sharply. Almost totally quiescent
since the moment Gavida collared me, the Heart of the Forest was

glowing, its deep green light expanding and contracting. When I gripped it in my palm, it throbbed, warm to the touch.

"What does it mean?" I whispered.

"I don't know." Wayland was still looking at me oddly. "But as you said, my father did forge the Treasures. Perhaps there is some connection—"

I gripped the stone a little harder, then lifted it toward the door. It was a stupid idea—the divot in the door was far smaller than the Heart; the keyhole implied an actual latchkey. Besides its ambiguous glowing, there was little to suggest my Treasure had anything to do with the source of Gavida's power.

But I was out of other ideas.

The Heart struck the door with a faint tink. A moment later, green light vined along the swirling stone contours like embroidered moss. Down deep, the bones of the earth groaned. The walls shook and the floor shuddered, sending a few small stalactites skittering downward. I jerked in surprise and nearly lifted the Heart from the door. But Wayland folded his large fingers over mine, holding my fist still.

"Not yet. Something's happening."

He wasn't wrong. The whole island rumbled with the force of some internal struggle. With painstaking slowness—like a giant cracking an eye after millennia of slumber—the door split ungently open. Some of the carvings sheared off and crumbled to the floor. The aperture left behind was no broader than me. Wayland and I stared into the dark crack as the cavern ceased its shuddering. A tendril of dread wound tight around my chilled bones.

This felt like a forced entry—as if some magic I could not understand had wedged a lever beneath the door, then pushed. Less an opening than a cavity—a tooth wrenched from an unwilling mouth.

We were not meant to be here.

For the first time since arriving at Emain Ablach, I wondered whether the forces at play on this isle went beyond Gavida. Before the smith-king collared me, I'd sent my awareness as deep as I could into the spaces below Aduantas. And beneath the dreadful lifeless-ness of the city, I'd *felt* something. A sick, throbbing metallic core deep within these caverns. It had frightened me.

My hand—sandwiched between my Treasure and Wayland's cool, smooth palm—convulsed. Maybe I should have listened to that fear.

"Well?" Wayland's murmur lapped against me.

I exhaled and yanked the Heart of the Forest up over my head to hold its glow out in front of me like a lantern.

"No turning back now."

Chapter Twenty-Nine

I ducked, my braids grazing the raw, broken stone. Then stepped into the darkness beyond.

The green light of the Heart preceded me into an echoing space, doing very little to dispel the sea of shadow lapping around us. I held the stone higher, as if I could will my Treasure brighter. But as my eyes adjusted, I saw the space was lit by a faint but pervasive metallic glow somewhere between silver and gold. I dropped my Treasure back down to hang against my shirt. It pulsed comfortingly, lending me some measure of strength.

The vast chamber was an echo of Gavida's forge and throne room up in Aduantas, although not a perfect copy. It curved around us like a womb. Or—as the pale glow illuminated thick, sinuous columns placed at intervals around the room—a rib cage. In the place of Gavida's throne a huge statue loomed. I recognized it from the tournament arena—it bore the same visage as the Oak King, open-faced and strong-jawed amid his halo of leaves. I whipped my head around. As expected, across the room, in the space where Gavida's crucible hung far above, another statue stood—this one portraying the hollow-cheeked, frowning Holly King, wreathed in sharp leaves and plump berries. We stood in a pool of shallow, reflective water two or three inches deep, etched with expanding wavelets. The air smelled faintly of burnt iron, charged with a current of energy that raised the hair on the back of my neck.

"This..." Wayland's barely audible voice rang sharply over the flat water, birthing echoes as it went. "This is not a place of honor."

He was right. A terrible foreboding lingered here: a memory of some atrocity, long forgotten...or the premonition of some malfeasance yet to be performed. I shuddered, gooseflesh pebbling my forearms.

The low hum of energy in the air intensified. The diffuse glow lighting the room began to *move*, flecks of light joining one another until the air rioted with shimmering stars. I backed reflexively into Wayland, who put a protective hand on my shoulder. The shining motes scorched through the blackness toward one another, burning streaming afterimages against my vision. I blinked, and when I looked up again, the glow had coalesced into something. Some*one*.

The figure was perfectly exquisite and wholly alien. I could hardly comprehend, much less describe them. They were made of *light*...or metal...or both. An otherworldly glow suffused them, cascading along the flowing liquid silver and gold that made up their face, their body, their hair. Their eyes were smoldering orbs of molten steel, hot from the forge. A flowing mantle of blistering red-hot liquid rippled and re-formed around them, shifting and spitting crimson sparks to fizzle out in the water below. Adornments around their throat and wrists radiated a faint, captivating silver light. Their form was fluid—an interchange between the ethereal and the tangible. As if in this one place, this single moment, the boundaries between the material and the elemental realms were impossibly but perceptibly interwoven.

I stared, awe and shock and a curious sense of *knowing* slowing my reactions. Wayland got there first.

"Na Bliana," he breathed. *The Year.*

There was little space to imagine any other conclusion. Again, I floundered for words. All I managed was a whispered "What were you saying about bedtime stories, Prionsa?"

Wayland huffed a quiet laugh. "Why am I not shocked that your first instinct in this scenario is to say *I told you so?*"

"Are you calling me predictable?"

"Never." His voice rasped, ragged with awe. "But I can't believe she's real. I can't believe she's *here*."

"*She?*" It seemed impossible to gender this entity, who existed so far beyond either human or Folk. But otherwise, this *was* the legendary Year—the goddess of their myths, the consort to their mythic kings, the center of their traditions. "That strikes me as... simplistic."

Indeed. It was not speech that burned sparks through my mind. Nor was it Linn's brutal pictographic telepathy. It was something almost unnameable—a complex calligraphy of words and feelings etched searingly upon my innermost reaches. *My kind have no genders—not in the way you think of them. But I have been called such before and surely will be called so again. It matters little how you refer to me.*

The Year drifted closer, forming and unforming and re-forming again in recursive, fractal patterns that made me faintly nauseated. I fought the urge to back away, even as the veins of molten metal dripping off her steamed the water and singed the ends of my hair.

You. Her burning, depthless eyes—like coals, like rubies, like the heart of a bonfire—were fixed upon me. She didn't even glance at Wayland. *I do not know you. And yet you are known.*

Flustered confusion made me leery. I took an involuntary step back, even as I shot a helpless glance at Wayland. "Did you hear that?"

He gave me a strange look. "Hear *what?*"

He is collared. Her regard was intensely unwavering. *He cannot hear me.*

"So am I," I said out loud.

Yes. The Year reached out with hands like half-forged daggers, guttering flames. But the moment before she touched my collar, a shower of sparks dashed like glitter from my throat to burn out in the water below. *But you are different than him. You are star touched.*

"*Star touched?*" My voice came out more incredulous than I'd intended. As if I was in any position to doubt *anything*, in this particular moment. "What does that mean?"

She said nothing, only burned a brief but heartrending sensation through me. An emotion, a memory, a wish. It started in the center of my chest and exploded outward, expanding into every crevice of my being. The knowledge of what I was before I was born. Who I was meant to be now. What I would become after I died. Everything...and nothing. Roots burrowed deep through dark loam. Silver-tipped branches sifting through a thousand dusk-lit skies. It was instantaneous and excruciating and ecstatic, and I wanted—I *wanted*—

"That's enough!" Wayland's growl cut through my trance—I opened eyes I hadn't realized I'd closed to find myself half-collapsed against him. "You have no cause to hurt her!"

"I'm fine." I rediscovered my feet. I glanced back up at the Year, with wariness but also creeping hunger.

"Who are you?" I asked. "And what are you doing down here?"

When the Year communicated, it wasn't so much a voice I heard as a bell resounding inside my mind, deafening as it rang. There were a thousand lifetimes of memories, a million perfect emotions. But she distilled it all into something almost digestible—a series of metal memories strung together like a chain.

"The Year was..." I spoke aloud as the story looped around me like a jeweled necklace of immortal evocations. There was a chance I would not remember it after. I should at least try to share it with Wayland. "*Solasóirí.* The Bright Ones. They came here from the stars—with light, with love. And for eons they—" I swayed. Wayland steadied me again, and I swallowed, hard. I wasn't sure I could do this. Color and sensation and endlessness were painted on the inside of my skin. "They brought magic to this land. Eventually, they were enslaved by the Fomorians, bound by their own vast power. She was forced to build this island. No, not build. *Reinforce.* It was unlivable before—the ocean too strong, the cliffs unstable. She propped it up with bones of metal—"

"Further forward." Wayland's voice was urgent in my ear. "We need to know how Gavida has her trapped. We need to know how to set her free."

But that wasn't how the Year was telling me the story.

"Then *you* came—the Fair Folk came." I closed my eyes against the burden of bittersweet memories. "There were two Gentry brothers. Your kings of lore. They swore they loved her. Together, they bound her anew. To protect her and themselves. The three of them made the Silver Isle flourish. The things they built—" Glory and ruination made a massacre of my mind's eye. "But it could not last. Their empire crumbled as so many had before. And in the end, she was alone once more. Until Gavida came.

"He sought her out. He—" I reached for Wayland, then—as much for support as for grounding. Something real, something here, something *now.* His broad hands wrapped around my arms, supported the small of my back as I struggled against terrible duality. This ancient, elemental entity transposed upon my being. A palimpsest of self that threatened to blot me out completely. "Something to do with the forging of the Treasures. She was not involved, but afterward he searched for her; he *hunted* her; he—"

"He caged her." Wayland's voice dragged me out from the unfathomed depths of my visions. I opened my eyes to find him staring up at the Year, and I realized in an embarrassing flash what I hadn't earlier.

Those were not bracelets. That was not a necklace. The metals she wore around her arms and neck were not adornments—the Year needed no ornamentation for her awesome, mind-boggling beauty.

They were shackles.

Thrice times three am I bound, said the Year. *Three kings. Three tethers. Three elements. And three times three golden trees hemming me in.*

For a moment, I didn't see how the apple trees—growing hundreds of feet above in the Grove of Gold at the top of the isle— could affect her. But then my eyes found the uneven pillars I'd thought were stone ringing the perimeter like ribs. And I saw—not golden stone, sinuously carven. But ancient, gnarled *wood*.

"Roots?" I whispered, almost as impressed as I was by the Year. "Then those trees are truly ancient—as ancient as the Heartwood, as ancient as—"

Me? The Year's psychic persona sounded vaguely amused. *They are holy. They are my counterbalance—they fetter even as they feed.*

"I gcothromaíocht," I murmured, remembering the lessons I'd learned from the ancient warrior's journals I'd discovered in Dún Darragh, what felt like eons ago. And I thought of what Laoise had told us about the nemeta—the sacred groves. "Counterpoise. Your magic must cycle through the Grove of Gold, renewing and regenerating. That revel the other night—"

"I told you it was more than a revel, Fia." Wayland's hands were still on me, but I didn't mind the comfort of his closeness. "But *what* does the ritual regenerate? What magic does my father take from her? And how can we break the link?"

"Is it—" I stared back up at the Year—at her rippling, ephemeral features; her ember eyes; her molten gown dripping heat above the reflective waters. I thought of Gavida's crucible, flickering and spitting silver sparks. It seemed unconscionable, but— "Is he siphoning off your blood for his metals?"

Not blood. The Year's demeanor turned grave. *Life force. Consciousness. Self. Every weapon he forges, every machine he assembles, bears within it a piece of* me. *Again and again, I am splintered. Slivers of me carved away and parceled up and used.*

"It's...*her*," I repeated to Wayland in an undertone, even as bile excoriated my throat.

And I am far diminished from what I once was, she continued. *It matters not how many die as sacrifice in his tournament, how robustly his disciples honor the Year, how regularly they renew the grove. He uses more than he returns. And soon there will be none of me left.*

"She's dying," I whispered, although that was yet another simplification. "Gavida takes more from her than he gives. He's using her up."

"Then we have to find a way to unbind her." Determination hammered Wayland's voice to steel. "We must set her free. Before it's too late."

"But how?" Helplessness gripped me, the same feeling I'd felt that night less than two months ago—the night of the Ember Moon. Although I'd racked my mind a thousand different ways, I hadn't been able to see a solution to Irian's fated tithe. I had realized what I needed to do only in the final moments—the understanding coming upon me unexpected and wholly unforeseen. I could not hope for such a revelation again. And simmering atop that realization was a worry, only half-selfish. "If she's freed, what happens to this island? Is it not your inheritance—your birthright?"

Wayland's jaw flexed, almost imperceptibly. "My father's power must be broken, especially now I know from whence it springs. This is a wrong that must be righted—a wrong that *I* must right. If I, too, am rendered powerless in the doing, so be it. I do not wish such power—not at this cost. And if the island becomes unlivable, then we will all simply have to move somewhere else." He glanced at me, then up at the Year. "But we cannot waste any more time down here. If we are to set you free, we need to return to Aduantas. My father must not realize I am missing."

The Year nodded. *Anywhere my veins spread, I can send you. You must only tell me where.*

"Veins?" I repeated out loud as I turned to Wayland. "Do you know what she means?"

"My chambers," Wayland said slowly. "There is a vein of metal above the bed—is that what you mean?"

It is. She reached out her hands toward us, fingers outspread. *As you go, so too may you return. Call out my name—Talah—and I will hear you.*

Wayland gripped my palm. Then we both lifted our hands toward the ethereal entity reaching toward us.

"Wait." The thought occurred to me like lightning. "Can you remove our collars? We will be better able to serve you if we can access our innate magic."

Her molten skin undulated in the dark. *I cannot unmake what has been made...unbind what has been bound. I am but the source. Neither the conduit nor the vessel.*

I shivered in the moment before my forefinger connected with hers. The touch was like quicksilver against my skin.

A jolt...ripple...slide. The isle's pale stone closed around me like a crypt. I opened my mouth to scream, but there was only the soundless pressure of a million years weighing me down.

I fell to my stomach on soft, weightless eiderdown in a candlelit room.

Part Three

The Silver Crown

Sweetness be in my face,
Riches be in my countenance,
Comb-honey be in my tongue,
My breath as the incense.

Black is yonder house,
Blacker men therein;
I am the white swan,
Queen over them.

—"Invocation for Justice," from *Carmina Gadelica* by
Alexander Carmichael

Chapter Thirty

Wayland's bed swallowed me in luxuriousness as I whumped indelicately down onto the fine mattress. Its owner followed a moment later, his tall, heavy frame landing beside me before nearly disappearing beneath the lush satins and expensive brocades. The weight of his impact rolled me on top of him. Our limbs tangled in disarray as I attempted to extricate myself from him.

"Ow," he grunted as I smacked him with one flailing elbow.

"Sorry." I tried to sit up, kneed him in the ribs. "I'm only trying—"

"Hold still, will you?" He gripped me roughly around the waist, holding me in place as he kicked at the quilt twining our legs together. I fought to keep my balance with a hand anchored by his head, the pillowcase velvety beneath my chilled fingers. I glared down at the offending blankets.

"You know, if you made your bed once in a while…"

Wayland glanced up at my chiding, and the motion brought our faces closer together. *Much* closer. Our noses nearly brushed, and I could see every mote of blue in his fathomless dark eyes. Between the shock of what we'd found in the caverns and our rather inelegant landing, we were both breathing hard—his breath gusted over my lips, tasting of sea brine and warm honey. I inhaled sharply. Wayland's hands tightened almost imperceptibly where they still rested at the divot of my waist. But otherwise he barely moved, his broad frame going still as his awareness followed mine to all the places our bodies touched.

My thighs, clamped around his hips. My hands, fisted in the pillows behind him. My half-undone, still-damp braids mingling with his sleek locks. Our lips, merely a whisper-width apart.

Exhaustion and revelation and the strength of holding back an inevitable wave of bone-cracking sorrow made me weak. Temptation slid cunningly beneath my warming skin, prickling thorns of desire up my softening spine.

"Do it," I whispered.

Wayland's smile was cautious. "Do what?"

Of course he was going to make me say it. Donn's hell, maybe the magic binding us together *demanded* it. But still I hesitated, staring down at the Gentry prince and cataloging his features, still strangely unfamiliar to me despite how much time we'd been spending together these past days.

His golden-brown skin, gilded by guttering beeswax candles. His cobalt eyes, depthless as a midnight sea and fringed by heavy lashes the same mahogany silk as his hair. His high, wide cheekbones; his gently curved nose; the wry, sly bow of his laughing mouth.

And I had to ask myself, Did I want Wayland to hold me, or did I simply want to be held? Did I want him to kiss me, or did I just want to be kissed? Did I want *him*?

I *didn't* want to think about Irian. And maybe it was unfair to Wayland—maybe it was unfair to *everyone*—but could this be the thing to bury those cruel, complicated, slippery thoughts? To keep them from sliding sharp between my ribs and rending my heart from its careful cage?

"Kiss me."

This time, Wayland obliged. His gaze softened, the shallows of his eyes warming to azure, then lightening to something pale as dawn. He slid one hand up from my waist to tangle gently in my hair. His palm cupped the back of my head as he closed the bare distance between us. His lips brushed mine, soft and cool. A shiver of energy buzzed along my skin and popped my ears, as if the pressure in the air had changed. I sighed with an odd and unexpected sense of relief, and Wayland took it as an invitation. His fingers tightened at my nape. He deepened the kiss, his mouth opening as his tongue slid between my teeth. He tasted like salt and sand, his ragged desire rasping like grit over my tongue. His lips spoke a promise to mine—a prelude to something *more*.

There was suddenly too much of him—too much warm skin and grasping hands and seeking tongue. And somehow, too, there was not enough—a lacking I could not quite fathom.

Perhaps I could.

I placed a firm hand in the center of Wayland's chest and disengaged my mouth from his, pushing away the desire beginning to crystallize between us. His fingers convulsed against my skin, as if he did not want to let me go. Then his hands fell from my waist, my nape. I rolled to one side, sitting up in his rumpled array of blankets. I fought the urge to scrub his lingering kiss from my swollen lips.

No need to salt the wound.

He made no move to sit up beside me, reaching back instead to pillow his head in his hands. The look he gave me was heavy-lidded with guarded disappointment. "No?"

I shook my head. "No."

"While it's not implausible that one person in the world is immune to my charms..." He sighed. "I confess, rather indecently—I wish it were not you."

"It has nothing to do with your dubious charms, Prionsa." I tried to joke, but the jibe fell flat. "My heart belongs to another."

"I know." He rolled up to sit beside me. The look he gave me was raw—almost wounded. But a moment later, it smoothed away beneath a flash of his familiar insouciance. "When are you going to forgive him, Thorn Girl?"

I frowned and opened my mouth. But Wayland raised his hands before I could speak.

"I know it's none of my business. But you have not seen him in the arena these past days. I unfortunately have. He has been worse than usual. Borderline berserk. I wonder—if not for his sake, but for mine, when I am likely to have to fight him—have you not punished him enough?"

"You're right," I said icily, even as a flash of worry spiked a hot sizzle from my collar. "It's none of your business."

Wayland was quiet for a long moment. Then he pushed a length of his hair behind one ear and faced me on the bed. "Has Irian ever spoken to you about his father?"

"Ethadon?" Terrible curiosity awoke inside me. "Only a little."

"I doubt he would wish me to tell you this. But I think you ought to know." Wayland's eyes darkened nearly to black. "My father is a villain. Ethadon was...worse. Months after Deirdre died and her magic—*your* magic—was set free, Ethadon came to collect Irian from his mother's home. He barely let him say goodbye to the woman who had birthed him, raised him, loved him. When Irian fought, Ethadon told him, 'I swear by gods living and dead, boy— the more you think of her, the less she will remember you. Forget her. She is but a mother. And you will soon be a man.' Irian was barely eight years old."

Sympathy and fury blistered through me. "Do men not need mothers?"

"Ethadon's words, not mine. I have lived too long without a mother to believe such nonsense." Wayland paused, passing a hand over his eyes. "Irian came to us devastated and disheartened. A broken-winged bird. He had lost both a soul sister and a real mother in the space of months. His father deposited him in our care, then once more disappeared from his life. I tried to take

Irian under my wing—to be the foster brother he deserved. But he thought only of her—of his mother. By day he was the stoic little warrior our fathers demanded he be. But by night...I do not know what he dreamed of, but I certainly remember how he screamed."

I swallowed. "Why are you telling me this?"

"He ran away." Wayland continued, ignoring my interruption. "About a year after he came to Emain Ablach. It was an elaborate plan, perfectly executed. No one knew he was gone until days after he scammed me and all the servants, stole a currach, rowed himself across half an ocean, and hiked alone over the moors until he reached his mother's cottage. Only to discover that his father's words had not been an empty threat, but a geas. Just as Ethadon had sworn, every thought Irian spared his mother had stolen a memory of him from her. And he had thought of her constantly. So when he barreled into her cottage, wrapped his arms around her waist, and lifted up his face for a kiss...his mother had no memory of her son."

Wayland's story unhinged something excruciating inside me— an ache of horrible familiarity. Only, in my story I was the one who had forgotten. A childhood—a mother. Was she out there somewhere, knowing I might love her if only I could remember her? "What did he do?"

"What do you think he did, Thorn Girl?" Wayland's voice rang with bleakness. "He sat weeping in his own home while his kind-hearted mother made porridge for the strange boy who'd wandered into her kitchen. Then he returned to us, although he knew it would earn him a lashing. And he never screamed in his sleep again."

Something unwieldy rose up inside me, and I clenched my fists. "We all have traumatic pasts, Wayland."

"Everyone Irian has ever dared to love, he has lost," Wayland said gently. "Including you, if the rumors are true. I daresay that might make even the best man behave like a monster."

Heavy silence yawned between us, choking out my words. The beeswax candles guttered on the mantel.

"It's late," Wayland said. "Hopefully my father will believe I took someone particularly interesting to bed, then fell asleep. But since I know you do not wish the world to think it's you, then you should leave as you came."

"Must you really be so vigilant of Gavida's observations?" I cocked my head. "He seems secure in his position. Why should he suspect you now?"

"Because *you* are here, and that means the balances have shifted. If there is anything my father truly believes in—other than himself—it is the pattern written in the stars. Perhaps now I know why." Wayland's face grew tight with learned wariness. "If we truly wish to free the Year and break my father's power over us in the doing, we need to remain cautious of him. He may be old, but that has only made him wily. And despite all our caution, he has too many eyes and ears for me to believe we have fully escaped his scrutiny this past week."

"Understood." I rose slowly to my feet. "But now that we have found the Year, how are we to go about freeing her? There are only a few days left in the tournament."

"Three," Wayland confirmed, a muscle in his jaw jumping. "Tomorrow, the field will be whittled down to two contestants, after which my father will host a great feast—the Damhsa de Thrí. The day after, those two will compete for the position of Oak King. And on the Longest Night, I will duel with whoever wins. And lose, if we cannot find a way to unbind the Year...and my own destiny with her."

"It's not much time," I murmured. "But Chandi said she'd heard word of a library or archive. Perhaps I can find some information about the Bright Ones. About how your father might have bound the Year."

Wayland nodded, although he did not look particularly confident in this plan. "Until tomorrow, Thorn Girl."

I shrugged my damp, salt-stained mantle back on. "Until tomorrow, Prionsa."

I twisted the mirror on the mantel, spun the glass dial, and scouted down the dark, empty staircase. But as I prepared to descend into the passages below Aduantas, Wayland's voice stopped me.

"Fia?" I turned. He lounged on the edge of his mattress, his clothes rumpled and his hair mussed. His mouth curved up in a ghost of a smile. "I know you felt nothing. But if it was truly to be our first, last, and only? I could not have dreamed of a more perfect kiss."

I did not dream of perfect kisses. I dreamed of Irian—a black swan upon a black sea against a black night. And when the sky split with electric veins of silver, I saw *them*—an endless boreal deity of skies and winds and storms. They reached for him with colossal, thunderous hands. And when they turned to look at me with eyes like burned-out stars, I knew that they were angry to have been caged so long.

Chapter Thirty-One

I woke to my body aching like I'd been trampled by an overgrown king otter before nearly drowning in an underground cavern.

Oh, *wait*.

I slumped to the bathing chamber. My reflection in the mirror startled me—I was a *mess*. My hair was a snarled, matted bird's nest; grime streaked my neck and cheeks; a purpling bruise peeked from beneath my hairline.

A dart of embarrassment pierced me. How had Wayland been willing to kiss me looking like this? I shook my head. It was done now. And everyone better off for it.

I peeled off the clothes I'd never bothered to change out of last night. My right side screamed when I lifted my tunic over my head. A massive contusion stretched from hip to rib, gruesome in shades of moss and mallow. I touched the wound gingerly, but the lack of excruciating pain told me I hadn't broken anything. Lucky. If there was ever a time I missed the healing powers of my Treasure…

I lifted a hand to my collar, shocked by how accustomed to its weight I'd become. I supposed with enough time, anyone could get used to anything.

The scalding bathtub was halfway full before I belatedly remembered—I'd promised Sinéad a dawn training session. I cursed, peering out at the pearly sky. It was halfway to midmorning, if I had to guess.

I had approximately five friends on this island. In the whole *world*. Forgetful or not, I was in no position to ditch any of them without explanation.

I stared longingly at the suds gathering in the tub before forcing myself to drag on a new pair of breeches. I pulled a fresh shirt gingerly over my torso, belted my skeans at my waist, then dashed out into Aduantas. Sinéad had likely already returned to her rooms or gone about her day. But if I could catch her—

To my great relief, she was still in the narrow little pleasure garden we'd earmarked for our exercises. Albeit sulkily. She'd apparently taken her ire out on a once-manicured topiary. Hundreds of tiny petals littered the snow at her feet, and the bush now looked like a dead man's skull—gaping eyes and a twig-filled mouth.

"Not sure the shrub deserved it," I said. "Fancy stabbing me instead?"

The honey blonde whirled on her heel at the sound of my voice, her expression softening toward relief before hardening again to careful anger. "You're here."

"I completely forgot," I admitted, shamefaced. "But I came as soon as I remembered. Thank you for waiting."

"Well," she said after a beat. "I didn't want to lose the bet."

"What bet?"

"Chandi said you'd forget. I said you'd remember. We wagered a bottle of that rainbow liquor on whoever got it right."

"All right, I deserve that." Guilt coiled sickly in my stomach. I attempted to lighten the mood. "And Laoise? With a bottle of rainbow liquor on the table, there's no way she'd turn down a good bet."

"She wagered you'd be so banged up from hunting that king otter that you wouldn't be able to block *this* feint."

Sinéad unsheathed her daggers and spun toward me in one fluid motion, dropping her shoulder at the last moment so she cut through my guard at an angle. It was a good move—my right arm came up too slow, instinctively protecting my bruised side. Sinéad's arm skidded down my own, jarring my collarbone. I winced as her blade came to rest an inch below my throat. I froze, raising my arms in surrender.

"The bottle goes to Laoise. Although next time tell her to earn it herself." I whistled, impressed. "You've been sparring with her?"

"A little." Sinéad stepped back, looking pleased with herself. "Her forms and variations are different from yours. It's a good balance."

I crooked a finger at her. "Show me."

The taller girl happily flung herself into training, and I did my best to keep up with her enthusiasm despite my injuries. She'd improved, in just a few days—her footwork showing more confidence and her strikes pulling more power from her core. We moved through all the variations I'd shown her, then the ones Laoise had taught her, until both of us were sweat gleamed and panting. Despite the dull ache curling a fist around my abdomen, it felt good to exercise—to pull sharp cold air through my lungs and force my muscles to their trembling limits. But before too long, I was finished. I planted my hands on my knees and helplessly shook my head.

"Enough," I gasped out. "Have mercy on me."

"Good timing." Laoise's melodious accent floated through the crisp air. I straightened. The Gentry maiden wound her way into the pleasure garden, followed closely by Chandi, who seemed more interested in Sinéad's butchered topiary than in me. Behind her, a huge hulking shadow loomed ominously—

I jerked my skeans out of their scabbards, then resheathed them just as quickly. Surprise and then delight wreathed through me. "Balor? What are you doing here?"

The Fomorian stomped forward, rattling the walls of the gardens and shaking the ornamental trees in their pots.

"Hello, lady! I was eliminated from the tournament again," he said in that slow, measured way of his. "During the Trial of Wits. I am not so clever, I'm afraid."

"I'm sorry to hear that, Balor." I glanced over at Laoise and Chandi. "But how did you all meet up? I didn't think you knew each other."

"We did not." Laoise made a rueful face. "But Balor went asking all over town about the 'kind, beautiful Gentry lady' with the 'scary husband.' We took pity on him."

"It's true." Balor wrung his hands together, looking sheepish. "Every year for twenty years I come to this island to compete in the tournament. Every year I get kicked out. Every year I go home again. This was the first year I made a friend."

"Balor, I'm touched." I pressed a hand to my chest, but the throb of the Heart of the Forest beneath my tunic made me think suddenly of the Year, trapped deep beneath the city. And of all that could go wrong if Gavida discovered what Wayland and I were planning. I glanced at Laoise, unsure how much she'd told the Fomorian. "But I'll warn you—my friendship may not be to your liking. I'm...not very popular with the smith-king. I would hate to get you in any trouble."

"I live for trouble!" Balor laughed—a terrifyingly loud boom that startled a nest of fledgling owlets from a tree and bowled over an ornamental bench that sprouted feet and began to sneak away. "And good company!"

"Then I suppose you may join our party." I glanced from him to the girls, who were looking at me as if they expected an update. But how could I explain to them what Wayland and I had found last night? More importantly, how could I be sure we wouldn't be overheard? I liked Balor, based on the three interactions we'd had, but could I trust him?

"You seemed close to finding a library," I said to Chandi instead. "Any luck?"

"Yes." The other girl finally looked up at me. Her usually

sparkling amber eyes were dull and shadowed—as if she hadn't slept much. Too much carousing, perhaps. "But you're not going to like it."

My heart instantly plummeted toward my boots. "Tell me."

"There is a rare-book repository in the Shielings," Laoise cut in. "But it's owned by our old friend Master Blink."

"Shite," I groaned. "We'd better give it a shot, though. It's time to do some research."

"About what?" Sinéad spun her daggers aimlessly around her fingers. The gesture jarred me, until I realized it was my own nervous habit she was mirroring.

"I'll tell you when we get there." I looked down at myself, then grimaced. "On second thought, why don't you get started without me? I'll meet you there in an hour."

"Why?" asked Chandi.

"I really, *really* need a bath."

Back in my chamber, I finished running my now-lukewarm bath, unbraided my matted hair, then submerged my throbbing body for the better part of said hour. Once I surfaced, I unplugged the bath before swaddling myself in three layers of fluffy sky-blue towels. The drapes opened to a sky like enamel glazed above the ceramic city. For a long moment I stood frozen, staring out over what Gavida had built with power he had stolen. I stared until dappled leaves shaded the inside of my skin and my collar spiked a warning to my thrumming veins. Then I slurped down half a cup of mushroom tea—which I'd strangely begun to crave—and dressed in a buttery-soft kirtle magically provided by the wardrobe.

My hand was almost to the door latch when I caught sight of a rectangle of white parchment nearly camouflaged against the pale tile. The letter had no markings on the outside. When I opened it, what could only be Irian's handwriting stared up at me—the ink black as his hair, the lines sharp as the Sky-Sword, the vowels fletched with barely contained passion.

Come back to me.

I clutched it until my fingernails cut divots into the parchment. Then I let it flutter to the floor. I stalked from the room.

I loved him, gods forgive me. But I wasn't ready to go home.

The Shielings were harder to navigate without Laoise's expert guidance. I hurried through alleyways winding like tangled necklaces and between listing buildings thatched with moss and seashells and houses that looked like seabirds' nests. The slums were beginning to clear out—Folk heading toward the distant hive-hum of the Tournament of Kings. After a half hour walking in circles, I finally found a tavern that looked vaguely familiar. I peered between its driftwood shutters and waved over a surly ghillie, one of the last patrons, who was nursing a goblet of dewdrops.

"Do you know Blink's bookstore?"

The creature swiped dripping lichen out of its eyes, then gestured one street over.

I marched toward where the ghillie had indicated. Blink was clearly waiting for me—he threw the door open as I approached, waving me into the tall building listing halfway over his curiosity shop.

"Come in, come in—your friends are inside!" Blink crowed, gesturing with his overlong arms at the towering stacks of books I could already see from the threshold. "Tales to spin and knots to untie."

"I swear to the gods, brùnaidh," I said pleasantly. "If you start speaking at me in rhymes, I'll put your tongue in a knot you'll never be able to untie."

Blink grumbled but ushered me inside—I supposed the prospect of wheedling another bargain out of me made him amenable.

I sighed and stepped into the greatest collection of books and manuscripts I'd ever seen.

Compared to Blink's bookshop, the archive I'd discovered in Dún Darragh was a piddling thing. This collection was indescribable—wobbling stacks of tomes nudged against looming mountains of scrolls; loose parchment sifted between piles of tablets etched in strange letters and symbols. Unsurprisingly, it was neither particularly well tended nor well organized—the whole labyrinth smelled of ancient dust and mildew-streaked paper. I sneezed, then followed the sounds of conversation deeper into Blink's maze of books.

They were all there—Chandi had a volume almost as wide as her arms spread out on a table in front of her, while Sinéad inadvisably tried to climb a teetering bookshelf in pursuit of some particular tome. Laoise was holding delicately illuminated scrolls up to the light and peering at them while Balor laboriously sorted through a stack of huge chronicles that looked like children's books in his massive hands.

"There you are," said Laoise, rather more cheerful than the rest of them looked. "This place is a disaster. Mind telling us what we're looking for?"

I swallowed. I still didn't quite know how to put Talah into words. The secret of her existence coiled inside me like a fern fiddlehead—curled so tight I worried unfurling it at the wrong moment might damage its survival. Besides, I mistrusted Blink—how could I be sure he wasn't listening? I decided to keep things as superficial as possible—at least for now.

"Let's focus on bindings," I said, as casually as I could manage. "The power of threes. And I think the Grove of Gold must be important too."

Sinéad and Laoise glanced at each other, then went back to perusing the books. Balor seemed not to hear me at all, humming atonally as he thumbed through books barely bigger than said thumb. Chandi, however, looked preoccupied. I stepped carefully over a stack of parchments seemingly inked in human blood on human skin, and sat on an uneven stool beside her. She was perusing a page heavily illuminated in deep, dark pigments—so intricate it took me a few long minutes to glean its meaning. When I did, cold water puddled in my stomach.

It was some kind of Folk grimoire, and the page Chandi was looking at depicted an arcane ritual for resurrection. On one folio, a triquetra whirled around a dead man curled like a fetus in an egg. Each arm of the spiral depicted a different bird—peacock, albatross, cormorant—spatchcocked with a blade through its neck. And on the facing page, the man stood resurrected but transformed—his skin no longer pink but a peacock feather's iridescent blue, his hair no longer brown but an albatross's white edged with black, his eyes no longer green but a cormorant's staring turquoise.

I looked from the page to Chandi, sympathy warring with hazy warning. She flipped the page to something more innocuous.

"I understand why it must be tempting," I said softly. "But if I know anything about magic, it is this: Even if you found a way to bring them back, they would not return the same as they had been before."

She glanced sideways at me. "You did."

The chill clambered up my ribs to caress my heart with cold fingers. "Did I?"

Chandi was silent for a long minute. *Flip.* Pacts and portals. *Flip.* Night-blooming flowers and eclipses. "Don't worry. I couldn't really read the spell, if that's even what it was. You know, I didn't even learn how until a few years ago. Most of the other swan girls learned—back in their old lives, in the human realms. But I was too little. And there wasn't much for me to read. I still can't write."

The revelation slapped me in the face, bringing an uncomfortable flush to my cheeks. It had never occurred to me that she would have been so uneducated. So deprived. But of course, I'd never asked.

"I didn't know." I slid my palm toward hers across the table. "I can help—"

Her hand lifted in the moment before I could grasp it. She turned the next page. *Flip.* Shadows and elixirs.

"It's all right, Fia," she said. "This book has lots of pictures."

After a moment, I stood and moved off between the stacks.

It was hard, unpleasant research. Many of the scrolls crumbled to dust at a touch; some of the books grew teeth and snapped at your fingers. The rest of the material was written in languages I only half spoke, and was illustrated in pictures I preferred to banish to nightmares. I'd thought my translations at Dún Darragh had been arduous, frustrating work—this was worse by far. After an hour, my fingers were nipped raw by cantankerous novels, my hair was clotted with dust, and I was running out of patience. When I spied Blink lurking in the stacks, I took drastic measures.

"You." He tried to hide himself, but I stalked him through the shop until he couldn't outrun me any longer. "Help me find something."

He spread his too-long arms in a placatory gesture. "What you seek, you shall find. For a price, of course."

"Of course," I ground out. "What price? And how can I be sure you'll actually find me what I need?"

"Name what you seek. Then I'll name a price."

Making a bargain with Blink was ill-advised—I knew that. But my patience was wearing thin. I rolled words over my tongue and tried to be precise. "How may I break a geas bound by threes? And know I will not pay the price until what I seek has been delivered."

Blink gave me a theatrical bow, then bounced off between the listing stacks. I'd almost grown annoyed enough to start searching again on my own when he finally slunk back.

"Lady," he said mockingly, as he held up a tome marked with one long finger in the middle.

I reached for it, but he clicked his tongue upon his too-small teeth. "Shall we discuss cost?"

"Go on."

"In return for this rare and valuable volume, I would ask for the first kiss—"

"No." My reaction was knee-jerk. "I'm not bargaining any more kisses. Name another price."

"Not with *me*, you enormous hairless weasel," snickered Blink, rather insultingly. "The first kiss *you* ever gave...in love."

Something cold touched the back of my neck, even as warmth bled into my cheeks. "I don't want to give you that either."

"Then I demand three hairs from your head."

The chill clinging to my spine intensified, making me shiver. After the Year's revelations and Laoise's warnings, it did not seem well-advised to relinquish any part of my body, especially not in threes. "What else?"

"I will not barter with you all day, lady." Blink's childlike smile was not kind. "Did you think the cost would be cheap? I have set the terms. Make your choice."

Shite.

Like nearly all my firsts, my first kiss had been with Rogan. I was fifteen, in the first flush of womanhood; he, seventeen, and rather obnoxiously arrogant with all the new muscles fleshing out his suddenly over-tall frame. It had been summer on the verge of autumn, a deceptively hot day with a high, brisk wind scudding white clouds across an azure sky. We had been out riding and had stopped to pick wild blackberries in the hedge. They'd been perfectly ripe, bursting warm and sweet and tart on my tongue. I'd picked one handful, then another, as Rogan swiped at the vines with his claíomh and bragged about some serving girl in the fort who'd been making eyes at him. I'd kept silently shoving blackberries in my mouth, the taste nearly drowning out my jealousy. He'd finally stopped prattling. I'd looked up at him, but he'd been watching me strangely.

"Sorry." I'd thought him angry at me for eating all the black-berries. I'd still had a few in my palm; the juices had stained my palms like wine. "Do you want a taste?"

"I do." He'd kissed me without warning—fullmouthed and overeager. I'd of course kissed him back, helplessly. The taste of ripe blackberries had mingled with the sharp liquor of my want for him until we were both drunk on each other's lips.

Later, Rogan had laughed it off. I'd been forced to swallow my tears while he flirted with—then eventually bedded—that long-lashed, full-lipped serving girl. And although part of me hated remembering how deferential I'd been to everyone else's wants, while simultaneously disregarding my own...it didn't mean I wanted to pretend it had never happened. I wasn't that girl any-more. But I *had been* her. And part of my transformation into who I wanted to be meant accepting—maybe even loving—the choices she'd made along the way. I wouldn't barter that away. Not for a book. Not to save a trapped deity. Not even to save myself.

"I assume the *given in love* element is the key." I feigned a casual tone. "The emotion makes the memory, does it not? I confess, my first amorous kiss was clumsy and boring. So let me offer you a dif-ferent, more valuable memory: my first kiss given in *self-loathing*. For don't you agree, Master Blink? Hatred is always stronger than love."

The brùnaidh cocked his domed head, considering. Finally, he held out his long hairy fingers and said, "Done."

I shook his hand briskly. When he handed me a dull nugget of quartz, I somehow knew exactly what to do. I lifted the crystal to my forehead, closed my eyes, and remembered.

Fionn, the blacksmith's apprentice. The forge, banked and darkened. A jug of poitín—homemade moonshine—poured into chipped, cloudy glasses. He'd been flirtatious, loquacious. I'd been almost flattered when he'd brushed my wrist, touched my waist, slid an errant strand of hair behind my ear. Then he'd reached out and simply palmed my breast. I'd frozen in place, the liquor slowing my thoughts. He'd slid a thumb over my nipple, worrying it like a bead, and smiled with anticipation.

He hadn't bothered to kiss me. He'd touched me, wheedled with me, worn me down. Then bent me over his workbench and taken me without looking at my face. It hadn't lasted long.

After—after I'd slid my breeches back up and rearranged the bodice of my shirt and finger-combed my hair away from my face— I had tried to kiss him. His lips had been hard, inflexible. He'd nudged me away after a moment, then pinched my arse roughly.

"None of that." He'd grinned. "Let's not make this something it isn't."

How I had hated myself. Hated myself for letting him convince me to give him what I hadn't wanted to give. Hated myself for almost liking it. Hated myself for wanting more from him when he clearly wanted so little from me.

I opened my eyes. The hunk of quartz in my palm now glowed a sickly vermilion; its surface stuck to my palm as if it were coated in grease. I handed it to Blink, and as he took it, something peeled away from me—a single rotten layer from an otherwise fresh onion. I clung to it for a moment—it may have been a bad memory, but it was *mine*.

Blink slapped the heavy volume down into my limp hands.

"Page seven hundred and eleven." He gleefully scampered off between the stacks.

Between two listing pillars of books, I curled myself into an alcove window and propped the volume on my lap. Through the smudged panes, the sky began to gather pink edges. We didn't have much time before the Trial ended. The book was densely illuminated, but the ink was faded, which made for difficult reading. I scanned the page Blink had indicated with as much focus as I could muster.

There.

In shadows deep, thrice threes a curse define;
Three elements, three kings, nine trees intertwine.
Only by the fourth, 'neath winter's darkest skies...

No.

The following passage was fully smudged out—as if someone had taken a wet paintbrush and smeared it repeatedly over the ink. I flipped the page, as if some remnant of the words might have imprinted on the reverse. But those words had been ruined too. I slammed the book down on the floor, raising a cloud of dust motes to sift like gold through the streaming light.

For all my negotiations with Blink, *this* was all he had given me.

What had I expected? Some perfect explanation or recipe for how to release an ancient elemental entity from vast, vicious magic? This was not a puzzle that could be solved in an afternoon. I had already performed one thoughtless miracle in my lifetime. Could I truly hope to repeat such a feat within weeks of the first?

I had changed. But I hadn't changed that much.

I stomped back out into the reading room, where the three girls and Balor were still dutifully attempting research.

"Stop." My voice sounded surly even to my own ears. "Thank you all for your patience, but this is a waste of time."

Laoise twitched an auburn eyebrow at me. "What makes you say that?"

"Gavida may be old, but that has only made him wily." I repeated Wayland's own words about his father bitterly. "He will not have left behind any breadcrumbs for us to gather. Even if he has, they will only rot away to dust in our mouths."

Chandi closed her book with a thump. "What would you have us do instead?"

"Nothing," I said tiredly. "Enjoy the last few days of tournament revels. I'll tell Wayland we've reached a dead end. And after the Longest Night, we'll all leave this cursed place the same way we came to it."

My words were met with a trickling silence. At last, Balor boomed, "And me, lady?"

"I don't know, Balor." I favored him with a faint smile. "Do you enjoy camping on clifftops and eating mangy seabirds for lunch and likely being hunted to your death by any number of unseen enemies?"

He considered this. "I do not *dislike* those things, lady."

"Then you may leave with us, if you so choose."

He broke out into a massive, toothy grin. "Thank you, lady."

I did my best to smile back at him. "Well, at least one of us is happy with this outcome. Now, shall we escape before Blink wheedles another cursed bargain out of any of us?"

The five of us exited Blink's bookshop hastily, doing our best not to trip over grimoires or step in puddles of living ink. Outside, the air was blissfully fresh and cold, smelling of salt water and rimed frost. I inhaled, even as my gaze sought the outline of the arena above Aduantas. The distant thunder of stomping feet and unrestrained cheers sent vines of distaste and dismay to wring my bones.

How many more people had been slaughtered in today's Trial to feed a dying Year? How many people would die tomorrow? Next year? And for what? So Gavida could cling to his misbegotten power? Enslave his own son?

I clenched my fists to keep from touching my collar.

Chandi caught up to me as we climbed through the winding streets toward Aduantas.

"I'm sorry about earlier," she said. "I was feeling sorry for myself. I shouldn't have taken it out on you."

I looked at her in surprise. "Please—don't apologize for that. I was being thoughtless."

"I cannot expect you to know what I haven't told you," she said, a little tightly. Then: "The power of threes—what was that about?"

I glanced sharply at her.

"I understand," she clarified. "You don't fully trust Laoise. You've only known Sinéad for a week. Balor is hilarious but an unknown quantity. But surely you can tell me."

I hesitated, if only because I still wasn't entirely sure *how* to explain what Wayland and I had found in the caverns. But there was no reason I couldn't trust Chandi with this information. Perhaps it might even be the very thing to bring us back on the same page—to salve the deep but festering wound lingering between us that I otherwise didn't know how to heal.

Tersely, and in an undertone, I told her everything that had happened yesterday—from hunting the dobhar-chú, to using the servants' passageways below the city, to nearly drowning in the tunnels, to meeting the Year in her prison cell. I even told her about kissing Wayland. When I finished, we'd reached the gates of Aduantas. Chandi halted in the shadow of the threshold as the others spilled around us into the bowels of the citadel.

"I think you're right to call an end to it." Her voice was soft. Intent. "You took this as far as you could. To pursue this further might put you in danger."

"That's not why—"

"I know." She held up a hand. "Do you remember when I told you how you ought to run away with Irian and try to live...*How* do the stories always end?"

"Happily ever after?" I supplied, with a little laugh.

"Yes—that." Her smile seemed sad. "You still could, you know. After everything you've done—all that you've fought for? You deserve it."

"Maybe so." I reached for her hand. This time, she let me squeeze it. "And so do you. Whatever that looks like."

"Sometimes I just wonder why my happy ending—" She paused, as though she wasn't sure how to end the sentence. "Why does every happy ending always seem to come at the cost of another person's tragedy?"

I looked at her, hard. I suddenly remembered what she'd said to me the night I'd seen Eala and Rogan in Gavida's forge. *Being a swan was always*—always—*easier than being a girl.*

"Chandi," I said, as gently as I could, "I promise you this: If something makes *you* happy, it can't be all that bad."

Briefly, she squeezed my palm back before following the others into Aduantas.

Chapter Thirty-Two

A letter waited for me in my chambers. I recognized Wayland's ornate handwriting from the invitation he'd sent four nights ago—I eagerly plopped down on the edge of my bed and cracked open the seal.

Thorn Girl—

I ask you attend me at the Damhsa de Thrí—the masquerade of the final three. Moonrise, in the ballroom. Understand: You will be my guest. Dress accordingly.

—W

And, in postscript:

In case you do not hear it elsewhere: He was badly injured.

My pulse leapt in my throat, and for a moment I wasn't sure who Wayland meant by *he*. But Wayland knew little of my history with Rogan—he had to mean Irian. I willed my pulse to level off. Irian was a Treasure, recently renewed. Ten months ago I had witnessed him nearly flattened by an ollphéist twenty times his size, only to recover in full a month later. And some vicious part of me was *glad* he'd finally met some semblance of opposition in the match. Hopefully being eliminated would make him rethink this untenable scheme to unforge my Treasure.

I crumpled the letter in my fingers, trying to maintain my composure. Dusk had fallen beyond my windows—moonrise would not be long after. If I was being honest, I didn't want to go to the feast—I didn't want to be anywhere near Gavida. Or Eala or Rogan. Or Irian. Or, even, Wayland.

But I understood what his invitation was trying to tell me. It corresponded with every other warning he'd given me—Gavida was watching. I could no longer sneak into Wayland's rooms without consequence.

Understand: You will be my *guest.*

A sharp-thorned vine of rebellion snagged me. Swiftly, I scrawled my own note, then stuck my head into the hall to flag down one of Gavida's puppets. I sighed before flinging open my wardrobe doors.

A kaleidoscope of silver and blue stared back at me, beautiful but impersonal. Every one of these gowns would be perfectly tailored to my figure, but that was hollow comfort. I did not want perfection— I wanted Corra's unique confections designed from moths' wings and cobwebs, flower petals and pine needles. I wanted my own battle armor designed from goldenrod and asters and brambles. I wanted something as real and raw and ragged as my beating heart.

But I did not have Corra. I did not even have my own magic. For the next few days, I had only what Gavida gave me. So I plucked a deep blue gown from the wardrobe—with translucent lace skimming over the bodice; a wide, sweeping skirt; and a deep, plunging back. I dressed sedately. Then swept out into Aduantas.

I didn't need directions; the citadel churned with well-dressed guests all heading in one direction, like water spinning down a drain. I was not alone in my finery. If anything, my gown—backless though it was—numbered among the more demure outfits sported by the merry Gentry host spiraling through the nacre-lined halls. I saw bosoms heaving over tightly cinched corsets, bared midriffs and lithe legs. Wild headdresses scraped the ceilings; gowns with living trains clung to the stairs as they descended. One Gentry man wore nothing more than an elaborate mask and a chain around his neck...attached to a tight circle of metal around his half-erect member.

I averted my eyes and brushed past him, trying not to blush.

The ballroom was ethereal. Exquisite. Haunting. Guests entered through a towering archway of twisted golden branches still bearing plump, perfect fruit. Icicles spangled down like crystal daggers. Beyond, the ballroom floor was a mirror of midnight polished to an obsidian sheen. Frost glimmered across its surface, reflecting the false stars bathing the room in Gavida's favored silver glow. Chandeliers crafted of shining metal whelks and gleaming crystal periwinkles dangled from high above, casting fractured patterns of light and shadow across the floor.

And in the center of it all—nearly bashing his oversized head into the delicate lanterns—danced Balor, his broad mouth laughing. He whirled Laoise and Sinéad over the gleaming dance floor with more vigor than they seemed prepared for, judging by the nauseous look on Laoise's face and the way Sinéad kept slamming dizzily into his legs. Chandi had wisely elected to stand off to one side, nursing a goblet of fizzing purple liquid. I caught her eye across the hall and flashed her a grin, the words of my impromptu note to my friends echoing through my mind:

Attend Gavida's feast tonight. You'll be my guests.

But before I could cross the room to join Chandi, a hand caught my elbow, dragging me out onto a dance floor already seething with revelers. I looked up sharply—it was Wayland, looking very much like the first time I'd ever seen him, just over a year ago. A mask cast in waves of silver and azure concealed his upper face. His long mahogany hair was braided intricately back from his sleek, burnished features. A formal cobalt mantle swirled around my legs as he spun me expertly into the center of the crowd. He definitely noticed when I stepped on his feet. Twice.

"You're not very good at this," he commented as he slid a hand onto the small of my back and propped my wrist upon his elbow. "Are you?"

"No," I ground out, even as I pasted a smile across my face. "I was educated in the arts of human warfare and espionage. Folk dances were not on the syllabus."

"Is that why you invited your friends?" Wayland asked wryly. "To draw attention from the fact that you can't dance?"

"Feasts are always more fun with a few friendly faces in the crowd."

"What am I, if not friendly?"

I made my tone breezy. "You don't want me to answer that, Prionsa."

Wayland laughed and bent me back in a spine-cracking maneuver I was sure would end with my face on the floor. A moment later, he scooped me safely back into his arms.

"Did you discover anything?" he whispered into my hair, even as he coiled me out of the center of the dance floor toward the shadowed pillars beyond.

"Not really." I curved my arms lightly around his neck, for show. "I discovered a line of poetry—or prophecy—but the bulk of it was erased."

"Erased?" Wayland's voice tautened. "What did it say?"

I'd committed the three lines to memory—it was easy to repeat them. " 'In shadows deep, thrice threes a curse define; three elements, three kings, nine trees intertwine. Only by the fourth, 'neath winter's darkest skies...' "

"Then what?"

"I told you—it was erased." Annoyance prickled me. "There wasn't anything more."

Wayland cursed, even as he slid me easily behind one of the massive marble pillars veined with silver and gold. He folded his long frame beside me in the shadows. " 'Only by the fourth, 'neath winter's darkest skies...' What do you think it means?"

"I think it means we've been outwitted." It was what I'd told the girls and Balor; it was what I believed. "I have no mind for riddles— I was raised to stab where I was pointed. Without my Greenmark, in a strange city, in an unfamiliar culture, beset by enemies on all sides? I have to confess, Wayland—I am finally at sea."

But Wayland wasn't done.

"The Year said she was bound by three elements; perhaps a fourth would set her free. Three shackles? Perhaps, somehow, a fourth could be key." Wayland's voice was uncharacteristically grave. "But three kings? I know no fourth. And the trees? It's certainly a puzzle. Perhaps if we speak with her again—"

"Sister?"

The voice was light, bright, and girlish. I recognized it instantly—Eala. I went rigid against the pillar at my back. Wayland put a gentling hand on my forearm, but I shook him off, stepping out into the light beneath the archway.

"Eala." My voice might have been as pleasant as hers—if I hadn't wanted to murder her. My sister was dressed all in white— a pale gauzy gown drifting delicately around her perfect petite frame. Her platinum hair cascaded down her back in curls spangled with diamonds, and her skin was frost pale. Had it not been for her eyes—blazing like sapphires in features nearly identical to mine—she might have been one of Gavida's silver-clad attendants. My gaze drifted—almost without my consent—to her shoulder, where Rogan stood. On the surface, he looked handsome and well groomed in a fine velvet mantle, with his golden curls brushed back from his face. But his expression—dead eyed and deferent—chilled me to my marrow.

A flurry of motion behind me whipped my head around. Sinéad had caught sight of Eala and was flinging herself toward the other woman across the ballroom, her turquoise dress catching around her legs as her honeyed hair winnowed behind her. Twin blades scythed from her hands. The lesson I'd learned too late screamed through me—Gavida's geas of hospitality.

"Balor!" I shouted. "Please—!"

The Fomorian reached for Sinéad, but he was too late. It was Laoise who intervened, spinning the taller girl with a brusque hand around her waist and a terse word I couldn't hear. Sinéad's daggers lowered; so, too, did her head. I stared at her, relief heating my bones, before turning to Chandi. She remained at the edge of the great hall, sipping steadily on a dwindling goblet of shining ambrosia, her eyes downturned.

I forced my eyes back to Eala before they could threaten me with tears. "What are you still doing in Aduantas? Most people know when they've outstayed their welcomes."

"Always the sense of humor, Sister." Eala's laugh glittered like frost in the starlit air. "Everything is as it ought to be. Your husband…battling mine. Our champions. Who shall be the Oak King? Only destiny may decide."

The realization hit me like a punch to the chest, and I fought the urge to double over. Somehow, I'd assumed if Irian had been so badly injured, then he'd been eliminated from the tournament. But the final three were Wayland, Rogan…and Irian? Nausea climbed up from my stomach. No. This couldn't be. That meant that tomorrow—

"I look forward to watching Rogan and Irian fight to the death for the honor of representing the Oak King." Eala gleamed with bright dignity. "But I must say—you have been notably absent from the Trials, Sister. I do beg your presence tomorrow—it will be such a spectacle. Say you'll come?"

Words rose up in me, but when I opened my mouth to speak, I feared they might come out as vomit.

"That is enough." Irian stepped out of the shadows and moved between me and Eala—leisurely, threateningly. He towered over both of us; the swirl of his night-blue mantle made enough of a screen for me to scrub at my suddenly stinging eyes. "Take your place, Princess. The feast begins."

Eala huffed but didn't press her luck. A moment later, Irian turned toward me. Dread and delight tangled around my bones, thrumming my heart to a fever pitch.

The sheer perfection of his face caught me off guard. Gods, how had I forgotten how utterly *magnificent* he was? He was poise and peril, wrapped in lean muscle and powered by a magic no one could match. Part of me hated him for how inescapable my attraction to him was, how continuously captivating his allure. But another part of me *wanted* him—his height, his power, his beauty, his touch—

I must have been staring. Wayland's hand ghosted against my elbow. "We should go up."

Irian lurched toward me, and I realized how stiffly he was holding himself—one arm looped protectively over his left side. I remembered Wayland's note: *He was badly injured.* I raked Irian's torso with my eyes, but beneath the midnight brocade of his ceremonial tunic, there was nothing to see.

If he was feeling well enough to perform stupid acts of unnecessary chivalry in defense of my honor, surely he couldn't be *that* hurt.

"Yes." Irian's leather vambraces gleamed in the silver light. But his outstretched hand shook, just slightly. That—more than anything else—burned worry up my spine. "We should."

"She is my guest," Wayland said, gripping my hand.

"She is my—" Irian began, voice low and dangerous before it abruptly died. He did not seem to know how to finish the sentence.

My eyes flicked helplessly up to his, silver in the dim. It had been mere days since we had last spoken, and yet all the moments we'd ever shared spooled out between us. I did not want to give him any power over me. And yet he already had it—in his words, his touch, his eyes, his body. I was his—had *been* his almost since the moment we'd met. But this last month, he had treated me poorly— kept secrets, tried to control me, *hurt* me. Part of me understood why he'd done it. But the rest of me couldn't help but ask whether it would be like this forever—him standing a half step in front of me, dictating the rules of the game while he decided when I got to play.

That wasn't a marriage.

But what *was* our marriage? Something delicate and still unde- fined. I remembered him cupping my face and asking me to be his widow, so sure he was going to die on the night we were wed. I remembered kissing him—both of us thigh-deep in cold dark water swirling with black feathers—as dawn touched the horizon. I remembered—

I sighed and hardened my expression. I looped my arm through Wayland's elbow. Then, tentatively, I reached out and gripped Irian's forearm. Beneath the dark leather of his vambraces, his skin jolted as the feathers marking his skin lengthened. A spark shivered up my arm as I slid my palm around his stiff elbow, until both men flanked me, like the Year and her legendary kings.

It was what the tableau demanded of me, was it not?

"There," I said, with more humor than I felt. "Has no one ever heard of compromise?"

But I didn't dare look at either man as we walked to the high table on the dais at the end of the hall.

Bedecked in his most elaborate Holly King costume yet, Gavida held court at the high table. He wore a heavy velvet mantle in shades of pearly frost and evergreen; tiny silver charms were braided in his graying beard and hair. Where they might have looked ridic- ulous on a less impressive figure, on Gavida they only heightened his regal power and eldritch resplendence. Upon his head, a vast crown of braided holly and ivy nestled, dusted over with an illusion of snow. When he saw us approach, the smith-king waved our odd trio forward toward the dais.

"Ah! My sons," Gavida boomed, spreading his arms wide to indicate both Wayland and Irian. "One by blood, one by fosterage. Both in honor."

Wayland and Irian bowed to the smith-king—Irian's little more than a stiff incline of the head, almost an insult. Wayland's sweeping flourish seemed obviously mocking to me, but if Gavida noticed, he didn't care. I stood frozen, staring up at the cruel, conniving, power-hungry king and hating him with every ounce of my being.

"And the little changeling girl." Gavida's deep blue eyes skewered me. "Who has made herself quite scarce of late. I worry you have not enjoyed my tournament this past week. Or have you simply been preoccupied? Sampling the delights of my illustrious bloodline, eh?"

A flush burned green behind my eyelids and spiked thorns against my throat. Beside me, Irian stiffened.

"Bow, Thorn Girl," Wayland muttered, with his head still bent. "And keep that pretty mouth closed. Lest you wish to discover what else your collar can do."

I hesitated a moment longer, then swept into the deepest curtsy I could manage, folding myself in half so my skirts pooled around my legs and my forehead almost touched the floor.

"Indeed, my lord," I managed. "This island has made me quite sick with delight. But such excitement does my nerves no good. It rather makes me feel as if I am being strangled."

Silence strung moments like jewels upon a chain. Then Gavida laughed, a violent booming chuckle that chattered my teeth in my skull.

"Rise, children, and take your seats." He indicated the high table. Eala and Rogan were already seated to his right—he meant for us to take the chairs to his left. My pulse accelerated—I had not realized Wayland and I would be spending longer than a few moments with the smith-king. Or with Eala. Or with Irian. But we were to *dine* with them. I looked at Wayland with a helpless kind of panic. He gave me a minute shake of the head, sitting directly to his father's left before ushering me toward the seat next to him.

My skin prickled as Irian folded his tall dark-clad figure into the chair on my other side. I fought not to look at him, but I couldn't help it—my eyes slid toward him. He sat rigidly, still favoring his left side. His gaze slashed toward mine when he saw my head turn, eyes quicksilver in the glittering dim of the ballroom. But beneath the sudden blaze of yearning lighting his gaze, a deep well of barely contained pain lurked. He stared at me like he wished to memorize me—as if he feared he might never see me again.

"You're hurt," I said softly, reaching out to brush the back of his hand. He flexed his fingers before his hand convulsed into a fist. "What happened? Wayland only said—"

"It is nothing." He reached for the goblet of glittering lavender liquor set before his plate, then threw it back in one long swallow. He scrubbed his hand over his mouth and set his gaze forward. "You never responded to my note."

Regret burned bile against the back of my throat when I remembered those four scrawled words. *Come back to me.* I swallowed hard. "Irian—"

But a sudden raucous cheer went up through the ballroom, drowning out whatever words I might have said. The doors opened to admit a parade of silver-clad attendants borne down with vast platters of extravagant, lavish foods piled in excess; with great glittering tumblers full of rainbow-hued wines. A hidden ensemble struck up a vigorous reel, and the noise of laughter and chatter and music muddled my thoughts.

I lowered my gaze, folded my hands in my lap, and set my jaw as a servant refilled Irian's glass and piled food upon my plate.

The feast had begun. And until I could find a way to escape this charade, I was going to have to behave myself.

Chapter Thirty-Three

E asier said than done.

Perhaps if I had not been able to hear Eala's delicate, fluting voice over the cacophony of the feast, I might have clung to my composure. But once I started listening to the way she tittered and simpered and joked with Gavida, I couldn't stop. I tried shoveling food into my mouth so I wouldn't be tempted to say anything I might regret. The dish in question appeared to be a series of smaller and smaller fowl stuffed one inside the other, layered with chestnuts and bread stuffing, but it tasted like ash on my tongue. I washed it down with some of the hazy lavender liquor Irian was seemingly trying to drown himself with, but that only made things worse—the drink fizzed down my throat with an intoxicating floral fragrance and shimmered across my vision with surreal radiance. When I glanced around, everyone in the room was briefly and delightfully transformed into rainbows. The sight elicited an involuntary high-pitched giggle from between my lips. I clapped a hand over my mouth and choked in horror.

"All right?" Wayland leaned over and patted my back as I coughed.

"What *is* that stuff?" I demanded as my vision slowly phased back to normal colors.

"Áthas." A wicked grin ghosted over his face. "Joy juice."

"Ugh." I pushed away the goblet, even as I slid a glance toward Irian, who had been steadily imbibing the liquor since the feast began. Despite the incongruous shimmer of the bright liquid against his stark dark clothing, he seemed unmoved by its marvels—his metal eyes sliced methodically over the revel, and his jaw was dangerously set. I almost laughed—only Irian would be able to maintain a steadfast steely glare while the world around him was transformed into dancing rainbows.

I couldn't help but watch him a moment too long as his sensuous mouth parted along the lip of the goblet—

"Indeed, it is essential for rulers to maintain a code." Eala's lilting, hateful voice sliced through my awareness, jerking my gaze toward her. "Kings and queens must rigorously embody honor. Although perhaps not always ethics."

A shudder of furious indignation puckered my spine. Eala was queen of nothing but bloodshed and betrayal.

"Why not ethics?" My voice spilled out of me before I could think better of it. "What is the point of a code of honor if it has nothing of morality in it?"

Eala and Gavida both turned from their conversation, contrasting bright blue and deep blue eyes settling on me. Rogan didn't so much as flinch, keeping his blank eyes on the table as he shoveled bite after bite of quadruple-layered roast fowl into his mouth.

"Because we are not priests, Sister," Eala said, with some asperity. "Ethics and morality are for holy men and scholars to argue over—to interpret the will of the gods or the universe into laws for people to follow. Rulers have a greater—and far more difficult—responsibility."

"What's that?" I asked acidly. "To steal as much power as they can, no matter who it might hurt?"

Gavida narrowed his eyes, and Wayland kicked me sharply

under the table. I flinched, set my jaw, then kicked him right back, all the while keeping my eyes fixed on my sister.

"No, Sister." Eala's voice held disdain. "To set themselves above and beyond the people, for the *good* of the people. A ruler cannot worry herself about one person or ten people or even a hundred people. A ruler must concern herself with *all* the people she is tasked with protecting. She must be willing to be cruel to some, if that is kindest to all. She must be willing to go to war, if that will bring violence to the least number of people. She must be willing to kill one to save many."

A vision of Eala ripping the still-beating hearts from her maidens sent blank rage to roar in my ears. "You are saying the ends justify the means?"

"I am saying a virtuous ruler must live two lives," argued Eala. "A private one and a public one. In private, she may believe whatever she likes, pray to whomever she likes, keep whatever morals help her sleep at night. But in public, she must be willing to act immorally at the right times. Her reputation and her honor as a ruler depend on it."

"What of fairness? Justice? Kindness?" My hands were fisted so tightly in my lap that my nails cut into my palms. "Are these not virtues a ruler must also embody?"

"Should peace and prosperity allow it," Eala replied. "But fairness does not keep bellies full. Justice does not inoculate against plague. And kindness most certainly does not keep the wolves of war from the gate."

"So every ruler is a villain?" I fought to keep my voice from shaking with indignation. Beside me, Irian sat up straighter. Wayland kicked me again beneath the table, harder than before. I ignored them both. "The price of power is corruption?"

"No." Eala's voice was ironclad. "The price of power is moral isolation. A ruler does not live by the same rules as everyone else, because they do not—*cannot*—apply. A good man may make a weak king, just as a wicked woman may be a strong queen."

Was that a dig at Mother? I fought the urge to laugh. What would the woman who raised me think of her perfect, shining princess, if she could see her now? Would she be repulsed? Or proud?

I honestly wasn't sure.

"And the more power we wield," Eala continued, "the less we must fear the censure of the delicate minded. For they can never understand what must be sacrificed to rule. How much it costs to be extraordinary. How much the powerful must be willing to change in order to be strong enough to carry the burden of our own lonely exceptionalism." Eala's pale, glittering eyes raked me, lingering for a moment at my collar, ever cold against my throbbing throat. "Or do you disagree, Sister?"

I jerked my eyes away from Eala to Rogan, who—now that his plate was clean—had stopped eating. He sat unnaturally straight, his hands neatly folded in his lap. Then I glared over at Gavida, who had watched the exchange with interest and was now waiting for my reply. Almost helplessly, I glanced at Irian, who had ceased swilling joy juice and sat with one forearm braced on the table, tendons corded as he stared down at his fist. I suddenly remembered something he'd said to me—little more than a week ago, and yet it felt like a lifetime.

Our power is great, but the cost is high. You and I—we are both waiting to die.

I stood abruptly, the feet of my chair scraping loudly along the marble floor.

"A most marvelous and welcoming feast, honored smith-king." I forced another overly deferent bow to Gavida. "But I am accustomed neither to such strong wine nor to such riveting dialogue. I require fresh air. Please excuse me."

I turned on my heel and fled the ballroom before I could do—or say—something I might regret.

I should not have assumed it would be so easy to outrun my sister.

Eala caught up to me as I turned down a narrow arched hallway inlaid with stained-glass windows. Or rather, Rogan did—his heavy, freckled hand clamping down on my shoulder and spinning me, not ungently, to face the princess. I jolted at his unexpected presence but mastered myself. In the moment before he let me go, I spun toward him, grasping his wrists in both my palms and staring up into his expressionless face.

"I know you're in there, princeling," I whispered. Rogan's eyes—flat and gray as darkened windowpanes—did not so much as flicker. But I swore—I *swore*—his pupils dilated. "You're strong enough, Rogan. You've always been strong enough. You have to *fight*. Please."

"It's no use, Sister." The corridor framed Eala in silver silhouette. "He is not that strong. And he never had much fight in him. Did he?"

I blinked heat from my eyes and stared her down. "Maybe he wasn't strong enough to fight for me in the way I wanted him to. But he did fight—for his people, for everything his forefathers had built. For Bridei. He wanted a better future for them than he was willing to take for himself. Is not that your definition of a virtuous ruler?"

"You were actually listening, then." Eala's wide eyes raked me as she stepped a pace closer. But as the dim light glazed over them, they had lost their usual assessing cast. Instead, her gaze was frantic, almost desperate. She smiled, but it was brittle lacquer over porcelain. "Is that why you hate me? You think I do not care?"

"That is only one among many reasons."

"I *care*." Her vehemence shoved me a cautious step back. "How could I not? I was not so young when I was taken from Fódla that I do not remember how badly it was ruled—how petty and violent its kings, how brutish and short the lives of its lowest citizens. And I have not spent so long in Tír na nÓg that I cannot recognize the cunning and cruelty of the bardaí, cannot see how their feuds and bitter magics have warped them."

"And yet you ally with villains like the bardaí. Like Gavida."

"Don't you see, Sister?" Eala's voice, usually sweet as sugar, curdled with insistence. "I have lived in both worlds and seen the worst of them. Only I know where they fall short, how they can be improved. Under my guidance, both realms could be better, stronger, more powerful than either stands alone. Fódla and Tír na nÓg, united. Humans and Folk, one people."

"With you as queen of everything?" The words pushed grit between my teeth. "You forget—I, too, have lived in both worlds. I am *made* of both worlds. I have been forced to confront all the terrible, wonderful things flowing through my veins. To confront, then learn to love them. Power-grasping mortal kings…and cunning Gentry. Mortal passion…and ancient magic. Brief, precious things that live but a moment before dying…and endless, unknowable entities echoing through the cosmos. And I can tell you, *Sister*—you are not the thing to make our worlds better. You are the worst of both combined."

Her mouth twisted, its red varnish cracking, the porcelain of her expression splintering into fury. "And you're so much better?"

"Yes!" I gestured almost helplessly at Rogan. "You have allowed the idea of control to corrupt you, Eala. But you cannot force loyalty through oppression. You cannot force peace through war. You cannot build unity through division. And you cannot rely on your hatred of both realms to guide you. If you cannot see all the good hidden among the bad, how can you hope to sustain it? That would be like despising the night instead of learning to love the stars shining from the darkness."

"Is that still your grand message?" Eala trembled, a frenetic energy seeming to vibrate along her limbs. Standing halfway between us, Rogan twitched. "*Love conquers all?* When Rogan refused to fight for you? When your own beloved husband tried to kill you in the arena?"

The viciousness of her words jerked me back. My hands instinctively dropped to my hips, but I'd traded my skeans for a ball gown. I flexed my fingers, then turned on my heel and walked away.

"Fia!" My name on her lips—perhaps the only time she'd ever used it—unleashed strange yearning inside me. The memory of the first time I'd ever met her splintered behind my eyelids and raked broken glass down my spine. She'd embraced me, held me, spoken gently to me. I'd naively thought she and I could truly be friends. Sisters.

I hated myself for turning back to face her. "Eala?"

"There are villains who do bad things for the right reasons. And there are villains who do good things for the wrong reasons." Her mask of control reasserted itself, the cracks of her expression smoothing away. Only the vein pulsing at her temple betrayed her emotion. "I know which one I am. And when you realize you are the other? Then—then you will finally stand beside me, as you should have done from the beginning."

"Stand beside you?" Revulsion made my tone harsh. "After all you have done? All you continue to do? No, I will never stand beside you. Because I am not a villain at all."

The chiming of her laughter chased me the rest of the way down the hall.

Chapter Thirty-Four

The corridor spilled me out onto a shallow balcony overlooking Emain Ablach. Unnaturally blooming white roses glowed, icy, in the light spilling from a quarter moon. Sheer diaphanous drapes stirred sinuously in a frigid breeze, but I didn't mind the cold—it needled beneath the delicate lace of my gown to cool my skin and slow the overgrowth of emotion tangling inside me. I stepped to the edge of the terrace, gripping the frost-spangled balustrade with trembling fingers as I stared over the Silver Isle. Light and music and laugher filtered up toward Aduantas, a thousand tiny revels glittering like captured stars in the city below.

When steps trod in the hallway behind me, I feared it might be Eala again, come to drag me back into conflict. But a moment later, I felt *him*—his presence heavy as a storm bearing down on the horizon. A confusion of exhilaration and resentment and desire sizzled through my veins like lightning. I gripped the railing even tighter and kept my back resolutely slanted toward him.

Irian paused in the threshold.

"Are you all right, colleen?" he finally asked, his voice almost inaudible.

I exhaled, my breath clouding pale in the darkness. "Not really."

"You should not let her rile you so," he rasped. "You said it yourself—she is wily. She knows where the chinks in your armor lie. And she has no compunctions about exploiting them."

He must have followed us from the feast—must have witnessed the whole altercation between me and Eala. Seen every furious tear and heard every angry word. Yet he had not intervened—had not tried to shield me or speak on my behalf. The notion prodded at my heart with devious little fingers.

"That's not what upset me," I whispered.

Irian stepped closer. I could almost imagine the pale drapes swirling around his dark boots; the way the moonlight silvered his eyes and glossed his hair. I wanted him to keep coming closer. I wanted him to go away. I clenched my eyes shut as he said, "What did?"

"I fear she is not wrong. About power. About bad queens and cunning Gentry. About villains." All my muscles felt rigid as tempered steel. "Have you ever known anyone who has not been transformed by proximity to power? I have not. The high king of Fódla, who thought he had the right to steal away Deirdre's future for his own gain. His queen, who let her thirst for vengeance bring two realms to the brink of ruination. The bardaí, who slaughtered countless innocents. Eala, who executed those who loved her most. All for the chance to wield terrible, forbidden magic. Even Gavida, who—" I bit down on words I couldn't—mustn't—say out loud. "The worst part is that none of them would ever admit what they did was wrong. No matter how the power corrupts, they all long for more. It is never enough—can never be enough. And when I think about you and I..."

Irian paced another step forward. Hesitantly, he trailed a hand against my bared back, his touch like a blazing star in the frigid night. "What do you think when you think about us?"

I tried to focus, but it was hard to wax philosophical with him touching me like *that*. "I worry that our own proximity to power has already brought out the worst in us. We have both been so sure that we are right in wanting the things we want—that no matter what we do in pursuit of those goals, the end benefit will be worth whatever the cost of our actions. But how long before we truly become what Eala spoke of—a person who is willing to do bad things for good reasons? Or good things for bad? A villain who has forgotten they are a villain?"

"I already am that villain, colleen." The cold self-loathing in Irian's voice contrasted with the scorching path of his skin on mine. I shivered helplessly as his fingertips grazed down the divots of my spine with excruciating slowness. He stilled with his hand barely skimming the small of my back, his touch burning away my self-control. When he spoke, his voice rasped with barely contained emotion. "Tell me to stop, Fia. And I will stop."

But I didn't want him to stop. I bit my lip and said nothing. After a moment he circled his scathing fingers around the indent of my waist, his large palm sliding over my bodice to splay across my stomach. His other hand glided up my spine between my shoulder blades to nudge my mass of unbound hair to one side. I sighed and leaned back against him, reveling in the sensation of his bulk bleeding heat into my chilled skin. He nuzzled his face into my hair, breathing me in even as his hand tightened over my waist—as if I was something he feared he had lost forever, instead of for a mere three days.

"Once, in a time of short cold days and long fearful nights, a stupid man did not know how to love the woman he had waited his whole life for." His breath warmed the shell of my ear and sent another tendril of heat to climb my spine. "Fia, when I first fell for you, it felt like discovering something I never knew I lacked. Not an addition but a subtraction—a hollowing out of the places I never knew needed filling. And when I lost you, I lost part of myself too. Those empty spaces you had opened inside me swallowed me whole."

The ragged edges of Irian's voice spun me fully toward him.

Even as I moved in his arms, he held me—his palm sliding from my waist to the small of my back; his fingertips sliding along my chin to cup the nape of my neck. And gods, his *face*. Sculpted from moonlight and shadow, a perfect symmetry between darkness and light—stark brows above candescent eyes; bladed jaw hard below that sensuous mouth.

"But you are not my lack, colleen. You are not the thing to patch the empty spaces inside me. You are vastly, exquisitely whole. Somehow, losing you made me forget that." His gaze on mine was so intent I feared he could see inside me, down to the perilous battle between my resentment and my desire. Down to the tender folds of my heart where my feelings for him still throbbed. "I did not stop loving you because I lost you. My love for you is something that will always be mine. Yours, too, if you wish it. But I cannot force it on you—I cannot let my fear control me."

"Do you truly mean that, Irian?" I whispered. "Make me believe it."

"Forgive me, Fia." He choked on the words, leaned down to rest his forehead against mine. He clung to me, his voice dropping even lower. "I tried to prune a wild rose but only cut myself on her thorns. I tried to capture starlight but only engulfed myself in shadows. I tried so hard to keep you from dying that I forgot about living. I love all of you. And I cannot—I cannot live without you."

"Then live *with* me." I lifted my hand to his face. A muscle feathered beneath my palm as he leaned into my touch. "Talk to me, instead of keeping secrets. Fight beside me, instead of battling for some notion of what you think will keep me safe. Live for me, instead of trying to die for me."

"Tell me how, colleen." Somewhere, high above, crystalline clouds formed like scales upon the belly of a fish. "I care only for you. I will do *anything* for you, if it means I get to hold you a little longer, stand beside you one more day, kiss you one more time. Do you wish me to surrender the Oak King's Crown? I will do it, and gladly, if it proves that I am yours. If it proves that I can be different. Better."

"Lose—" Shock pushed the word from my mouth, even as an excruciating image of Rogan and Eala burned across my mind's eye. *Our bond is complete—a finer marriage than free will ever would have allowed.* "No. We have moved beyond that. If you forfeit tomorrow's duel, Rogan becomes the Oak King. The Holly King always loses—meaning Eala will get her boon. And gods only know what she plans to ask Gavida to forge as her prize. No—we must not let Eala win. You must vanquish Rogan tomorrow, no matter the cost."

"Truly?" Surprise pushed Irian back an inch. "You should know, colleen—this duel is not to the blood. It is to the death, unless the opponent yields. And..."

Irian trailed off, but his unspoken words echoed through me nevertheless. *Eala will never let him yield—not to me.* I jerked, my fingers convulsing against Irian's shoulder. A terrible foreboding rose inside me, and for a moment I stood frozen. Memories pounded between my ribs, bitter mallow and poison rue. Rogan's bleak words at Lughnasa sliced tough thorns along the inside of my skin. *Life hurts. Death levels. But love—love destroys.*

"Do what must be done," I whispered. "I would but ask one thing. I know you hate him, but please promise me...you will make it quick."

"Fia." Irian cupped my face. "I do not hate him because you loved him. I hate myself for not being able to forget it. I swear to you I will be as merciful as I know how."

His thumb found my chin, gently tilting my face up to his. His eyes dropped to my lips. But he did not move farther. He kept himself achingly, painstakingly, indecently still. High above us, in the sheer clouds draping themselves over the moon, thunder grumbled. I hesitated. So much had passed between us, and there was still so much to address. He had done inexcusable things to me; I had said contemptible things to him. And yet I wanted this. So much. Wayland had asked when I planned to forgive Irian.

Perhaps I already had.

I tilted my face up toward his, dragged him down by the shoulders, and—

He groaned, his hand jerking away from my waist to convulse against his left side. I pulled away, narrowing my eyes at his brocade tunic, where a line of silver was beginning to seep through the expensive embroidery.

"Gods alive, Irian." I swiftly undid the pewter toggles fastening his mantle, pulling open the garment. His undershirt was already dribbled through with silver; beneath it, I could see the outlines of a heavy bandage wrapped several times around his torso. That, too, was soaked with blood. "What in Donn's dark hell happened to you?"

He gritted his teeth. "It is nothing—"

"It's not nothing!" I glared up at him. "Tell me."

"The Trial of Wits." Irian looked away, opal eyes gleaming. "Gavida bespelled some of his battle puppets to mirror our every move. If we slashed, they slashed...If we feinted, they feinted. If we stabbed, they stabbed. It was almost impossible to prevail. But I did."

Dread spangled through me as I envisioned the scene.

"The easiest way to defeat your opponent was to hurt yourself." Concern made me tender—I reached a tentative hand out toward the gaping wound marring his side. "Irian, what a foolish—"

A brisk, belligerent tap on the stone threshold dashed the moment like a rock hurled through glass. Irian turned; I peered over his shoulder.

Wayland stood framed by white flowers and pale curtains.

"Sorry to interrupt." He looked apologetic but steadfast. I realized he had probably stood there for several moments, listening—then decided to interrupt us nevertheless. "But I beg a moment with Fia. Alone. Do you mind?"

By the way Irian's jaw clenched and he roughly refastened his tunic, I gathered he minded. Very much. I did too, honestly. But perhaps it was a blessing in disguise. There was still so much that he and I needed to address before our relationship could move forward, and we had a horrible—well, *wonderful*, ecstatic, addictive—tendency to fall into bed with each other before our troubles were fully resolved. Something especially ill-advised considering his injury. So I laid a gentling palm on his bicep and stood on tiptoe to brush a feather of a kiss along his jaw.

"It's all right," I said. "You need to rest and heal. All will be well."

He caught me before I could walk away, clutching me briefly to him. "Promise?"

I summoned a smile from somewhere I wanted badly to be real. "I promise."

～

"Brighid's forge, Wayland!" I hissed the moment we were alone. "You couldn't have waited ten more minutes?"

"Is that how long it would have taken you two to fall back in love with each other?" Wayland's tone was crisp, his jaw set. He took me by the arm and steered me through Aduantas at a brisk pace. "Your little outburst with Eala did nothing to endear you to my father. I *warned* you he had his eye on you. I *told* you—"

I shook off his hand. "*What happened?*"

"I think he knows." Wayland stopped, raggedly ran a hand over his braided mahogany hair. "He has formally requested you attend him for the remaining Trials. The letter will be in your rooms when you return to them. Which means we only have tonight and *maybe* tomorrow to return to the Year's cavern, to further interrogate her about how to save her, to—"

"Wayland." I gripped him at the shoulders, shaking him a little. "Take a breath."

He inhaled roughly. His hand lifted to cover his eyes.

"I should never have gone along with your mad plan," he muttered. "I should have known when the human prince started doing so well—"

"What do you mean?" I asked, my interest piqued. "About Rogan?"

Wayland dropped his hand from his face. "My father has always wanted a way back into the human realms. I've never known why—I suppose it doesn't really matter. But if you think it's coincidence that Eala's champion has gotten this far, then you don't give my father enough credit for the sheer, unflagging control he wields on this island."

"She won't win," I promised him. "*We* will. Gavida can only keep me so close. We will discover how to free the Year. We will give you back your magic. Irian will beat Rogan tomorrow. For the first time in remembrance, the Holly King will win the Tournament of Kings. And your father won't forge anything for anyone ever again. *You* will. All right?"

Wayland gathered himself slowly. Then nodded.

"Come, Thorn Girl. Let us bring your half-finished riddle to the Year. Perhaps she has something to say about her freedom."

Chapter Thirty-Five

It was mercifully easier to get back to the Year than it had been to discover her. Now that we knew what she was and where her influence extended, it was easy to spot the veins of her metal embossed throughout Aduantas, edging along door lintels and cross-sectioned in slabs of pale marble and slicked beneath our feet. She was everywhere, and it made me wonder how much she must have seen over the years, how much she must know about the terrible creatures who had seen fit to cage her for an eon.

At last, we were back in Wayland's chambers.

He climbed up onto his bed, held out a hand to help me beside him. He touched the vein of silvery metal bisecting the wall above.

"Talah," he murmured carefully. "We seek counsel with you."

The transition was no easier this time—a vicious wrenching through water-molded basalt; a harsh scraping of marrow from bone. I cried out as my feet landed ankle-deep in cold water; in my extravagant gown and delicate slippers, the damp chill of this prison felt more oppressive than it had before. But I forced myself to standing, still gripping Wayland's palm.

As before, the only light was the subtle glow of our collars, the dull green throb of the Heart. My eyes adjusted slowly. Together we walked forward, our steps rippling across the still water. I braced myself for the surge of energy that heralded the Year's arrival. The scent of petrichor clung to the insides of my nostrils as the air began to churn: scorched metal and cold water. Once again, the Year seemed to coalesce from the threads of metallic light shimmering amid the darkness; her outlines were limned in quicksilver as she slowly took shape. She was no less terrible and exquisite and otherworldly than the first time we'd met her—I could hardly bear to meet her molten eyes blazing through the dim.

Her mind touched mine with a fierce, amorphous, wordless question.

"We found nothing but an unfinished rhyme." Guilt made my voice tight. " 'In shadows deep, thrice threes a curse define—' "

Boom.

The deep, hollow thud startled me. The words trembling on the tip of my tongue died. I whipped my head around, only to meet Wayland's own widening eyes, black in the dim.

Boom.

"What is that?" I asked the Year, panic threading through my voice.

Her own scorched, inhuman eyes flared brighter. She reached for me, her arms like half-forged daggers. I fought the urge to jerk away, but she simply curved her hand gently around the Heart of the Forest, not quite touching it. It blazed green over my breast, and a shower of sparks scattered down to die upon the water.

Remember what I told you, star child. Remember!

She dematerialized as swiftly as she'd appeared. Inexplicable horror carved a sword through my intestines.

"Something's not right," I cried softly, gripping Wayland's hand in mine as some instinct raised the hair along my spine. "We shouldn't be here. Let's go back—"

It was too late.

Boom.

Across the subterranean cavern, broad arched doors I hadn't even noticed flew open with a noise like thunder. A blast of heat wrinkled the water and blew my hair back from my face. A moment later, Gavida stepped into the Year's prison, stomping across the shallow water. His steps were more forceful than ours—insistent wavelets collided with our gentle ripples. Behind him, a half dozen blank-faced attendants waited in the shadows. And someone else— someone gleaming like a white feather in the dim.

Eala stepped out from behind Gavida, her pale hair and white clothes shining. She caught my eye across the cavern, then smiled.

Panic gripped me. How were they here? My fingers curled tighter around Wayland's hand. How had they discovered us? I turned, spinning toward our own half-broken doors as if I could somehow swim back through the caverns, escape this terrible twist, rewrite the past three days. But an inescapable compulsion gripped me, a grotesque sizzle at my throat contorting me back toward the smith-king. Beside me, Wayland underwent a similar struggle—his whole body buckling as he fought whatever magic his father was forcing upon him. A moment later, we were both released, but I shuddered with the repercussions of Gavida's terrible magic.

"My son." Gavida's voice boomed out across the cavern. "I expected such shenanigans from you. But you ought not to have brought your paramour into your dramas."

I glanced up at Wayland, helpless and confused. His gaze was equally fraught, but he held himself painstakingly still as his father splashed steadily closer. Eala remained against the back wall, her toes dry and her face brilliantly lit with that serene smile.

"Why is that, Father?" Wayland lifted his jaw, defiance and dread sculpting his already handsome features into something heartbreaking. "Must I be alone in my wish to make something of myself, outside your influence?"

"No, my son," Gavida said with jollity. "But you must have known, should the two of you be caught, that I would punish her instead of you."

The pain came out of nowhere, a screaming agony that tore down the back of my throat and roasted my spine. I could not even scream, pain blotting out my voice as my fingers tore at the circle of metal collaring my throat. A moment later, the sensation was gone. I dropped to my knees in the shallow water, scrabbling at my neck and whimpering like a dog that had been thrashed.

"Stop." Wayland's voice rang harsh. "Punish me for my disobedience. Not her."

"You have always been a soft, foolish boy." Gavida had reached us now. He glanced briefly at his son before turning to me. He wrapped a massive hand around my collared throat, dragging me up to standing. His fingers gripped no harder than necessary, but my collar nevertheless spiked, burning lines of fire along my collarbones and up into my skull. I gasped and kicked out. My foot struck Gavida's knee, and I brought my arms up into position to break his hold on me, no matter the magical cost.

Then blackness overtook me.

When I woke bare moments later, my arms and legs were bound with silver shackles similar to my collar. Gavida's attendants were melting away into the dim; Eala's smile still shone like a star from the far wall.

"She has nothing to do with this, Father," Wayland was arguing. "She was a means to an end—surely you, of all people, can understand that."

"You still cannot believe that I loved your mother?" Gavida's laugh was syncopated with scorn. "How else could I see how much you cared for *her*? You wear your heart on your sleeve, boy. And it is a weakness."

I rolled to all fours, testing the strength of my binds as I slowly rose to standing.

"Little one." Gavida shifted his attention to me. "It is not often that one such as you graces my court. Newly made, wholly untested. I collared you selfishly, out of an abundance of caution. But now I see I was correct in my suppositions."

"And what are those?" My voice was little more than a snarl. "That I have a mind of my own? That I dislike being controlled? That I wish to make my own destiny?"

"Yes," Gavida said after a beat. "In a nutshell. But all that might have been tolerated, had you not somehow regenerated a Treasure from the ether."

He came at me swiftly, his speed and his bulk catching me off guard. He slammed me back against the cavern wall, dislodging a shower of pebbles to skitter to the floor. His hand latched around my throat. He might have strangled me had it not been for the collar.

"*I* forged the Treasures, little one," Gavida whispered, his breath like scorched metal and the darkness at the edge of a nightmare. I couldn't help but shudder as his long beard brushed my cheek. "*I* bound the sources to the vessels via the conduits. They were destroyed—but none save me should have been able to remake them. What did you do? *How* did you do it? Tell me now."

"All right." Gods, but the smith-king was strong—he'd lifted me fully off my feet to pin me to the rough cavern wall. I slid my bound hands reflexively to my hips, but my skeans were back in my room—Gavida's stupid laws of hospitality had demanded I keep them from the feast. Which meant now I had only my body and my wits. Both of which were stunningly outmatched by my present company. I stalled, my mind racing. "It's a complex equation. I must whisper it to you."

Gavida's brow furrowed, but he leaned his huge grizzled head close. Wayland stared at me, trepidation and hope tangling in his gaze. I gritted my teeth, fairly sure my plan was the worst kind of stupid. I brought my lips next to Gavida's ear, pitched my voice low, and said with gravity, "Bite me."

Then I snapped my teeth around the curve of his ear, sinking my incisors into flesh and cartilage. Blood burst in my mouth, metallic and faintly sweet. The smith-king grunted with shock and pain, jerking away as his hand slipped halfway down my neck. I kicked out sharply, connecting with the old man's knee. Bone cracked. Gavida stumbled, crumpled. I fell from his grasp, landing in a crouch before lunging for Wayland. But both of our hands were now bound with Gavida's metal; even as I scrambled at our shackles, I could feel how magically stunted we both were. I desperately lashed out with my Greenmark, but the pain just bounced back at me. I collapsed against Wayland, who did his best to hold me up as we both sagged toward the floor. Around Gavida, blank-faced attendants clustered like bees around an injured queen.

"*Bite me?*" Wayland muttered in my ear. "Really?"

"Listen," I said around the sickly sweet taste of Gavida's blood. "We've been betrayed. Someone must have told Eala what we were doing. Laoise—"

"No," said Wayland urgently. In my periphery, I saw the smithking drag himself upright. "I think it had to have been—"

Wayland's voice cut out as an attendant clobbered him over the head. But his swift, unfinished utterance trickled a slimy, distressing thought through me. I reached for it slowly, even though part of me dreaded it. Then something struck me very hard in the back of the skull. And blackness sucked me down.

I followed the doe through the woods. She did not seem to notice me as she moved through the undergrowth, nibbling at evergreens and pawing at tufts of grass. At last, she came to a hut nestled between the trees. Smoke spiraled up from the chimney; a garden lay fallow in winter's chill; instead of straw, a thousand bird wings thatched the roof. Through the window, I glimpsed a man's profile. But no matter how I stared, I could not see his face.

"Why did you bring me here?" I asked.

"I told you, little deer," said the doe, parting her lips to show me a melancholy human smile. "He is to blame for your troubles. Not I."

Chapter Thirty-Six

I slid upward through dream-glow into waking. My head pounded and my body ached. I had been stripped out of my impractical gown and nestled naked beneath cloud-soft covers in what I vaguely recognized as my room in Aduantas. A distant, amorphous feeling of violation curled me in on myself. I grasped for clarity. I lifted my face toward the window, trying to gauge the height of the sun behind gray clouds. Noon, perhaps—I had not meant to sleep so late.

No—not sleep.

I struggled against the spill of memories, fractured as a broken mirror.

An almost kiss on a frozen balcony. Splashing footsteps in a deep cavern. The smith-king, all threats and violence and venom. Eala, smiling and smiling and smiling. And a club to the back of the head.

Gingerly, I touched the contusion knobbed on my skull. I supposed I should be grateful they hadn't left me where I'd fallen. But I didn't appreciate being tortured. Lugged around like a sack of potatoes. Undressed and put to bed like a child—

A moment later, all thoughts of potatoes vanished. As my fingers prodded my head, the dull gray light struck filaments of silver on my arm. I glanced sideways, then froze. A second band of metal—very like my collar in appearance—wrapped tight around the slenderest part of my wrist. I hissed as I remembered, and jerked my other arm from beneath the blanket, although the movement felt strangely ponderous. Another slender bracelet. I gripped it, slid my fingers beneath it, did my bloody best to undo it. My efforts were for naught.

Like the Year, I was now thrice collared.

I reached for the comforting weight of the Heart of the Forest.

Only to find that it was gone.

Fury and a feather of fear propelled me up. I kicked out of my bedsheets and crossed to the wardrobe, angrily pulling on the first trousers and shirt I could find. Yet again, my movements felt oddly ungainly. Then I was standing in front of the mirror, watching my fingers play over the triple bands of mystical metal wrapping my throat and wrists. I smoothed my palm over my chest, resting my hand on the spot where my Treasure usually hung. My heartbeat throbbed unevenly at my touch, as if syncopated without its second heart.

First, Gavida had stolen away my magic. Now he had stolen the emblem of my Treasure. What else would he be willing to take from me?

I crossed to the door, jiggled the knob. It was locked. From the *outside.*

"Hello?" My voice was hoarse, quiet. I pounded on the door as loudly as I could. But my fists felt weak—they barely struck the wood. What I meant as a boom was barely a tap. A moment, two. No one came. I tapped again. "Is anybody there?"

Finally, the door opened. Two of Gavida's puppets stood shoulder to shoulder in the nacreous hallway, blocking my path. I tried to edge by them, but they were having none of it. Although their faces remained perfectly impassive, they corralled me back into my room with surprisingly strong arms. Once I was back over the threshold, they held out their cupped hands. One held Wayland's mother's signet ring. I hadn't even noticed the ring was gone; I plucked it up, then glanced at the second attendant. He proffered a strip of parchment inked in bold handwriting.

You have angered me, little one. Were it not for my sons' affection for you, you would already be on a boat to the mainland. Or at the bottom of the sea. But you are still of use to me, at least until the tournament ends. Neither Wayland nor Irian will defy me so long as I hold your life in my hands.

As you know, the first collar curtails your magic. The second controls your voice—you may speak only in low, calm tones. The third limits your movements—any sharp or violent motions will be tempered.

Your Treasure, I have borrowed for safekeeping. It will remain with me until you leave my island.

There is no need for extreme measures, little one. Join me, your sister, and my son in my box for today's Trial. Behave, and we can all have our happy endings.

Misbehave, and I can promise you an altogether unhappy ending.

I cursed, crumpling the note in my fist before smoothing it out again. My fingers trembled with rage; my blood burned green and black behind my eyelids.

You may speak only in low, calm tones... Any sharp or violent motions will be tempered.

I had been reduced to little more than a thrall, then. I remembered Wayland's comments about his father's *efficient systems*—the smith-king had certainly proved his son's point. Without my magic, my voice, or the freedom to react as I chose, I was little better than Rogan. A marionette operated by strings Gavida controlled—a doll for him to pose in his grand pantomime.

I reread the note, again and again. *Join me, your sister, and my son in my box for today's Trial.* My anger rose again when I thought of Eala, bright and beaming in the Year's prison last night. I had no doubt my sister had been the architect of our betrayal, but I still didn't know how *she'd* discovered us.

My fists clenched. It had to have been Laoise—what did we know of her, truly? We had been far too swift to trust her, to let her into our little entourage. She had acted suspiciously since the moment she'd found us on that bluff. She must have been spying on us this whole time—working for Eala since the very beginning.

Wayland's rushed, interrupted words to me in the caverns burned between my ears. *No,* he'd said. But who else could he have meant?

Again, a perilous thought slithered upward from the back of my mind. But I didn't want to look at it. I couldn't.

The attendants were still at the door, as if waiting for my reply.

"Well?" I said, softly but icily. "Are you going to help me get ready for the Trial?"

The two puppets said nary a word as they helped me dress in an overly embellished silver gown that fit me like a glove yet suited me very poorly. The color and shape were all wrong. The stiff-boned corset was spangled with jewels and pearls arranged to look like snowflakes against a dark background; the vast fluffy skirt floated like a blizzard around my legs. I fought back fury as they draped a pale blue cloak over my shoulders and drew the white-furred hood up over my dark hair.

Gavida's doll, dressed up like my sister for his amusement.

Finally, we left my room. One attendant led me out through the winding halls; the other followed me, pacing me without deception.

My honor guard? No—my prison wardens.

Beyond the gates of Aduantas the city churned with a thousand revels. I tried to make my way down the steps into the crowds, but one attendant stopped me with a surprisingly strong grip. The other waved me toward a delicate silk-draped palanquin waiting in the shadow of the gates. I balked, grinding my heels into the marble.

"I have feet," I managed, between my clenched teeth. "I have no desire to be carried through the streets like a sack of—" Why did I keep thinking about potatoes? "Please. Let me walk."

But they were implacable. So I reluctantly climbed into the palanquin, settling myself rigidly on the plush cushions within. The litter lurched away into the crowds. I peered between the gauzy curtains, watching the festivities roil around us. A hundred escape fantasies tangled in my mind, tantalizing me with possibility. I could kick my way out of the window, steal a weapon from a passerby, disappear into the crowds, fight my way down to the harbor.

No matter how many ways I plotted my escape, I could not leave. I was thrice shackled, bound to the smith-king's whims. He held the emblem of my Treasure hostage. But dragging me most inexorably toward the arena...were the contestants.

Today, Irian battled Rogan for the Oak King's Crown. And although I could hardly bear the thought of watching the only two men I'd ever cared for fight to the death in a Folk arena for the entertainment of the masses...well.

How could I bear to be anywhere else?

At last, the palanquin stopped swaying and lowered with a thud. One of the attendants handed me out before the smith-king's box. The noise of the arena swelled around me, a throbbing, thunderous melee of laughing and chattering and singing and cheering. The sky was cold and leaden; needles of freezing fog lashed my face beneath the hood of my cloak. I climbed the dozen stairs up to the raised platform, navigating my voluminous skirt over the steep, icy steps. I was so focused on not falling onto my face that when a large, meaty hand folded over my wrist and dragged me toward the center of the dais, I did not protest. I could only cringe away from

Gavida's breadth—his scorched metal scent and blistering forge heat. My collars and both my bracelets spiked a cold shock along my bones.

Fortunately, he did not keep his hands on me for long. He deposited me in a chair beside Wayland, who sat very still and totally expressionless, his polite smile vacant and his deep blue eyes inscrutable. I stared at him a moment too long, trying to determine whether he was simply *behaving*—as I'd been instructed to do—or whether his father had further curtailed him as he had me.

Perhaps that was why it took me a moment too long to see who else had joined us in the smith-king's box. Eala, I had expected. Although the sight of her enraged me—her ice-white gown fluttering like feathers in the stiff breeze, her pale blue eyes and constant smile—it did not surprise me. But the sight of who sat beside her did. I almost didn't recognize the tall brown-skinned girl sitting next to her, with black velvet hair bound back in a severe bun—

"*Chandi?*"

If the other girl heard me, she did not show it. But Eala did. She turned to look at me, her smile growing ever wider.

The realization I hadn't wanted to look at—the terrible, nauseating fact growing like a cancer in my mind—punched me right in the face. If I hadn't been sitting down, I would have fallen. As it was, something unhinged inside me, releasing a torrent of weakness to burn alternating skeins of heat and cold through my veins.

"No," I whispered, desperate to suppress the unwelcome certainty pounding through me. But no matter how much I wished to place this betrayal on someone else—*anyone* else—there *was* no one else. Not Laoise, whom I had never fully trusted. Not Sinéad, whom I liked but still did not know well. Not even Balor, who would have been an easy scapegoat.

There was only one person I had told about the discovery I'd made with Wayland in the caverns beneath Aduantas. Only one person who knew why I sought to unbind thrice threes, only one person who knew about the Year. The one person who'd been with me from the start. Who'd fought for me the night of the Ember Moon. Who'd brought me pastries from the Summer Twins. Who'd ridden with me through woods and over cliffs. Who'd brushed my hair and held my hand and—

"Chandi!" I choked out, around the thick surge of tears threatening to drown me. "*Why?*"

Her head began to turn, but Eala gripped her wrist with a forceful gesture. "You do not answer to her, my love."

But Chandi shook Eala off, facing me fully across the dais. She was silently weeping—tears made her eyes round and glassy; moisture streamed down her wide cheekbones and dribbled off the angle of her chin. She looked haggard with grief and exhaustion, her eyes red and her face drawn. But that wasn't exactly new, was it?

How many times had I looked at her and refused to see what was staring me in the face? How many times had I noticed her moments of hesitation, of reticence, of despondence...and ignored them?

Might I have seen this coming if I'd bothered to spend a little more time thinking about what she was going through? Instead of my own dramas?

"I love you, Fia," she said. "But I loved my swan sisters more. And unless Eala wins the tournament—"

"Enough of this tragicomedy!" boomed Gavida as he sat down in the middle of the raised box directly between Eala and me, blocking my view of my sister and Chandi. "Let the Trial begin!"

A roar went up as he motioned toward the center of the arena. Slowly, the platform he had previously used to open the tournament laddered up out of the lower levels of Aduantas, revealing the two contestants. The crowd cheered louder, their garbled words winging like sharp-beaked birds to bombard the men.

One Gentry, one human. Both tall. One with hair black as night, one with hair the warm gold of a summer afternoon. Both already carried unsheathed swords—the late-afternoon light caught the metal and turned it bloody.

My pulse ratcheted, the base of my throat beginning to throb with fear. Despite the frigid wind pushing icy fingers through my cloak, a sheen of cold sweat gathered beneath my arms and along my clenching palms. I sat forward in my chair, staring desperately down at the two fénnidi as they stepped off the platform and moved a few paces apart.

"Welcome to the penultimate Trial!" Gavida's voice boomed, loud enough to shake the mountain. "Today, it will be decided: Who will have the honor of wearing the Oak King's regalia in the final battle? The Gentry heir with his legendary sword?" The clamor of the crowd shrieked higher. "Or the handsome human prince come to avenge his betrothed from the wicked tánaiste who cursed her?" They cried even louder, an ululation of delight and impending violence.

I glanced sharply at Gavida, then around him to Eala. Was *that* the story she was spreading about Rogan? About *Irian*? That this was some kind of battle over her honor? A virtuous quest for justice against those who'd wronged her? But what did she have to gain?

Popularity? Sympathy?

Loyalty.

The revelation thundered through me, and I almost had to admire my sister for her calculated, thorough cunning. It was not enough for her to control Rogan, half the gates, Chandi. She wanted to be in control of the story, too—the narrative that would ultimately shape her image when she finally went to war for both realms. Eala would not go to battle unprepared—she'd already propagandized herself into what she believed herself to be.

The hero. Instead of the villain.

"Never underestimate the power of pageantry, little one," Gavida said to me, quietly but jovially, as the crowd frothed themselves to frenzy. "Perhaps if you and Irian had tried to tell a better story, they'd be cheering like that for you. But no one wants to listen to a story that *starts* with happily ever after. They want to believe there will be one, in the end—but they want to have to chase it. First they want conflict and sorrow and yearning and tribulations—that's what makes them *believe*."

"Believe what?" I snarled, as loudly as my bracelet would allow me. "Outrageous lies?"

"Whatever we want them to believe," Gavida corrected. "No one wants truth. They want diversion. You can distract them with opulent truths or outrageous lies, but in the end it must only be a very good story." He glanced over at me, considering. "Now. That's quite enough talking, I think." He raised his fist. "Begin!"

Irian smoothly flicked off his outer mantle, exposing lean, sculpted arms sinewed with stark black feathers. Neither flowers nor thorns remained. Rogan followed suit, more slowly, dropping his bold-checked cloak onto the frosted ground. He circled Irian carefully. Irian might have been made of stone, he stood so still—no inch of him moved save for his raven's-wing hair feathering in the breeze.

Without warning, Rogan attacked, lashing out with his steel. Irian barely seemed to move, and yet his guard came swiftly up. Claíomh met Treasure with a clash like havoc. A knell like death. The hairs stood up on the back of my neck as I leaned forward, craning to watch the men I loved finally face each other in combat.

Rogan fought with a familiar disciplined style. His claíomh clanged with determined force against Irian's blade, a testament to a lifetime of training. I recognized every strike and parry before he even performed them—they were the same forms and variations I'd had drilled into me since childhood. He was good—he'd *always* been good. But I'd sparred with Rogan a thousand times—I knew every humorous flourish and insouciant flick of the wrist that he usually added into his fights. There was none of that today. This was different—a brutal single-mindedness that reminded me yet again who was twisting his strings.

I swallowed and looked at my new partner instead of my oldest friend.

The fact that Irian had been nearly mortally wounded the

day before seemed immaterial to his performance. As always, he moved with otherworldly grace. His fighting style was a waterfall of intention—the flicker of a half step curving his torso, the slight twist of his hip echoing in the arc of his arm, his blade sliding out like an afterthought. There was power in his movements but also grace, his measured steps taking on a serpentine quality as he danced and parried with Rogan across the arena. The Sky-Sword sliced the air like sunlight or poetry, a crystalline gyre sending an almost inaudible melody shivering through the crowd. But there was also an inexplicable hesitation to Irian's fighting, a lack of enthusiasm I had never witnessed in him before. It was only when his dazzling blue eyes lifted to find me between one step and the next that I began to understand.

Despite what I'd said to him last night—or perhaps because of it—he didn't want to hurt Rogan.

That was the only thing that made it a fair fight. Rogan's strikes—determined as they were—were no match for Irian's effortless finesse. Irian easily evaded Rogan's most relentless forays, weaving between his ferocious slashes with little more than puffs of dust rising between his boots. Still Rogan pressed him, unfaltering, unflagging, resilient. The song of their conflict rose in crescendo and flogged the energy of the crowd with it. Rogan lunged forward, hammering Irian with all his strength. Irian gave up a pace, then feinted sideways to slash up. The tip of the Sky-Sword sliced along Rogan's mantle, rending a gash in the fine fabric. A spray of blood flicked rubies across the frosted sand. Rogan barely reacted to the pain that must be screaming across his shoulder, simply barreling forward toward his opponent.

But he wasn't indefatigable. His steps were beginning to slow; his parries weakening. His temples had gone dark with sweat; the bared skin of his biceps gleamed with moisture. Still Eala's compulsion drove him on.

Nervous energy propelled me to standing, despite Wayland reaching once more for my wrist. I spared a swift glance over at

Eala. She appeared as unflappable and smiling as ever, sitting prim and poised like the princess she was. But after last night, I'd begun to recognize the cracks in her perfect porcelain facade. The deepening of the lines around her mouth, the tension around her eyes, the tiny beads of sweat gathering at her hairline. Something like hope clambered up the ladder of my ribs, and I returned my gaze to the duel raging on below.

Fight her, I screamed silently. *You are strong enough to* fight *her.*

Irian blocked Rogan's wild, wide swing; he stepped inside his guard and slammed his elbow into Rogan's face. Blood burst from the prince's nose as his head snapped back. Spinning away, Irian flipped his grip on the Sky-Sword and pummeled back toward Rogan—*slash, slash, slash.* Rogan barely parried the strikes; his steps fumbled in the sand.

Irian slammed up against Rogan's guard again. And again. Rogan pivoted on his back foot, but he was finally flagging; Irian was barely winded. My fingertips dug into the wooden railing draped in silken pennants, willing Irian to disarm him without bloodshed. Willing Eala to let Rogan yield.

Without warning, Irian crouched, spun, and kicked out. Rogan's knee buckled, and Irian drove up through his defense. He caught the edge of Rogan's blade along one vambrace, jamming the hilt of the Sky-Sword sideways until steel screamed against steel. He twisted and heaved up, wrenching the sword from Rogan's hands and disarming him. Rogan fell back. The blade arced up into the sunset; Irian reached up and caught it, then sliced it down to quiver an inch from Rogan's throat. A moment later, the Sky-Sword slid down to join it, until Irian collared his opponent's neck with two razored edges: one silver, one the bloodied gold of the setting sun.

"Do you yield, human prince of Bridei?" Irian asked passionlessly, pitching his voice to carry with unsettling clarity upon the lofting breeze. "Yield, and I will be as merciful as our host, the venerated smith-king Gavida."

The sounds of the crowd bottomed out, lowering to a tense,

seething murmur. Bloodlust beat like a silent drum beneath the deceptive stillness of the arena—the spectators yearned for death. Whose, I did not think it mattered.

Irian held himself statue still as Rogan lay half-supine beneath him.

"Yield." The same word, more forcefully.

I swayed forward, blood hammering at my temples as greenery beat green-gold wings against the sizzling metal at my throat and wrists. My hands on the railing felt like ancient gnarled vines, twisting and crumpling as my rigid forearms hardened. I glared over at Eala, even as a silent scream rose up in my convulsing throat.

Let him yield!

Her smile had dropped a half inch from her beatific face. A veil of concentration dulled her normally blazing eyes. Her fingernails dug into her palms. I whipped my head back around to the tableau playing out in the arena, those green-gold wings unfurling larger with my desperate hope, hammering at the cage of my heart.

Fight her, Rogan.

"Yield!" Irian shouted, his voice like the crack of a whip upon the wind.

But when Rogan still did not respond, Irian faltered. For an instant, his eyes lifted to mine, azure paling toward silver. Even from halfway across the arena they pierced me with violence and regret and worry and the barest edge of desperate indecision. Then—deliberately enough for me to know it was no accident—Irian lifted the tips of both swords two inches away from Rogan's throat.

Rogan didn't hesitate—he exploded upward with what must have been nearly the last of his strength, thrusting into Irian's torso with the full force of his right shoulder. He collided directly with Irian's still-healing wound. Irian crumpled from the impact, his spine bowing as pain knocked a groan from his lips. Rogan drove him bodily back against the frozen sand. Irian's head struck the ground with a sickening thunk. His hands went boneless around his double swords.

I leaned so far over the railing that the edge cut into my abdomen and my fingernails shredded the silken awning. I tried to cry out—to say Irian's name, to warn him, *anything*—but my voice was a caged bird, and no matter how it fluttered, it could not break free.

Rogan thumbed his steel sword back into his palm. The tip of the blade flicked out, kissed Irian's chin. Irian's eyes slid open; his lips parted. His hair fanned out behind him on the pale sand. He didn't move.

But neither did Rogan. He was panting silently, his chest rising and falling as dusk painted fire across the sky. I silently begged him to say the customary phrase: *Do you yield?*

The Rogan I'd known all my life would have, in a heartbeat. Brighid knew he had his faults. Dishonor in battle wasn't one of them.

But Rogan wasn't in charge anymore. And Eala had no intention of letting Irian yield. She would drag this fight out as long and as bloodily as she could, for the story she was telling. For the *spectacle*. If Irian was truly the villain she was painting him as, then he did not deserve mercy.

She was going to have Rogan kill him. *She* was going to kill him. Which meant I had to tell my own story.

Slowly—my bracelet forced me to move so *slowly*—I awkwardly propelled myself over the railing. The drop was farther than I'd anticipated—I landed hard, tweaking one ankle as the other knee thunked down into the sand. But I gritted my teeth and forced myself to stand. Gavida's compulsion was like moving through mud—every step ponderous, labored, achingly sluggish. My arms were dead branches; my legs wanted to grow roots. I drove myself to a staggering, plodding run before my mind could catch up with what my body was feeling. For the first time, I was glad of Gavida's doll clothes: The wind seized the voluminous train of my absurd skirt and dramatically flung it out behind me. Snapped up the edge of the blue cloak and pushed the hood back from my head. Streamed my long dark hair back from my face like a pennant of shadow.

Once more, the energy of the crowd shifted, curiosity and renewed bloodthirst keening higher. I pressed myself as fast as Gavida's magic would let me; Rogan's sword was dragging slowly down Irian's throat, trailing silver in its wake. But even if I got there in time, what was I supposed to do? I wasn't armed; I was thrice collared—

My rage roared high enough that I could taste it in the back of my throat. My arms, desperately pumping by my sides, felt so restricted, as if some giant hand was reaching out and dragging me backward. I tried to scream, but I was still muzzled, silence suffocating me from the inside out.

No.

Gavida had gone too far. He had stolen my magic; he had restricted my movements; he had taken my voice. But I was no man's puppet. I closed my eyes as I dragged myself toward Irian, painting every fleeting moment I had spent with him against the backs of my eyelids.

An unnecessary bandage on a barely wounded finger. A touch like a forge.

A kiss stolen beneath trees frothing with white flowers.

Bluebells and spring water and the feeling that I'd found something I hadn't known I'd lost.

Cold stone steps and skin so hot I thought I might ignite. *I am . . . savoring.*

A rushed handfasting beneath the Heartwood. The terrible, wonderful realization that if I wanted my ending to change . . . I was going to have to do it myself.

We'd been through so much. I couldn't lose him now.

You . . . are star touched.

The thoughts—memories—exploded through me in a confusion

of green veined with molten lines of silver. Something rent the skin on my left arm. A moment later, answering pain shrieked up my other wrist. My collar snapped teeth at my neck, sizzling white-hot toward my brain stem. Then I was screaming—my voice bursting from my throat in a wordless keen of protest. My steps exploded forward until I was sprinting across the arena. Irian jerked his head toward me, and a moment later, Rogan looked up at me too.

I swore, for the barest instant, that his eyes were not the flat, blank stare of a man enthralled to a heartless woman. But the glittering, anguished green-blue of a man who had nothing left to lose.

I flung myself between them with clumsy, jolting impact, knocking the blade aside as I folded myself as a shield over Irian.

"He yields!" I cried out, and the wind picked up my voice and flung it into the stands. *"He yields!"*

The noise in the stands rose to a fever pitch, even as the wind around us intensified, sending sand flying. Rogan instinctively shielded his eyes, and when he looked back down, he was empty again—Eala had exerted control once more, if she had ever really lost it at all. I tore my eyes from him and looked down at Irian. His throat was silver with blood, and his eyes twined with pain and ebbing violence and the barest edge of wounded pride. But mostly, they brimmed with fear and awe and love—the same all-consuming, staggering emotion I'd seen in his gaze the night I'd splashed back to life in the lough beyond the fort.

"You are wonderfully mad, colleen." Then his palm was at my waist, and his other hand lifted to my nape. He dragged me down for a seething, simmering kiss that stole away the last of my breath. I slid my own sand-choked hands into his hair and kissed him back, tasting the wonderful curve of his perfect mouth as his tongue slid against mine.

Only minutes later—when Gavida was loudly proclaiming Rogan the Oak King over the thrumming, insatiable hum of the crowds and blank-faced attendants were tearing me away from

Irian and dragging me back up toward the smith-king's box—did I notice what I hadn't before.

Both my wrists were a mess of leafing, flowering vines piercing my skin and smearing green-black blood all the way down to my fingers. And the bracelets Gavida had put around my arms...were cracked.

Chapter Thirty-Seven

Gavida bundled me into his personal carriage drawn by six white horses—more spacious and comfortable by far than my little palanquin. He was angry; the fury radiated off him like a stench, mingling with the scent of burnt metal and rotten flowers.

I didn't care. Well, I *did*. Nothing had gone as planned. Gavida had discovered my scheme with Wayland and punished us both. Irian's affection for me had stayed his hand, and he had spared Rogan's life at the cost of his own victory. I hadn't wished Rogan dead. But now Eala would get her magical boon after all. Wayland had told me the final contest was rigged—there was no way for the Holly King to win. The Oak King had to vanquish the Holly King for Gavida's grand ritual to be complete.

Yet I was also strangely buoyant. My antics in the arena had made me drunk with defiance and foolish hope. And my heady kiss with Irian had been its own liquor, warming the deepest, most secret parts of myself until I could think of little beyond our next reunion.

I glared back at Gavida as if daring him to punish me further.

"You could put another collar on me," I suggested levelly. The smith-king continued glowering at me over his beard as we rattled back toward Aduantas. "Both my ankles are still free. And I have lovely, elegant little ankles. Or so I've been told."

"You are adorable, little one." Gavida leaned forward in his seat and gripped my wrists. The greenery I'd inexplicably summoned from beyond the power of my first collar had retreated, leaving long, deep gashes and livid scratches from my elbows all the way down to my palms. The smith-king examined the wounds, impassive, then folded his massive hand over the cracked bracelets. When he lifted his fingers, they were gone—crumbled away to flakes of metal and ash. The smell of bog tar and ozone intensified. "You should not have been able to do what you did."

"You told me to make them believe the story I wanted them to believe," I reminded him. "You cannot blame me for taking your own advice."

The smith-king stared at me a moment longer before scraping a meaty palm over his face and sighing. "Perhaps it is for the best. Neither you nor Wayland would have forgiven me if I'd let the human kill Irian. And it would have been a shame to let my foster son die simply to avoid disappointing him yet again."

Curiosity flared to life inside me. "What does that mean?"

"The Treasures are unlike anything I have forged before or since. I know not how to unforge them. I am not even sure it can be done. Not the right way—not without warping the source by destroying the conduit or the vessel." His cobalt eyes, so like his son's, slid outside the window as Aduantas's crenellations and twisting spires rose up to meet us. "Bindings are always easier than unbindings. All the pieces of the cosmos want to be connected, even as they fall apart. Prince Marban taught me that an eon ago." His eyes drifted back to me, and there were questions lingering in their fathomless, ancient depths. "Do you know, little one...I have never met a human who did not change the course of my life."

My heartbeat stuttered as I tried to parse his disjointed musings.

Who was this Marban, who knew of bindings? Was Gavida imply-
ing he'd been *human*? Did he have something to do with the Year's
imprisonment below the city? The questions scalded my tongue,
but I somehow doubted Gavida would answer any of them directly.
So I simply said, "I'm not human."

"No, little one." His eyes narrowed. "But neither did I mean to
imply you were the one changing the course of my life."

The carriage ground to a halt. The door swung open to half a
phalanx of Gavida's silver-clad puppets. Arms reached cloyingly
for me. But I resisted.

"I beg you." I tried to keep my voice calm. "Please give it back
to me."

"What? This?" A slow smile creased Gavida's face. He slid the
blue-green jewel from beneath his collar, dangling it in front of me.
"No. It is my insurance against your behavior, now that I know
my weaker collars are not strong enough to restrain you. I have
granted you leniency for dramatic acts of love performed upon a
public stage. I daresay it was good fun for everyone. But you have
tested the edges of my patience, little one. No more sneaking,
snooping, plotting, begging, or snarking. Tomorrow is the Longest
Night and the Trial of the Oak King. If all goes smoothly, you,
your husband, both your Treasures, your remaining ladies, your
friendly giant, and your aughiskies will leave this place unscathed.
If it does not...? Well."

He tucked the Heart of the Forest back beneath his clothes and
stepped down from the carriage. He bowed mockingly and handed
me down after him.

"The door to your room will be locked until the morrow, at
which point I will allow you to attend the final Trial. The day after,
you all may leave Emain Ablach." His stare was piercing and com-
manding. "So *behave*."

I swallowed hard. Curtsied. And let the attendants guide me
back up the grand steps into Aduantas.

Gavida was right—I had much to lose. Everyone and everything

I'd ever cared about, for a start. And what did I stand to gain by defying him?

An unknowable entity freed. An heir uncollared. My sister defeated.

Was it worth the risk?

I stared down at my arms, marked by dark vines studded with thorns and ragged scratches where my power had overcome Gavida's bracelets.

I had learned many things in the past year.

And not one of them was how to behave.

I changed out of the horrid silver gown as swiftly as possible, then took to pacing my room. My door was, as promised, locked. I tested the window, but it had neither hinges nor a latch—it was simply soldered fast to the wall. Looking out, I could see why. The tower overlooked a gorge plunging a hundred feet deep before rising steeply toward the amphitheater and, above it, the Grove of Gold. I stared for a long moment at the shining crown atop the Silver Isle, glowing like a beacon amid the fallen darkness. The half-finished rhyme Blink had given me slid through my mind, needling me with frustration.

> *In shadows deep, thrice threes a curse define;*
> *Three elements, three kings, nine trees intertwine.*
> *Only by the fourth, 'neath winter's darkest skies...*

The fourth *what*? Element? King? Tree? I cursed Gavida and his aggravating pattern, his wicked tournament, his unholy chokehold on everyone and everything on this island. There had to be a way to circumvent him—

My treacherous thoughts were interrupted by sudden aggressive tapping on the window. A moment later, huge, heavy black wings buffeted the glass.

Irian.

I wasn't surprised he'd come to me like this—after my stunt in the arena, I'd assumed Gavida would feel the need to sequester me. But as the attendants had dragged Irian and me bodily apart, I'd clung to him long enough to whisper, "Find me."

And he had. But this damned window wouldn't open. I once more ran my fingertips over the finely soldered panes, looking for some latch, some flaw, any way to open the window short of shattering it. Outside, Irian's anam cló tapped more urgently at the glass, his black beak a loud staccato in the night.

I cursed, stepped back. Beyond the window, the Grove of Gold once more caught my gaze.

I had an idea. A *bad* idea.

I dashed away from the window, throwing myself to my knees in front of my wardrobe. I scrabbled it open, digging through the careless mound of discarded clothes humped in the bottom. Gods, what had I done with it? I'd wrapped it in a shawl or scarf—but where had I shoved it?

Finally, my fingers collided with something firm. I unrolled the golden apple from the hem of one of my mantles. It was still fresh, firm, and plump despite being days old; the only marks it bore were the ridges of my teeth where I'd bitten it once before. I stared down at it for a long moment, weighing my options.

I had no real desire to experiment with the apple's dubious wishes ever again. But I *did* want to see Irian. *Needed* to see him, to talk to him, to touch him.

Before I could second-guess myself, I dashed with the apple to the casement. Irian's frenzied tappings were slowing, his beating wings slacking as he fought the wind outside the glass.

"I wish to open the window without breaking it," I whispered. I sank my teeth into the crisp, sweet flesh of the enchanted apple and swallowed its nectar down. As before, it tasted like summer days and solace with a bare hint of bitterness, like a well-disguised poison. Or a warning I should have heeded.

The window cracked open down the middle, the panes yawning inward with a rush of freezing wind and a tangle of feathers. Almost in the same instant, the middle finger on my left hand broke, the phalange snapping in half without warning. Pain screamed up my arm to the elbow, and I cried out as I dropped the golden apple to the tile. Irian lunged for me, his transformation only half-complete—his arms still furred with inkblot quills, his dark hair like a ruff of feathers. But I didn't mind—his embrace was blissfully warm and tight even as the window hurled ice-flecked wind around us. He pressed his lips against my hair and murmured something, but I couldn't hear him over the howling gale.

He released me only in order to nudge the window shut. When he turned back, his expression was thunderous. He knelt before me, cradling my injured hand between his own broad palms.

"You should not have done that, colleen."

I grimaced around the pain. "I wanted to see you. I couldn't think of a better way."

Irian's silver gaze was conflicted as he lifted his eyes to mine. But he smiled, just a little. "I wanted to see you too."

He stared back down at my broken finger, then took in my scratched and bloodied wrist from that afternoon. His eyes jumped to my other arm, then darkened to the ominous iron of a thunderhead. He reached up and traced the slender metal around my throat before cupping my face with his hands.

"I will kill him for what he has done to you," he promised me, flatly and dangerously. "The next time I see him, I am going to *fucking kill him.*"

"We're going to do better than that," I countered, still gasping from the pain in my finger. "We're going to take away the source of his power. We're going to destroy him. And we're going to make him watch as everything he's built burns away to ash."

Irian's eyes lit with deadly intensity. But the next moment, he softened, once more cradling my injured hand between his palms. "We need to set and splint this."

He led me into the darkened bathing chamber, rummaging through the cabinets for medical supplies. Finding nothing, he simply ripped off his shirt and began methodically tearing it into strips. I inhaled at the sight of his glorious expanse of sculpted muscle, a savage burst of desire igniting inside me. A moment later, my fervor cooled. He was still injured—badly. Rogan's rough treatment of him that afternoon was evident—a massive bruise purpled beneath the livid edges of the ragged cuts slowly healing across his torso.

"That doesn't look so good," I said as he began examining my broken and throbbing middle finger.

"It is a straight break." He misunderstood my words. "It will heal cleanly. And swiftly, once your magic is restored."

"Not me." Exasperation streaked through me. "*You.*"

He glanced down at the half-soaked bandage barely covering his cuts, then back up at me. Something lightened in his gaze, like humor or tenderness. "I told you not to worry about me."

I made a noise in my throat. "That's worked so well for both of us."

He hesitated, his lips parting as if he wanted to say something. Instead—and without any warning—he neatly snapped my middle finger back into place. I cried out as renewed pain flashed up my arm, then clapped a hand over my mouth and pressed my teeth into my palm.

"Breathe," Irian told me gently. "Just breathe."

I closed my eyes and obeyed, counting my inhales and exhales until the pain waned. When I opened them once more, Irian was methodically splinting my middle finger to my ring finger with tight strips of his now-ruined shirt. The finger still throbbed—terribly so—but at least it was back in position. I glared over at the golden apple, two bites gouged out of its perfect flesh, and resolved once more to never use it again.

When I looked back, Irian was gazing up at me, his eyes blisteringly bright. Emotions stirred within me—lingering resentment and lurking regret and burgeoning desire. I had *missed* him, these last few days—missed him with a yearning I had hardly let myself name. Because to have admitted that to myself would have been to admit how much I cared for him. How much I loved him, even when we were fighting. But here he was before me once more, and we were finally *alone*.

"Why did you let Rogan live?" I whispered before I could stop myself. "Why didn't you take his life, and with it the Oak King's Crown?"

"Because it would have broken your heart, colleen. And that would have broken mine."

I leaned down, grasped his angled jaw in my hands, and kissed him. There was none of the desperate, wild clash of tongues and teeth we'd shared in the arena. This kiss was a question. His lips moved soft under mine, but there was resistance there too. I had expected that.

"Fia," he began, his face an inch from mine.

"Me first." I slid the thumb of my uninjured hand gently over his plush lower lip. His breath gusted over my knuckles. "We have both done things we regret...said things we would take back if we could. Perhaps, in due time, all our apologies will spill from us like autumn leaves falling from a tree. But for now..." I hesitated as words bubbled up inside me. "The night of the Ember Moon, I was indelibly changed by the choices I made. But I am beginning to understand how you, too, underwent your own transformation. We two are not the same as we were when we met. Not even the same as when we were wed. And we are likely to keep changing, with every day and every month and every year. Gods willing, we will live long enough to transform a thousand times—rising and falling and twisting like the seasons."

I paused, my throat tightening around the words I had been so unsure of. Words I had kept caged inside me for too long. Words I so badly wanted to speak—and to hear—but had learned to mistrust.

I slid my hands over Irian's feather-marked shoulders. I gazed into his opal eyes and thought about Mother, who had told me she loved me a thousand times but had never once meant it. Rogan, whom I had loved so long but who had never truly loved me back. Wayland, whose fate seemed etched beside mine in a way I could not quite fathom. Wayland, who had relentlessly flirted with me. Wayland, whom I had kissed...and in the end, felt nothing for.

And Irian. Irian, who had dared love me for all my thorns and shadows. Irian, who had held me beneath the Heartwood as the life bled from my limbs. Irian, who had tried so hard to protect me that he'd lost me.

I thought about what marriage meant—what it truly meant to choose someone over and over and over again. Was it a palimpsest—a layering of loyalty until the original choice became obscured by the ones that came later? Or was it a palindrome—the beginning and the ending recurring simultaneously? Or was it a single choice—the one you made now, in this moment? Forever.

"I love you," I whispered. "Irian, son of Ethadon, tánaiste of the Sept of Feathers—I love you. I choose *you*. Today and tomorrow and the day after that. No matter who you become or how you change—you are my home. And I am yours. We are stronger together."

"I told you once—I was only made for one love." The silver of his gaze was moonlight breaking from behind dark clouds. "One great, terrible, consuming love. A savage, scathing, sublime love. *You* are that love." He swallowed. "Yes, we will change. But I will love you in the tender warmth of spring. I will love you in the hot bright heat of summer. I will love you through the slow wrinkling fade of autumn, to the cold depths of winter. And beyond. For if I have my way, death will be but one more change we two must weather together. And if anything exists beyond it, I will love you there too."

Heat burned the back of my throat, and I blinked my eyes against an unexpected sting. This time when he kissed me, there was no hesitation—only hope. He tangled his hands in my long messy hair and cupped the back of my head. But even as our bodies collided and heat burned in my veins, Irian tensed at my touch—the muscles of his stomach rippling not from desire, but from pain. And my own left hand was tentative on his skin, my instinctive fear of bumping my broken finger making me clumsy. I drew back.

"Colleen?" His eyes were bruised dark with want, pupils dilated with pain. "Do you not want...?"

"I do." I laughed a little. "Oh, how I do. But we have a lifetime to explore each other. And I wouldn't want you to tire of me too quickly."

"Impossible." Irian's dazzling, full-fledged smile was like a long-awaited dawn—I couldn't remember the last time I'd seen it. He hoisted me against him as he stood—regardless of his injury—and I clung to his shoulders as he carried me gently to the bed. He laid me softly back on the pillows, then slid his arm around my shoulders as he climbed in beside me. Together we nestled between the clouds of soft, downy blankets. Outside the window—wind still whistling through the tiny gap left by my wish—it had begun to snow again over Emain Ablach. "Or did you not hear what I said about the afterlife?"

For a long, contented moment, I reveled in his closeness—the hard, protective loop of his bicep over my shoulders; the press of his powerful torso next to mine; the way his breath stirred my hair. But then the world crept back in—deceptive little quivers rushing up my arms and creeping beneath my collar. I angled my head to Irian, and he looked down at me, his dark lashes shadowing his eyes.

"We should talk," I said.

"Go on, then, colleen." His voice was low, mild. He pulled me even closer. "Talk."

❧

I started at the beginning—or, perhaps, the middle. I told him about the revel in the Grove of Gold. About Eala and Rogan and how much our encounter had broken my heart. I told him about my charade with Wayland. About discovering the caverns with the girls. About Blink. The dobhar-chú.

The Year.

Chandi.

I told him everything. He listened intently to my every word. Sometimes he tensed, his bare muscles flexing against my skin as if he wished to leap into my past and strong-arm my memories. Sometimes he looked away from me, his gaze gliding out to watch the snow angle down along the sill. Sometimes he made that wordless sound low in his throat, although I never knew quite what it meant. And in the end—when I'd run out of words, laid everything that had happened over the last week on the table—he was silent.

"Well?" His quiet threatened to overwhelm me. "Aren't you going to scold me?"

"No." He looked down at me, his eyes like pearls in the dim. "I cannot agree with all your choices. You must know that by now. But I think perhaps you were always going to make them."

"I'll try to be less reckless."

"That would be excellent. But I will not hold my breath." He sobered, his eyes once more driving past the window. "Tell me again of the rhyme you found in Blink's bookstore."

I repeated it to him. " 'In shadows deep, thrice threes a curse define; three elements, three kings, nine trees intertwine. Only by the fourth, 'neath winter's darkest skies...' And that's where it ended."

His jaw flexed. "What do you think it means?"

"My best guess?" I sighed, scrubbed a hand over my tired eyes. "Today, Gavida let slip that bindings were easier than unbindings. What if we need to override his binding with a new binding? Rather than thrice threes... four fours? Four shackles, four elements, four kings?"

One of Irian's stark eyebrows slid upward. "And the trees?"

"I don't know." I sighed. "I don't know about any of it. I was made to stab where I was aimed. This is all a bit beyond me."

"Do not say such things, colleen. You know you are obnoxiously clever." Irian traced his finger along my collarbone, quiet with thought. "When the Treasures were originally forged, Gavida was the younger brother of the first chieftain of the Sept of Fins. Between that bloodline and Wayland's mother's affinity, Wayland's innate magic is tied to the element of water."

"Potential tánaiste of the Un-Dry Cauldron." I gamely followed his train of thought. "But between me, you, and Wayland, that still only makes three elements."

"And three heirs." Irian's gaze sharpened. "Although if you are truly Deirdre and Rían's child, then you are doubly so. Heir to the Heart of the Forest... and the throne of Fódla, after Eala."

My dream from the other night shuddered through me. The faceless man in the cottage in the woods... I blinked it away. I could worry about my nightmares later. "I doubt that's enough. Surely we'd need a tánaiste of the Sept of Scales too. A fourth heir. A fourth element."

Irian stilled. His eyes flicked down, then back up.

"What?" I pushed away to sit fully up on the bed, trying to read his expression. "I've told you everything. Please don't keep another secret from me."

"It is not a secret, colleen." He reached for my hand, waylaying my retreat. "It is an educated guess. One I think you have also made."

I stared at him, trying to parse his words. I remembered how he'd once told me of the long years he'd searched for other heirs after the bardaí had slaughtered the Septs. How more than a decade of searching had left him with nothing...but *me*. But that hadn't been quite true, had it? He'd known about Wayland, although I understood why he'd kept his distance all these years. But who else...?

I forced myself to think back over the blur of the past weeks. I remembered a night when the forest had failed to warn me of an intruder. Rough scales, dry heat. Two days later, a Gentry woman without an oath had stumbled upon our camp and offered to join our party. A woman with old ties to the Sept of Scales. A woman trained in elite combat. A woman with red hair, ember eyes, and a touch that *burned*.

"*Laoise?*"

"I believe so." His gaze was guarded. "She has tried to be so very subtle—I did not see a reason to expose her against her will. But I have suspected almost since the moment we met her that she was an heir of the Sept of Scales. A potential tánaiste for the Flaming Shield, should she ever be in a position to inherit it."

"Irian!" I breathed. "You should have told me."

"I know, and I am sorry." He grimaced, regret and self-loathing warping his beautiful features. "But I knew if you discovered her true nature, it would only drive your ambition to resurrect the other Treasures. And selfishly...well. You know."

I did know. My pulse throbbed with renewed thirst to reforge the lost Treasures. An heir to both the Sept of Scales *and* the Sept of Fins? Right here in Aduantas? But I controlled myself. If Irian could choose me despite my penchant for the reckless, then I could choose him despite his desire to crawl away into a hole with me and wish away the outside world.

"I promise you this," I said, gripping his fingers with my good hand. "Once we defeat Gavida, resurrect the Treasures, and renew the balance of magic between the human and Folk realms...*then* you and I can have our lifelong honeymoon."

"Is that all we must do?" He smiled despite the sorrow and dread gathering behind his eyes. We both knew that unless another miracle happened, our honeymoon wouldn't be very long. Thirteen years, decreasing by the day. It wasn't enough. But it was more than either of us had ever hoped for. "Very well, colleen. Tell me how."

Chapter Thirty-Eight

It must have been two hours past midnight when we left my room. Irian flung himself from the casement in the shape of his anam cló, black wings melting into a blacker night. His job was simple—locate Laoise and Sinéad, who had so far escaped Gavida's dire notice, and bring them to the Grove of Gold.

My job was harder. Much harder.

I changed into practical clothes, then stuck my head out the window I'd wished open. A gust of freezing wind burned across my face, whipping hair from my braid and teasing sharp tears from my narrowed eyes. I gritted my teeth and looked down. Aduantas was built on a rise—our tower dropped precipitously down stark cliffs before rising once more toward the hill crowned by the Grove of Gold. Frost sparkled from the pale white stone, and fresh snow lumped along windowsills. My bravado bled toward something closer to despair. Without access to my magic, trying to climb down the side of this building would be suicide.

But what about climbing *up*? I spun, gripping the edge of the window as I craned my neck toward the roof. We were much closer to the top than to the bottom—only two floors separated my window from the sleek, sharp crenellations edging the peak of our tower. I followed the line of its roof with my eyes, registering the flimsy covered bridge slinging toward the next tower, which was encircled by a narrow serpentine staircase. Far below, the fortified curtain wall rose up to meet it, like two snakes twining together in the night.

I grinned madly. This was a very bad idea.

Ducking back inside, I braided my hair more tightly, reset my splint, drew on my gloves, then looped a scarf over my mouth, nose, and forehead, until only my eyes were exposed. Thanks to my original collar, both the cold and the wind were going to be a challenge. I jumped back up onto the sill, loosening my daggers in their hilts before palming the edge of the window. I eased outside, the panes barely allowing the width of my hips to scrape by. My boots connected with the narrow ledge. The wind instantly screamed at me like a bean sidhe, grasping the hems of my clothing with cold fingers and tugging at my scarf with deadly fervor. I hesitated one last second, then reached up for the ledge above the window.

I kicked up, aiming one of my skeans for a vein of mortar bonding the stones of the tower together. It struck true, lodging deep even as it rained grit on my face. I jiggled it experimentally, then kicked up again as I lashed out with the other dagger. This one glanced off stone, jolting my arm. My broken finger throbbed as I flailed for purchase. A moment later, I found it. I jerked myself up onto the next story's windowsill, breathing through the pain in my hand and pining for my Greenmark.

I climbed the rest of the tower hand over hand, regretting it more with each passing minute. My broken finger screamed at me. My palms, encased in their fur-lined gloves, began to sweat and cramp. Conversely, my toes were nuggets of ice in my swaying boots. Tears burned from my wind-whipped eyes. My biceps trembled. I keenly missed the familiar comfort of the Heart of the Forest humming a slow, near-silent melody between the percussion of my ribs.

Finally, I wrapped my arms around a narrow crenellation and

hauled myself up onto the vertex. The roof was narrow and sloped; I edged along it until I could dance across the bridge slung between two towers like a necklace. The staircase snaking around the shorter tower was iced over and had no railing. I crept down it with my back to the stones and my daggers braced to catch my fall.

When my boots touched the solid stones of the curtain wall, relief unspooled the tension clenching my muscles. Dizziness forced me down to one knee as my collar spiked a numb thorn toward the base of my skull. I shook my head to clear the vertigo, even as the tramp of heavy footfalls announced an approaching patrol. I folded myself into the shadow of a parapet and waited until the guards passed me by. Then I took off in the opposite direction, circling Aduantas until I'd nearly reached the main gates. I grinned when I spotted it—the impossible flowering vine I'd grown, then climbed, less than a week ago.

Wayland's pleasure gardens were still and silent. I was glad— I wasn't sure I could have borne another revel, another desperate charade. But then I saw the pair of attendants guarding his chamber doors. And I understood.

I crept forward through the snow-draped courtyard, keeping to the shadows. The wall rose up to meet me, and I slid along it, bathed in shifting pennants of moonglow and darkness. I paused an arm's length from the taller attendant, then swiftly dragged him into the shadows. The back of my hilt struck his temple; he slumped down at my boots. But the second attendant had heard the struggle—she lashed out to meet my attack, her hands striking my raised wrists. Pain skeined up my left arm and jolted my bad finger; I hissed and jerked back. She pressed her advantage, slamming her knee up to collide with my hip. I caught her leg with my good arm and used her momentum to slam her into the wall, pinning her body with mine. I slashed out with my skean.

But when my dagger parted the skin above her collarbone, she didn't so much as flinch. She didn't blink, didn't cry out. Didn't bleed.

She broke my grip, shoved me backward. I stumbled on a patch of ice, fell to the flagstones. She was on me in an instant, her hands scrabbling at my throat. I threw my arms outward against her elbows, trying to break her grip. But she was *strong*. She throttled me, and I was suddenly afraid—

Afraid that this, of all ways, was the way I would die.

A heavy boot slammed into her torso and knocked her bodily away. She was back on her feet in an instant, but the tall male form caught her in a brutal chokehold, twisted, then simply ripped her head off. I raised my hand up to my face, bracing myself for the spray of blood. But it never came. Wayland carelessly discarded the two halves of her body on the ground. Instead of muscle, fascia, bone, there was only metal. Wires and mesh and metal rods and rivets.

"I told you they were forgings, Thorn Girl." Wayland's face was impassive. He hesitated for a moment before reaching down and helping me to stand. "Did you expect them to have blood and bones like you and I?"

"I didn't expect *that*."

Wayland looked at me. His eyes were shadowed in the dim— behind him, the door to his chambers yawned dark and cold. Surprise wavered up through me—it wasn't like Wayland to spend his nights in silent contemplation.

"What are you doing here?" he asked, low. "Do you wish my father to collar your ankles too?"

I almost choked—the suggestion was nearly identical to the one I'd made to his father earlier. But when his face contorted, my mirth disappeared. "We need your help."

"No." He turned and made his way back into his chambers. I followed a step behind. His rooms—usually flooded with honeycomb light, smelling of beeswax and liquor and sex—were dark and silent. "We tried. We failed. And now we're done."

"You'd give up that easily?"

"Easily?" He half turned, his profile stark. "I have spent years trying to thwart my father. To live my own life...to carve out my own destiny. This year, thanks to you, I came closer than I've ever managed before. But that has only served to enslave me to him further."

"I'm sorry, Wayland. But we now have a chance—"

"To do what?" He passed a hand over his brow. "Fia, you are breathtakingly beautiful and bewilderingly bold and profoundly beyond my reach. I would follow you into a volcano and thank you for the opportunity to warm my toes. But in two days, you and Irian and the rest of your lucky entourage will leave this place. Will leave *me*. I...I will be forced to stay. I *must* think about what my life will look like once you are gone. I do not blame you for the punishments my father has hammered down on us. But I cannot risk further restrictions, lest I lose what few privileges I still enjoy beneath his thumb."

"There is another heir," I blurted out. It was already late—if we did not return to Aduantas before dawn, all would be for naught. "At least, Irian believes so."

Wayland blinked. Then reluctantly nodded. "Laoise?"

I swallowed wounded pride. How had I been so blind? "Then you'll come."

He leveled me with a reluctant stare. "Come where?"

"To the Grove of Gold," I said. "We're going to free Talah from her prison."

By the time we'd clambered up from beneath Aduantas using the attendants' passageways, the night weighed heavy. Dawn was not far off. Wayland was unusually twitchy as we emerged near the Grove of Gold, and when he spotted the hulking outline of a massive Fomorian blotting out the stars, he nearly fell back down the stairs. I caught him.

"That's Balor." I recognized the gentle giant's terrifyingly massive skull silhouetted against the horizon. "He's a friend."

Wayland recovered himself but shot me a curious glare. "You have a way of making strange acquaintances, Thorn Girl."

A moment later, a willowy form rocketed down the slope and launched herself at me. I rocked back on my heels, glimpsing honey-blond hair limned with the gold of the enchanted apple trees. But it was the slender daggers gripped hard in her hands that tipped me off.

"Sinéad," I whispered, folding my arms around her. Wayland gave us space, climbing the rest of the way to the grove. "Morrigan, I'm so sorry I couldn't see you sooner—"

"Don't you apologize." She hugged me harder, then drew back. Even in the dimness, I could see she'd been crying—her blue eyes red ringed and bleary, her dimpled cheeks swollen. But none of that compared to the anger blazing over her face and shaking her limbs. "*She's* the one who should be apologizing to me. Chandi is my sister—how could she do this to me? To us? After the night of the Ember Moon, she swore she'd never go back to Eala. We all did. We promised each other we'd never believe another word out of her lying mouth. I could *kill* her, Fia!"

"Calmly." I gripped her wrists, gently lowering the daggers she held before her. "I understand how you're feeling. I understand your anger—I do. But try not to judge Chandi too harshly. This is Eala's fault—she is the only villain in this story. If you want to rage at anyone, let it be her."

"But *why* did Chandi return to her?" The ragged plea nearly broke my heart. "Why, after everything, did she betray us?"

"I think—" I bit my lip. I remembered how focused Chandi had been on my resurrection, how our conversations had kept circling my death and rebirth like water down a drain. I remembered the spell she'd pretended not to read in the Folk grimoire at Blink's bookstore. And I remembered her words to me earlier—*I love you, Fia. But I loved my swan sisters more.* "The night of the Ember Moon, Eala promised to resurrect you, did she not? In return for your willing hearts?"

Sinéad nodded. "She vowed she'd use the magic she bought with our hearts to bring us back. Our deaths would be sanctified; our resurrection, divine. And gods help us, we believed her. But she was lying—my sisters are just dead. They're not coming back—she can't bring them back."

"I fear Chandi doesn't feel the same way. Eala must have told her she could resurrect your dead sisters if she won the tournament. And Chandi's grief must have made her believe it."

Sinéad's face twisted with heartbreak and outrage and the barest edge of hope. "But that's madness. Is it not?"

"I don't know what Eala has planned," I told Sinéad honestly. "But if I know my sister, then yes. I believe it is certainly madness."

Sinéad swiped at her eyes, nodded to herself. Then finally—finally—sheathed her daggers. "Come on. They're up this way."

The three heirs faced off between the golden apple trees. Irian, stark and dangerous as a bird of prey. Wayland, sleek and dark-eyed as an otter. And Laoise, deceptively harmless and winsome, with her gently curving figure and sweet smile. But now that I knew who—what—she was, it seemed so obvious. The flaming glint of her auburn curls; the firelight lurking in her ember eyes.

She looked up as Sinéad and I crested the rise.

"So—I've been discovered." Her face twisted into something that wasn't quite a smile. "Was it you, Fia? You're too clever by half, you know."

"It was Irian," I admitted, a little reluctantly. And Wayland, apparently. "You're lucky he kept your secret for as long as he did."

She glanced back at him, a little surprised. "Why did you?"

"I will tell you." Irian canted his head in the way that always made my blood run cold. "If you tell us why you kept it from us."

For a long moment, Laoise considered her options. Then she crossed her arms over her chest and said, "I never lied to you. I did need a good cover to get onto the island. I was telling the truth about the nemeta—they used to flourish everywhere magic gathered, with the power to imbue objects with wishes or enchant the weary or heal the sick. But the nemeton in my home is dying. I thought perhaps if I could examine this one, with its mythical, wish-granting golden apples, I might learn how to revive the one we are losing."

"But that wasn't the whole truth," I guessed. "Was it?"

"No." She looked at me, canny. "Word of the Heart of the Forest's resurrection spread like wildfire through Tír na nÓg and beyond. It spread so far it even reached me, in my self-imposed exile. I have never been interested in my Sept's inheritance—not even before the Treasures were destroyed did I wish to fall heir to a Treasure. But the stories I heard made me curious. I wanted to see what you were made of." Her gaze scorched from me toward Irian. "Both of you. Now, if you don't mind telling me what you plan to do to me?"

"*Do* to you, No-Oath Laoise?" Irian laughed, the sound so shocking to me that I nearly lost my footing. "We are going to fold you in, of course. Welcome you to our no-good, harebrained, accursed band of outcasts, desperate dreamers, and miscreants. Provided you are willing to join the side most likely to lose, of course."

"I've never particularly cared about winning." Laoise scanned over me, Wayland, Sinéad, Balor, until finally returning her gaze to Irian. "Go on, then. I think I know about two-thirds of this story. Who's going to tell me the ending?"

I did. I filled her in on the Year, the rhyme Blink had sold me, and my theories about what it meant. After I finished, Laoise was silent for a long moment.

"It's plausible." She seemed skeptical. Briefly, she lofted her hands, sending red-gold arcs of crackling, sizzling fire spinning through the dark. I gasped. Beside me, Wayland also inhaled. "The elements, fine. But the kings? We may all be tánaistí, but half of us are heir to nothing. And what of the fourth shackle? And the trees?"

"We're all just guessing," I said. "But it's the best shot we have.

Otherwise, we sit back and let Eala win the Oak King's Crown. I don't know exactly what she plans to ask Gavida to forge her. But I know it won't be good."

Laoise narrowed her ember eyes. "Will the Bright One—the Year—become bound to one of us?"

"I don't know. Maybe." I glanced around our awkward circle. "If she binds to anyone...Laoise, it may be you. Down in the caverns, the three elements she was bound by seemed to be earth, water, and air. Fire might be the thing to set her free. There was something *molten* about her. Are you prepared to be bound to one of the Bright Ones?"

"Is that not what the Treasures are? Sources of elemental power, bound through conduits to vessels?" Laoise asked. I glanced sharply at Irian; he gave me an imperceptible shrug. But he knew little more than me about our inheritances—he had been a sequestered child, barely schooled and underage, when he received the Sky-Sword in the midst of slaughter and war.

"Then you are prepared?"

"I am prepared. Although I confess I am dubious about this whole endeavor."

"Fair enough." I threw my hands up. "But we will not know unless we try. Sinéad, Balor...will you keep watch beyond the grove?"

Sinéad hefted her twin blades, seemingly glad for the distraction. Balor gave me a broad, craggy smile.

"Gladly, lady."

They moved down the slope, leaving our strange quartet alone. Without discussion, we moved to the center of the grove. Everyone looked at me. I swallowed.

"In shadows deep, thrice threes a curse define," I said, a little uncertainly. "Three elements, three kings, nine trees intertwine. Yet a fourth, the key to unbind..." My skills at poetry were negligible— the rest of this wasn't going to rhyme. "Four dynasties...four heirs... four kings and queens to be." I slid Wayland's mother's silver-and-gold ring from my finger and, shooting him a slightly apologetic glance, leaned down to set it in the middle of our square. "A fourth shackle." I remembered my own binding I'd spoken beneath the Heartwood, seven weeks and yet a lifetime ago. "Four elements. By fire and by sky, by fast water and by ancient golden trees…we bind you, Year. We bind you, Talah."

For a long moment, we waited. The only sounds were the sighing of the wind between the golden boughs and the distant, constant crash of the waves against the tall white cliffs.

"Blood." I remembered how Cathair had once opened the Gates. How I myself had once bled for them. "A heart is powerful magic."

I drew one of my skeans and nicked the tip of my finger, letting four droplets green as moss fall to the ground. Irian mirrored me a moment later, his blood silver as cirrus clouds and lightning. Wayland followed suit, his blood dark as midnight seas. Finally, Laoise pricked her hand, her blood so bright a crimson it glowed in the dark.

We waited.

Nothing.

I had expected dramatics. Visions or sideways worlds, explosions or ignitions. Rumblings, at the very least. But there was nothing—only the four of us awkwardly standing amid a magical grove of wishing trees as false dawn grayed the horizon.

"I'm sorry," I finally said. "I really thought that was going to work."

"It was worth a try." Wayland clapped me a little too jovially on the shoulder. "But now we should all try to get some sleep. Tomorrow comes too soon."

"He's right." With more kindness than I probably deserved, Laoise leaned close. "I also thought it was going to work."

It made me want to cry.

They both moved off, leaving Irian and me alone amid the glowing grove. I slowly bent to retrieve Wayland's signet ring, a little surprised he hadn't picked it up himself. I slid it onto my uninjured middle finger, and when I rose back up, Irian wrapped his arm around my shoulder. I leaned into him, hiding my disappointment in the breadth of his musculature.

"You are not omnipotent, colleen," he said gently. "You have already enacted one improbable miracle this year. A second was rather a tall order."

I sighed. "I know. But what do we do now?"

"We go back to your room." He pressed a kiss to my temple. "We sleep. Tomorrow, we witness the end to a rigged tournament. Then— we go home."

"Home?" The word tore something jagged from my throat. "Where's that?"

"Wherever you wish. You are my home now. As I am yours."

I looked up at him. But despite the softness of his words, his sharp silver eyes were deadly serious.

"Less than a day," I said. "And Wayland yet again loses a rigged tournament. Eala wins her prize. And we just…leave?"

"It is not victory." Irian once more betrayed the faintest hint of wounded pride. "But it is living. And I am trying to find ways to live for you, colleen, instead of fighting so hard to die for you. As instructed."

I slid my hands around his neck, drawing him down for a simmering kiss.

I didn't have much. But I had him.

Chapter Thirty-Nine

The day of the Longest Night dawned diamond bright and crystal cold. Flowers of frost had bloomed on the windows, clouding the world beyond to shades of blue and white. I nestled deeper into Irian's embrace, sleep still clinging to my eyelids. It had only been a few hours, surely—exhaustion weighted my bones, and pain throbbed dully in my left hand. He pulled me closer, his heavy arm snug around the curve of my waist; his sculpted chest against the wings of my shoulder blades. We drowsed for a little longer, until the realities of the day crept close on serrated little feet. I groaned, turning toward him in our nest of pillows and blankets.

"We should get up," I said softly. "We should get ready."

"Ready?" Irian's blue-gold eyes were heavy-lidded with lingering sleep. "The final Trial does not take place until the afternoon—for the forging of the Oak King's Crown must take place at sunset on the Longest Night. The moment between one year and the next. That is the tradition."

"Oh." I glanced out the window at the morning sunlight slicing down like golden spears. "That's hours away. Do you want to sleep more?"

"No." His hand, looped over my waist, flexed—his finger-tips gliding over the divots of my spine. I shivered, my awareness shifting toward the easy, languorous way our naked bodies were entwined: my ankle looped over his calf, my hip pressing his stomach, my hands idly twining in his hair. "I want you."

"Oh?" I smiled a little, tilting my chin up in a silent request for a kiss. "How so?"

"I want you warm and willing," he murmured, brushing his plush lips softly over mine. "Sun glazed and sighing. Soft limbed and moaning."

"How very poetic."

"Fine." His mouth twisted with wicked humor. "I want you to scream my name in the moment before you forget your own."

I opened my mouth beneath his, delving my tongue between his teeth. He shed all his morning softness in an instant, his sculpted physique hardening. He slipped his knee between my thighs, gripped my waist. I arched myself toward him, molding my stomach to his now mostly healed torso and pressing my peaking nipples into his smooth, carven chest. He exhaled roughly, his mouth dragging down over my jaw and along the column of my throbbing throat. His tongue carved out the hollow where my pulse leapt. His hands explored my body slowly, precisely, adoringly—his fingertips reacquainting themselves with every angle and curve, memorizing every line and dent and scar.

He settled himself lower, propping himself on one elbow as his mouth skated hot over my nipple, then dragged downward, gliding past my navel to nip at my hip bones. His hands curled possessively around my thighs, hooking one up around his ear as he splayed me out like a feast. He tasted me reverently...devoured me slowly. I moaned at the hot, slick pleasure of his mouth gliding over me. An ache burned a path upward from my core, igniting my veins with skeins of silver and gold. I bucked my hips, wanting more speed, more pressure, more heat. But he just smiled against my skin, lifting eyes dark with lust and longing to pin me over the plane of my stomach.

"I have no gods to pray to, colleen," he growled. "Will you not let me worship you instead?"

His words reverberated through me, carving out the echoing spaces of my cavernous heart. I climaxed a few moments later, the crescendo of my pleasure wringing something raw and primal from my throat. My back arched as I rode wave after wave of gratification until my bones were molten from the heat burning a path through me. At last, the sensations abated enough for me to twine my fingers in his dark locks and tug him toward me. He obeyed, skimming his tongue over my body until his mouth met mine.

My hands dropped to his hips, guiding him forward as I bucked my aching core up against his hard length. But he pulled back onto his knees and drew me with him, folding me in his sinewed arms. I bit my lip, intuiting what he wanted. I curled my arms around his neck and slung my legs over his thighs, his growing need pulsing against my slippery heat.

I lowered myself onto him slowly—achingly slowly. Irian exhaled with a sound like homecoming, his body going rigid as I slid down upon every inch of his glorious length. I cried out, my fingernails digging into his biceps as my still-simmering desire sang higher—a sizzling glissando I almost couldn't bear. I felt hot and nearly fluid, surging above him as he began to rock his hips. But I forestalled him with my hands pressed to his chest.

"Oh, no," I whispered. I leaned down and dragged my teeth up the throbbing column of his throat, then slid my tongue around the seashell of his ear. He groaned. "If you want me to ride, you have to give me the reins."

I pushed him back onto the bed. His hair spilled over the pillows, black as ink on white parchment. He circled my waist with his palms, tendons flexing beneath the dark markings fletching his arms. I rocked against him, slowly at first and then faster, as I found the joined rhythm of our pleasure. His jaw flexed as his abdomen tightened. His hands lifted from my waist, dragging lines of fire up my ribs to brush the curve of my chest. I arched my back, pushing my breasts forward. He palmed them, sliding rough thumbs over my peaked nipples and sending lightning spiking through my veins.

The heat inside me burned toward a crescendo. I threw my head back as I came apart once again, the backs of my eyelids exploding with stars. I collapsed on top of him, trembling with the aftereffects of climax, crying out his name into the hard ridge of muscle connecting his shoulder to his neck. The sound triggered something feral in him. He smoothly flipped me onto my back. His hands slid up my arms, pinning my hands above my head. He kissed the helpless noises spilling unbidden from my mouth—roughly, raggedly. His neck corded with tension as he chased his own peak, his motions growing forceful until he spent himself inside me, finishing with great shuddering thrusts that nearly rent me in half.

For a long moment, we lay together, panting and trembling as our heartbeats slowed. Then Irian tugged me even closer—hip to hip, chest to chest, face to face. His gaze roamed my features, as though memorizing each angle and curve, every freckle and eyelash and mote in my mismatched eyes.

"Is tú mo chuisle, Fia." It was almost a question, as if he wished me to fill in the next clause. But I was boneless with satiation; my thoughts caged behind the live-wire tangle of my still-sparking veins. "You are my pulse."

"And you are my heart." I curled my palms around his jaw and drew him to me for the faintest, sweetest kiss. Then smiled, remembering an ancient journal in a dust-choked archive. An endearment that I had not invented but that nevertheless felt like it belonged to me. To *us*. "Mo chroí."

"Mo chroí," Irian repeated, rolling the syllables over in his low burr. "My heart."

"For we are bound by ties no one can sunder—not living gods or trickster kings or devious princesses. Not even each other." My smile grew. "I'm afraid you are rather stuck with me."

"No place in the world I would rather be," he said, his smile rising to meet mine. "Mo chroí."

We spent the remainder of the morning pleasantly, lounging in bed and watching the ice whisper strange patterns across the window glass. We sent for mushroom-mud tea and pastries and picked at them idly as we spoke of simple, mundane things. I told him about the epic snowball fights the trainees in the high queen's fiann had engaged in on the rare occasions it had snowed in Fódla. He recounted a rather harrowing tale of the time he and Wayland had constructed an intricate luge course down the side of the mountain and had both wound up severely concussed.

I huffed out my breath. "You two sound like quite the handful."

"We were." Irian flashed that rare, wide smile before sobering. "He did his best to be there for me, all those years ago. I regret that after I inherited the Sky-Sword, I could not return the favor. And that we were not able to once again be close friends...in the way you two seem to have become."

"I doubt you would have appreciated the level of flirtation I was forced to endure," I said dryly.

"Did you fulfill your oath to him, at least?" Irian's eyes flicked to mine, then away. "Never mind. You are not obliged to tell me."

"I did." I reached out and glided my fingers between his, then pulled our joined hands over my heart. I considered telling him about it—Wayland and my cavern-damp clothes and scorched-metal skin. How I'd thought, in the end, only of Irian. But I decided the less said, the better. "There is nothing between him and me anymore. In any shape or form. Save—as you say—friendship."

Relief burned blue over Irian's lingering curiosity. But he asked me nothing more.

"He told me—" I hesitated, not sure how to broach Irian's past when he had not brought it up himself. "Perhaps he should not

have. But he told me more about your mother. And the geas Ethadon placed upon her."

Irian arm jumped, slopping some of his barely touched mushroom tea over his fingers. But when he looked up at me, he was
composed. "I have wanted to tell you, colleen. But I have spent
so long alone that I do not always know how to flense those old
wounds without butchering myself in the process."

"I do not begrudge you that secret. I only hope you know you
may speak of your past to me, if you find the words. I can only love
the things that made you who you are, no matter how awful or
brutal or cruel."

Irian's eyes flicked away, and he was silent for a long minute.

"Would you—" He cleared his throat. "Would you ever want to
meet her?"

Surprised jerked through me. "Meet her? But I thought...?"

"She has no memory of me as her son. But she still lives and
retains all her faculties otherwise. After that first desperate escape
back to her cottage, I have gone back from time to time to visit
her. I bring her fresh cockles or weaving supplies or storybooks,
for she always loved a good yarn. She makes me tea and sits with
me beside the hearth, and we talk of the weather or her loom or
her garden. She thinks of me only as a somewhat inconstant friend.
But I would like for you to meet her, and her you. If you think you
could tolerate the awkwardness."

"Mo chroí." I gripped his hand so tightly I thought our skin
might meld together. "I would far rather know her as a friend than
never know her at all. We have so few mothers between us—it's
only right that we should share where we can."

Our time ended too quickly. The bells over Aduantas tolled afternoon. We dressed reluctantly, Irian in his familiar black raiment
with his dark armor buckled over it. I took rather longer, mulling

over my wardrobe options. The clothes I'd come to Emain Ablach with were all gone by now—Corra's gowns abandoned in the room I'd previously shared with Irian, my well-worn fighting leathers and boots stripped away by the attendants who'd put me to bed after Gavida discovered Wayland and me with the Year. The armoire was filled with extravagant gowns in the smith-king's chosen color scheme. But I was tired of being his marionette—tired of jumping when he snapped his fingers and dancing when he clapped his hands.

I spun to Irian. "Give me your outer mantle."

Perhaps it was foolish to make a statement when we were so close to earning our freedom. But I wanted Gavida to know that while he might have beaten me...he didn't own me.

Irian gave me a curious look but didn't protest, merely unclasped the cloak from his shoulder and handed it to me. I pulled on a pair of dark blue leather trousers from the wardrobe, then layered the cloak over them, wrapping it around my waist before crisscrossing it up over my chest to tie around my neck, leaving my arms and most of my back bare. But the attempt was clumsy—disappointment thundered through me. If only Chandi—

Irian made a noise low in his throat.

"What?" I swallowed my grief and anger at the thought of my erstwhile friend. "I'd rather attend the last Trial as your queen, rather than *his* thrall."

"You misunderstand, colleen." A hint of mirth warmed his tone. "It simply needs a finishing touch."

Irian picked up the silvery confection I'd worn to yesterday's Trial from where I'd discarded it, inside out, on the floor. Briskly, he unsheathed his sword and cut away the frothy skirt from the bodice, then tore off the lace-and-pearl overlay. Beneath the bejeweled lace was a corset of dark satin girdled by stiff vertical boning of silver metal. I smiled, understanding, then turned. Irian curved the bodice around my waist and laced it swiftly, his fingers deft on the stays.

"There." His fingertips skimmed the black markings bridging my collarbones before dancing down my arms. "My queen of thorns. And perhaps again someday...my queen of feathers."

I turned in his arms, lifting my chin for a brief kiss. Then I braided my hair in a severe crown, smeared dark kohl on my eyes and red rouge on my lips, and buckled both my skeans around my corseted waist. Finally, I reached down and plucked up the golden apple, with one last dubious wish tucked away in its tender, tempting flesh. I hesitated, remembering my prior two wishes. Then nevertheless slid it into the pouch hanging from my waist.

I gripped Irian's arm as we stepped out into Aduantas and prepared to witness the last Trial of the Tournament of Kings.

Chapter Forty

The frigid afternoon on the shortest day of the year was edging toward sundown as we entered the amphitheater, which had been transformed into something altogether unexpected. By now I had come to despise Gavida's sense of spectacle. But not even I could resist being awed by the splendor of his imagination.

A massive crystalline dome now arched over the arena, articulated along lines and angles like a giant diamond. Its facets were limned by the dimming sun, transmuting its rays into spears of fire and frost stabbing down from the firmament. A thousand roaring braziers lined the amphitheater and circled the sandy stage, heating the air beneath the dome. And at the crown of the amphitheater, at the center of the Grove of Gold, there now stood a grand forge, with a massive, roaring furnace and the smith-king's unmistakable crucible propped upon its giant metal stand. I stared up at the white-hot vessel glowing with molten metal and spitting starry sparks into the dimming afternoon and thought of the Year, even as nausea rose in my gorge.

Every weapon he forges, every machine he assembles, bears within it a piece of me, she had told me. *Again and again, I am splintered.*

Tonight, another great forging would take place. Something wicked and terrible, if my sister had anything to do with it—a grand culmination of her schemes, an apotheosis of her ambitions. How much of Talah's life force would be stolen to create Eala's prize? How much longer could the Bright One survive, with all Gavida kept taking from her?

Irian's large palm in the small of my back urged me forward, and I realized I had frozen in the middle of the steps, fury radiating along my bones and heating my blood. Behind us, the blank-faced puppets who'd shadowed us from my chambers waited silently, brooking no disobedience. I glared at them, but they waved us forward.

"One more night, colleen," Irian whispered in my ear. "Then we are free."

I kicked the train of my makeshift dress behind me and climbed.

Whispers and glances hounded me and Irian as we paraded toward our seats. I supposed I shouldn't be shocked—my spectacle at the Trial yesterday had been neither subtle nor understated. Nor was my current outfit—the revealing sweep of Irian's cloak over my supernaturally marked skin; the tight black corset like armor over my torso; the silver of its boning perfectly matching the collar at my throat, exposed by my severe updo. But I suddenly wondered how much they really knew—how much of my relationship with Eala, and hers with Irian? What nefarious tales had spread of our deeds? But when I met the gazes following us through the amphitheater, I wondered whether it wasn't something else entirely. The eyes alighting on Irian and me did not quite betray hope. No, it was more ambivalent than that—more neutral. As if they were biding their time. Waiting.

Irian's and my story was still unscripted—the parchment of our lives barely inked with twists of fate and unknown destinies. And those eyes following us seemed almost to dare us to pen our own conclusion—one satisfying enough to carry us out of the shadows of the unknown into something that might one day become legend...fable...or cautionary tale.

But a tale yet untold promised infinite possibility or infinite danger. Like Wayland had once promised, we might one day be admired, envied, and desired. Or just as easily, we might be feared, despised, and reviled. Villains, instead of heroes.

The thought fled when we reached Gavida's royal box, and I saw my sister and Chandi again sitting beside her. She was candle-lit with yearning, staring avidly up toward the Grove of Gold, at the crucible burning steam through the air. Her torment was obvious in the jagged angles stringing her bones together, in the lines striping her lovely face, in the way her hands gripped her knees through the material of her dress, as if she might come apart if she did not hold herself together.

What had she said to me yesterday?

I loved my swan sisters more.

Something pushed me toward Chandi—a sudden and unexpected desire to comfort her amid the obliterating pain of her betrayal. But Irian caught me, spun me away from my friend.

"Come, mo chroí," he murmured into my hair. "Not here. Not now."

He thought I meant to accost my sister in front of the assemblage. When I glanced over my shoulder back toward her, I saw why—Eala was glaring at me with a vivid, vengeful triumph that ignited something grim and glittering in my veins. I stared back at her for a long, unpleasant moment before Irian's touch once more prompted me to look away. But before I tore my gaze from Eala's, I realized—with a certainty bordering on prescience—that whatever Eala planned to do with her boon, it was far worse even than what I could imagine. In her eyes, I could see the coming war. Destruction, famine, ruined fields. Blood and death. She made me afraid—not for myself, but for everyone and everything I loved.

Boom.

Down in the arena, Gavida's platform rose in a thunderous waft of forge light and steam. He was not alone—Rogan and Wayland rose with him. When they stepped forward into the center of the arena, I gasped—for this, the last Trial, they had been truly transformed into the Oak King and Holly King from Gavida's pageant. Wayland wore hammered silver armor over robes of violet and evergreen; atop his sweep of mahogany hair a headdress of sharp emerald leaves bedecked with gleaming rubies shone. And Rogan— oh, Rogan. My heart slipped down between the cage of my ribs and festered in my stomach. He made the perfect Oak King. Golden armor hugged the heavy musculature of his chest; green and golden silks swirled over his freckled shoulders. His dark blond hair was braided back from his face and decorated with a spectacular crown of green oak leaves and twisting golden branches.

But his river-stone eyes were empty as a waiting grave.

I shivered and reached for Irian's hand.

Boom.

"Friends!" Gavida's voice thundered unnaturally loud. "Welcome to the final Trial of the Tournament of Kings!"

The crowd cheered with resounding fervor.

"Every year grows older before finally coming to an end. Such is the cycle of the seasons, the balancing of the natural world that governs us all. The Holly King came to power at Midsummer, heralding this year's slow decline. Now he has grown old. The Oak King is reborn in the promise of the light returning, the covenant for new growth. This night—the Longest Night—marks the inflection between the two. It is when light battles dark, when summer battles winter, when life battles death. It is inevitable. And yet these champions are no gods—they are but men. A human prince...and my own son. So perhaps the outcome is not as predetermined as all that!"

Again, the crowd howled havoc. I clenched my fists at his blatant lies.

"Let the battle begin!"

Boom.

Rogan and Wayland met with a clash of swords and armor and the roar of the crowd above. I tried to force calm through my

thrumming veins, reminding myself that by Gavida's own rules neither man would die today. Wayland would lose, as he always did,
by yielding—after all, if he died, who would perform the pageant
next year? Neither he nor Rogan were in any real danger from each
other. But somehow, the knowledge did not sit easy. I quivered
with each strike of the blade, each block and parry and blow. As if
something was coming alive inside me, rattling against the boundaries of my skin and threatening to burn me alive. I swallowed and
clutched harder at Irian's hand.

"Are you all right?" he asked in an undertone.

I nodded, but I wasn't sure.

The duel was spectacular. I had not yet seen Wayland fight, and
I recognized some of Irian's fighting style in him. Or perhaps, considering their upbringing and ages, it was his style I saw in Irian.
A louche ease with which he held the sword, as if it weighed nothing and he might drop it at any moment—totally at odds with
the lightning-fast strikes he rained down upon his opponent. The
unpredictable footwork he employed to use Rogan's momentum
against him—ducking and sliding to force him to move just as fast
but twice as far. His easy transitions between a front-handed and
back-handed grip, sending his blade slicing with both edges at double the angles.

But Rogan—or Eala, controlling him like a puppet—was
dogged. I was once again astounded by the single-minded and
humorless persistence of his assault. He fought like a hammer
pounding on a nail—his unfaltering strength coming down again
and again.

But Wayland's heart wasn't in the fight. And the crowd soon realized it, beginning to stir restively, eager for fresher stimulation—
some new spectacle. It was not long before Gavida realized it too.

Wayland's neck jerked. His foot slipped in the sand. His blade
swung wide, missing a parry. Rogan's own sword swung dangerously close to Wayland's throat—Wayland barely lurched beyond
its unstoppable arc. Rogan kicked out, his boot connecting with

Wayland's flailing arm. The blade clattered from his fingers. Rogan kicked out again, sending Wayland to his knees. He lifted his claíomh to his opponent's throat.

"Yield." Rogan's voice was so guttural and unrecognizable that it nearly tore a scream from me.

"I yield!" Wayland's words carried easily and pleasantly over the assemblage. "Tonight, on the Longest Night, the Holly King must ever yield to the Oak King. I cede my crown to you, Brother, and cede the new year with it. May the light return!"

The cry went up all over the amphitheater, resounding. *"May the light return!"*

Rogan reached down, helping Wayland to his feet in a gesture so *Rogan* that it made my throat close. Gavida strode down between them, his hands aloft not with his customary tools, but with an actual crown—the circlet he had worn on his brow when the tournament opened. He handed it to Wayland, who bowed excruciatingly low before proffering it to Rogan. Rogan took it, then stared down at it for a long moment before turning on a heel and pacing briskly across the arena toward our box. It was too tall for a person to reach—I expected him to come around the long way, using the steps. Instead, he climbed up, hand over hand, along the ruffled silken banners hanging down from the box, with the crown clenched in his teeth. He paused a half dozen feet from the summit and reached it up to Eala.

Regal and elegant, she strode to the lip of the box. The setting sun amid its salmon-striped sky caught her waving blond hair and turned it gold. She leaned—delicately, slowly, formally—to accept the crown from Rogan's hand.

A champion offering up a token to his lady—a prince bestowing his hard-won prize upon his princess. A storybook ending, a happily ever after.

The crowd went wild with a riotous hum of victory.

"Your champion has fought well, Princess!" Gavida's voice boomed across the amphitheater. "Name your prize!"

"Thank you, honored smith-king!" Eala's voice did not have Gavida's magical enhancement, yet it carried—a sweet fluting lilt. The crowd quieted almost to a whisper to hear her words. "I have given this matter much thought, as your generous boon is no small thing. Especially not for one such as me—a human princess trapped in the Folk realms, bereft of magic in a place that is so effortlessly magical." The crowd undulated, although I could not be sure whether the surge carried sympathy or distaste. "But your speech this night about the role of the Oak and Holly Kings has moved me. Nature is indeed a balance—light rises in the dark, only for the dark to return. Day gives way to night; summer always turns to winter; heat must fade before everlasting cold. And death—death inevitably conquers. Why is that?"

Another wave of sound carried through the crowd, and this time it echoed the sensation buzzing a chill along my arms. *Unease.*

"You forget my terms, Princess." A note of command threaded Gavida's voice. "I said I would not bring anyone back from the dead."

"You need not compromise your morals for me, smith-king," Eala said easily. "You will not be the one to resurrect anyone. I will."

"I cannot—"

"You have promised that anything you can forge, you will. Were you not the master smith who forged the four legendary Treasures of the Septs?"

She waited, even as Gavida's face grew tumultuous. But he eventually answered, "Yes. It was I who forged the Treasures."

"That is what I ask for, then." Eala was exultant, luminous. "I wish for a Treasure of my own."

"The Treasures are...bound...in complex ways, Princess." Fury striped Gavida's face, underlaid with a sudden strange helplessness—as though the smith-king was realizing he may have been outwitted by a human girl a fraction of his age and power. His words from yesterday echoed through me: *I have never met a human who did not change the course of my life.* Another time, it might have brought me some grim satisfaction to witness his degradation. But watching Eala, I felt nothing but dread. "And were never designed for a human to inherit."

"Can you forge one, *smith-king*?" Eala crooned. "Or is all this pageantry merely a display? Smoke and mirrors meant to aggrandize you while your own dubious powers dwindle away to nothing in isolation?"

Gavida's fury warped into frenzy; we all witnessed the moment his pride overcame his common sense. Horror burned through me, igniting fire over my skin and softening my bones like metal heated too long in a forge. Irian's hand was welded to mine in the space between our bodies.

"You wish to wield a Treasure, Eala Ní Mainnín, princess of Fódla? Then a Treasure you shall have." Gavida cut a deep, almost-mocking bow. "But all the Treasures I have previously forged have been tied to elements. Earth...air...fire...water. What element would you like to bind to, Princess?"

I half rose in my seat, my head whipping around to Chandi as everything came clicking into place. Her words from seven weeks ago, when she nearly gave her willing heart to my sister: *Eala will find a way to resurrect us.* Her words from yesterday: *I love you, Fia. But I loved my swan sisters more.* Eala's words from bare moments ago echoed back through my mind: *Death inevitably conquers. Why is that?*

No.

"You mock me!" she cried out. "You surely know as well as I do that there are not only four elements. There are nine dúile, or elements of magic, originally carried to our world by the ancient, mythic Bright Ones. I wish to wield the element of spirit, smith-king!" The crowds began to rise, surging and shouting in the lowering sunset. Gavida's army of puppets held any dissenters at bay. For now. "I wish to claim mastery over the element controlling life, death...and the passage between them."

"There must be balance, Princess," Gavida warned. "Not even

I can forge a Treasure that does not abide by its laws. Your life will be truncated—you will be bound by its thirteen-year death sentence. This new Treasure must live beyond you—you will have to find an heir willing and able to inherit it after your life is tithed, lest the wild magic warp beyond its control."

For a moment, Eala wavered. Her head bowed, as if pressed down by a massive, heavy hand.

"I can forge you something else, Banfhlaith," Gavida wheedled, pressing his advantage. "A knife to cut through fear. An arrow to destroy bravery. A mirror to show you your destiny. Magic you need not pay your life for. Power you need not stagger beneath."

"Do I seem like someone who staggers beneath the weight of power?" Eala's voice was deathly quiet. The crowd held its collective breath, a tense and terrified silence louder than any wail. "Or someone unwilling to shoulder the cost of magic? I have named my boon."

A moment later, Gavida bowed theatrically.

"What shape, lady," the smith-king asked, "would you have your Treasure take?"

Her laugh was a glittering, grievous thing. "A crown, of course!"

Gavida climbed heavily up the amphitheater, the eyes of a thousand Folk following his every step. The glow of the grove bathed him in gold; the crucible between the trees sparked silver. The smith-king took up his apron, his vast hammer, and his raw length of metal. Bellows flared at the base of the fire; flames leapt up against the dimming sky. The red sun lowered toward the flat black line of the distant sea.

Boom.

Around us, the crowds grew chaotic—some Folk fleeing down the steps toward the relative safety of the city. Others churned up toward the grove, colliding with the narrowing line of Gavida's attendants. Many simply sat in the stands, unable to tear their eyes from the spectacle unfolding before them. I tried to claw my way toward Eala and Chandi, but Irian held fast to my sweat-slick hand.

"We should go, Fia," Irian said gently but firmly. "Now."

But I couldn't leave. Something rose inside me, unwieldy as a sword I was not strong enough to heft. I no longer cared how this night cut me. I had to see this through to the end.

Boom.

I glanced up toward the Grove of Gold, where Gavida's crucible cursed the night, spitting stars to shine against the lowering dark. This should have been *my* prize—a new Treasure resurrected, warped magic renewed from its corruption. Not Eala's perverted triumph—a depraved subversion of everything I had fought for.

I once told you, Sister—I am the stronger weapon.

Boom.

I gripped the barrier before me. When the wood splintered beneath my fist, I smiled. Irian's gaze nailed to the side of my face. The wood burst at my touch, growing tiny green leaflets. My throat screamed with pain. The tattoos around my wrists felt thorned with metal.

Boom.

"Fia." Urgency rasped along Irian's voice. His eyes—sliding from blue to silver—birthed shadows as night fell. "*Now.*"

Boom.

Still Gavida hammered, his forge a furnace of outrage and stolen magic.

Boom.

"*No!*" Something was twisting inside me, something that I could not push down no matter how hard I tried. My words came out torturously. "Stop this, Eala. Please. It isn't right."

"Oh, Sister." Eala slid around to face me. Her eyes glittered like sapphires in the hammered-gold light, bright with anticipation and hard with conviction. "Can you not see how fate has brought us here together for a reason? This place, this moment, this triumph?"

I could not force words around the inexorable feeling rising in me like a tide.

"I was angry with you at first," Eala continued calmly. "You stopped my ritual beneath the Ember Moon. You somehow spared Irian's life when he ought to have died. You inherited a power far beyond your meager capacity. You set yourself against me instead of serving me as you were meant to."

I clenched my fists harder around the wood of the barrier, reveling in the sensation of it splintering and flowering beneath my fingertips. Pain glittered up from my collar, bursting behind my eyes like falling stars.

Boom.

"But I have since realized—there is a larger pattern at play." She returned her gaze to the grove, where silver flashed and flared amid glowing gold. "A greater purpose both of us must fulfill."

"What, pray tell, is that?"

"Why, you are my counterpoise, of course!" Her serene smile gleamed bloodily in the last rays of sunset. "Every action requires an equal, opposite reaction. The eternal balancing all nature demands. And we two—so similar yet existing in perfect contrast—were born to be each other's balance."

"You're mad."

"Sired by the same father...raised by the same mother. Our fates entwined since birth. I, a human stolen away to the Folk realms; you, half-Folk, abandoned to the human world. Our faces like mirror images, yet our coloring so different. Me, fair as moonlight; you, dark as shadow. The white swan, the black swan. Don't you see, Sister? We complete each other."

Her words throbbed through me, heavy as a millstone around my aching neck. "We are nothing alike."

"Yet so perfectly aligned." Bright, insatiable sentiment wreathed her expression. "And that is just how it is supposed to be. We were always going to stand here together. Your Treasure gives you power over living things; mine will grant me the power to vanquish death. Together we are unstoppable."

"I will *never* stand willingly beside you." The words came out in a surge, a rush, an irrevocable current.

"Perhaps. But it matters not whether you are my enemy or my ally. You are my sister. My other half. And only together can we be made whole."

Boom.

With a gasp and a sigh, the sun slid away beyond the blood-stained horizon. New stars pricked needle-sharp against the tapestry of dusk, and the sudden darkness felt leaden. An omen, not a promise. Silence fell once more as Gavida's forge burned out in a shower of sparks and guttering flames. The craven, heavy feeling building in my chest tangled with sudden hope—perhaps there had not been enough of Talah left. Perhaps he had not been able to forge Eala the Treasure she wanted. Perhaps, perhaps, perhaps.

Gavida strode down from the Grove of Gold to stand at the peak of the amphitheater. He lofted an exquisite silver crown—a pale gleaming tiara etched all over with a stylized emblem of frost and feathers. Slowly, Gavida paraded it down the steep amphitheater steps, and the crowd rose humming as he passed, following him with ravenous eyes. At last he stood before Eala.

My pulse hammered in my throat, as if my blood wished to escape my body.

"Daughter of kings," Gavida cried, "on this, the Longest Night of the year...don your crown! And let the world see what Gavida the smith-king has made you."

Eala reached out, curved her hands around the tiara.

Still the sensation laddered inside me, so powerful and profound I had experienced it only once before.

I suddenly remembered unstitching myself through an endless twilight. Sweeping silver-tipped fingers against the dusk.

That time, I had died.

This time...

Eala slowly, theatrically lowered the crown onto her head. It glimmered down above her pale hair, even as whatever was rising inside me crescendoed, slamming along the inside of my skin with a force that threatened to overwhelm me. Wayland's mother's signet ring, which I'd thoughtlessly placed back on my hand after our misbegotten ritual last night, flared molten silver and gold before sinking into my flesh. I gasped as pain lanced up my arms. Stumbled, fell down to one knee. Irian's hand was at my elbow, but I pushed him away, craning forward across the dais toward Eala. Words ricocheted up my throat, but I couldn't match them to my voice.

The language was all wrong.

Star child.

Boom.

The crown came to rest on Eala's head with a force so concussive it blew us all backward. I slammed into Irian's chest even as he fell down onto the decking. I swiftly struggled back to my feet, veins sparking, to see the rest of the stadium had been similarly affected. Gavida and Wayland crawled to their feet nearby; above us, the crowd erupted back to their feet as a sudden icy wind buffeted the trees of the grove. Behind Eala, Chandi must have hit her head—she lay sprawled on her back like a corpse. I lunged toward her, but something caught me around the middle and squeezed.

For a moment, I thought it was Irian. But then: *Star child. Let me in.*

And I suddenly knew—something had gone terribly wrong. Or, perhaps worse...

Terribly right.

I froze, my awareness traveling along every muscle and tendon and vein in my body. And I knew—*she* was already there, that strangeness I'd wanted to simply ignore. Welded to my bones, soldered through my veins, amalgamated with my mind. I slapped my palms to my temples, fighting the familiar, terrible voice seeking all my secret crevices.

You bound yourself to me. So let me in.

This was no homecoming, no leafing path guiding me toward a destiny I had always longed for. This was something else—something that threatened to overpower every ounce of my self-control. My identity. It warred with the dappled green forest within me, fighting for dominance.

I fought back.

Across the dais, Eala underwent a similar struggle. Beyond the black smoke of my darkening vision, I saw her bow down, as if the crown on her head was crafted from something far heavier than metal. I thought perhaps she cried out, her voice ragged in the dusk. But maybe it was me—a scream ripping something potent and primeval from my deepest reaches. Beneath our feet, the earth gave a treacherous, speculative shake—a vast, vengeful beast testing the strength of its bonds.

I wondered, distantly, whether it was Eala... or Talah making it shake. I did not know which would be worse.

After a few more tortured moments, Eala finally stood. Her spine straightened. She lifted her crowned head toward the blackening sky. And smiled.

"Shall we see what I can do?"

Chapter Forty-One

My veins surged with power. Talah's conquest was slow but inexorable—blistering waves of molten metal overwhelming every defense I tried to throw in her way.

I clutched at my throat, where Gavida's collar still held fast. For the first time, I did not wish to break it—instead, I prayed that it would hold. The smith-king had kept the Year captive for an eon—perhaps his forged devices would keep her at bay a little longer. Keep her from taking me. *Devouring* me.

But it was a foolish hope.

"Colleen!" Irian threw himself down on the platform beside me, his voice rutted with concern. "Is something wrong? Did Eala—"

But his words died away when he truly looked at me—saw the circle of molten metal glowing like a star from my finger; the tangled greenery beginning to climb my arms in desperation; the veins of silver and gold edging the stark outlines of my markings, limning the thorns in burning metal.

Below us, the ground rumbled another warning.

"Gods alive." Irian's worry transformed into alarm, the fear shadowing his eyes mirroring my own dark dread, increasing with every inch of control Talah wrested away from me. "The Year."

"I was...an idiot," I ground out, around the ratcheting panic making a muddle of my throbbing thoughts. "I thought...she would choose...Laoise."

"No." He gripped me bruisingly. "You cannot channel the power of the Heart of the Forest *and* the Year. Not if you hope to survive. You have to fight, mo chroí. *Fight*."

The platform beneath us shook, boards rending away from the scaffolding as silken pennants flew off into the wind shrieking over the ocean. I longed to look beyond the circle of Irian's arms to see what my sister was doing. But I feared if I lost even an ounce of focus, I might lose myself.

"What do you think...I'm *doing*?"

"Apologies." Irian clutched me closer, even as Talah's empyrean will rose inside me. "You are so strong, Fia. You are made of mountains and forests and fallen stars. You saved two Treasures. You saved my life. Please fight. For you know I cannot live without you."

Molten metal coursed through my veins toward my heart. What would happen once Talah took control?

"Irian," I managed, even as my voice began to sizzle in my throat. "Promise me...something."

His voice cracked. "Anything."

"Well," I amended, ridiculously. "Three things."

"I will make you a thousand promises, colleen." Again, the ground spasmed beneath us. Distantly, I thought I saw a portion of the cliff face shear away into the ocean. "But we are running out of time."

"First—do not...let my sister win." My collar vibrated along my throat, hot as a brand. "Second—you have to get my Heart... back from Gavida. I...need it."

"Yes," he growled lowly. "I promised you, colleen—I will kill him for what he did to you."

"Never mind that." Veins of silver and gold netted against the backs of my eyelids. My vision blurred. Irian clutched me tighter, although it must have hurt him—my fingernails left scorching crescents on the sculpted, tattooed skin of his biceps. "Third—please..."

Talah surged up and swallowed my voice whole. But I still had some fight left in me. I lashed out at her with all my waning strength. Images slashed through me—memories and moments that had shaped me—and each one lent me a modicum of strength.

A cruel-eyed mother who pretended to love me...and the not-father who hated everything he was forced to do to make me strong.

A golden-haired princeling brushing wings of snow off my shoulders and racing me over the moors and kissing me in the hedgerows and leaving me in the blue of dawn.

Corra flitting from carving to carving in a crumbling fort at the edge of nowhere.

A great leafing figure with arching antlers and a face like the forest path disappearing into the hollow trunk of the Heartwood. And walking beside them was a graceful doe with depthless, despairing eyes.

A raven-haired tánaiste who had loved me so violently he had almost lost me because of it. And I saw how he had tried to change himself—how he had tried to learn to love me more gently. To love me how I needed to be loved.

Finally, I saw myself. A slight, strange, dark-haired changeling with mismatched eyes sitting up in a bedroom that did not belong to her. I saw myself turning my nursemaid into a tree; picking up my twin skeans for the first time; riding bareback through the marsh while wielding a bow I had carved by hand. I saw every trial I had forced myself to overcome, every skill I had hammered into my bones, each sharp edge I had forged upon myself.

I *was* strong. But not because I'd been born that way. Because I had transformed myself to be so. I had transformed from child to girl to woman, and each stage had demanded a price.

Perhaps this would be my last transformation. Or perhaps I would keep changing, a hundred thousand Fias evolving over the course of a lifetime.

Not yet! I screamed at Talah, beating her back from my ebbing consciousness.

I am sorry, star child, she whispered inside me, her regret genuine. *But you should not have bound yourself to me if you did not wish to join with me. And you should have known two would be too much to survive.*

One more moment, I begged. *Please.*

She hesitated, then obliged, ebbing away. But only a brief respite—the sucking calm before a tidal wave.

My eyes snapped open. Irian cradled me—his arms cupped around my neck and my knees, my arms limply curved around his neck. All around us, the island had begun to implode—stone shattering and earth grinding and sea screaming over falling cliffs. I gripped him tightly. His gaze snapped down to mine, shadow and silver and salvation.

"Promise me," I managed, even as molten tears sprang to my eyes. "Promise me that no matter what happens—no matter what I become, no matter how I transform—that you will love me. Promise me you will not let me go."

"Never." Irian smoothed the hair from my face, his motions jerky with haste and horror. "I will love you today, tomorrow, and always. I will love you until the sun fades and the moon cracks and the stars burn away to husks. I will love you even after the world has forgotten our names and ground our bones to dust. You are my blood, my marrow, my heart. *Not in a thousand lifetimes will I ever let you go.* But you must promise me something in return."

"What?"

He tilted my chin with one trembling thumb, then pressed a frantic, precarious kiss to my buzzing lips. "You must live, Fia. *Live.*"

I scrabbled for the pouch hanging around my waist. The golden apple came free in my palm, clinging to my burning skin. There was just enough plump, juicy flesh left on its core for one last bite. One last wish. I stared at it, my hesitation scored bright against the looming specter of Talah's terrible presence.

This would not be a small wish. Which meant the cost of it would be great—far greater than anything I wished to pay.

But I also remembered Talah's words from the night Wayland and I had met her.

The trees are holy. They are my counterbalance—they fetter even as they feed.

Thrice three trees bound Talah. We had newly bound Talah with fours—a fourth shackle, a fourth element, a fourth heir. It was a long shot. But could a wish born from the Grove of Gold be enough to keep her from wresting control from me? From flooding my body with power it could not contain? From blotting me from existence?

I did not know what to do but try.

I cradled the apple before my face, inhaling its perfumed, tempting fragrance. "I wish...I wish to become whatever I must be to withstand her."

I took the last bite from the apple. The nectar burst in my mouth, intoxicatingly sweet and redolent with promise.

Then Talah reached up and dragged me down into a dark, depthless abyss of my own creation.

After

Irian

I *should never have brought her here.*

The wave of that thought crashed against him, relentless, his regret foaming and frothing atop it. It was almost enough to make him want to surrender—to wrap his arms around his unconscious wife and bury his head in her hair and allow the world to implode around them.

But he had made Fia a promise. Three, in fact.

He was not a good man. But he was a man of his word.

He forced his gaze up. Only a few moments had passed since Eala had placed her newly forged Treasure upon her blond head. It might as well have been a lifetime. He could *feel* the magic radiating off her—all the power and rage and pain and fear barely contained in her petite form. It clashed with every instinct of control he had painstakingly taught himself over the past thirteen years. It hummed along his bones and whispered into the wind swirling through his hair. But there was another song abrading the length of his spine with its wrongness, its atonality—one he had not let himself hear until this very moment.

Footsteps. Heavy, lumbering, scraping. Different from the crowds dispersing in every direction, flying with fresh fear.

Irian's eyes found the rim of the amphitheater, which was beginning to crack and splinter beneath the force of the convulsions rhythmically shaking the island. A moment later, he saw *them.*

He had never bothered to wonder what happened to the contestants who did not survive the tournament—where they went, whether they were buried or cremated or callously thrown off the cliffs to the sea. He had been too focused on winning—too focused on *Fia.* Too focused on securing her safety, their future. He was once more reminded of his foolishness when he saw the hundreds, perhaps thousands, of reanimated corpses marching down the steep steps of the amphitheater.

Irian had known battle. He knew the ratcheting gurgle of death on a man's lips. The metal stink of viscera, the inexorable bloodstains that soaked clothing and skin and grass. The moment life fled behind staring eyes, the relentless stillness that lingered after.

But he had never known anything like this. These were men and women he had already faced in battle—some he himself had slain. Their patchwork bodies should not have been able to move, and yet they did, cascading down the grinding, gasping stones in lumbering rows. He glimpsed throats he had cut, armor he had rent, limbs he had sliced off. Every death a sacrifice, every pound of flesh carved from his own conscience. And yet here they were again.

And he feared this time, they would be far harder to kill.

He rose in a rush, holding Fia's motionless, scorching form tightly to his chest. The apple core fell from her limp fingers, rotting away to dust now that its magic was spent. The Sky-Sword hummed against his thigh, eager even through its sheath. He longed to draw it, to square his body toward the approaching host. But he had made Fia a promise.

Three promises. But the last was the only one that truly mattered to him.

A tall figure barreled toward him. Irian whirled, nearly colliding with Wayland. The earth rumbled again beneath their feet, and his erstwhile foster brother grasped his shoulder to steady him.

"What happened?" Wayland's voice was urgent; his dark blue eyes, wretched. "What happened to Fia?"

"The Year," Irian told him roughly. When the four of them had performed the ritual in the Grove of Gold, he had never imagined this might be the result. But they all should have known better than to tamper with magic they did not understand. "The binding worked. Only not in the way any of us anticipated."

Wayland's face contorted with desperate hope and miserable remorse. He looked down at Fia, who was clutched in Irian's arms. Registered the veins of silver and gold embossing her pale skin like lace; the circle of Wayland's mother's ring glinting from where it had melted into the skin of her ring finger; the hammered metal still circling her throat. Wayland slowly lifted his hands to his own neck, tearing at the expensive green and violet silks of his costume until they were tattered around him. His fingertips found his own collar, wider and stiffer and more intricately carved than Fia's.

He gripped it, tugged it. When it held fast, he exhaled, his eyebrows winging together in defeat. But a moment later, the ramifications thundered down on him, even as his eyes registered the army of dead marching down toward them.

His gaze shifted from the undead army to Gavida's own fiann of puppets standing guard over the arena. "This will be a slaughter."

"It will be worse than that." Irian shrugged to encompass the crumbling cliffs, the listing amphitheater, the rumbling earth. His ragged breath tasted of iron and creeping loss and relentless death. The smell of decay hung heavy in the air, a prelude to more destruction.

"Talah," Wayland said slowly. "The Year—when she spoke to Fia, she said that she was originally bound to this island as a way to protect it. To shore it up. Without her—"

The end of his sentence hung in the thrumming air between them. *The island will take its due.*

"Your father." Irian tried to keep his fear from carving out his insides with visions of quaking rocks and rising magma and seething seas. This would not be how it ended—not while he still held *her* in his arms. "Where is Gavida?"

"Last I saw, he was fleeing back toward Aduantas with some of his puppets." Wayland frowned. "Why?"

Fia's second promise swept through him, as did his own to her last night. *I am going to fucking kill him.* He wanted so badly for it to be true—he longed to hunt down the man who had taken him in only to throw him out; the man who had orchestrated his wife's unwilling submission like a prodigy played an instrument; the man who had embroiled and entangled him in this terrible, violent charade. Irian wanted to put the Treasure Gavida himself had forged through the old man's gut and watch his face as he died.

In his arms, Fia twitched, her mouth parting as a single word haunted her lips: *No.*

He held her tighter. He would not let her go. Not for pride. Not for vengeance. Not for *anything.*

"He still holds Fia's Treasure. She needs her Heart. Can you retrieve it?"

"And relish in the opportunity to face him, one last time, with his power broken?" Wayland's hand skated once more over his collar. Irian saw vengeance surging to life in his foster brother's eyes. "Gladly."

"Then go. Hurry." Below them, the platform gave a warning groan, which they both heeded, dashing sideways onto the cracking stone steps. "Do you know where the aughiskies are stabled?"

"In the caverns below Aduantas."

"We will meet there in an hour." He hoped they had that much time. "And if you see Laoise or Sinéad—"

"I know." Wayland clapped a heavy, familiar hand on his shoulder, then slid off through the rioting crowds of panicking Folk and the blank-faced puppets and the river of oncoming dead.

Irian paused, lead creeping into his bones as his wife lay motionless in his arms. He glanced toward Eala, who stood like a conquering queen twenty paces away, staring down her dread army as it slowly descended toward her. He could still feel the power blistering off her in invisible waves—a shallow, serrated scrape against his soul. She was smiling, but her face looked brittle, tight—as if her skin was a poor cover for the radiance hollowing her from the inside out. Beside Eala, Chandi had risen back to her feet, blood on her face and fear in her eyes. Behind Eala, as always, stood the human prince, dead eyed and unmoved by the unfolding chaos.

The earth in the middle of the arena screamed, shuddered, then split. A silver geyser arced like cold fire through the near-black sky. Stones groaned and plunged off the cliffs, sinking as foaming water rose. Screams mounted from the spectators stupid enough to linger in this cursed arena.

Irian lurched forward, plummeting down the stairs to slam into the wall of Gavida's puppets. They parted around him with little protest and re-formed behind him—he was not their target. Fia jostled in his arms as he ran for the towering statues guarding the stadium exit. He swore and shifted his grip on her so she was curved around him—her limp legs around his waist; her chest against his chest; her head lolling upon his shoulder. But she seemed heavier in his arms than ever before—dense with impossible, ancient, unstoppable magic. Her limbs were iron, her skin molten where it rested on his.

But he refused to set her down, even for a moment. Not while there was strength in his limbs or breath in his lungs would he let her go.

The bones of the earth creaked and moaned beneath him. The sky pressed too close—the last fingers of sunset streaking fire over the black. Beyond the gates of the amphitheater, an exodus had begun—thousands of Folk streaming through the perilous night in all directions. Surging toward Aduantas, rampaging through the city, spiraling down along the precarious cliffs. Irian hesitated, glancing first at the city, where streams of molten metal criss-crossed cobblestones and silver flames danced along eaves. Then at the cliff path, where a rising sea pummeled angry fists against the fragmenting stone.

The cliff path would take him to the aughiskies faster. Very fast indeed, if it crumbled away beneath him.

He tried to shove through the retreating crowd, his long legs ready to outpace any who dared stand in his way. But this kind of desperate stampede was treacherous—Irian knew if he stumbled, he and Fia might both be trampled. So he consigned himself to threading wildly through the throng, hoping he could somehow outrun the destruction snapping at his heels.

When he almost ran headfirst into a familiar twenty-foot-tall Fomorian, he let himself hope the living gods were on his side after all.

Or, perhaps, just Fia's.

"Balor!" he roared up at the giant, who turned with excruciating slowness to glance down at him. "Balor, do you remember me?"

Recognition slid over the Fomorian's features, followed by ponderous horror when he registered the figure Irian held clasped to himself. "Well met, scary husband. But what has happened to my lady?"

"She is...unwell. We must get her off the island." Irian dodged Balor's stomping footsteps. "Have you seen her friends? Laoise? Sinéad?"

"Yes, lord." Balor seemed stunningly unconcerned by the vast boulders beginning to roll off the cliffside to slam into the crowd of spectators attempting to flee the arena. "Last I saw, they were headed toward the Shielings."

"Can you find them?" A fissure opened in the cliff face, dragging half a dozen screaming bystanders down into a vein of molten silver. "Then meet us in the caverns before the hour is through?"

"I can, lord," said Balor equably. *Stomp, stomp, stomp.*

"Good," Irian said. Then, haltingly: "Thank you."

He slid forward through the seething mass of Folk.

The island was coming apart at the seams. Even were it not for the rifts splitting like wounds in the flesh of the land, Irian would have known by the way the wind screamed through the chinks opening between rocks, the way the sea sang stormy warnings to the breezes.

They were running out of time.

Fia's stillness had transformed into something new. She writhed in his arms as he picked his way down the crumbling cliff face, his steps sure but his mind reeling. There was a time when he had known these pathways like the back of his hand and had traversed them like a mountain goat. But he felt suddenly old with caution, ancient with concern—as though the woman he held against him had made him immeasurably more aware of all that he had to lose.

He had never feared death—often, in the past thirteen years, he had yearned for it. But here, now, with the island groaning at his back and the sea gnashing its teeth at his boots and molten veins of impossible metal vomiting through the stone, Irian was afraid. Of dying, yes. But mostly, of *her* dying. He could sense the power coursing through her in the same way he had felt it in Eala—the magical struggle playing itself out over the battlefield of her bones. And there was nothing he could do to help her.

Nothing but what she had asked. *Promise me you will not let me go.*

Only the wind was a comfort. It sang around his trembling limbs, whispering the same promise since the day he was born—a paean to the day and an elegy to the night; a song of bright buoyant oceans and sharp silent forests. The words were unknowable, and they would go on, silently, long after he was dead. It was a requiem for undoing, a prayer for new birth. But just now, it was a promise.

There is still time.

When he at last reached the caverns, they were nearly under-water. Dark waves smashed over pale rock, sloughing off layers of stone as they retreated. The aughiskies were in a frenzy—lashing tails and stomping hooves and gnashing teeth. Irian almost laughed when he saw what had prevented them from striking out into deep water and abandoning him and the women to their fates.

It was Fia's vicious sea-foam mare—the one who now insisted on being called Linn—herding the rest of her drowning like wayward toddlers. She had her delicate legs planted at the front of the cavern and her double rows of shark teeth bared beneath her dark, dripping forelock. Her tail was bannered behind her, whipped by the rising wind.

She caught sight of Irian, sallied sideways. Then lunged forward when she saw whom he held in his arms. The aughisky nuzzled her nose up Fia's spine, whuffed at her neck. When she got no reaction, she buried her teeth in Fia's hair and savagely yanked. Irian batted her away, not ungently.

"She will live, fiend." He could not muster much humor. "If we can get her off the island in time."

Linn sent him a sharp question. *Now?*

"You waited for her," Irian told her firmly. "Now we wait for everyone she loves."

Scree rattled between footsteps descending the shattering stairs. Irian turned swiftly, hope and trepidation warring within him. Would it be Wayland? Balor? Laoise and Sinéad?

It was none of them.

Few things had the power to shock Irian—he had seen too many horrors and lived through too much pain to be often surprised. But the last person he had expected to come down those stairs was...

Eala.

Much like the island falling to pieces around them, the swan princess was coming undone, although she was trying very hard to pretend that was not the case. Beneath her shining new crown, her pale hair whipped around her in damp, windswept tangles. Her outer mantle had come loose; her bejeweled dress floated around her like frost and fog. Her eyes shone with the same bright hunger

Irian had seen the night of the Ember Moon. Behind her, a horde of the reanimated dead plodded along the cliff path, careless of the sea frothing at their feet and the wind dragging at their bodies. Irian searched their number for Rogan and Chandi but saw neither.

"Irian." Her voice was lilting, half snatched by passing breezes. "Give my sister to me. I need her. I need Fia."

Reflexively, he clutched her—as if Fia's body, already molded so tightly to his, could get any closer. "Never."

"Did you not hear what I said?" She held out her arms, placatory. Almost pleading. "I need her. She is mine. I am hers. We cannot exist without each other. We are bound, in ways neither of us understands. She is my counterpoise."

"That may be true." The words rose up in Irian almost without his permission. "But not in the way you think. She is kind where you are cruel—effortless where you are full of guile. She has borne a lifetime of blows, and it has only buoyed her toward the light; you have borne the same blows, but it has driven you toward darkness. You have chosen death over life, Eala—that, more than anything else, proves who you are."

"No!" Again, Irian had the impression of skin stretched too tightly over luminous bone. Hairline cracks fissured over Eala's face as if she were a doll that had been dropped, then badly patched. "I have chosen to *overcome* death. And that—that can only be life."

"Are you sure?" Irian stared at the army of corpses lurching ungainly down the steps at her back—their ragged mouths and jagged wounds and terrible, staring eyes. "You were once a princess of swans. Now you have made yourself a queen of death."

"Always better a queen than a princess." Eala's voice rose as the lingering remnants of her composure began to fracture. "Now. Give me my sister. Only by her may I be made whole. And she, me."

Around her, the undead swarmed, flinging themselves mindlessly toward Irian and the aughiskies.

He stumbled back, grabbing for the hilt of his sword even as he held Fia against him with his other arm. The position was ungainly; the pressure of her body on his torso threatened to reopen his barely healed wound. But he did not care—he slung the tip of his sword haphazardly into the oncoming horde, his decades of training frosting cold over the terrible fear burning up his spine.

Not in a thousand lifetimes will I ever let you go.

From the cliffs above, a figure dropped, landing squarely on Eala. They both tumbled down the last few steps, landing awkwardly in a heap. They scuffled together, limbs flailing. Irian squinted, making out the figure of another woman locked in combat with Eala. Long, slender limbs; honey-blond hair; twin daggers flashing in the wind-whipped dark.

Sinéad.

The two women grappled amid the havoc of attacking undead and thrashing aughiskies. Eala was no fighter; Sinéad, barely trained. The fight was clumsy but deadly serious—both women seized by a violence they could not control. Sinéad yanked Eala's long blond hair back, slammed her head repeatedly into the cliff face—once, twice, three times. The princess recoiled, dizzy—but not unconscious. Graying hands and splintered fingernails grabbed at Sinéad's arms, tore at her braided hair, dragged her away from the princess. She faltered, stumbling over loose scree and fallen stones. Gasped, as if afraid she would be trampled beneath their unflagging onslaught.

Her blue eyes skimmed desperately over the heads of the undead. Latched on to Irian's. Dropped to the woman lying limp in his arms.

Sinéad's mouth hardened. She tensed, then abruptly dropped, flinging her legs out in a whirling kick. Irian almost smiled— that was Fia's favorite feint. The two nearest soldiers went down, unhinging at the knees. Sinéad threw herself forward. She collided again with Eala, catching the other girl around the waist and bearing her to the ground. This time, she did not bother with incapacitating her erstwhile swan sister.

Sinéad struck Eala with a killing blow.

Her daggers curved high, then slammed down into the princess's chest. She wrenched the blades back up, blood arcing over her chest and hair before she brought them down again. Eala's new-forged crown rolled away into the shadows. Almost instantly, the undead horde came to a halt, stopping where they stood, as if a lever had been flipped. Sinéad lifted the daggers one last time, but another woman caught her by the arms. Folded her hands in her own. Curled her back against hers, sliding auburn hair over honey gold.

"That's enough, Sinéad," Laoise whispered to her friend. "It's enough."

Sinéad slowly subsided, although tremors racked her form and blood dribbled down her face to collect along her jaw. After a long, tense moment, she sheathed her twin daggers. Rose to her feet, blood spattered and vengeful.

The next few moments were a desperate blur of greetings— Sinéad and then Laoise reintroducing themselves to the sallying herd of aughiskies; Balor stomping down the cliff path and knocking most of the undead fénnidi into the rising tide as he came. But there was little time for salutations; the island was unstitching itself, thread by broken thread. The caverns shuddered, stalactites spearing down to shatter upon freezing stone. Great furrows opened along the island's ridges, belching cascades of molten silver to heave crackling and steaming into the sea.

Linn sent a brisk, wordless message into Irian's mind. *We leave. Or we all die.*

"Wayland." Irian could not abandon his foster brother. But in his arms, Fia once more began to flail and thrash against him. He glanced down at her in desperation—her eyelids were the luminous color of a sunset; her lips, the color of bone. "Did anyone see him? He went up to Aduantas—he went—"

A terrible crash—the caverns collapsing in on themselves. Light blazed up over the isle; distantly, Irian saw the Grove of Gold catch fire in a terrific conflagration. The ground beneath them slanted precipitously toward the raging waves. The aughiskies sallied—even Linn was edging toward the sea. And Irian knew—if he wanted to save Fia, he was running out of time.

"Laoise, Sinéad," he commanded. "Find a mount. Balor—can you swim?"

"No." The giant displayed all eighty-seven of his slanted, serrated teeth. "But I can float, lord."

"Good enough." Irian grasped the mane of his black aughisky stallion—Abyss—and clumsily hoisted himself and Fia atop his back. "We wait no longer. Wayland is strong and wily—he will find his way."

"I'll fetch him," said Laoise, unexpectedly.

"There is no time—"

"Let me tell you about my anam cló, tánaiste."

She did not tell Irian anything. Nor did she give him time to protest. She simply flung herself from the edge of the caverns above the rioting sea. A blast of dry, unseasonable heat. The sudden beat of wings upon restless air—shifting and soft, leathery yet scaled in a way Irian could not quite grasp. And that sound—a low hum of power, an undulation of magic—

The serpent rose up on the wind with wings of rose gold and scales like the shifting red coals of a dying fire. She was a bloody comet against the night, brilliant and bold, and they all stared as she streaked up over the crest of the cracking, dying island in search of Wayland.

"Go," Irian urged after a moment. "We have not a moment to lose! To the whale road!"

The aughiskies surged into the sea, navigating the rough, rising waves crashing upon the cliff face. Frigid salt water lapped Irian's thighs, kissed Fia's bare feet and uncovered arms. Ice already crusted over his armor, rimed frost along the length of his sword. In horrid contrast, Fia was hot as a forge. Lines of molten gold edged the contours of her markings; streaks of bright silver slowly laddered away from her temples through her sable hair.

If Fia died tonight, it would not be the cold that killed her.

They plunged through the dark and the cold. Destruction chased them—sheets of rock pitching down into the dark, devouring sea; great tongues of silver fire leaping up through the cracks left behind, licking at hovel and mansion and palace with hungry, devouring flames. It was hard for Irian not to look behind—not to watch Emain Ablach dissolve into the sea, sucking a thousand glowing currachs down in its wake. Not to watch the amphitheater slide off the side of the island in one clean sweep. Not to watch Aduantas crumble in fits and spurts, crenellations and towers and spires caving in on themselves as the caverns below collapsed.

The Silver Isle had hurt him, hurt the woman he loved. But he did not relish watching it burn. There were tens of thousands of innocent Folk who lived there—another ten who had visited for the tournament. Many of their boats were already smashed upon the rocks; their screams keened on the breeze.

He had spent the bulk of his childhood here, and this felt like erasure. The few happy memories he had cherished cleaved away; the dark moments he had loathed drowned abruptly in dark water.

One more loss to add to the pile.

A line of bright fire arced through the sky toward them. And hanging precariously from Laoise's golden, shimmering, sinuous neck—*Wayland*. He landed neatly upon the back of Linn, who rewarded him by tearing off the cuff of his trousers with her shark teeth.

Irian accepted Wayland's arm, shook it. Around Wayland's neck, a familiar blue-green stone hung. And above Fia's Treasure, Wayland's throat was shockingly, significantly barren. Irian inhaled, observing the pale outline where for years Wayland's collar had rested.

"The old man removed it?" Irian asked, surprised. He had come to believe Gavida would never free his son.

"Yes," Wayland said after a beat. The grim set of his mouth and the violence in his tone told Irian it had likely not been so simple. He nodded toward Fia. "How is she?"

Irian refused to say Fia was dying. But he did not know what else could be happening to her. She was somehow both heavier and more malleable in his arms—her skin less skin than hammered metal, her bones less bone than forged steel.

"I do not know." He reached for Fia's Treasure, hung it gently around her neck. Prayed to any god, living or dead, that it would be the thing to save her.

They struck off into the ocean. But Irian could not help looking back at Emain Ablach, one last time.

And there, upon the shifting, sinking beach, he swore he saw a small pale figure staring after him. She shone bright as a star, gleamed white as a swan's stark wing. Even from this distance, the tremors of her power rattled his teeth and sang curses in his ears.

Before she blinked out of view...Eala smiled.

⁓

Irian held Fia through the night. He held her as Emain Ablach finally drowned in a torrent of pale rock and sparking metal. As the shock waves roared over them, soaking them to the bone... As the herd of aughiskies doggedly ferried them across a dark sea on the longest, coldest night of the year.

He held her when they finally found the whale road and sheered toward a shore they had begun to fear they might never find.

He held her as they collapsed on the beach. Held her as Wayland crouched beside them, his dark eyes intent on Fia.

"Do you want...?" Wayland's hands flexed with some impulse Irian could not fathom. "I think I could remove her collar. If you think it would help her."

The words struck Irian like arrows, fletched first with hope, then with fear. He glanced down at his motionless wife and the circle of carven metal marring her perfect throat. He had wanted the cursed collar removed from the moment it had snapped around her neck. But now he wobbled with desperate indecision.

"What if it is the only thing protecting her?" His low words were nearly soundless above the shrieking wind and pounding surf. "What if it is all that is keeping the Year from taking complete control?"

"When you asked me to retrieve Fia's Treasure, you said *she needs her Heart*." Wayland's words were gentler than Irian deserved. "So, too, does she need the magic it channels. If anything will save her in this, it will be the power of her Treasure. You know that."

Perhaps he did know that. Irian thought of those ragged, wretched moments before Fia had fallen unconscious. What she had murmured, before she sank her teeth into the wishing apple.

I wish to become whatever I must be to withstand her.

Perhaps Fia already was exactly who and what she needed to be to withstand this second entity using her as a vessel. He had come to the Silver Isle in the hopes of unforging his wife's Treasure so she might live, even if he could not. But that had not been his decision to make. The Heart of the Forest belonged to Fia as truly and indelibly as her mismatched eyes or her lilting laugh or her keen mind. And she—she belonged to *it*.

The Heart of the Forest would not let her die.

He just had to set it free.

Slowly, Irian nodded. "Do it."

Wayland wrapped his tan hands almost tenderly around Fia's throat, closing his eyes in concentration. A moment later, a charge of energy pulsed through Fia's body and into Irian's, thrilling through his veins and raising the hairs along his arms. Threads of light sizzled over Wayland's fingers and tangled in Fia's hair.

Snick. The latch cracked open; two half-moons of carven metal came away in Wayland's palms. Fia twitched in Irian's arms; faintly sighed.

And as dawn bloodied the horizon, she began to change.

First her skin exploded with sharp dark pinions, lustrous as midnight. Her neck lengthened, her mismatched eyes going cygnet black.

But as soon as the form held, it changed again.

The swan's long neck growing longer, her webbed feet disappearing. Until, at last, she became a serpent, snapping venomous fangs mere inches from Irian's face.

The fangs, still snapping. But the scales melting into fur, the eyes savage with predatory intent. A wolf.

The eyes rounding into dinner plates, staring golden as feathers fletched her skin once more. *Owl.*

Long slender legs and sharp hooves, kicking at him. *Doe.*

He held her as she changed. Every shift, each transformation. Although his arms shook and his skin chilled and his eyes burned. He did not care whether it was Talah or the Heart of the Forest or Fia herself thrashing in his arms. He did not care whether she was a deer or a serpent or a bear or a fish or a swan. He had made her a promise—and he was a man of his word.

Not in a thousand lifetimes will I ever let you go.

The story continues in...

A Heart So Green

Book Three of the Fair Folk

Acknowledgments

Next time I decide to write a sequel, will someone please remind me how hard this book was? I won't listen, but remind me anyway.

To Jessica Watterson, my rockstar agent and evergreen cheerleader, for never being more than a frantic text away. And to everyone at SDLA—I'm so fortunate to have such a wonderful team behind me and my books.

To my US editor, Alyea Canada, for your insights, encouragement, and insanely fast read times. To my UK editor, Nadia Saward, for fielding and facilitating my most random requests. To the amazing teams at Orbit, whose hard work, incredible commitment to quality and consistency, and unflagging support have made my return to publishing an absolute dream.

To Shauna Granger, for never pulling your punches—you legitimately saved my leading man this time around. To Kara Quinn, for being the best IRL writing buddy I could ask for. To Roshani Chokshi, the OG demon horse. To Ryan Graudin, for speed reads and encouragement.

To Steve, Freya, and Kepler—I love our little family.

Last—but most certainly not least—to my readers. Everyone who has read, reviewed, posted about, or supported my books—THANK YOU. I feel so lucky *A Feather So Black* found its readers, and I hope this has been a satisfying next chapter in Fia's story. I can't wait for everything to come!

Glossary

Amergin (AH-mer-ghin)—founder of Fódla; god of poetry and law

Aduantas (AH-doon-tes)—the capital of Emain Ablach

anam cló (AH-num klow)—soul form; animal avatar

áthas (AW-huss)—joy juice; rainbow liquor

aughisky (AW-ih-ski)—shape-shifting carnivorous water horse

banfhlaith (BAN-lah)—princess

barda (BAR-dah), **bardaí** (bar-DEE) (pl.)—gate warden

brùnaidh (BROO-nee), **brùnaidhean** (BROO-nee-in) (pl.)—small, secretive household Folk who tidy homes in exchange for leftovers or milk

Bridei (BREE-dye)—Rogan's home kingdom

Brighid (BRIDGE-id)—goddess of husbandry and healing

Cathair (KAH-her)

Chandika (CHUN-dee-kaa)

chiardhubh (KEER-va)—sable; nickname roughly meaning *dark-haired*

claíomh (clayve), **claimhte** (CLEV-tah) (pl.)—longsword

Corra (KORE-ah)

currach (KUH-rach)—a rowed boat

dobhar-chú (DOE-wur Hoo)—a giant amphibious carnivorous monster; also known as a king otter

dúil (DOOL), **dúile** (DOOL-yuh) (pl.)—magical element

dún (dune)—a fort or fortified castle

Dún Darragh (dune DAH-rah)

Eala (AY-lah)

Emain Ablach (EM-in AB-luch)—an island nation ruled by Gavida, the smith-king; the Silver Isle

Fia (FEE-ah)

fénnid (FAY-nidge), **fénnidi** (fay-nidge-EE) (pl.)—warrior

feis (FESH), **feiseanna** (FESH-uh-nah) (pl.)—a festival with music and dancing

fiann (FEE-in), **fianna** (FEE-nah) (pl.)—band of warriors; army

Firbolg (FEER-bull-ug)—ancient inhabitants of Tír na nÓg, conquered then enslaved by the Fomorians; their origins faded into legend

Fódla (FO-lah)—an island nation ruled by a human high king or queen, with four major provinces ruled by under-kings

Gavida (gah-VEE-dah)—smith-king of Emain Ablach

geas (GESH), **geasa** (GYES-sah) (pl.)—a magical binding or obligation; a curse

gruagach (GREW-ah-gak), **gruagaigh** (GREW-ah-guy) (pl.)—big, hairy, aggressive Folk

Irian (EER-ee-in)

leipreachán (lep-reh-HAWN), **leipreacháin** (lep-reh-HAYN) (pl.)—diminutive, mischievous Folk

lough (loch)—lake

mo chroí (muh-CHREE)—endearment meaning *my heart*

nemeton (NEH-meh-tin), **nemeta** (NEH-meh-tah) (pl.)—holy grove or site of power

poitín (po-CHEEN)—home-brewed liquor; moonshine

prionsa (PRIN-sah)—prince

Rogan (ROE-gin)

Samhain (SOW-wen)—a high holy day occurring between the autumn equinox and the winter solstice; November 1

Sinéad (shi-NAYD)

skean (skene)—a small single-edged knife

Solasóirí (SULL-ah-SO-ree)—another name for the Firbolg; loosely
  meaning *Bright Ones*

Talah (TAW-lah)

tánaiste (TAW-nisht-uh), **tánaistí** (TAW-nisht-EE) (pl.)—heir apparent of a Sept's Treasure

Tír na nÓg (TEER na NOGUE)—the realm of the Fair Folk; the
  otherworld

About the Author

Lyra Selene was born under a full moon and has never quite managed to wipe the moonlight out of her eyes. She grew up on a steady diet of mythology, folklore, and fantasy and now writes tall tales of twisted magic, forbidden love, and brooding landscapes. She lives in New England with her husband, daughter, and dog in an antique farmhouse that's probably not haunted.

Find out more about Lyra Selene and other Orbit authors by registering for the free monthly newsletter at orbit-books.co.uk.